LOVE & OTHER CURSED THINGS

KRISTA & BECCA RITCHIE

CHAPTER 1

ZOEY DURAND

People always say you can't outrun a curse, but I've been running for six years. So far misfortune hasn't caught up and dragged me down yet.

But today, I finally stop running.

No one ever really returns to Mistpoint Harbor once they leave. Hell, even I would keep my ass firmly planted in Chicago if I had a choice. Only a handful of reasons could get me to board a plane back home.

When Parry called me last night, all the air suctioned out of my apartment. An invisible rope wrapped around my waist and started yanking and yanking and yanking. *Pulling* me home.

I have to return.

As I heave a beat-up suitcase out of a Kia's trunk, the phrase *no turning back now* is cemented in my core and practically tattooed to my ass, and I realize the Uber driver is standing a foot away, hypnotized by the town sign.

Welcome to Mistpoint Harbor.
The Most Cursed Town in America!

I tug, and as the suitcase wheels *thunk* hard on the cement, he wakes from his stupor and combs a hand through his tousled, chestnut-brown hair.

"Hey, do you know someone who lives in Mistpoint Harbor?" He jabs a thumb towards the cobblestoned pathway. No cars allowed down the main walk of the tiny town center. "I heard the whole 'curse' thing is bullshit to drive up tourism. But never had a first-hand account."

I shake my head. "Sorry to disappoint. I'm just passing through." I don't love lying, but I better get used to it. I can't exactly tell everyone the reason I'm back. As Parry said, *keep this shit on the low. I mean it, Zoey. Don't tell Brian or October.*

My brother, Brian, is easy to lie to.

But even *trying* to deceive October is like trying to fool *Zoltar*. You know, the robotic fortuneteller in the 80s movie *Big*. October is neither robotic nor psychic, but she can stare through me with unblinking, soul-eating eyes, and I unravel into a fucking mess.

She's a lot prettier than a robotic dude with a mustache too.

Like a diamond-studded glamazon. Wonder Woman in the flesh.

A Wonder Woman who I can't lie to. I can't remember what her gold rope is called: an honesty lasso, a *fuck-you, give-me-the-truth* weapon? Honestly, I only saw the superhero movie because Wonder Woman is hot—my geek card is mostly swiped in Star Wars lore. But Mistpoint Harbor's very own Wonder Woman will probably strangle me with the *fuck-you, liar* rope, so I have that to look forward to.

I try to exhale a mountain of apprehension. The Uber driver frowns at the sign, then back at me. Crestfallen at my declaration. "Well, damn. Thought I'd finally figured it all out."

I wish I could tell him the real truth. There's nothing to figure out. It's a legend—you either believe or don't—but no one will tell you where to put your faith.

Some people who live in Mistpoint think just like him—it's all bullshit. A legend created generations ago to attract tourists to the harbor. Others, like me, don't spit in the face of fate. Some things can't be properly explained.

Like how Mistpoint has more accidents, more missing persons, deaths, and all-around misfortune than any other port in the country. And yet, it takes a whole unearthly energy to uproot yourself from this town just to leave. I got out when I was eighteen. I almost didn't go.

Shit, I was a *breath* away from staying.

Sometimes I wish I did. This town has a magnetic pull, an energy that I don't understand. Brian, my oldest brother, used to tell me that being born here is like adding another root to the family tree. We're tangled underneath the earth with the generations before us. Only way to truly leave is to hack yourself away. And when you do that, you leave the ground rotted. You leave the tree decaying.

My stomach churns, and I shake that image from my head.

My hand tightens on the handle of my suitcase. "Thanks for the ride," I tell the Uber driver.

He closes the trunk. "Don't forget to rate me. I'm a five-stars kinda guy." He gives me a wink—and I can't tell if it's friendly or flirty. And one thing is for certain, I don't need to be in a relationship right now. Not even a *flirt*ationship.

Nothing's worse than falling in love in a cursed town.

So I avoid eye contact and mumble out a noncommittal, "Yeah, definitely."

He lingers for a second, and I'm quick to casually pull out my cell. I try to manifest my destiny. The one that says *leave me alone!*

Sure enough, I hear the slight bang of a car door. When I glance back up, the car is peeling away.

I sigh heavily. What the fuck am I doing? I'm back home for zero-point-five seconds and I'm already on edge. Living here is like trying to play whack-a-mole with fate—and I'm the kind of girl that doesn't like to go down with any ship. I will jump overboard and swim my way to shore before an ocean tries to drown me.

People in town probably think I left to avoid a curse.

As the legend goes, live here long enough and misfortune befalls.

The curse never scared me growing up. Ultimately, I had a very different reason for leaving, but avoiding a curse was like a little consolation prize that I don't take for granted. Being back here now, I feel the weight of the risk I'm taking. Six years. I've avoided a curse for *six* whole years. I can't forget that.

I'm getting in. Getting out.

I'll do what I came here to do, and I won't stay long enough to get fucked over by some generations' old legend.

That's the plan.

Let's just hope fate doesn't fuck with it.

CHAPTER 2

ZOEY DURAND

Two minutes. That's all it takes for someone to spot me walking down the main path towards the old docks. As soon as the five-foot-nine girl does a double take, she doesn't go about her day. No. She *speeds* up her pace towards me like she spotted prey, and I'm just that dumb rabbit caught doe-eyed in the forest.

Awesome.

I should have known that I'd receive an *un*welcome party on my arrival. This party of one has a name.

Amelia Roberts.

Reddish-brown hair in a neat fishtail braid, a J.Crew wardrobe, and perpetual snotty attitude—she's made my life absolute hell since the ninth grade. The Roberts own The Mistpoint Harbor Historical Museum of Curses & Curiosities near the east side of town. A tourist hot spot in any season.

I had the unfortunate experience of working the ticket booth when I was in high school. But people treat Amelia and her family like royalty in this town. They ass-kiss to ensure the museum records their own families *favorably*.

Believe me, there's a whole section on the Durands in that museum and *none* of it is kind. No amount of ass kissing could change that.

It made me an easy target growing up.

And right now, that bullseye is growing hotter and angrier on my chest. Screw it. She's going to have to chase me. I grip the handle of my suitcase and *bolt* towards the docks.

"Zoey Durand!" Her shrill voice calls behind me.

Cold March wind whips against my cheeks. My grin spreads. And then I hear a *snap*. The wheel of my battered suitcase breaks off from the uneven cobblestone. The corner of the hard case skids across the ground.

"Fuck," I groan, slowing to a stop in pathetic defeat.

Amelia lands behind me as I turn around. She's not breaking a sweat. Barely panting.

I remember she's literally *Miss Mistpoint*. She won the contest the year I left, and it's not even some small-town beauty pageant. No. It's a fucking expert-level treasure hunt that the elders in the town put together. Classic Nancy Drew shit, and Amelia won in record time.

Under the cold overcast, coastal sky, we have a thirty-second staring contest. Birds chirp and fog rolls over the lake not far from our stand-off, but I know better than to flee again.

I blink.

Shit.

"You can't be here," Amelia says, breaking the tense silence. She crosses her arms over her cashmere sweater.

My stomach twists. I didn't expect anything kind to leave her lips, but I wish those words weren't the first thing I heard since I've been home.

"Take that off," Amelia suddenly says in disgust.

"What?" I frown, confused until I realize she's fixated on my bracelet.

"Take. It. *Off.*"

Don't worry, my jewelry isn't cursed. Amelia is just wearing the identical bracelet. Translucent beads strung together; every purchase gives 50% to a marine wildlife charity. It's become a basic bitch bracelet with about a billion Instagram ads, and I actually *like* it.

I make a noise. "*You* take it off."

Amelia is taken aback by my courage. "Seriously?"

"Did I stammer?" I say roughly, and I can't help but think October might be a little proud of me.

After a long, awkward beat, Amelia tugs her sleeve to hide her bracelet. Acting like the exchange never happened, she repeats, "You *can't* be here."

"Too late for that, Amelia," I say. "I'm back."

Her pink lips purse, and her eyes drop to the suitcase in my hand. She inhales a sharp, choked breath. "You're planning on staying?" She looks mildly horrified.

Like big bad Zoey has come to wreak havoc on the town. Only I know she's never seen me as a big baddie. Most people only relentlessly try to crush things smaller than them.

People are cruel that way.

And I know better than to think she's worried that me staying here means I'm opening myself up to being cursed. Amelia couldn't care less.

"I don't have to explain myself to you." I bend down and grab the orphaned wheel from the cobblestone.

She huffs. "You're going to have to explain yourself to *everyone* in this town. If you think you can waltz back like nothing happened and we all embrace you with open arms—"

"No worries there, Amelia," I cut her off. "I definitely don't want to be embraced by *your* arms." I rise to my feet, a good five inches shorter at five-foot-four. I try to tower.

"Stop hunching, Zoey." I hear October back when we were just teenagers. *"You know what you look like?"*

"Short?"

"And like a frightened doe."

"I am frightened." Not of her. I was in *awe* of her. This cursed town with these gossiping, judgy people—that's what scared me. Even if I was born here. Lived here all my life until I left.

"Frightened deer end up mounted on walls. You want to be mounted on someone's wall, Zoey?"

"No."

"Then stop hunching." Her voice was hushed, icy breath, but her fingers were soft, warm. They skimmed my waist, slipped up my spine, traveled with gentleness along my shoulders. And before I knew it, I was standing straighter.

If only to reach her height.

Like I'm evoking the memory of Mistpoint's Wonder Woman, Amelia's eyes heat on me as she says, "October won't want you here either."

October won't want you here either.

Those words are the equivalent of unsheathing a sword and sticking the point at my throat. I go stone cold, and my chest deflates at the mention of October. If the Roberts are royalty in Mistpoint, the Brambillas are gods.

October Brambilla was a goddess herself back in high school, and Amelia reminded me every day how *lucky* I was that someone like October would even dare give me a second of her prized attention.

How lucky I must be.

"You don't know that," I mutter weakly under my breath.

Amelia must hear because she says, "Did you lose brain cells in Cleveland?"

"Chicago," I correct.

She ignores that. "October and I are best friends. *Still* best friends. I know her better than you ever did. Like I said, she won't want you here." She places her hands on her hips and appraises me slowly. Starting at my worn leather boots and up to my black turtleneck. "Save yourself the embarrassment, Zoey, and just leave now."

My nose flares.

I'm not here for October. So even if she *allegedly* won't want me here, it changes nothing. Other than blossoming hurt in my chest. But that feeling can be drowned out with a bottle of red and singing some 70s hits at the top of my lungs.

Right now I have neither liquid courage nor Stevie Nicks to help me through this. So I can't stop the anger from bubbling. And there's nothing and no one who will stop these words from coming.

"I don't know how many times I'm going to have to say it," I snap. "I'm *not* leaving. And if you have a fucking problem with that, Amelia, then you can go eat a bag of dicks."

My anger carries my feet, and I turn around, headed back towards the docks. Leaving Miss Mistpoint in a stunned puddle.

Fuck, that felt good. I hardly ever stuck up for myself in high school. It was easier shrinking into the shadows than pushing back. But I wished for those words to leave my lips thousands of times.

Maybe not *exactly* those words...phrased so...ineloquently. Bag of dicks? Could've had a better punch, but hey, at least it was *something*.

Endorphins start pumping through me. I feel high, and I let that electric feeling carry me further and further through town. Seagulls squawk and fly towards the pier. The boardwalk along the docks is dotted with shops, bars, and restaurants. Further up the walk, multi-colored houses splatter across the cliffs, creating a picturesque landscape that many visitors love posting on Instagram. The fresh water is endless. Only boats visible in the horizon. But somewhere on the other side of the great lake is Canada.

Closest to the entrance of the pier, two pubs face each other like an omen to their generations' long rivalry. Fisherman's Wharf has an upscale appeal with a blue and white safety ring artfully tangled in a fish net hung above the door. *Fisherman's Wharf* letters glow in a soft, watery turquoise.

As much as I'd love to go in there and ask October herself if she's pissed I'm back, I'm banned from the Wharf.

As Effie Brambilla so crotchetily put it, *"You Durands step foot inside Fisherman's Wharf and you'll be kicked out faster than Mitch Montague lost the regatta race of '84."*

He lost in five seconds. His boat sank. From what the museum has recorded, everyone in the town thought the embarrassment of the loss was his official curse. Turns out his calf sliced open from the pier as he was trying to swim onto the rescue boat.

He died a month later from an infection.

And it's just like Effie to bring up someone's literal *death* to threaten us Durands. She's dramatic as hell, and also carries way too much sway in this town.

I kind of hate that she's October's aunt.

Crossing off Fisherman's Wharf from my list of options, I turn towards its rival bar. *The Drunk Pelican.*

The door needs a fresh coat of paint.

The *d* and *c* are tilted and practically falling off the shitty hand-painted sign. And I'm allowed to call it shitty, since it's my handiwork. My dad enlisted me for the job after the last sign fell off from rot.

A part of me will always love this little shithole of a pub.

The other part despises its very existence.

The Drunk Pelican is the cause of a lot of my problems.

Yet, I'm about to walk through those doors. Against better judgment—probably. Definitely. I inhale a breath, taking in the fresh air.

I'm here to see the guy who called me from across the country, begging me to come home. Parry DiNapoli should be inside these doors. There really is no turning back now.

CHAPTER 3

ZOEY DURAND

The Drunk Pelican hasn't changed one bit. I could've taken a photograph six years ago, and it'd be a replica of what I'm staring at today.

Torn vinyl booths, graffiti-covered walls, an old jukebox, and Christmas lights that eternally dangle from the ceiling all add to its shabby allure.

Unsurprisingly, it's also empty.

I guess not much has really changed.

When the door sways closed behind me, the little bells jingle. I wince at the sound. It's loud enough that I feel like a blowhorn announced my arrival. On the list of people I don't want to see, Brian Durand's ass is parked near the top. To be honest, I don't even know if he's here.

He took over the pub when our dad ditched this place to become a mariner, working mostly as a deckhand. I don't expect to see my dad. The Great Lakes shipping season has already started, so it's more likely he's on some lake freighter right now.

But Brian…my brother is uptight and relentless enough that he's still probably spending every hour of the day at the Pelican. Trying to keep this shithole afloat.

Then again, six years is a long time for me to be away, and it's not like I kept tabs on my brothers. The only person I stayed in contact with was October, and even then, she wouldn't talk about my family. At my request.

I tried my best to cut out the things that would make me miss home. To make it hurt less being in Chicago.

Don't ask me why I couldn't cut her.

I shuffle further into the pub and carry my suitcase so it doesn't skid noisily on the floor.

"I'll be with you in a second!" someone calls from behind the kitchen doors.

I recognize the deep smokiness of that voice immediately—the kind that sounds sensual and like a come-on, even when he's just talking about rainstorms and sailing conditions.

Definitely *not* Brian, who just sounds like a pissed crab caught in a net.

All the worries from earlier today start to leave. My muscles loosen, and I set my suitcase on the ground.

Pots and pans clank together before the kitchen door swings open. Parry's eyes meet mine, and he freezes *in* the doorway. The door swings back and hits his ass. The impact stumbles him, and the tray of glass beer steins drops out of his hands.

Glass shatters violently on the floor. I flinch.

He doesn't make a move to clean the mess. His bottomless, seafoam green eyes survey me like he's seeing a ghost.

I can't take my eyes off him.

Parry DiNapoli used to be one of the hottest people who graced Mistpoint High. Older than me (graduated before I attended), his beauty was another legend whispered in the hallways. Olive skin, sun-kissed golden-blond hair, lean muscles, and carved jawline.

He's all of those things still. Even his hair has the silk and charm of those 90s California surfers. Tucked behind his ears. Skirting his neck.

He's never surfed, as far as I know, but if I ever went searching for Parry growing up, nine times out of ten he'd be on the lake underneath the bright sun and likely cleaning a local's sailboat for an extra buck.

But now—now I'm stuck on the new *thing* on his face. The scar that slices down the left side. Thick, puffy, distinctive—it begins at his forehead, cuts through the edge of his eyebrow, and descends to the base of his jaw.

What happened to him?

I've missed six years.

That invasive thought wreaks havoc in my head. I've missed *so* much. I left, but everyone else I cared about stayed. Everyone I went to high school with or who attended school with my brothers— they've most likely already been through some kind of misfortune.

Shit, Parry is *thirty* now.

He's my brother Colt's childhood best friend.

And even though Parry is six years older than me, he's been close like family. There were times I'd rather run to Parry than to Colt. His edges aren't as serrated, and his diehard loyalty to town scum like us, Durands, is questionable on his part—but revered on mine. I always looked up to Parry as someone to aspire to be like.

To maintain good morals, a good heart, and be someone to trust. Someone to depend on.

Did not exactly achieve those Parry DiNapoli levels of dependability. I ransacked and murdered that part. I haven't been dependable for anything since I left.

But I'm here now.

And I can't get over the time lost and his scar.

My chest rises and falls heavily. "Parry—"

"You came." His surprise is unmistakable.

My brows knit together, confused. "Of course I came. You called. Don't you remember?"

He lets out a long breath. "Yeah…but…" His smoky voice tapers off like he's considering his words carefully, and he rubs the back of his neck. "I didn't think you'd come back. No one ever does."

"For Colt," I say my brother's name. "I'd come back."

He nods strongly. "I'm glad you did." He grabs a towel and bends down to the broken glass. "Scared the shit out of me though. Could have texted, you know?" He smiles, the movement pulling the scar.

I try not to stare, but he's inspecting me head-to-toe too.

Through his eyes, I've gone from eighteen to twenty-four in a blink. How different do I really appear? I swallow my feelings and manage to say, "I haven't texted you in six years. Didn't want to break the cycle."

He tosses some broken glass and cracked steins back into the tray.

I step closer to help.

He whips his head up. "Zoey, do-do-doon'tttt!" he stutters, his voice caught in the *t*. Frustration crests his brow, but fear and something more forceful and protective are clearer.

I stop cold, feet away from the broken glass.

Parry has had a stutter ever since his parents died. As the story goes, his nature-loving mom and dad camped at Edge of the World one night. The primitive campground, located among a wooded cliffside in Mistpoint, is home to urban werewolf legends and a lot of wildlife. Bears, wolves, foxes.

Don't go camping at Edge of the World on a full moon, locals will tell out-of-towners, hoping to entice them into the Supernatural Oddities shop. Just to spend money in our shabby tourist traps.

The only supernatural thing here is October Brambilla's catlike balance. Perfectly agile. Never trips. Never falters. Quick and swift with soft hands that've caught me before.

I think about how when Parry's parents were killed from an animal attack on a full moon, they became a staple in the Harbor's history.

Don't go camping at Edge of the World on a full moon. You'll die like Mr. & Mrs. DiNapoli.

I believe bad fates reoccur here. Animal attacks happen, and this one just happened on a perfect full-moon day to spin a tale.

But Parry—he never believed a pack of wolves ripped their tent and killed them. He's convinced they were murdered from a stranger passing through. A stabbing in the dark. And what better place to hide a killing than a town full of ghost stories and shitty detective work?

He was fifteen back then.

His older brother became his guardian, and Enzo DiNapoli even took over their parents' job. Cemetery caretakers. Enzo is the local grave digger, and I've rarely seen him. He only comes out at night.

Parry only comes out during the day.

Our eyes meet again, and his soften a fraction. "Just…don't get close." He manages to speak without the stutter this time. Glass shards still scatter the floorboards.

Realization hits me. "Jesus, Parry, I'm not going to get cursed touching some broken glass." I shuffle closer and squat across from him.

"You don't know that." He's quick to scoop more glass in a rag. "This place has a way of making a one-in-a-million freak accident become a sure thing."

Impossibly true.

And *definitely* true.

I'm not that confident a piece of glass won't impale my heart. But when you grow up in Mistpoint Harbor, you learn quickly not to let that kind of fear consume you.

"I know I'm not indestructible, just like no one here is," I say like he's forgetting I grew up in this town too. "Don't baby me just because I'm back."

He holds my gaze with more softness.

Like I said, he's Colt's friend. Where you found one, you'd eventually find the other. They even sailed together on the high school team. But in a way, Parry has always been like a third brother to me.

When I knew I was bisexual, Parry was the first person I told. I love Parry, and he's the kind of person that'd take your secret to the grave.

At fourteen, I wasn't really ready to come out to anyone else.

Now, though, I'm fairly sure most people in town know I'm bi.

Parry says quietly with that natural smokiness, "I'm not babying you." He stops for a beat, then sighs heavily. "Okay, maybe I am. But fuck, Zo, you *left*. And you've avoided getting cursed this far." He throws the last bit of glass in the tray.

I see where this is going and my stomach sinks. "Parry—"

We both stand up, and he cuts me off quickly. "*I* asked you back here, Zoey. *Me*. And you fucking came." He laughs like he still can't believe his own eyes. "So if anything bad happens to you…"

"It won't be your fault."

His green eyes pierce me. "We both know that's not true. Just do me a favor and *try* not to get into trouble." He sets the tray of glass on the bar. Shards clink like windchimes.

"Avoid broken mirrors, black cats, and walking under ladders, got it," I joke.

"I'm serious, Zo."

I know.

Agreeing to staying out of trouble in Mistpoint is basically agreeing to be locked in a bedroom. I can't do that.

That's not why I came home, but I don't want Parry to regret asking me here.

I leave my suitcase on the ground and take a seat on the barstool. "You didn't force me home, Parry. I could have said *no*. Hell, I could have told you to *go fuck yourself*."

He grabs a fresh glass from the shelf. "I wouldn't have blamed you if you did."

"Because you're nice."

"Because I'm used to it from Durands. Your brother tells me to *go fuck myself* on a daily basis."

Brian.

My oldest brother is also Parry's boss. And the only reason Parry continues to work at The Drunk Pelican is his greatest trait and his biggest flaw.

Loyalty.

"You still hate Brian?" I ask.

"Some things don't change in six years." His brows rise. "Some things are everlasting." He pours me a beer from the draft. "Like my hatred for Brian. Like the busted jukebox only playing Frank Sinatra."

"Like the rot on this roof," I add.

"Like your blonde hair." He eyes my hair as he slides me the beer. Maybe I should've dyed my hair blue or green to be less predictable.

I focus a little harder on his scar. It looks healed. Can't be new. "Some things have changed."

Our gazes meet in a heavy beat.

"It was a sailing accident," he breathes in a panty-dropping voice. But I know he's not trying to drop my green Yoda panties. For one, Parry DiNapoli is gay.

For another, Colt would kill him.

I cup the glass of beer. "You don't have to talk about it, if you don't want to."

He smiles softly. "It's in the fucking museum now, Zo. There's no hiding anything. Plus, everyone here is nosy as hell—*that* hasn't changed."

"You mean we don't live in *Gossip* Harbor?" I feign shock.

He lets out a small laugh. "Exactly." After a beat, he continues, "Colt and I were sailing in the Spring Royal Regatta, and he got ca-ca-cauught up in the lines." He clears his throat, then says, "I cut him free from the rope, and the wind just picked up at the worst time. I got knocked back and my knife..." He waves at his face.

I want to say *I'm so sorry.* But something else leaves my lips. Something worse. "You're still hot."

He laughs. Those full-bodied kind of laughs that shake the ground.

I try hard not to smile, already feeling the guilt spring up from being completely and utterly tactless. "I didn't mean to say that."

He can't stop *laughing.* He braces his fist on the bar, bent over. "You definitely did."

"I have no tact," I remind him and take a large swig of the beer to stop my word vomit. To be honest, I just don't do well with those somber situations. Where people need condolences and hugs. I don't know how to be *that* person. No one ever gave me those tools. And here, in Mistpoint, it feels like everyone goes through so much shit that the words *I'm so sorry* don't seem to carry any weight. So many of us are fucked up here.

Parry holds a stitch at his side, trying to gather himself. "Thank you for that. I needed it."

"No one's told you you're still hot?" I wonder into a deeper frown.

He cocks his head in thought. "Let's just say my ego has been chipped away these past few years."

"Let me guess, Brian is doing the chipping?"

"He calls me Frankenstein about fifteen times a day, and I've told that asshole Frankenstein is the doctor, *not* the monster. Jackass still doesn't care."

"Sounds like he's still pissed you taught Colt how to sail." Parry even introduced Colt to the sailing team. If Mitch Montague—the guy who *died* from the '84 regatta accident—is any indication, sailing is dangerous here.

But some people were born to be on the water.

Have the wind in their faces.

You can't stop that kind of love.

"Yeah, Brian's still carrying a raging hard-on against me," Parry says. "Pissed I'm Colt's best friend. Pissed I'm the cook at his bar." He looks me up and down. "He's going to be even more pissed I asked you here."

"He doesn't have to know you're a part of this. I've come up with a bulletproof excuse for being here. One that doesn't involve the truth." I lean forward on the bar, closer to Parry. "To Brian and the entire town, I'm here on behalf of a publishing deal. I'm writing a book about Mistpoint Harbor."

"*Zoey.*" Parry is near a grimace and a groan. He threads a concerned hand through his pretty boy hair. "Do you have a death wish? A Durand snooping around and profiting off the town's history—the town she abandoned?"

"I know it'll piss some people off."

"*Some* people?"

"Okay, a lot of people—but isn't pissing people off kind of the point? In their anger, they'll get so caught up in the lie that they won't even question why I'm *actually* here."

Parry is still wincing, but he nods. "Maybe you're right." He pours himself a beer while I take a sip of mine. His eyes flit to me. "I still can't believe you're over twenty-one now. Don't have to give you a coffee cup for your beer."

I smile sadly.

I don't like having missed everything.

"It's good to be back," I say. Despite my run-in with Amelia earlier, I do believe this.

He takes a swig from his beer. The small silver hoop in his left earlobe glints a little in the light. "How was Chicago?"

"Alright," I say into a shrug. The six years in Chicago feel like another life. Not mine, really. Someone else's. It hurts thinking about *that* life when I'm here. "I don't want to talk about me," I say. "I'm here for Colt, remember. Ever since you called last night, I've thought about a million tragic things that happened to him. Is he okay? Do we need to go to the lighthouse now?"

"He's okay right now." Parry grips his beer tight and glances to the window. "It's going to get dark soon. He's pretty particular about not being disturbed during nighttime. I think it'd be better to visit him tomorrow morning."

"Have you…tried visiting him at night?" I wonder, tension spooling between me and Parry. The unsaid thing drawing a discomfort that I'd rather barrel through.

October taught me that.

Don't just sit in discomfort. *Do something.* So I prod, "I mean, do you still avoid the dark?"

He lets out a frustrated noise. "No, you mean, *are you still* afraid *of the dark, Parry?*"

I don't disagree. "Well, are you?"

"Yes," he admits tensely, then adds quickly, "but I've *tried* visiting him at night with Enzo. This isn't about my fear of the dark. Like

I said, he doesn't like being disturbed at night—it's better in the mornings."

The pressure on my chest still hasn't released. "On the phone, you said he's pretty messed up. What does that even mean?"

"It means he's messed up. I don't know how else to describe it. Tomorrow—you'll see tomorrow. Maybe you can snap him out of it." He lets out a heavier breath. "That's what I'm hoping anyway."

And what if I can't help him? I keep that thought to myself and take a larger swig of my beer. Then I ask, "Do you get off work before sundown?"

"No, I'm the only cook. And I'm the only host. And sometimes the only bartender and waiter."

A pang shoots through my heart. Of course he's the one keeping this shithole from sinking. My dad always had trouble staffing the bar, and Parry is still coming to the rescue. "My family doesn't deserve you, Parry."

"Yes, you do," he refutes with ease. Like it's just known. "Brian doesn't deserve me though."

"Hear, hear," I agree with the raise of my beer.

He wipes up a sticky spot on the bar. "He has done one semi-nice thing, even if it's mostly for his benefit."

"What's that?"

"He agreed to walk me home every night, just so I'll work until 2 a.m. It's slight torture keeping his company, but at least I'm torturing him."

I smile. Glad that Brian is getting a taste of his own bitter medicine.

Parry stares harder at me. "I don't even know what you're doing now. Are you really a writer? You graduated college a couple years ago, right?"

"Not a writer. I actually suck at grammar." I smile at myself. "Honestly, I'd rather stick my finger in a pencil sharpener than write a five-page essay, let alone a whole book." My cover story might be a shit one if anyone realizes I'm no Virginia Woolf or Agatha Christie, but it's the best I have. I barely glance up at him, a little sheepish about my past. "And yeah, I did graduate two years ago."

He tilts his head, waiting expectantly for me to keep going.

I stare down at my beer. "I'm not even sure where to begin, Parry. It's been so long. And anyway, I didn't come here to tell my sad story. I just want to help Colt."

And then I'll be gone again.

Parry frowns harder. "What s*ad* story? Was everything alright back in Chicago?" His gaze sweeps me earnestly and swiftly like he's trying to find a broken bone.

Concern furrows his brows off my silence. "Were you dating anyone?" he asks.

I knew this question might come up.

It's also the one I wasn't sure how to handle.

"I—" I start but I don't get the words out.

A jingle echoes from the pub door.

Parry and I whip our heads toward the sound.

No.

I'm groaning internally.

My oldest brother is here.

Brian stands inside The Drunk Pelican with a box of frozen crab claws. A dark raincoat on, beanie over his chocolate brown hair, and thick but neatly groomed beard makes him appear even more like a gruff local than the last time I was here.

Like the Lady of the Lake birthed him.

He doesn't even acknowledge me. His first order of business is turning to his cook. "Get the fuck out," he tells Parry.

Parry barely blinks. "We're open, Brian. What if a customer comes in? You burn everything you touch. But if you want to serve *char* then by all means." He nods to my brother.

Brian saunters to the window and flips the *Open* sign to *Closed*. "Crisis averted. Now leave."

Parry grumbles under his breath and tosses the rag onto the bar. His eyes flit to me. "I'll text you, Zoey."

My brother's intensity bears down on our interaction. Like he's gathering every morsel of information he can.

"Sounds good. See ya, Pear."

Parry gives me a nod. On his way out, he passes Brian and says in smoky anger, "Eat shit and die."

"Get bent, Parry," Brian shoots back.

Parry kicks the door open with his shoe, and Brian glares at his shadow as he departs.

I grimace.

Six years ago, they might have hated each other but it was a quiet, simmering hatred. Whispered curses and eye rolls. Now everything seems to be messy and exposed. Like there's one string left holding things together before they just explode on each other.

One thing is certain: Brian can't know Parry asked me here.

My cover story better hold up. It's the only thing keeping the pin in the grenade.

With Parry gone, the tension thickens the closer Brian approaches the bar. He sets the box of crab claws heavily onto the stool beside me.

Confusion wrinkles the edges of his eyes, and his hair is starting to gray at his temples.

Thirty-nine.

Shit, I can't believe my brother is almost out of his thirties. He was only thirty-three when I left.

We have a fifteen-year age gap, but it's not really strange considering we're biologically half siblings. Brian, Colt, and I all share the same dad. Different moms.

He still hasn't looked at me. Instead, he digs into his raincoat and unearths his cell. He intently scrolls, clicks, and types. It's *unnerving.*

"You're really not going to say anything?" I ask him.

"There's a Greyhound leaving tonight. I'm booking you on the first one out of town."

The floor might as well drop from underneath my stool. "What?"

For the first time, he finally meets my gaze. We share the same blue eyes. Rough and turbulent like the lake outside these doors.

"When you turned eighteen, I told you to stay," he says each word with a precision and sharpness like he's brandishing a razorblade. "I told you what would happen if you left."

The roots are rotted underneath our family tree. Decaying. Gone.

"You told me I'd have no home here," I say in a soft whisper. "I remember, I just thought—"

"You thought I was lying?" he says coldly.

"No, I didn't think that."

"But you thought I'd change my mind and accept you back with open arms." He doesn't phrase it like a question. Because it really isn't.

Brian has always been a stern, angry person. But he's been a decent brother. So maybe I did think that seeing me would trigger a change of heart. Especially since I always thought it was more of an empty threat to get me to stay.

He was the biggest cheerleader on Team Mistpoint Harbor and aggressively against those on Team Chicago. He needed help with The Drunk Pelican, and my college plans weren't part of the familial responsibility to the pub.

And maybe I was the selfish one, running out.

So it's hard to blame the anger that rolls off Brian in waves, but I'm still his little sister. We're both still Durands. We grew up as outcasts in an already cursed town. There's got to be some solidarity in a single cell in his body.

"Aren't you even going to ask why I'm back?" I snap.

"I don't want to know. I don't need to know. You'll be gone in…" He checks his motherfucking watch. "An hour."

"I'm not leaving, Brian. I'm here to write a book."

"A book. You?" he states like it's absurd. Me writing a book.

"Yeah, me," I almost shout. "I'm Agatha fucking Christie. Have a problem with that?"

"No. Just go Agatha-Christie-yourself someplace else."

"I can't. It's about Mistpoint Harbor."

"What is?"

"The book!" He's exhausting me.

I'm rattling him. "No. *No.*" His gaze darkens. "You're not. Not here."

"Yes, I am, and I'm *not* leaving."

He takes a long breath like he can't ingest enough oxygen to fill his lungs. And then he glares at me. "Well, you're not staying here."

"My room—"

"Is gone. I turned it into my office after you left."

I try and ignore the pain that flares in my chest. Can't blame him—I remind myself. I chose to leave.

That's on me.

"So you're kicking me out?"

"That's not how I see it. You have a place to go: the bus station. And I'm happy to buy your ticket if you're strapped for cash."

"How sweet of you," I say sharply and jump off the stool. I almost ask him if he knows anything about Colt—but that's doubtful. My brothers have their own tempestuous history with each other.

I grab my suitcase. "I don't need your cash. I'll find another place in Mistpoint to stay."

His scowl darkens. "None of the inns will house a Durand. That hasn't fucking changed since you've been gone."

I could call Parry, but if I have any hope of mending this rift between me and Brian, then I shouldn't be asking favors from Parry DiNapoli right now. It'll only stir the pot, and I need this boil to come to a low simmer.

"I'll figure it out," I tell Brian. "Thanks for nothing."

I leave him in the pub. Hoping he'll come rushing out. Telling me to *hold on! Wait!* Something that a big brother would do to protect his little sister. But then again, I grew up being bullied by a lot of people in this town and there was only one person who'd ever come to my defense.

And it was never my brothers.

CHAPTER 4

ZOEY DURAND

Ten Years Ago
Age 14

There has to be some sort of mistake. I stare at my course schedule with wide eyes. The dreaded *D* word stares back at me. I didn't sign up for *drama*. In fact, I remember picking my top choices for electives. Drama did not make the cut. Not even close.

I wanted an elective where I could sit in the back of the classroom and disappear into the wall. Be invisible.

Drama is the antithesis of *invisible*.

So how the fuck did I get put in this class?

It's what I want to say to the lady in the school office, but I don't think that'll help my cause. While she chats on the phone, I rock on the balls of my feet impatiently and regrip the long stick of my black umbrella. *First period is Drama 101.* If I don't get this sorted out pronto—I'm going to be late for class.

First day of high school.

First day at Mistpoint High.

And I'm already seconds from screwing up my one goal: *blend in.*

Just…blend.

It really can't be that hard.

Elementary and middle school, I skated by with only a few hallway pushes and shoves. Sure, in fourth grade Macie Byrne tripped me in the cafeteria, and my tray of mushed carrots and a hockey puck hamburger went sailing. Everyone laughed.

Didn't want that disgusting food anyway.

Oh, and there was that one time in seventh grade where Aiden Gray sat behind me in class and stuck gum in my hair.

I needed a haircut. Anyway...

Up until (possibly) today, I blended pretty well. All things considered. And I had a friend back then. Now Vittoria is gone. The Romanos made a surprise move to Milwaukee last month, taking my only friend with them. Leaving me to face this town and ninth grade with *no* friendly companion.

I'm on my own.

Mrs. Shields keeps chattering away on the school's landline, pretending like I'm not right here. Her fire-engine red raincoat squeaks as her arms shift. Her hair is twisted in a stylish top-knot, and she bites on the end of her pencil.

Maybe I'm blending *too* well.

I clear my throat.

She shoots me a nasty look and holds up a manicured finger. "One minute. This is an important call, honey." She swivels around in her chair, back turned to me.

Great.

I blow out a nervous, tensed breath. A Mistpoint High sky blue and white pennant flag hangs proudly on the wall. A picture of Mistpoint's mascot, the Seagull, rests on the front desk. He's hoisting a *Go Mistpoint!* sign during a football game.

Brian played for the team growing up, and surprisingly, he said he enjoyed it.

Maybe it was just a good, healthy way to expel his aggression. He bought me a Mistpoint Seagulls T-shirt to commemorate my voyage into high school. I think he was trying to bolster my "school spirit"—but being a part of the spirit squad doesn't work into my *blending in* plan.

The phone clicks loudly, and Mrs. Shields spins around, a fake smile plastered to her face. "Now how can I help you, honey?"

I slide my schedule on the desk. "I'm not supposed to be in drama. Is there any way I can get this changed?"

She examines the paper intently. "Let's see if we can sort this out." Her lips slowly downturn. "Zoey Durand?"

I suck in a breath. "Yeah, that's me."

She purses her lips and slides the paper back. "I can't help you."

"But—I didn't sign up for drama. It's supposed to be an elective—"

"You're a freshman. You get what's available."

I'm not sure that's the complete truth. But I go with it. "There has to be *any* other open elective available. I'll take anything."

She shakes her head. "It's too late for schedule changes." Now that is a lie.

The first warning bell rings.

Shit.

One minute to get to class.

With a defeated sigh, I reclaim my class schedule and adjust my bookbag strap.

"Zoey," Mrs. Shields says.

I'm not dumb enough to be hopeful as I glance up. "Yeah?"

Her eyes flame. "Tell your dad to stay on the lake. It's where he belongs."

Cold slips down my spine.

I'm unsurprised she knows my dad became a deckhand just a few weeks ago. It was the biggest gossip in town. *Nicholas Durand will be away for nine months out of the year!*

My dad's decision to work on a lake freighter wasn't easy. He loved The Drunk Pelican so much he put every dime of his personal savings into that place. But I know he loves Brian, Colt, and me more. He must've thought leaving town would make things easier for us. Part of me thinks it'll just be harder. Not having a dad around.

I already don't have a mom.

Tell your dad to stay on the lake. It's where he belongs. Her words echo in my head. A snarky retort dies in my throat. So I just give Mrs. Shields a nod and slip out of the front office.

The hallway is almost empty, except for a janitor. He mops up wet puddles and unfurls yellow signs that warn of slick floors.

I tuck my umbrella under my arm, walking brisky. Slipping.

Only in Mistpoint Harbor would I need an umbrella when it's not even raining outside. The first day of high school marks the death of Lenard Doyle and Madeline Mackay in 1894. After a vicious rainstorm, the school flooded, and the two students drowned in a locked broom closet.

Legend goes, Mistpoint High has been cursed ever since, and the first day of every school year, ceilings spring uncontrollable leaks. And it's not like ghosts walk these hallowed halls and summon downpours.

I just think it's some strange destiny. Some sort of magnetic shift on this one spot in the world that makes bad shit happen.

Like deaths in broom closets.

Like leaky ceilings.

Catching my balance, I bypass posters on the walls that read:

IN MEMORY OF DOYLE & MACKAY,
GRAB YOUR UMBRELLA.

I manage to pick up pace and jog towards the Fine Arts hall, all without face-planting. The final bell rings when I'm a foot from the doorway.

And I watch as the teacher closes the door on my face.

"Wai—"

Slam!

You've got to be kidding me.

Fuck.

Fuck.

Fuck.

Why didn't I just stick my umbrella inside and jam the door? Regret pummels me about as much as fear.

Now I have to make a grand entrance.

Okay, I can do this.

No, I have to do this. There is no alternative. I'm not planning on skipping class forever and flunking out of ninth grade.

I cage a breath and open the door.

All the students are already seated. And they're staring at me. Heads turn like I've swiveled a spotlight over my bowed shoulders and flushed neck.

Water drips onto my hot cheek.

I look up. Ceiling tiles concave with moisture. Droplets drip throughout the classroom like a light shower, and students have already drawn the hoods of their rain jackets. Others hold their opened umbrellas, as though bad luck is such an occurrence here, opening an umbrella indoors couldn't possibly add more.

Only in Mistpoint Harbor, I think again.

"You're late," the teacher barks from his desk. Mr. Owens is a wiry man with curly strawberry-blond hair and a red beard. His blue Mistpoint Seagull umbrella shadows his angered eyes.

I'm burning up under the attention.

He can't be any older than Brian. Late twenties, probably.

"I'm sorry. I was, um, in the front office." I scope out an open desk. Shying over the intrusive gazes of my peers. Teenagers I've seen all my life, yet they've avoided me like I've carried the bubonic plague.

They still stare at me like I'm a walking infection.

I spot a vacant seat in the back. One foot towards my freedom from this horrible spotlight—and Mr. Owens approaches me.

"Wait right there," he demands.

Shit.

He crosses the room, clasping his umbrella and a mason jar filled with slips of paper. My stomach overturns.

Nooooo.

Please, nooo.

"I didn't think I'd have to get this out on the first day, but there's a first for everything." The surliness in his voice shrinks me another two inches. He directs his attention to the entire class. "If any of you are late for the final bell, there will be consequences."

He extends the mason jar to me. "Take a piece of paper."

I dig into the jar.

Mr. Owens eyes me harder. "Your name?"

"Zoey." I pluck a folded slip.

"Last name?"

"Durand."

Several students who didn't recognize me at first glance—they noticeably squirm in their seats. Others lean into their friends, whispering.

Side-eyeing me.

Water wets my cheek, my hair, my black baggy Patti Smith band tee. Artfully ripped. I thought it was cool. Retro. Maybe I just look like I stepped out of the dumpster everyone wants to throw me in.

Too nervous to unfurl my umbrella, I'm slowly getting soaked.

"Durand," Mr. Owens says in thought, going a little stiff. "I played football with your brother."

I relax a little. Maybe this won't be so bad then. Brian can be a jerk, but as far as he told me, his high school teammates never hated him.

Mr. Owens returns to his desk. "Do you know how to play charades, Zoey?"

I wish I didn't.

I wince and nod halfheartedly.

"Good. Read the paper silently and then begin." He focuses on the class. "Whoever guesses correctly first will receive five extra points on the next quiz."

I unfurl the paper. Typed out are the words Zombie Cheerleader. Greeeaaat.

How should I start?

Before I even move a muscle, a student—Marc or Mattie or something or other (I can't remember his name from eighth grade)—he shouts, "A corpse!"

Laughter fills the classroom.

"Scared girl!"

"Blonde girl?"

"The daughter of a murderer," a girl in a yellow raincoat guesses cruelly.

I'm frozen. Cheeks flaming.

"Amelia," Mr. Owens scolds.

Amelia feigns disbelief. "What? That's what she is. Technically, I should be getting five extra credit points, Mr. Owens."

The teacher disregards her and nods towards me. "Keep going, Zoey."

Keep going? I haven't even started.

I lick my dried lips and shuffle around the front of the room awkwardly. People shout in wild succession.

"Snake!"

"Loser!"

"Bigfoot!"

My eyes skirt around the faces. Some in my grade that I remember. Others are upperclassmen that I've never met, never paid much attention to. Everyone's voices start melding together. My heart pounds harder and harder. Palms sweating. The temperature climbing.

And then my gaze lands on her.

Holy shit...

October Brambilla. Town royalty. One year older than me—ten times more put together, braver, prettier. She's in my class?

Loosely gripping a cotton candy pink umbrella over her head, she sits with gracefulness and dignity—like she owns the room, the town, the world. Brown hair cascades in perfect waves along her shoulders. A pink sweater matches the color of her full, kissable lips. And why am I thinking they're kissable when she's staring at me like I'm a rodent traipsing through her universe? Her iced gaze pushes through me, punctures me. Makes me feel small. And weak.

She seems like an utter bitch. Exactly what my friend Vittoria used to tell me before she moved. But then...why isn't October shouting at me like everyone else?

Why isn't she making a guess?

I almost stumble.

"One-legged pirate!"

"Idiot!"

"Hey," Mr. Owens barks at that.

I do feel like a bumbling idiot. Everyone knows the Brambillas. Just like everyone knows the Durands. Only, October has never cast a glance in my direction. Not whenever we crossed paths in town. Not in middle school or elementary. Not as kids. Definitely not as teenagers.

I'm gross.

Trash.

She's a gem.

Wanted.

Desired.

Not only is she a Brambilla, but the girl literally ran into a burning building three years ago. The old library in the square went up in flames, and October stormed inside and saved her younger sister. Plus one of the town's oldest history books.

She's a legend.

I force myself to shuffle again. Arms outstretched. Lumbering forward like a ghoulish, ugly thing.

"A zombie," October finally says in a cool, commanding tone.

I stop moving, and the students make a show of cursing and huffing. With wet hair and the damp tee suctioning my flat chest, I hand the soggy paper to the teacher. Trying not to shiver.

Since no one technically guessed the cheerleader portion of the zombie, Mr. Owens could make me continue. But I'm hoping he'll cut me some slack.

He frowns a little at the paper, then nods.

"Alright. Good job, October."

Hearing her name short-circuits my brain. And I unfortunately ask a question I know the answer to *out loud*, "October Brambilla?" Maybe she's siphoning all of my oxygen. Asphyxiating me. Making me say stupid things.

Snickers fill the classroom at my dumb question.

Of course she's the one and only October.

Amelia snorts. "You're in the presence of royalty, Durand. Bow down to the queen."

I ignore that, about to head to the open desk, but I'm stuck struggling to open my black umbrella. The sharp points snap back at me. Jesus. Come on, come on.

Everyone laughs more.

"Durand," Amelia snaps louder. "I said bow."

What the fuck? I glance to the teacher. Mr. Owens pretends not to hear, busying himself with something on his computer. Maybe he thinks he can't give me another pass since he just did with charades.

Umbrella half-unfurled, I suck down my pride and look to October.

She doesn't say anything. Her eyes, shaded beneath the pink umbrella, are as demanding as Amelia's words.

Slowly, I bow.

Under my breath, I say, "Your highness."

And I swear I hear her hiss just as quietly, "Stand up."

My chest inflates with something I can't understand. When I rise again, the classroom is in a fit of irrepressible laughter. My eyes are on hers.

They haven't softened. Not even a fraction.

Shame and heat color my cheeks as I find the open desk. Bumping into umbrellas and apologizing all the way to my seat, "Sorry, sorry...sorry, I'm really sorry."

I finally sit, take a breath, and manage to easily open my umbrella. Droplets ping and slip off, and I can barely think about drama as Mr. Owens hands out the syllabus and starts class.

My mind spins with other things.

October.

My dad.

Amelia's words still puncture me. The daughter of a murderer.

My dad's curse feels like a part of mine. But that's not how this town works. Technically, I can't be cursed until I'm over eighteen. To protect the children, I think the town made that ridiculous rule. Like they can control the meaning of misfortune.

To anyone that asks, I'll never stop repeating the truth. Nicholas Durand is not a murderer. His curse is just morbid.

His first wife died in childbirth. Brian's mom. Dead.

His second wife died giving birth to Colt.

And then there was my mother. She died during my labor.

After I was born, the town decided it was too much of a coincidence that three different women died all the same way. They think my dad had a hand in it.

It's a cruel rumor, not based on fact. And for a town that loves legends and the unexplainable, they've decided our family needed to have an explanation.

Really though, having a murderer lurking around town just adds to the "cursed" allure. It's a game to a lot of people here.

The bell rings, signaling the end of class. I take my time gathering my things. Avoiding eye contact. Avoiding everyone.

Even the one and only October.

The rest of the school day goes by according to plan. Blend. It nearly lifts my spirits, but the residual embarrassment from this morning still lingers. No matter how hard I try, I can't stop replaying the events in my head. I effing bowed to October Brambilla.

In front of an entire classroom.

God, could I be more pathetic?

The end-of-day bell rings and students crowd and loiter in the wet hallways, chatting with friends before heading out to the parking lot.

Shuffling my way into the hall, I reach my locker without much notice. Success, I think. Until I perch my umbrella handle on my shoulder and open my locker.

A pastel pink paper bag rests on a stack of textbooks.

Looking around, I try to spot the girls or guys giggling in the corner. This has to be some practical joke.

Right?

Carefully, I open the paper bag and pull out a homemade fruit tart. Little blueberries and raspberries center the pastry. I skipped lunch today. Hid out in the library to avoid having to choose a table, not that I suspect many people would've wanted me to join theirs. My stomach grumbles at the sight of the tart.

Why would someone give this to me? Is it poisoned or something? I take a second look into the bag. There's a note.

I slip out the pretty stationary paper—woodland creatures like birds, wolves, rabbits decorate the border—and I stare at the neat, beautiful handwriting.

Chin up. – OB

OB.
October Brambilla.

CHAPTER 5

ZOEY DURAND

♡ *Present Day*

Twilight settles into town. Oranges and pinks bathe the lake, the colors reminding me of my dad.

He used to warn Brian, Colt, and me about the most dangerous time to be outside. Twilight is the time between dog and wolf. When it's too difficult to distinguish which animal you face, and it's easy to mistake a dog for a wolf. Or a wolf for a dog.

"Inter canem et lupum." Our dad would say the idiom in its original Latin form. He'd always end with, "Return home before then."

A distant howl echoes across the winds and sends a shiver over my arms. Dog or wolf, I don't want to come upon either right now. I have enough going on than facing any kind of creature.

I wheel my broken, wobbly mess of a suitcase down the boardwalk. Unruly wind rocks and sways the docked boats at the harbor.

I find the familiar, orange-painted house nestled behind Fisherman's Wharf. October and I kept in touch mostly through texts and the occasional phone call. I cared too much about her not to check in, and I think she felt the same way about me.

But we had rules.

Rule #1: Never discuss family.

Rule #2: Never talk about relationships.

Rule #3: Never ask about the curse.

Rule #4: Never meet again. Never ask for it.

That last rule was always the hardest, but we never did break it. Hell, we never broke a single one.

Until now.

I pull out my cellphone and dial her number. The wind howls… or is that a dog? A wolf? I check over my shoulder, a chill creeping in.

Strange noises lurk within the empty town. Old wooden docks are creaking, and beach glass windchimes clink on front porches while skeletal tree limbs scrape against houses.

My breath smokes the cold air, and I hug my free arm around my waist. She's not picking up. My phone rings again.

And again.

Fuck.

A second passes and I'm listening to her answering machine. "If you meant to call October Brambilla, you almost found her. Try calling later."

Almost found her.

I expel a heavy breath, about to call again just to hear her voice a second time.

My answering machine is just an automated voice. I've never even bothered recording a personal message. Not that many people are ever trying to find *me*.

What if Amelia already ran into October and told her about my arrival into town? What if she's purposefully screening my call?

Hurt punctures my confidence, but I'm still holding out some hope that October won't be pissed if she sees me. We're still friends.

At least we were yesterday.

I ditch my suitcase on the sidewalk and creep into her yard. Light still glows from her bedroom window. Top left. Lacey white drapes obscure the inside.

Okay, time to find a stone. Or a pebble. Definitely not a rock. I scope out the bed of purple pansies and quietly tiptoe through them to snatch a flat stone.

I brush the dirt off because if I'm going to throw a stone at October's window, it should be a clean one.

How absurd, Zoey. I almost laugh at myself.

Seriously, if I told myself three days ago that I'd be creeping through the Brambilla's flower bed, I'd have also told myself to seek professional help.

Too late for that.

I lick my dried lips and eye my target.

The stone sails out of my hand and connects with the window. What I think is going to be a light *tap* on the pane in reality is more of a soft *crack*. I hold my breath.

It didn't shatter, thank God.

But a nasty fissure runs through the glass.

Note to self: *don't underestimate your own strength.*

I see a shadow move, and then a girl shifts the lacey curtains and opens the window with two hands.

October sticks her head outside. Brown hair billows around her heart-shaped face. The strands flutter in the wind. Ethereal sort of exquisiteness that causes my lips to tick up, blush to rise. She's six years older than I remember, but she carries the same self-assurance. She's the kind of beauty that'd be carved out of wood and attached to the bow of a ship. She'd lead Vikings into battle and pirates out to sea.

"Zoey Durand." She says my name like I've been caught in her web. Neither friendly nor coarse. More cold and unfeeling, like she's calculating how to eviscerate her prey.

Her icy gaze is just as ruinous.

I blink slowly. My eyes pinned to her. "Amelia told you."

She assesses me in a slow up-and-down. "Stay there."

I don't have a chance to reply. She closes her window and disappears. Cold nips at my neck and I rock on the balls of my feet.

"She doesn't hate you, Zo," I whisper to myself. "Amelia is wrong. She got it wrong." My words do little to pump up my spirits and sunken morale. October Brambilla is kind, even if she seems like a cold ice queen. She's the person who broke into my locker just to give me pastries and an encouraging note. Every day.

For three years.

I cradle that truth close to my chest as I blow out a nervous breath. This will be the first time we've been face-to-face in six years.

It's my last thought as her front door opens. Now in a white faux-fur coat and knitted mittens, she steps over the flower beds to meet me on the small patch of grass.

October stands tall and confident like she was birthed on Mount Olympus. At least she carries herself with the raw grace of a god.

I can't mistake what's on her shoulder. Two tiny *birds*. She's not just a Wonder Woman, Aphrodite, supreme beautiful being—she had to go and become a Cinderella too? She *would* be a Disney princess. Do the birds flit around and dress her in the morning?

It's unfair.

How awesome she is.

How lackluster I am.

The bluish-feathered birds perch on a place I wish I could touch. Her shoulder. Chirping with their tiny beaks. Both have white heads with blue bodies, but one appears more violet-colored.

As soon as October approaches, the birds fly *at* me.

"Fuck, *fuck*." I duck as her birds flap at my face. Going for my eyes! "Are they attacking me?" Did October just sic her pet birds on me?! I shield my face with my forearms and wiggle left and right to avoid being pecked to death. "Octo—"

"Figgy, Rosemary—bad girls." Concern pitches her voice. Is she scared I'm going to smack her pets out of the air? "Come back here now." She whistles a tune repeatedly.

One pecks at my cheek. I wince.

"*Figgy.*" October rushes closer.

I'm crouching, hands over my head. Face in my lap. Waiting for the Death by Two Tiny Birds to end. And a breath later, the flapping and chirping stops.

I open my eyes to see October calming her birds, nestled back on her shoulder. Her eyes are a little distraught.

She's another person I've rattled since returning. "October…"

"Lovebirds are territorial," she cuts in, her voice somewhat tight like she's caging breath. "You're just a stranger to them."

I sense the attack wasn't intentional.

Slowly, I rise. Still unsure of where I stand with October. "I wasn't trying to hurt them…I didn't even know you had pet birds. What happened to Strawberry?" Her bunny.

"She died."

A knot forms in my throat.

Okay…I don't ask about the little ducklings she'd been raising before I left. Just in case those are gone too. I'm unsurprised she never brought up her animals in our text conversations. If they were filled with grief, she wouldn't have mentioned them.

October stands tall, only a foot or two away, her three inches on me adding to her allure. "And I wasn't worried about you hurting them."

So she was concerned about me. Warmth floods my cheeks, and she takes an assured, threatening step forward. Barely any space separating us. All the oxygen in this town swirls around October. Feeding her.

Still asphyxiating me.

"You broke my window," she says pointedly.

I glance up at the fissured glass. "Uh, yeah. Sorry. I'll pay for it—"

"I don't need your money," she says curtly. "You're just lucky that rock didn't ricochet back and hit your head." She says this with as much sincerity as Parry when he didn't want me to help clean up the broken glass.

"I think if my curse was *concussion by stone* I'd get off easy," I say into a laugh. "A better fate than even *death by lovebirds*." I'm grinning into another laugh, staring at those feathery assholes who almost pecked my eyes out.

October doesn't even crack a smile. "It's not funny." Her brown gaze strikes me cold.

My laugh dies. "Sorry."

October cringes at the word. I used to say "sorry" a lot in high school. Apologizing for accidentally bumping someone in the hallway. Apologizing for looking at Amelia the wrong way. Apologizing for being born a Durand.

And then one day, October had enough. She just turned on me and said, "If you say *sorry* one more time, I'm going to lose my fucking mind. Spare me so you can spare yourself in the very least. You don't owe anyone anything. Least of all an apology."

Now in the cold, in front of her house, I expect her to say something about the apology, but she skirts around it.

"Amelia told me you're back. But you couldn't at least call me yourself?"

"We made a promise. Never meet again. Rule number four—"

"Which you're breaking."

"That is true," I say, sucking in a breath. "You're not why I'm here though, so I figured this fell under the Exception Clause."

Her lips twitch, fighting not to smile. "We don't have an Exception Clause."

"We probably should have made one though," I tell her. "I mean if we went through the lengths to make up rules, we should have added a clause or two in there. Right?"

She opens her mouth to reply and her front door whips open.

"Fuck," October curses. And then she shoves me. *Hard.*

I fall into a bush.

Let me rephrase: She pushed me into a fucking bush! Leaves and branches scrape my arms, and I'm about to pry myself up in hot anger when I hear a voice.

"October Brambilla, I heard *people* out here." Oh God. I recognize that voice. Effie Brambilla is not only October's aunt but she's hated the Durands for longer than I've been alive.

October sidesteps to block the bush…or me *in* the bush. "I was on the phone, Aunt Effie," she replies quickly. "I'm the only person you heard."

Effie scoffs. "I can recognize a Durand's voice if it was five-hundred miles across shore. Zoey was right here—"

"Aunt Ef—"

"But she's a smart one. Probably already fled like the frightened little rabbit she is. But if I catch the stink of her near my home again, she's going to wish she never returned to town. You hear?"

Looking between a couple branches, I can see October nodding slowly. And at the sound of the front door shutting closed, I let out a long breath.

After a measured moment, October extends a hand. "Sorry about that."

I grasp onto her, and she helps me out of the bush.

Feet planted firmly on the ground, my gaze drops to our hands. Skin-to-skin, they're still intertwined. Fingers bridging together. We should break away, but we're fused. Like I'm exactly where I'm supposed to be.

She's where she's meant to be.

Sweetly chirping lovebirds fill the quiet. And those feathery assholes don't seem so bad anymore. I tell her that out loud.

Her brows crinkle. "They nearly pecked out your eyes and you're already trusting them again?" She says it like I'm a fool.

"Maybe. Yeah, I guess."

She eyes me in a long, tender sweep. One that feels like an eternal hug. A caress. The softest, sweetest, most everlasting kiss, and she whispers, "After six years, you still make me want to…" She lets out a noise of frustration.

"To what?"

Her eyes snap up to mine. "Protect you—make sure you don't get yourself killed, you idiot."

Oh.

I do my worst at stifling a smile.

She rolls her eyes. "It's not funny."

"You keep saying that."

Her lips almost tic up. Our hands are still together. Warm and soft and wanting. We both look down. Noticing the simple yet devastating embrace. One we can't shake off that easily. We're destroying each other.

Annihilating our tenacity and the persistence we'd cradled for six years.

The determination to *never* meet again.

And now we're touching.

Now we're not letting go.

And the minute passes in a long beat. Too long.

Because when we both do finally break apart, thick tension strains the air. She glances away. Can't look at me for a second. Hurt punctures my heart, and I'm waiting for October to cast me out. The anticipation wrenches my soul.

"October—"

"I'm not done talking with you," she interrupts quickly. I let out a deep breath before she says, "But we have to go somewhere more private."

"Where did you have in mind?"

CHAPTER 6

OCTOBER BRAMBILLA

She's back.

It's hard to believe I'm seeing the blonde-haired, blue-eyed girl in the flesh. My aunt called her a frightened little rabbit—and for the most part that's how I've always seen Zoey. Fragile. One good kick away from shattering completely.

But she does seem different now. She'd have never even risked coming to my house when we were teens.

Swiftly, I shut the door to the small shed. No one but my younger sister and I use this old, wooden solace. A canoe and a couple bicycles lean against worn siding. While a small cot, nightstand, and lamp are shoved in the corner. A table takes up the middle of the uneven floor where different shells, beach glass, and trinkets are scattered.

I watch Zoey appraise the beach glass and shell windchimes that cascade from the wooden ceiling.

"Babette has really improved from making earrings..." Zoey says with genuineness that compels me towards her. She's always been sincere, even naïvely so. "These are beautiful."

She remembered my sister's hobby. A part of me craves to take Zoey's hand and draw her down onto the cot, to spend hours catching up. *Truly* catching up.

But I can't.

Things are different now.

I'm different.

Even if we kept in touch through texts, we never dug deep enough to uncover the depth of what happened here.

"We're not talking about my sister," I say with force, urgency. I don't love that the importance I carry derives from my lineage. From the Brambilla name. But instead of shying away from who I am, I've had to embrace it.

Aunt Effie—bless her wretched heart—once told me, *no one listens to cowering, stammering little girls. Speak well and like you're someone to fear.*

I couldn't have been older than five. And she was right. So I don't try to soften my words as I say, "Why are you back, Zoey?"

Her cheeks flush as she spins to me. "I'm...I..." She crosses her arms over a black turtleneck. Pushing up her breasts, and I imagine what it'd be like to lift off her sweater. To snap off her bra—to press my lips to her lips and shove her against the shed wall.

To feel her smooth skin beneath my fingers that've longed for warmth. To consume Zoey like she's been silently consuming me.

You shouldn't think this.

But I can't stop.

Does she still wear those thick razorback bras? Her sun freckles along her nose and cheeks have faded. Does she still have the constellation of freckles on her lower back? Or have those faded too?

Has it all disappeared?

Just as her blue eyes begin to drip down me, I snap, "Spit it out."

Hurt crosses her striking features. Features made of genuine, delicate things that completely, masochistically *shatter* me. Hurt is followed quickly by a flash of concern. "October—"

"You can't ask," I interrupt her quickly. "Rule number three. You can't ask about my curse, Zoey. And there's no Exception Clause to that one."

Her concern just churns through her. She's always been terrible at hiding her feelings. She wears them on her face like the world's worst poker player. I fell hard for that.

"Have you been cursed?" Zoey says.

I arch a brow. "Way to rephrase."

"But have you?"

"Yes." That one word feels hollow. Not enough. Not the full gravity of the situation. So I do a ridiculous thing and spill more. "I'm a ghost, Zoey. I died months ago. So whatever it is that made you come back, I promise it's not worth being here. You need to leave."

Zoey steps closer to me. And then closer. One more step. I cage a breath, unable to drop my eyes off hers. Something unexplainable strings her to me and me to her. I felt the tug the moment she entered drama class years ago. The moment her eyes locked on mine with confusion and questions and need.

She stops a breath away.

And then slowly and carefully and nostalgically, Zoey places her smooth palm against my cheek. Warming my skin, and I struggle not to sink into her hand like a fool.

"You don't feel like a ghost," she whispers sweetly.

"I'm not a *literal* ghost, you idiot." I roll my eyes, wanting to smile but not having the effort. It almost hurts to lift my lips. Like I've forgotten how those muscles work.

She drops her hand, leaving the imprint of her warmth behind.

"Figuratively, you died," she breathes in that realization. "What hap—"

"You can't ask," I remind her.

It's her turn to roll her eyes. "Then how about a trade? I tell you the real reason why I'm here, and you tell me about your curse."

I tilt my head. "You have changed," I muse and hop on the table. Carefully, I cross my legs and then grip the edge of the table on either side of me. She watches every movement with raw intrigue. "The old Zoey wouldn't have tried to barter with me. She would have known better."

Zoey snorts. "You *did* just call me an idiot. Twice now."

"You are one, if you think you hold any power here."

Arousal flushes her cheeks and heavies her breathing. We're both under each other's compulsion, feeding off the desire, but she has no idea how strong hers is to resist. "How in the hell do you do that?" she whispers.

"Do what?" I arch another brow. "Make you wet?"

She groans. "You're really insufferable, you know. *You* haven't changed, even if you think you're a ghost or whatever."

I am a ghost.

A ghost who's found someone to play with, which shouldn't be the case. I shouldn't want Zoey around. But light breaks through her gaze whenever she simply *looks* at me. Like I'm Helen of fucking Troy.

I'm beautiful, but I'm not going to cause a thousand ships to sail from my beauty alone. Unless all one thousand belonged to Zoey.

She would try to do that.

My heart clenches and aches.

I shouldn't be turned on by the way she looks at me. Just like she shouldn't be turned on by the way I talk to her.

But I bask in her reverence and awe of me. It's different than others in the town. She's seen a different part of me. She's already pulled back my layers once. She knows what lies underneath. The thaw under the ice.

My fingers brush over a shell. "New deal," I tell her, sidestepping over her insult. "You tell me the truth why you're here, and I let you sleep in this shed tonight."

Her nose wrinkles. "That'll only get me to tomorrow. I might be here for a week."

What?

"*Might?*" I repeat that word. "So you don't know how long you planned to stay?"

She sighs heavily. "Not exactly."

I wait for her to keep going.

She lets out an even heavier sigh. "Parry called me. Told me Colt's messed up. In trouble. I don't know. He seemed *really* worried about him, so I just booked a flight back here. No questions asked. But now I'm starting to think I should've probably asked some questions. Seeing as how Parry won't tell me anything until I see Colt in-person tomorrow. That's…basically it."

Parry?

He's the cause of her return.

Ugh.

I blink. "You risked coming back here because Parry DiNapoli asked you."

She nearly laughs. "That's an oversimplification."

He's going to get her killed.

He's placing *Colt* above Zoey. And that's not okay with me.

"You should have demanded a better explanation. Fuck, Zoey, what if Colt's fine?"

"I know." She sighs. "But…maybe…I don't know…" She stares at her hands.

"What?"

"Maybe I was waiting for a reason." She looks up at me underneath her eyelashes. "A reason other than you."

Because I couldn't be her reason to come back.

We have rules.

She swallows hard and adds, "And anyway, if Colt really is in trouble, I'd never forgive myself for not coming. You'd do the same for Babette."

"I'd do anything for my sister," I say.

"Exactly."

Our siblings have always meant everything to us. In this town, family is your lifeline. Your blood and soul.

I nod slowly, thinking this over for a half second. "Alright." I push off the table, back on my feet. "You can sleep here as long as you need. On one condition."

"Deal."

I give her a frosted look. "At least make this a little hard for me."

She smiles. "I need somewhere to stay, so whatever you want, you can have."

I eye her from her feet to the top of her head. The air thickens again with tension formed years and years ago. "Don't make that deal with me, Zoey." The severity in my voice sobers the room.

She blows out a soft breath. "Okay." For a second, she sounds like that frightened little rabbit. Then I watch her shoulders pull back. "No deal," she says with a newfound confidence.

I like this Zoey.

"I'll let you sleep here," I explain. "But as long as you stay in Mistpoint Harbor, I'm going to be following you around everywhere you go. Someone has to protect you."

Fondness washes over her face. A deeper nostalgia.

My heart twinges with pain like it's fighting to come back to life. "Don't look at me like that," I whisper in distress.

She blinks. "Sorry. I just…okay. Yes. I'll let the ghost follow me around and protect me, if that's what the ghost wants."

Oh God. "*You're* the insufferable one," I shoot back.

She smiles softly and looks around, her gaze pinging to the cot. Appreciation flashes across her face. "Thanks, Kenobi," she breathes.

Kenobi. Most people call me OB. My initials. Zoey, the smartass that she is, would always try to slyly mutter "Kenobi" to me after someone called me OB. She'd have this cute grin like she made the best fucking joke. A joke only we shared.

I knew she was a Star Wars fan and loved Obi-Wan Kenobi. She said Kenobi suited me more than OB anyway.

That cute dork nicknamed me after an old man who flings around a light saber.

I want to smile.

I want to tell her I still love that nickname.

I want to tell her that I still think about her.

That I've thought about her every day since she left.

But I can't do any of those things. Instead I say, "Get some sleep." And I head towards the door, leaving her behind.

CHAPTER 7

OCTOBER BRAMBILLA

"Holy hell, OB, are those what I think they are," my younger sister says as she enters the kitchen sniffing the air.

Same glossy brown hair and heart-shaped face as me, we'd almost look like replicas if it weren't for the dark red birthmark above her left eyebrow. If you squint hard enough, the birthmark resembles a crescent moon.

Babette Brambilla is my lively twenty-three-year-old sister. And she completes my world.

Since she was little, she's had an appetite for people. Making friends easier than Durands can make enemies, which is a feat around here. But she loves strangers and tourists more than locals, possibly due to preferring small talk over deep conversation. Or because strangers tend to be more honest, less cutthroat and desperate to be accepted by the town hierarchy.

By us.

When our parents disappeared, she was just seven. She vaguely remembers the search parties and the moment when the town's sheriff declared the case closed after a short month. For Babette, she more vividly recalls the *after*. Being raised by Aunt Effie. Having our aunts, uncles, and cousins dodge every question about our parents that we could throw at them.

It wasn't until I was in high school that Aunt Effie finally fessed up.

Our parents never disappeared.

They left.

Moved away.

They live in a small town in Canada. On the other side of Lake Erie. Occasionally I gaze out over the water, imagining if they ever think about us. I wonder if they're fine to be written into our history books as missing persons. Another lie to add to the mystery of Mistpoint Harbor.

But that's what we Brambillas do.

We keep the legend alive.

No matter the cost.

Grabbing a *sculmacadoon*, I carefully strain frying cookies from a pot of oil. Then I reach the butcher's block island and place the cookies on a paper towel lined plate where over a dozen more are cooling.

Babette gasps. "It is them. *October.*" She nearly sticks her nose in the Italian cookies shaped like bowties. "I forgot how nukadells smell. Doughy fried deliciousness. So...*so* fucking good." She's about to bite into one like a wild animal.

I want to smile, but the movement is difficult and practically lost in time. I tear the sheet away from her teeth. "Were we raised in the same household?"

"We were," she says coolly, leaning against the kitchen island, "only you listened and I laughed." She reaches for a cookie. "Especially during cotillion."

I smack her hand away. "These are not for you."

Babette collects her glossy hair in a pony. "Then why would you make nukadells? They're a Christmas cookie that you haven't made in years. And it's past Christmas." She gives me a matter-of-fact look. "But you know they're my favorites."

They're also her favorites.

I refuse to say that.

Instead, I say, "I also know that Aunt Effie hates when you call them nukadells," I remind her. "They're *frappe*."

Babette makes a show of slumping on the island. "God, she's such a b——"

I glare.

Babette says softly, "*Bore*. She's a bore." She buttons the front of her black blouse. Add in the matching black slacks, and Babette is a shining example of a Fisherman's Wharf server. "Why does she care what most of us call them? The cookie has no real name. We could drive to Cincinnati and another Italian would call them something completely different."

It is true. "She believes some of what we were taught is more uneducated. It can't be found in any books. You know this."

"And I hate this," Babette says quietly, sadly. We share a brief glimpse of knowingness. That our mother taught us how to cook.

That our mother called them nukadells.

That Aunt Effie has little love left towards her own sister-in-law.

Our paternal and maternal side descend from two different parts of Italy. Aunt Effie, our father's sister, likes to believe she's "proper" Italian and our mother was poor, uneducated. At the end of the day, we're all Italian-American. We're all part of a culture taught dusted-in-flour in the kitchen and spoken through unwritten words.

And I can't hate my mother—no matter how hard I've tried to *loathe* her. My memories of her were always kind. She was the warmest person in my family. Sometimes I think that I refuse to wipe her from existence because I believe it's what she wanted.

To be a missing person.

To be gone.

So I've decided to keep her alive. Vindictive, possibly.

But does she deserve anything sweeter? She left two young daughters: a seven-year-old, a nine-year-old. Why? How could she possibly think that was okay?

How could our father think that was right?

Babette would force herself not to cry after I told her the truth in high school. How our parents weren't killed by hitchhikers or eaten by bears. How they're still alive.

How they aren't looking for us like we'd been foolishly looking for them.

And she'd whisper to me, "They're evil. To do what they did. *Truly* evil, October."

"Or maybe they had a reason," I'd whisper back. We theorized for years. We still do some days. The possibilities of *why* they left have shrouded the hurt. Have muffled the pain. Have silenced the heartache. All that's left of our mother and father is a mystery.

One we're not eager to solve.

I open a cupboard, hearing the faint chirps of my birds in the house. "I always thought you'd agree with Aunt Effie. Destroy every trace of Mom in the house. Burn the cookbooks."

Babette sighs. "I did think about it. But I saw Aunt Effie go off the deep-end when she torched Dad's clothes. She hates her own brother for leaving town."

"Or she hates him for leaving us."

She's more cynical. "You think so good of bad people, OB."

"We're all bad, Baby." I use her nickname, and I grab the container labeled *powdered sugar*.

Babette watches me return to the cookies at the island. "All I know is that I don't want to be her. Cold. Snooty. *Mean.*"

I'm like her.

Can't you see that?

A chill snakes through me, but I don't shiver. "She might not be kind, but she showed us kindness when she took us in."

Our other aunts and uncles already have loads of children, and if we'd gone to live with one of them, we could've easily been overlooked. Aunt Effie married young, and her husband left early. A divorce. Not "the right fit"—she'd say. And "I'm not meant for marriage"—she'd decree.

She gave us all her attention and all the love she could muster. Like we were her own daughters.

I add, "And she'd do absolutely anything for us."

"Anything?" Babette says with a scoff. "She won't even let you make other desserts, October. I'm *so* sick of crème brûlée and peanut butter cheesecake." She reknots her sleek ponytail. "And don't even get me started on fried crullers." She gags dramatically and leaves the bowtie cookies untouched.

I let out a laugh. My sister is my biggest fan. As I am hers.

Babette grins. "She laughs."

"She listens," I reply. "And I understand where Aunt Effie is coming from. The menu at Fisherman's Wharf hasn't changed in years. The more I make other pastries and desserts in my spare time, the more I'm just sticking a knife into my gut. It won't change Uncle Milo's position."

Uncle Milo owns the restaurant and is also the executive chef. When he hired me on as a pastry chef after high school, he explicitly told me that the menu isn't up for negotiation. Every day I'm to make the same three desserts.

Crème brûlée.

Peanut butter cheesecake.

Fried crullers.

It's been my life for seven years.

"Uncle Milo sucks," Babette says pointedly. "You're better than peanut butter cheesecake."

I don't disagree, but I'm imprisoned in cheesecake purgatory. No one will pay me as well as Fisherman's Wharf for baking.

I pop the lid of powdered sugar. "Meet anyone new?"

"Sure did." She tucks her blouse into her slacks. "Cute boy coming into town for a couple days. He's passing through on a road trip to Niagara Falls. He saw Mistpoint on Trip Advisor as a place of interest."

"Don't they all." I pick up the bowl of homemade icing. "How old is he?"

She mumbles the number.

Oh no.

"Baby." I give her a look.

"Thirty-nine-ish."

I set the bowl hard on the counter.

"*-ish*, OB," she emphasizes.

"So forty?"

Babette bites her lip. "Possibly, slightly forty."

"That's not a boy—that's a fucking *man*. And what is he doing talking to a twenty-three-year-old?"

"I engaged first," she mentions. "He was alone at Harbor Perk. He seemed interesting, sitting there. Drinking coffee. Reading *Into the Wild*."

Oh God. I cast her an iced look. "He sounds like a cliché."

"So judgy of you, Oc-to-ber," she playfully emphasizes the syllables. Of course she approached this *man*. She'd approach just about anyone who she didn't recognize.

"Anyone who comes within an inch of you, I'll *gladly* judge." No one fucks with my sister.

"I love you too," Babette smiles, one that fades after a few seconds. "He's not sticking around…it was just one conversation. That's all."

I know that's all she wanted.

"Baby Brambilla," I muse while I work on the cookies, "the girl who can befriend just about anyone. It's your gift."

"And yet, I've been cursed."

I hate that banter, yet I always fall into it with Babette.

She sniffs the air again and practically salivates. "I missed this." And she reaches again.

I swat her hand with an oven mitt. "They're not done yet. I have to powder them."

Babette narrows her eyes at me. "I thought you said they weren't for me."

"They aren't," I refute. "But you're my sister, so I will allow you to have *one*."

Her lips lift slowly. "These are for Zoey, aren't they?"

My stomach nosedives and color drains from my face. "What?" I croak.

"They are!" Babette points at me with too much glee. "I *knew* it."

My face sets to stone. "You are wrong. Zoey's in Chicago. Why would I be making her cookies?"

Babette's eyes grow. "Whoa. Wait, you really haven't heard?" She puts her hands on my forearms. "You're going to need to sit down, OB." My tenderhearted sister literally guides me around the kitchen island and to the cushioned barstool.

I should feel bad I'm lying.

But I don't.

Babette takes a step back and inhales deeply, preparing herself for dropping the news. "Naya heard from Ilsa who heard from Sebo that Zoey is back. Apparently, Frank saw her through the window of The Drunk Pelican."

At least, I know Amelia didn't betray me when I told her to keep Zoey's arrival to herself. Not that there was any question about that. Amelia would rather throw herself off a cliff than do me wrong. She's a rare kind of friend, and I'm not certain I deserve her.

"Frank isn't very credible," I remind Babette. "He sells mushrooms to the tourists. It was only a matter of time until he started eating his own product."

"He didn't hallucinate Zoey Durand," Babette says strongly. "I promise, October. I don't want you to get hurt or blindsided when you see her. And it's going to happen."

You're too late.

I nod slowly. "Okay. Thanks for the warning, Baby."

She lets out a deep exhale, and I finish sifting powdered sugar over the cookies. Dusting the fried dough with expert focus. It'll be the first thing Zoey probably has eaten since she's returned, and they have to be *perfect*.

"Fuckfuckfuck." Babette's sudden alarm pops my focused bubble.

She paces around the kitchen, opening and closing drawers. "What's wrong?" I ask.

"My gloves." She panics, slamming more drawers. Wafting her hands like her skin is crawling. "I can't find them. I swear I left them on the kitchen chair. "Oh God, *fuck*. OB."

Immediately, I abandon the powdered sugar on the counter and dash away to the laundry room. We live with Aunt Effie in the house our parent's left behind. Left us, really. It's three-stories with a rustic attic and lakeside charm. Quaint and clean and feminine.

Not even Aunt Effie's boyfriend is allowed inside.

"Not while you girls are here. This is *our* home," she'd say.

She's been dating the town's only lawyer. He's like bland, weak coffee. Something I'd rather spit out. But I'm not the one "involved" with him.

Easily enough, I find a pair of black velvet gloves deserted on a hanger to dry. I snatch them quickly and return to the kitchen. "Babette."

She sees them in my hand. "Oh thank God."

I pass them to her and watch as she rolls the fabric all the way up to her elbow. My heart twists.

The most extroverted person I know…hates to be touched.

When I carried my sister out of the smoldering, *burning* library, she was ten. Flames licked the roof, the walls. She had passed out behind a bookshelf.

I'd never felt something so blistering hot. Never been choked so cruelly by smoke. The smoke…God, there was so much smoke.

I was only twelve. Taller than my sister. Stronger.

It was a miracle neither of us had more than a few second-degree burns.

But the fire still haunted Babette. Weeks, months, *years* afterwards, she would flinch from hugs, recoil at handshakes. Shy from most touch. I'm not sure what aspect of the fire affected her this way. Why she seemed to retreat physically from people.

She just said, *"I can't handle it. I don't want it. Isn't that enough?"*

And then came her eighteenth birthday party. Hug after hug after hug. Kisses on the cheek from grandparents and aunts and uncles. All wishing her a happy birthday. She finally just broke down. I wiped her tears in the freezer of Fisherman's Wharf while the rest of our family ate her birthday cake in the dining room.

After that, she demanded not to be touched by anyone. Except me. It's been five years, and I've fended off the Roberts from putting

Babette's anxiety and trauma into the history books. But I know it's only a matter of time until it's written in stone.

Babette Brambilla was cursed at eighteen. Unable to touch a living soul again.

"Here." I place a couple cookies on a napkin and slide it across the bar.

Her face lights up. "*Yes.* Thank you, OB." She takes a deep sniff and just as she goes to bite, her phone pings.

Carefully, I pile the rest of the cookies in a round stationary box for Zoey. I watch Babette's smile grow as she reads her phone.

"Good news?" I ask, hoping for some.

She nods. "Seagull95 just bought another windchime on my Etsy shop."

My brows rise. "That's the fifth one this month. You said the PO Box is local?"

"Yeah, it's in the post office right down the street. It has to be someone from high school. Seagull, you know? Mistpoint High's mascot." She scrolls on her phone. "It's probably just Naya. Maybe she's hoping that I'll be smitten over some secret admirer."

Her friends are a bit pushy to get her to date, so I could see Naya playing that cruel game. Or this could be a stranger she befriended. One who remembers her more than she remembers them.

"Be careful," I warn.

"It could just be a family member," Babette theorizes. "Supporting my art."

"Then why would they stay anonymous?"

"Our family likes their secrets."

I consider this with the tilt of my head. "True."

Her eyes flit to mine and they soften considerably. "I wish you could tell me the whole story about your curse."

"Babette—"

"In time, I mean," she says quickly. "Take your time, OB. But I'm here if you ever want to talk about what happened. Whatever that is. I'll *listen.*"

"I'll laugh," I tease.

Her lips rise before she pops the whole cookie into her mouth, chewing with chipmunk cheeks and a smile.

I haven't even told Amelia everything that happened.

I'm not ready.

I don't know if I'll ever be.

CHAPTER 8

ZOEY DURAND

"Your cover is blown. Everyone knows you're back in town." October delivers this news with a round box of freshly made Italian bowtie cookies. My absolute freaking *favorites.*

Have I dreamed about these bad boys for the past six years? *Yes.*

Have I thought about asking October to mail me some? *Double yes.*

Did I chicken out ten or twenty times and hang up the phone? *Undoubtedly and stupidly yes.*

So gazing longingly at them, *smelling* them, and hopefully mere minutes from tasting them—my stomach is a grumbling, beautiful mess and October's news isn't as devastating.

"I wasn't exactly hiding my arrival." I stand quickly from the squeaky cot. "Just *why* I'm here."

She seems hesitant. Like she knows she should ship me back to Chicago with the box of cookies. (Shit, I hope these aren't goodbye cookies.) But she's making no move to throw me out of the shed.

My limbs ache from sleeping on the rickety cot, but it's much better than the alternative. Outside. On the freezing ground. At least a space heater and sleeping bag kept me warm.

Though I do wish October would have stayed. Back in high school, there were nights we'd spend at the end of the fishing pier, cuddled up under a blanket. Our bodies heating and warming and surviving together.

We never did date in high school.

But we weren't exactly *just* friends either.

October is commanding. Just standing there at the shed's door with her soul-eating gaze and *I'm in charge* posture. Maybe that's why I expect her to command me to leave again. Or maybe she planned to drop off the food and make a quick exit. She hasn't moved further inside.

She clutches the box of cookies closer to her chest. And I notice a frown tugging her lips.

"I survived the night," I say with a lighthearted smile on my way to her.

She's lost in a thought, and I'm grateful when she finally shares. "You really want people to know you're back?"

"Not exactly, but I always figured it'd be hard to hide. Anyway, I came up with a good cover story, so people won't ask me too many questions. Are those for me?" I point to the uncovered box.

Her gaze doesn't soften, but she does hand me the cookies. "They're probably cold by now. And if they're too soggy, let me know. I can alter the recipe on the next batch—"

"Hush." I put my finger to her lips. "I'm sure they're perfect."

Her eyes grow wide. I can tell October is caging breath. My finger still on her soft, pink lips.

My chest suddenly tightens, and I swiftly drop my hand. "Sorry, I don't know why I did that." *Liar.* I totally know why I did. Her lips are all I can think about.

"You wanted to touch me," October just says it. "You don't have to apologize for that." With a relaxed, casual hand, she brushes her brown hair over her shoulder.

She knows she's hot.

I know she's hot.

We all know.

I bite the corner of my lip. "Fine...um, just...fine." I shake out a mental image of kissing October. My face on fire. "I don't apologize for wanting to touch you." I can't believe I haven't even shoved a cookie in my mouth yet.

She notices too. "You're not going to eat them?"

"You're better than any sweets." It just came out! I stare at the canoe and beach glass trinkets, grimacing. "Yeah, I'm not taking that back." *Roll with it, Zoey.* "So sue me."

I swear her lip twitches upward. "I think I'd win the lawsuit."

"Probably."

"You give up so easily."

"To you," I say pointedly. *To you, I'd give up everything.* God, am I that willing to just lie down for October?

Yes.

I hate and love that I would. Just like I think she hates and loves that I'd surrender to her too. October casts a glimpse down my body. "Eat your cookies, sweets." Her voice is a breathless whisper, somehow still compelling me.

I grab a cookie. "Did you just call me *sweets*?" I'm smiling like I've been awarded a Pulitzer for the fake book I'm writing.

She doesn't deny. "You're the sweetest of sweets, and you think I'm better than you."

She does have a point. "I don't just think it, you know. You *are* better than me."

"I'm not." Her face sobers. The slight smile just *gone*. Light vanished.

I decide not to dig deeper (which is exactly why I'm never winning a Pulitzer in journalism on the Life of October Brambilla). But I just can't prod as she focuses her gaze elsewhere. Like *away* from me. Far away. My stomach knots and grumbles again.

As I bring the cookie to my mouth, I smell the familiar scent of *sweet* fried dough. "Fucking hell, I've missed this."

October eases at the change of topic. "You're not the only one. Baby nearly drooled over them this morning."

I pause.

She almost, *almost* smiles. "Don't worry, I didn't let her drool on any of yours."

"These are all mine?" I hug the pretty box closer to my chest.

She nods like it's nothing.

It's not nothing.

My heart floods with hope.

Amelia made me think October would be cruel to me, but in reality, all October really wants is to protect me. Sure, October would probably love to banish me out of town like Brian tried to, but she knows better.

I'm strong-willed.

She's the one who helped forge my strength after all.

"So what's the cover story?" October asks as she watches me devour the cookies. I haven't had anything to eat since the plane ride yesterday. Just a snack-bag of pretzels. I keep using a hand gesture to make sure she knows they're perfect because there's no fucking way I can speak as I shovel them in my mouth.

"Easy, Zo," October says. "You're going to choke."

"Am not," I mumble with a mouthful, then swallow to show off my success at not choking. But I proceed to eat another cookie, then another and another. I lick my thumb, not wasting any crumb.

October watches. "If I remember correctly, I'm the one who held your hair back after a Fourth of July party because you ate an entire tray of scones. By yourself."

"And you should have made them less delicious. It was really all your fault."

She snorts with a *slight* smile. "It's my fault you have no self-control?"

"Yeah."

The room stills for a second. Neither of us taking our eyes off each other. And then she pulls her *shoulders* back like she's reinforcing barriers and walls. "We shouldn't be doing this," she whispers with frost.

"Doing what?" I frown.

"Flirting." She crosses her arms over her chest.

I smile. "I thought we were talking."

She gives me an aggravated look. "Zoey. You're staring at me like you're ready for me to drop to my knees and eat you out."

Fuuuuck.

Am I?

I definitely am.

Would she?

My whole body heats and almost trembles at the thought. "You only did that once, so I don't expect it to happen again." Although, I have imagined the overwhelming act. About a million glorious times.

"Good because it's not happening again. I don't know what beds you've been in or who you've slept with—"

"I could tell you."

"That would break Rule #2. And I don't think we should be shattering anymore of those. Your time here has an expiration date."

My stomach twists, powdered sugar thick on my tongue. "You're right...I don't want to hurt you."

"You can't hurt me," she refutes swiftly, almost too nonchalantly. "But you'll hurt yourself if you fall for me again and then leave."

I let out a frustrated noise. October will tell you she's made of unbreakable things. But she's not built solely of steel and iron. She might be a diamond. Powerful and coveted and pleasing to the eye. Yearned for.

But steel and iron and diamonds—they don't *care*. They don't *love*. And I've never been loved the way that I *know* October used to love me.

To me, October Brambilla is made of compassionate things. Romantic things. Everlasting, affectionate, loving things.

She's all heart. And I know very fucking well that hearts can break. Mine was in pieces after I left town. After I left her.

I know she *feels*. I know she *cares*.

Yet, she thinks she's dead already. A ghost. Maybe there's no more damage I could do, and that just sends a shockwave of hurt cascading through me. What happened? What the fuck happened?!

I want to scream those words.

Shake her.

But I know it won't do any good.

She's a fortress.

She always has been. Yelling and shouting won't get her to open up.

I have to maneuver this differently. If only so she can see that she doesn't have to be a ghost the rest of her life. I now have two very important reasons to be in Mistpoint Harbor.

Task #1: Help my brother.

Task #2: Make October Brambilla come alive again.

I lick the remaining powdered sugar residue off my fingers. "So I'm *technically* not supposed to be telling you my cover story."

October rolls her eyes. "Parry?" She guesses correctly.

"I think he's just trying to lessen the casualties. He told me that if I get hurt while I'm out here, it'll be his fault."

"He's not wrong about that." She looks me over, eyeing my face for too long. "You have a little something…" She motions to her own lips.

"Here?" I rub my arm against my mouth, dirtying my black turtleneck with dusty white.

I must not do a good enough job. October steps so much closer, tensely—only an inch or so away from me, and I watch her soft fingers rise to the corner of my lips.

I inhale.

"It's right here," she breathes and then thumbs the corner. Her gentle, teasing touch flip-flops my heart. Melts me.

"Powdered sugar?" I ask like an idiot. *What else would it be?*

She has a smile in her eyes that turns more desirous, and I think, *just do it, October. Just kiss me.*

Please.

She suddenly retracts. Hand dropping. "You're going to get sick. You should've slowed down."

Slowed down? Us? Is that even doable?

She's not talking about us. This isn't some metaphorical, figurative convo. It's literal, and she pops the lid back onto the empty box. Yes, I ate all the cookies.

No regrets.

"Your cover story," October says. "Will you tell me even if Parry said not to?"

"You know I will." She's my exception. And I end up explaining how I'm telling locals that I've returned to write a book about the town.

With each word out of my mouth, October's face morphs into pure *horror*.

When I finish, she says, "Are you out of your fucking mind?"

"Like I said, if people are pissed at me then they won't ask questions. It's a win-win."

"I will be sweeping up your corpse from the town square and mopping up the blood, Zoey. They're going to kill you."

I frown. "Not like actual murder though."

74

"Someone will probably send you a message. And it won't be wrapped in a bow."

I think about this for a second. "Is it weird that I'm not scared?"

She lets out a heavy breath. "I don't know. Probably not. We're all raised to not be scared of terrible shit happening to us. And you…" She pauses for a beat. "You more than anyone had to be strong to survive this town, but I wish you would be a little frightened this time."

"I'm not."

She groans and runs a hand down her cheek. "Alright. Alright. I'll just have to keep my eyes open. If you really insist on this ridiculous cover story, you're going to need me now more than ever."

My first thought: *I've always needed you.*

But I let that one drift.

We have too many rules. Only one exception. And it doesn't involve me falling for her ever again.

I unzip my suitcase. Flinging out some wardrobe options since I've been wearing the same turtleneck and jeans I wore on the plane. I was so tired, I slept in them too.

"Do you want to take a shower before we go to the lighthouse?" October asks me.

My brows knit together. "Won't your aunt murder me?"

"The town council had an early meeting this morning. She's already gone."

A shower in *October's* bathroom? It's tempting, but I check my phone for the time. "Shit. I don't think we'll have time for that." I yank off my turtleneck. Changing fast. "Parry said to meet him at nine, and it's already eight-thirty." When I pick up my long-sleeved shirt, I brave a glance at October.

Her eyes drift over my bare skin and my bra that does a pretty bad job at pushing up my cleavage. I have no boobs in comparison to October, and I would've said that I'd rather our positions be swapped—me in a heart-flipping wreck as I watch October strip down to nothing—but I wouldn't trade seeing *exactly* how she's staring at me.

Like I'm the Wonder Woman.

Like I'm the goddess.

Like I'm so *impossibly* beautiful. I slip off my jeans, and I'm drawn to her gaze that caresses the curve of my hips, my mesh thong Yoda panties that reveal too much. But I can't be self-conscious underneath her rapt attention.

I heat all over.

As she focuses on my bra, her gaze reddens. "You still wear those?" I'm lost, even as she eyes the back clasps, but she's already adding, "The razorbacks."

"Oh…" I reach over my shoulder, barely touching the strap. "These reliable things. Yeah they're still a friend of mine." When I go to shimmy my panties down, October shifts her gaze quickly. Sadness washes over me.

She walks to the door. "I'll wait outside."

"You don—" The shed door shuts behind her. Leaving me alone. "You don't have to go," I finish to myself with a sigh. "Way to clear a room, *Zoey*." I hurry and get dressed. New panties. Same bra. Glancing more than three times at the shed door.

Hoping October will reappear.

But she doesn't.

Stop falling for her, Zoey Durand. I can't be late for a very important date with my second brother. The one I've returned for.

CHAPTER 9

OCTOBER BRAMBILLA

An overcast winter morning, the lake laps roughly against the rocks. Ominous, unfriendly skies. The weather hasn't been great since Zoey returned, and if I were a bigger believer of fate like her, I'd call that a sign.

I just think it's fucking cold.

Zoey checks her phone as we hop out of my baby pink Jeep. A gift from Aunt Effie on my sixteenth birthday. My sweater matches the color, but I make sure to grab my white faux-fur coat before shutting the door.

Water swells mightier against the rocks and splashes against the base of a towering lighthouse only a few yards to the west.

"We're two minutes early," Zoey says as she pockets her phone. I'm about to slip my arms through my coat, but she shivers, only wearing a black long-sleeved shirt beneath a cropped Star Wars graphic tee.

You watched her change. Yet, I don't regret staying in the shed for as long as I did. For a moment, I remembered the two of us in high school. How I pulled her shirt over her head and slid my hands along the softness of her skin, the dip of her hips. How she'd draw me closer—our lips a teasing, aching distance. Our eyes devouring first.

We were young. She was a junior. I was a senior.

We're older now, and things should be different. But she's still wearing those same razorback bras. She's still the Zoey I remember, but then again, she's tougher. Happier? *Has she been happier in Chicago without me?*

I push aside the thought, and I hold out my coat. "Here, sweets."

Her cheeks flush, then her lips part. "Kenobi, I can't—"

"Why?"

She's already taking the coat from me. "You're cold." She touches the soft fur to her nose. Inhaling my floral perfume. When she notices that I've caught her, she blushes. "Your smell is intoxicating."

It is. But that's not the point.

I eye her intensely. "If you melt anymore, you'll be a puddle at my feet."

"I thought you wanted me warm?" She smiles, slipping her arms into my coat.

"I did—I do," I snap, flustered. *Get a grip, October.*

Zoey hugs the fur around her, still enamored with my coat. *She does look pretty in my clothes.* I watch her bury her nose in the fabric again as she says, "I *so* prefer how a girl smells over man musk."

I nearly smile. "Me too. Only I *always* prefer it."

Before I can tell her I'm not as cold as she looked, the sound of tires on gravel whips our heads.

A beat-up white convertible parks next to my Jeep, and I watch the former Sailing Team Captain climb out.

PARRY DINAPOLI

Cursed at Age 27

Sailing accident that scarred the most beautiful face in town

The snippet written about Parry in the Museum of Curses & Curiosities stays with me. As do most of the curses of locals. I shouldn't know them word-for-word, but Amelia's mom likes to quiz us as a show of superiority.

I willingly play her game. Better to not make enemies of the Roberts—they have too much clout in the town, and Amelia is genuinely my best friend.

Parry shuts the door of the convertible. He doesn't make it five feet before stopping in place. Eyes pinned to me. He takes one step back like I'm made of dynamite.

Typical.

I'm not destructive like he thinks. I'm usually the thing that keeps people from blowing into smithereens.

I'm the shelter, not the storm.

Not the bomb.

Not the match.

Yet, a part of me believes Parry. Because I know I'm not all good, but I'd *never* blow up Zoey.

He swings his head to her. "What is she doing here, Zo?"

I step forward. "I came to protect Zoey, something you and her brothers have been failing at for years."

Parry grits his teeth. "You shouldn't be here, OB. This duh-uh-esn'ttt concern a Brambilla." He turns to Zoey. "This wasn't part of the deal."

Parry. I roll my eyes with an exasperated huff.

I used to tell Amelia that Parry is just a golden retriever. Deathly loyal. "To garbage," she'd reply. I would cast a glare, but she'd mock shrug with a snarky, "What?"

She knew I was fond of Zoey. She never understood why because I couldn't explain how or why I was drawn in her direction. Just that I liked her.

And Parry might be the golden retriever who protects the Durands, but I'm the arctic wolf that has always circled Zoey. The kind of wolf that's rumored to have killed his parents.

Parry dislikes me.

Greatly.

So our goals might be the same, but we couldn't be more different.

Zoey makes a confused face. "Did we have a deal, Pear? I thought I was here to help. And October is here to help too. Three heads are better than two, right?"

He exhales through his nose and glares at me. "For the record, I am trying to protect her."

Hot rage pours through my ice-cold veins. "By asking her to come back?" I growl. "How is that helping?"

"It's a risk, but I'm looking out for her." His smoky voice doesn't bite like mine. "I *have* done that."

"Where did she sleep last night?" I ask him.

"At home," Parry says like there is no other answer.

I cock my head. "Try again."

The phrase *oh fuck* drops his face. He whirls around to Zoey. "*Zoey.*"

"Ugh." She shuts an eye and bites her lip. "About that. Brian kinda threw me out before I could even crash there."

"Of course he did," Parry says angrily under his breath. He drags his hot gaze across the ground. "You should've told me." He lifts his eyes to Zoey. "You could've stayed with me."

"She was *fine* with me," I retort.

He glares. "So you let her in your house with your Durand-hating aunt?"

I hate admitting this, but I'm not choking on my pride. I understand that I can make mistakes. That I'm not perfect. That I can even be worse than wolfish. I can be monstrous. "You know I couldn't."

Parry looks murderous. "Where'd she sleep, OB?"

"A warm, comfortable place, *Parry*."

"Where?"

"Okay, let's just focus on Colt—not on me," Zoey cuts in while Parry and I are eye-locked. He never rips his glare from me.

"The shed," I answer him.

"A shed?" His brows rise. "Like she's some broken kayak—"

"She came to *me*," I snap. "I'm helping her the best way I can. She's not my broken toy." *I love her!* I scream the words in my head. My chest rises and falls heavily, and I'm uncertain what breaks through my features—what just broke through me. It scares me. The sudden burst of emotion—but whatever Parry sees is enough to divert his gaze.

More calmly, he asks Zoey, "Why didn't you tell me you needed a place to stay?"

"You would've offered, and I'm not messing things up between you and Brian."

"They're already messed up!" Parry yells, frustrated. He kicks a stone on the patchy grass. The sky rumbles above us. He rakes a hand through his shaggy golden-blond hair. "Last night, he came by my place. To apologize."

Zoey's mouth drops. "Brian? As in Brian Durand? Apologizing?"

"For what?" I ask curtly.

"For kicking me out of the Pelican when he saw Zoey," Parry clarifies, glaring out at the rough lake. "And he so conveniently forgot to tell me that Zoey didn't have a place to stay…and he kissed me—or maybe I kissed him. We kissed each other—I don't know." He pinches his eyes.

Zoey is horrified. "Parry…"

"I know…" He cringes. "It was a mistake—a lapse of judgment. For a second, I thought Brian had a soul."

"I'm just…" Zoey gapes. "You and Brian?"

"You do know he's…bi, right?" Parry says in worry.

"Uh, yeah…I think he dated some fisherman when I was fourteen…fifteen. I can't remember. He didn't last long." Her face twists in more emotions. "But Brian is…*mean*. And you're *nice*. Better than him—Jesus, you can do so much better than *Brian*." She grimaces into a gag.

Parry exhales exhaustedly. "I could say the same about you and October."

He's not wrong. She could do better than me. She's just figuratively hypnotized, but I should break the spell.

Zoey bristles. "October is the most—"

"He's right," I say to her, then quickly, I tell Parry, "We're not together."

"And I'm not with Brian," Parry explains.

"I don't care about what you and Brian do," I say bluntly, probably bitchily too. "And we all saw this coming from a hundred miles away."

"We?" Parry frowns.

"The town." I give him a look. He can't be that obtuse. "Brian Durand is the notorious loner who somehow *only* spends time with you."

"At work."

"You're the only one who has accepted the role of employee."

"Because Colt is my best friend," he refutes.

"Because you have the hots for Br—"

"*He* kissed me," Parry rebuts.

"Is that the story now?" I arch my brows.

"Truce, *truce*," Zoey interjects. "Let's call a fucking truce. Okay? We're not in competition. We're all cool. We all love each other."

"No, we love you," Parry rephrases.

"Agreed," I say.

"We're agreeing. See that," Zoey smiles. "All of us. On the same page." She lets out a breath. "Feels great, right?"

She's cute.

Parry eases too. "You can do what you want, Zo. But my door is open. You can stay with me."

She should.

I almost say the words. She should choose Parry. Not my dingy shed. But that'd mean seeing her less.

"Thanks, Pear," she says. "But I still don't want to get between you and Brian…maybe even *more* now. You guys need to…figure stuff out without me causing problems. So I'm going to kindly reject the offer."

He nods tensely, respecting her decision.

Zoey steps between me and Parry to cool the tension further, and to us, she says, "I can look out for myself." Her eyes soften on me. She knows that's only partly true. In this town, you can have all the strength in the world, but without allies, you're nothing.

It's why the Durand name is as good as dirt. Her dad never had enough people to support him and defend him against my family. The rumors. The gossip. It all but drove him out of town. Or at least as far as he could go without completely leaving.

Parry resurfaces his glare on me. "You know what your family has done to Colt. I don't see how you can help."

Pain lances my chest. "I'm not my family, Parry."

He looks me up and down. "Sure as hell look like a Brambilla to me."

Air is brittle in my lungs.

Colt Durand is a lighthouse keeper. An antiquated job these days, but Mistpoint Harbor is one of the last places that still employs a civilian to keep the wick trimmed, light lit, weather recorded, and to watch the coast for signs of distress. When tourists come, Colt's also responsible for giving tours of the lighthouse.

It's a thankless job. Long hard hours. Little sleep. No one wants it. But it's Mistpoint Harbor tradition to have a local take the position. So every two decades, a lottery is held. One name drawn from a list of qualified citizens. The qualifications are simple: Be in good health and at least eighteen years or older.

Eight years ago, Colt's name was drawn.

But it's no secret the lottery was rigged. Out of the seven people on the town council, five are Brambillas. Two of my aunts, two uncles, and one cousin have a large sway in this town, and their desires have always been clear to me.

Make sure Mistpoint Harbor is always seen as cursed.

Who better to man the lighthouse than the son of the famed *Mother Murderer*? The Durands are unequivocally the most cursed family here, and the moment Colt took the lighthouse position, my cousin Bernard posted about it online. It spread through the internet, reaching Reddit even. Tourists came in droves to be able to talk to Colt during a group tour.

I want to tell Parry that Colt could have turned down the position. No one forced him to become the lighthouse keeper.

But it wouldn't be completely true. No one pointed a gun at Colt's head, but if he refused, he'd have been shunned out of town. And while the hours and work are horrid, Colt is paid well. According to what Aunt Effie has told me, he earns more than Dr. Rhodes, the family physician, down the street.

In front of the lighthouse now, I realize Parry's not going to trust me. Maybe not ever. But I can at least put the truth out there.

"Parry," I say, "I can't deny the destruction my family has caused the Durands. But if I can help Colt, maybe I can make this *one* thing right. Let me do that."

His seafoam green eyes barely soften a fraction before looking to Zoey. "Your call, Zo."

Zoey looks to me, and for a second, I worry she might cast me out. Maybe she's remembering just how influential and cruel my family was…still is. And like Parry said, I'm still a Brambilla.

I can't change my blood.

I can only use what I am for good.

A silent beat passes between us before she turns to Parry. "Kenobi is with me. She goes where I go."

Her words are like liquid fire, trying to thaw my frozen heart.

Parry expels a tense breath. "Fantastic." He shoots me a warning look. I shoot him one back. The dog versus the wolf.

We're cautious of each other. Him of me, more so. He locks his convertible with the key fob. "Let's get this over with then."

CHAPTER 10

ZOEY DURAND

Darker clouds roll in just as we reach the base of the lighthouse. A small one-bedroom keeper's quarters is attached to the exterior. It's been my brother's home for eight years now.

My reunion with Colt will be different than with Brian. Colt never threatened me when I told him I was leaving Mistpoint Harbor. He helped me pack. He drove me to the bus station. He told me, "Your happiness is my happiness, Zoey. Do what you have to do."

In high school, he was never picked on like me. Colt was mostly ignored. Protected by his friendship with Parry. Much like October tried her best to protect me. Hell, Parry was even a grade above Colt just like October was a grade above me. Seniors while we were juniors.

Colt is a whole five years older than me, and as soon as I entered Mistpoint High, he'd already graduated. But maybe that was for the best. Two Durands together would've painted a bigger target than just one alone.

And Colt might not have been my protector growing up, but he was my home. My safety and comfort. Because only three people left in this town know what it's like to have the name Durand.

The wind picks up and thunder grumbles like a forewarning.

October steps closer to my side, the warmth of her body radiates against me, felt even through her fur coat that I wear. Her presence is a life raft that keeps me afloat.

I'm not sure what to expect when Parry knocks on the door. *My brother is a mess.* That's the most I know.

But we're all big messes. So why is he so different than the rest of us?

No one answers.

Parry knocks again, louder this time. "Colt!"

Nothing.

Parry combs a hand through his hair, and with his other, he pulls out his phone. "Pick up, Colt," he begs. His worry amps up my own.

I push ahead of him and bang a fist on the door. "Colt!" I yell, then I use the brass door knocker shaped like an anchor. Nothing.

No response.

"This is Colt." I hear my brother's edged voice from Parry's phone. *"I'm busy. Call back later. Or never. Don't bother leaving a message because I don't check 'em. Colt. Out."* An automatic beep follows.

Parry hangs up and curses under his breath. Golden locks fall to his forehead, and he brushes them away to look at the door. "We have to get in there."

My adrenaline spikes. What's wrong with Colt?

"Move." October pushes her way past Parry and to my side. In one aggressive move, she slams the bottom of her boot against the door. The wood lets out a slight *crack.*

"On three," I tell her.

She gives me a nod.

"One, two," I count. *"Three."* We both body slam the door and the wood lets out a deeper, angrier *crack!* Before we can barrel inside, the door swings effortlessly open.

"Back the fuck up!" my brother shouts, a baseball bat pointed threateningly at us. Shirtless, sweats hanging low on his gaunt bony waist, and dark-brown hair disheveled like he was woken from a deep, eternal slumber from inside a coffin.

October takes my hand quickly and pulls me back behind her.

Colt's anger is replaced by confusion. Brows drawn in a bunch as he pieces together what's happening. Parry. October. *Me.*

When his gaze lands on me, the color drains from his face. "What the…fuck?" His head swings to Parry. "What the fuck, Parry?!"

I don't ask how he knows *Parry* is to blame for my arrival. Colt knows him better than anyone. My dad used to say that Colt and Parry have been best friends for so long that their fates twisted together. Vines too tangled to tear apart.

Parry holds out a hand. "Let me explain—"

"Let you explain?" Colt points the baseball bat at him. "You brought my *sister* back to town, and you want to talk? I should put your ass in the ground right now, DiNapoli."

"Whoa!" I take a step forward, around October, coming into better view, but Colt still hasn't let us inside. "You don't need to put any asses into the ground, Colt. I came here willingly."

Colt keeps his glare on Parry like he doesn't want to look at me again. Like maybe actually *seeing* me will make it real. Colt's chest concaves heavily, anger still present. "Is that true?" he asks Parry.

Parry is calm. Casual. Not even worried about the rage spewing from my brother. He stuffs his hands in his jacket pockets, the breast embroidered with the words *Regatta '17*. It belonged to his dad. "Technically, I asked her to come—"

Colt takes a threatening step forward outside the lighthouse. Winds howling around us.

I slip in between Parry and the end of the baseball bat. Colt freezes instantly, and this time he has no choice but to look at me.

Nose flared, he holds back something raw. Anger. Concern. I can't tell which.

"I could have said *no*," I tell Colt. "Don't blame Parry."

Slowly, he lowers the bat. His eyes flit from Parry to me and then they finally register her. He lets out a cross noise. "You brought a Brambilla here?"

"Nice to see you too, Colt," October says, voice full of ice.

He flips her off.

She rolls her eyes.

Then my brother says to October, "If you ever loved her at all, you'd tell her to go home."

Those words crash against me. My pulse starts hammering in my ears, and I almost think I missed October's response.

Her lips draw into a thin line. "Zoey refused to leave."

"So?" Colt glowers. "Kick her the fuck out of town. Isn't that what Brambillas do?"

All the light drains out of October's eyes. "If we had that kind of power, your father would have been banished after he killed your mother."

I go still, my face falling.

She can't actually believe those rumors about my dad. I *know* she doesn't.

Colt charges.

Parry is quicker, side-stepping in front of him. "Stop. *Colt.*" He has a hand on his shoulder.

"You're just like the rest of them, OB!" Colt yells at her. "Don't fucking fool yourself, you heartless cunt."

"*Colt!*" Parry shoves him backwards into the lightkeeper's house, away from us. They tussle against each other. Pushing. Clawing. Until Parry, stronger, pins Colt against the wall inside. "Calm down."

Cold wraps around me, bleeding through the fur coat. My bones feel frozen solid. I can't move. Can't breathe. Colt's anger is less surprising than October's words.

She's always told me she never believed the rumors about the *Mother Murderer*. Betrayal chokes air from my lungs.

She doesn't believe it.

She can't.

But she'd be the first to remind me to not be so naïve. So fucking foolish.

October doesn't tear her eyes off mine. They're different than they were this morning when she brought me cookies. Colder.

I hold my arms around my body, around her soft coat. "Kenobi, what you said—"

"Colt is right, you should go home," she cuts me off quickly. "Get the fuck out of here, Zoey. Before something bad happens to you, too."

I shake my head. "I can't."

I have to help Colt…I have to help you.

She glares at the sky. "Well, you don't have a place to stay tonight, so—"

"We had a deal," I snap. "I tell you why I'm here, and you let me stay in the shed."

"It's off."

Anger vibrates through my body. "Why?" I try to reroute what went awry. "You were just telling Parry you're not like your family. That you want to right *one* wrong."

She nods. "If I do anything right, it's going to make sure you don't have a reason to stay here. It was foolish of me to give you a place to sleep. I won't make that mistake again."

She thinks she's the fool here?

"Kenobi—"

She's already walking away.

My heart feels shredded apart. October believes she's doing this *for* me. To protect me. Pushing me away for my own good?

The wind blows her brown hair as she climbs into her Jeep. She doesn't give me a single glance back as she drives away.

CHAPTER 11

ZOEY DURAND

Cigarette smoke and bourbon permeate in the lighthouse keeper's home, an overpowering combo as I slip through the half-broken door. The smell is...*nauseating*. But my stomach might be tossing from more than my brother's empty liquor bottles and unwashed laundry.

October's quick departure—her exit and words still sit uneasy. My head still pounds. Ugh, I'm still wearing her *coat*. The white soft fur caresses my cheeks as I hug the fabric closer. Tighter.

I'm an idiot for not tearing the thing off. But I can't just desert something of hers like she means nothing.

It takes a concerted effort to shake off October and finally look around me.

Piles and piles of dirty clothes decorate the sofa. Empty pizza boxes and Fizz cans scatter the ground. On the walls, Colt taped maps and hundreds of printed papers like a madman in search of buried treasure. A tornado might as well have violently swirled inside the lighthouse, leaving a disaster behind.

And then there's my twenty-nine-year-old brother.

Sitting on the second stair of a spiral staircase, he bites his fingernails and talks to Parry quietly. Dark circles outline his eyes.

I've never seen him so skinny and frail. He was an athlete growing up. Never drank more than a single beer so that he could be in "top form" during practice days on the water. His usually tanned olive skin looks pallid and sickly.

This isn't the Colt I left six years ago.

The only thing that I recognize is his anger. It's not new. When you're pushed down enough, you learn to bite back. Though it took me longer than my brothers to find the bite in me.

He goes quiet on the stairs, and his head swings to me. "Zoey."

It's the first time he's said my name.

"What's going on here?" I ask, motioning to his disaster of a living room. "What is all of this?" I eye the maps.

He doesn't answer, just looks over my shoulder. "Where's the bitch?"

I glare. "She has a name. Stop calling her a cunt and a bitch. You're no better than the people who shit on us."

He sucks in a tight breath. "*That*, I am reminded of every damn day."

My stomach sinks. *He didn't leave.* I have to remember that I haven't been living in this town like Colt. I left most of its cruelty behind.

He rubs harshly at his weary, tormented eyes. "I'm an asshole." Regret etches the words. "You can tell her that."

"You can tell her," I say, "and being an asshole isn't an excuse for—"

"I get that, Zo," he cuts me off, looking too pained, too tortured to dig into any harder. He searches the room for someone. And I realize he's trying to find October. Probably to apologize. Colt can be fiery and bitter, but he has a good heart underneath the toughened layers of self-preservation.

Parry frowns. "October left?"

I mutter, "Yeah."

Colt flinches in shock. His gaze softens on me, and he studies the fur coat. "Maybe she does love you."

I hate how much his words hurt. I hate how I can still smell her on me. And I hate how I don't want to stop thinking about her.

"You didn't answer me," I say quietly. "What's going on with all of this?" I approach the disorderly wall of maps and Sharpie marks. Circles. Lines.

I can barely make sense of it—except for the map of Mistpoint Harbor. The red circle around the lighthouse. The map of Lake Erie extending up the wall with numbers printed and scribbled. Latitudes. Longitudes.

"It doesn't concern you," Colt says, hopping to his feet. He's unsteady, wobbly. Parry catches him underneath his armpit so that he doesn't trip. I notice the half-empty bottle of rum on the end table.

"You're drunk," I realize.

"My little sister comes back to a cursed town," Colt says, swaying a little but maintaining balance like someone who's skilled on sailboats pitching at rough seas. "There's no better moment to drink."

He drank before he knew I was even here.

Parry slips him a look. "Not like you need a reason these days, Colt."

Colt laughs bitterly. "True…" He slaps Parry's chest. "Very true." He reaches the couch and sinks down tiredly. Is he even eating? His rib bones protrude in a way that gnaws concern through my own body.

"Can I grab you some food?" I ask and rifle through the pizza boxes. Empty. I open another. *Moldy.* "Colt."

He's swigging from the bottle of rum. "Zoey." He licks liquor off his lips. "My little sister…coming back to town…" He's lost in his head.

Parry and I exchange a worried look, and while he steals the rum from Colt—my brother putting up *zero* fight—I find a trash bag and clean the shit in here. Tossing the pizza boxes. The Fizz cans and empty chip bags.

Parry sets the rum bottle on a worn trunk near the door. "I'll go get some food from the Pelican. I have t-t-t-ttto tell Brian I'm missing my shift anyway."

"Oooh Brian won't like that." Colt kicks his feet up on the couch and pinches his eyes closed. "Careful, Pear, he might spank you."

Parry has no response. He's avoiding Colt's eyes, but Colt isn't opening them and looking at his best friend. Not even as my brother continues, "One of these days you'll both just hate fuck and get it out of your systems."

My eyes widen.

Parry tenses. "Well...we did kiss and that solved nothing, so I doubt fucking him will do much."

Colt opens one eye. "...you're screwing with me?"

Parry shakes his head.

"When?"

"Last night."

Colt closes his eyes, looking both tired but somehow relaxed.

"That's all?" Parry asks.

"Long time coming, man."

He shakes his head harder. "No it's not. I've hated Brian."

"We all hate Brian," Colt proclaims.

"I *still* hate Brian."

"Then go hate-kiss again until you hate-fuck each other and get back to me with that." He rubs his head like it's pounding. He reaches for a bottle and swipes air. We've repositioned all the alcohol out of his grabby drunk hands.

Parry mutters under his breath. "I'd say that'll only happen *in hell* but I'm not spending the afterlife with that bastard." He looks to me. "Want anything specific for lunch?"

I shake my head, and he motions with a tilt of his own head towards my brother. I'm picking up Parry signals. *Get Colt to talk to me.* Mission acquired.

I give him a nod.

Parry opens the broken door. "Later, Colt."

"See ya, man."

He leaves.

Colt ignores me. Purposefully, I'm sure.

I plop down on a worn club chair. Stuffing peeks from the plaid material. "Yesterday, I thought Parry and Brian were on worse terms..." I try and make small talk. "I guess Parry says nothing has changed even though they...kissed." I'm still in shock.

I didn't see it coming.

I couldn't have. I've been gone.

Colt keeps his eyes closed as he says, "If giving you the run-down of what happened here will get your ass out of town, I can give you the CliffsNotes version. All the juicy gossip here at Mistpoint handed to you on a silver platter."

"As tempting as that sounds, I'm not here to pick up the latest Mistpoint Harbor gossip rag." Plus, I've already had someone break a deal we made. I'm not stupid enough to take a second deal from anyone. I add, "I'm here to help you."

He's quiet, and his silence tells me everything I need to know.

He does need help.

I steer back to the safe topic. "You really think Parry and Brian should hook up?"

Brian has been out for as long as I can remember. He never hid the fact that he dated guys and girls. Hell, Colt and I even watched women and men leave Brian's catamaran in the early mornings after what looked like a raunchy night. We both witnessed the *goodbye* kisses and the *I'll never talk to you again after this* breakfasts.

The fisherman lasted the longest. And even that must've only been a couple weeks, at most. It's not like Brian dated a lot or hooked up on the regular. I think he was selective. Picky. Even when it came to one-night stands.

"Yeah, I meant it," Colt says. "The quicker those two can just find a way to screw out the hate, the better."

"Are you really in the market to give relationship advice?"

"It's sex advice, Zoey." He opens one eye to look at me. "Speaking of relationships though—if there's someone back in Chicago waiting for you, don't you think they'll miss you?"

"Nice shot." I lean back, crossing my legs like I'm the Solver of Mysteries in this chair. Miss Mistpoint better watch out. "But I'm not telling you about my life in Chicago while you get to be Closed Lips McGee."

He rolls his eyes dramatically, and when I decide to kick my feet up on the coffee table, Colt waves a finger at me. "No sitting. You're not staying."

I make a face. "I've been sitting."

"You don't need to get…comfortable." He seems more uneasy. Cagey. He slowly lifts himself a little higher on the couch. "You need to go."

What was he looking at? The maps? The door? "I'm here for *you*, Colt."

"I don't need you," he spits back.

"Look at you!" I yell. "You're drunk in the middle of the day. You're practically a fucking skeleton, and your house is a dumpster and ashtray and why the fuck are you covering your ears?"

He twitches, rubs his ears, cringes—and something like shame crawls over his face. He mutters something.

"What?" My heart is racing.

"It's not you," he says more clearly, his feet now on the floor. His knees jostling. He motions to his ears. "I was listening to you. You weren't who I was trying to tune out."

Is he…hearing things?

"Colt—"

"You should go. You can't help me." His voice is shaking. "Go!"

I don't move, and I lower my voice. "If our roles were reversed, you'd be right *here* in this chair screaming at me. So I'm not going anywhere. You're stuck with me until you tell me what the hell is going on."

He's quiet. I let him take as long as he needs. A minute turns to two and enters into three before he whispers, "You're not going to understand."

"Give me a fucking chance at least," I beg.

He slowly pulls out a pack of cigarettes from between the couch cushions. *Gross.* I watch him slam the pack against his hand a couple times before fishing out a cigarette. An old box of Drunk Pelican branded matches rest on the coffee table, and I lean forward to grab them.

He gives me a hard look, but before he can say anything, I'm tossing them to him.

He relaxes a fraction. "Thanks," he mumbles and lights his cigarette. I wait.

His knee jostles again. "It was around last December," Colt explains. "There was a bad storm, and a distress call came in over the radio." He stares at the ground like he's being pushed back to that night. "Her voice…she was terrified. The signal was garbage. The static made it hard to hear her, but she was saying *mayday*. Over and over. Like her life depended on it." He pauses. "I still hear her...I still replay it over...and over." His eyes redden before he sucks the cigarette, blows out smoke. "Last thing she told me was her name is Augustine Anders and her boat was sinking."

A shiver snakes through me, and I tighten October's coat. "You must receive those calls a lot during bad weather."

He shakes his head. "Most calls go to the Coast Guard unless the caller doesn't know which station to use. But I saw something in the distance that night. It looked like a flickering light..." He glares at the ground. "I radioed the Coast Guard—but they were taking care of a freighter accident. They didn't reach the area until the morning. By then, there was no boat. No girl. Nothing. They told me they couldn't do anything, so I tried bringing it up with Sheriff Carmichael—"

I let out a breath of shock. "Colt."

His bloodshot eyes flit to me. "I had to do something, Zo. You didn't hear that girl." He points towards the door with the cigarette pinched between fingers. "*I did*. And she was dying."

"Okay," I say into a nod. "You're right. You had to do something. So what did Sheriff Carmichael say?"

Colt sobers. "He laughed in my face."

I'm not surprised. The sheriff hates us. Mostly Brian. But I suppose we're extensions of our brother.

"That's bullshit. He has to take you seriously," I refute. "You're the lighthouse keeper."

Colt takes a breath. "I don't have any evidence, Zo. No one saw a boat leave the harbor that night. And I can't find any proof that an Augustine Anders exists. She's a ghost."

"What about the distress call? Is there a recording?"

"That's the weird part. The system is set to auto-record, but...it didn't that night."

I frown. "Colt. Have you ever thought that maybe this is some elaborate hoax?"

He shakes his head over and over. "No. No. *No.* You didn't hear her, Zoey. There was water and wind. Fuck, the wind!" He shoots up to his feet and paces. "She was on the water. I know what it sounds like."

"Okay, Colt." I rise slowly. Carefully. "I believe you."

He's already storming over to his wall of maps. "I just need to find some evidence. *Something* that'll get that fucker off his chair and out there looking for her."

Another chill creeps down my back. "It's been over three months. Even if you did find evidence that she exists, she's probably…" The word lodges in the back of my throat.

Colt has turned to look at me, his eyes still bloodshot. "Say it."

I can't.

In my silence, he says, "I know she's probably dead. That's not what this is about."

"Then what is it about?"

"They're letting their hatred of our family turn their back on a girl. On a human life. *They* need to see what they did to her." His face breaks. "And they think I'm crazy, Zoey." He chokes on the words and motions angrily towards the door. "The whole *fucking* town. I'm okay with being the son of a murderer, but I am *not* crazy."

"I know, Colt." I take a breath. "So let's do this. Let's find some evidence that Augustine Anders exists."

He shakes his head. "I don't have any leads, Zoey."

"No one in this town will talk to you, right?" I ask.

He nods.

"So maybe they'll talk to me," I tell him. "I'm a Durand, but I've been gone awhile. The gossipmongers are going to want all the dirt on me. I have leverage."

Pain lances his face. "I can't ask you to do this for me. You *need* to leave."

"I'm not leaving." I exhale roughly. "Jesus Christ, how many times do I have to say it?"

He touches his chest like he's hurting all over. "I don't want you cursed like me."

Cursed.

This is his curse.

I go cold. "Did...did the Roberts..."

He nods.

He's in the history museum.

"Already?" I breathe out.

He rubs at his swollen eyes. "Colt Durand, cursed at twenty-nine. Believes he saw a girl drown in the lake, and he let the madness consume him."

Anger ruptures through my chest. "Fuck them. They were just *waiting* with bated breath to put you in that fucked-up museum."

He snuffs his cigarette out in an ashtray. "Probably." He looks to me. "But that's why I don't want to encourage you to stay, Zoey. You know they'll find a way to write you in. You're the last Durand not in those books."

I'll be okay, I want to say.

I'm not the same girl who left, sits on the tip of my tongue too.

I'm stronger, I truly believe.

But all those truths are lost to what he said. The legend. The curse. The longer I stay in town, the more I'll play with my own fate. I'm willing to take the risk—even if I'm going up against Mistpoint Harbor itself.

CHAPTER 12

ZOEY DURAND

Colt won't let me stay with him. No surprise there since he basically told October giving me room and board was signing my death warrant. He doesn't want that on his hands either.

When I leave the lighthouse, I find my suitcase outside the door. Propped up next to a broken bench. *Thank you, October.*

I'm surprised she didn't include a bus ticket as a parting gift. No cookies accompany my luggage, but before I grab the handle, I see something wrapped in pretty pink tissue paper.

I unfurl the tissue to find a gooey cinnamon roll.

Still warm.

My heart elevates.

I try to find a note. Like the ones she'd put in my locker with pastries. But she didn't leave one this time.

My heart sinks.

She left me food. That has to mean something. Or maybe she just didn't want me to go hungry. I bite into the most perfect cinnamon roll just as my phone pings. *October.*

My eyes flit to my phone and hope is quickly replaced with disappointment. Just a friend from Chicago. Asking where I am. I haven't told everyone I'd be MIA.

The original plan was to get in and get out without anyone noticing I'd left for long. That might not work out, but I'm unsure of how to respond. So I just send a vague, I'm okay. Out of state for a bit. Be back later.

Settled with the text reply, I hike away from the lighthouse. It's a laborious effort trying to wheel my luggage over stones and grassy patches, since my suitcase is still down a wheel.

It feels a little like déjà vu. Being kicked out of another place.

Not far into the long trek, Parry's white Mustang rolls to a stop. Scratch marks and dents mar the driver's side door. Roof down, he leans a shoulder out of his convertible.

His eyes dart immediately to my suitcase. "You're leaving?"

"Not Mistpoint," I correct. "But Colt won't let me stay with him."

Parry nods, understanding. He gestures with his head to the passenger side. "Hop in."

"What about feeding Colt?"

"I'll be back before dark."

After shoving the rest of the cinnamon roll in my mouth, I heave my suitcase in the backseat next to a couple takeout bags from The Drunk Pelican. Then I climb into the passenger side. Still chewing, I buckle and finally swallow, licking icing off my thumb.

He zips off.

The brisk air pinches my skin, even with the warm heat from the vents. I once asked Parry why on fucking Earth he chose a convertible. It's not like we live in sunny Florida.

But he said, *to weed out the weak, Zo. Can't hack the cold then get the hell outta my life.*

That was years ago. And as I look at Parry now, I wonder if that's partly why he's chosen to befriend Durands. We might be the easy targets in this town, but we're not weak. We're people who were always meant to survive.

"Was October right?" I ask him as he drives. "When she said you work at the Pelican because you have the hots for Brian?"

Parry lets out a noise. "No." He glances to me, then the road. "I work at the Pelican because I love you and Colt..." He trails off for a long beat.

"And Brian?"

"I love your family," Parry says, "and what the town has done to all of you...it's not right. You don't do that to people." He defends us because he loves us—because his moral heart knows we've been wronged.

I smile softly. *I love you too, Parry.*

The Mustang has survived all this time as well, but the scratches and dents are new. I smell fried fish from the takeout in the back, and nostalgia overpowers me. Dizzies me.

Parry is driving towards the center of town. "You change your mind about staying at my place?"

"No," I tell him. "Take me to the Harbor Inn."

His brows jump. "Kelly won't give you a room."

"She will. I have a plan."

Parry doesn't protest; his eyes flit to the rearview, looking back at the lighthouse as it fades. "Did Colt talk to you?"

My bones chill. I explain everything he told me and end with, "So that's why you brought me here. To find evidence that Augustine Anders was on the water that night—or shit, that she even exists."

Parry frowns. "What? No."

"No?" My stomach drops.

"I called you out here to convince Colt that this girl *doesn't* exist." He glances to me, then back to the road. "He was tired that night, Zoey. He did about ten lighthouse tours back-to-back."

A wave of hurt presses against my chest. I always thought Parry would take my brother's side. On anything. "So you agree with Sheriff Carmichael?"

Heat touches his eyes. "The same sheriff who did an ass-backwards job investigating my parents murder? Who told me, *'It's a closed case, son. Animal attacks happen around here. Nuthin' we can do for you.'* That one?"

"Yeah," I say tensely. "That one."

"No, Zo. I don't believe shit that comes out of his mouth."

"Then why do you want me to convince Colt that this girl doesn't exist?"

"Because he's been set-up—they're setting him up to *think* he heard something. They knew how long he worked that night. They knew what they could do to him. What they could make him believe he heard."

"Who did?"

"The town council."

Damn.

I'm stunned silent for a second. "...so you think Augustine Anders is fake—that the town council created this ugly hoax," I realize, and partially, I begin believing this a lot more too.

It makes sense.

But I want, so badly, to also believe Colt. To be in his corner. But does being in his corner mean siding with Parry?

"And Sheriff Carmichael is in on it somehow. I know he is." Parry narrows his eyes on the darkened street. Clouds still gathering overhead. It hasn't rained yet. Shockingly.

I stuff my hands in October's coat. "Did you hear the sheriff say something?"

He shakes his head.

"Did you hear the Roberts admit to it? Did someone tell you the truth?"

Parry is more rigid. "Not-t-t-tttt exactly, no." He runs a distraught hand through his thick golden hair.

My mouth slowly falls open. "Parry, do you have any actual evidence they're setting him up?"

He's quiet until he says, "No—but I have a feeling." His gaze bores into me until he eyes the road again. "The town council have been fucking Colt over since they put him in that lighthouse."

"But it's just a hunch you're going on?"

"Yeah."

Jesus. "…and what if Colt's right? What if there was a girl?"

"What if there wasn't and he spends an eternity searching for something he can never find?" Parry is scared for Colt. It's clear just how much. "The best way to get him back to his old self is to help him move on. Hunting down an imaginary person isn't going to fix things, Zo. It'll just prolong…" His voice tapers off.

What was he about to say?

Prolong my brother's binge-drinking, chain-smoking, paranoia, anxiety, trauma, or how about his clear lack of eating?

All of the above?

All of the above. I nod slowly to myself, then wince a little. I'm not totally convinced Parry is choosing the best route.

If there's anything I know, it's the power of *belief.* Belief in curses and legends has fueled generations of wealth for certain families in Mistpoint, while it's left others to drown.

Belief can be even stronger than the truth.

So if Colt really believes this girl exists, nothing I say will change that. And I don't even have the evidence to back up a counter argument.

"He won't believe me," I tell Parry. "Not without evidence."

"It'll take too long, Zo. I've tried for months and I've already come up with as much as Colt. Augustine Anders doesn't exist, and the town council acts like Colt has lost his mind." He glances at me. "You were my only hope left. If anyone can get through to Colt— it's you."

To simply *talk* Colt out of his beliefs?

"That's not true. The only person my brother would drop to his knees and tunnel his way to hell for is a guy named Parry DiNapoli."

He grimaces. "It's been three months, and he hasn't listened to me at all. You're the next best shot."

I think for a long second. "I've never seen him so sure about something, Parry. We're not going to be able to help him without proof."

And a huge part of me wants answers too. If the girl is out there, then she needs to be found. And if Colt is being set-up, the prick who's fucking with my brother needs to be throat-punched.

But what if Parry *and* Colt are wrong? What if Colt didn't see anything and there is no nefarious hoax? I'll be helping him track down a girl that really doesn't exist, and I'll be wasting my time here. There really will be no closure for Colt.

In the end, Colt is a Durand. He's my brother. And the worst thing about not being believed is not being believed by your own blood. That's never happened to me before. Like hell I'll do it to him.

Parry exhales a big breath. He's wishing we could just *easily* convince Colt that it's all a hoax. But we can't.

"We have to prove that she's real or that she's not," I tell him.

"How are you going to do that, Zo?"

I don't think as I say, "October. She's connected to the town council. She can get inside the inner-circle. Places we can't."

"Will she really help you?"

We're both remembering her storming out earlier.

My stomach knots. "I don't know." I think harder. "...but I'm supposed to be writing a book about Mistpoint. I can ask around without appearing that suspicious."

He nods more. "I'll help any way I can." He swallows hard, his Adam's apple bobbing. "You know, I would've given anything for the sheriff to believe me that night."

The night his parents died.

He breathes, "I hate that Colt is going through this now, and I just want it to end for him. And you're right, he needs proof. I got mine."

I go cold. As far as I'm aware, his parents' death is still a mystery. "What proof?"

"I've only told Colt…and Brian."

Brian?

I swear Parry reddens, but he inhales strongly. "I wanted to tell you. I was going to tell you at some point…but then you…"

I left.

"You're going to tell me now?" I wonder.

"Yeah," he nods, lips lifting. For a blip, I can tell Parry is happy I'm here. That I'm back, and it feels good to be home.

Your time here has an expiration date.

A pain sits heavy. I know. I can't stay.

His smile wanes as he starts. "When I was seventeen, Enzo dug up our parents' bodies a day after he buried them."

My eyes grow to saucers. "Parry."

"I knew he was going to do it," he continues. "My brother and I paid a coroner from out of town to do an autopsy."

"What'd they say?" I ask, but knowing that Parry has *always* been convinced it wasn't an animal attack, the answer is clear.

"Stab wounds. Nothing a wolf or a coyote or a bear could've done."

He tells me the rest of the story. How he felt vindicated. But they didn't have the money for a lawsuit or the power to hunt a murderer

108

with no lead. So they buried the truth back in the ground with their mom and dad.

I understand now why Parry is so dead-set on the hoax theory. The town turned their backs on the DiNapoli boys when they needed justice and the truth. And the council never really disliked the DiNapolis. They were hard-working members of the community.

Still are.

But the council *loathes* my family. They could do worse to Colt.

Still, the side of me that believes in fate and strange coincidences thinks, *what if the girl is real?* She could be real.

Parry drives into town. We're on the last street that allows vehicles before signs start reading *no cars beyond this point.* Most pedestrians are inside as a storm brews. We pass the museum, and Parry tells me, "If Colt was in his right mind that night and he did see something, there are people in this town that wouldn't take his word just to spite him."

Sickness churns in my belly just thinking about that. People always say I look more like Brian than Colt, but it's an easy explanation. Colt has more of his mother's features than our dad's. Mia Vitale came from one of Mistpoint's more prominent Italian-American families. The Brambillas and Vitales have always been friends, but as the story goes, Effie Brambilla and Mia Vitale were thicker than thieves growing up.

At least that's how my dad described them.

So when Mia Vitale died giving birth to Colt, Effie blamed my dad. She shut out Colt, even if he was and *still* is the son of her best friend. The town followed suit.

People don't forget the past.

They sure as hell don't forget that Colt's existence killed Mia Vitale. It was even a worse sin in the town's eyes when my dad fell in love with Colt's young nanny years later. Bethany Reed. My mother.

What I've been told—it was a short fling, but she got pregnant soon after and also died in childbirth.

Parry stops the Mustang at a curb near a three-story bed & breakfast with a dark shingled roof, red bricked frame, and cobbled pathway up to a navy-blue door. The Harbor Inn has always evoked a quaint charm, but I've never stepped a foot inside.

Until today.

Parry helps me with my suitcase, then shields his eyes from a single ray of sun breaching the ugly clouds. He scrutinizes the Inn. "Call me if they don't give you a room. Pissing off Brian is better than sleeping on the docks."

"Deal," I say and hold out my hand.

Parry smiles and gives it a shake. Tender, long-lost emotion passes between us, and he lets go to hug me. I hug back just as tightly.

He whispers, "You're the little sister I never had. I'm glad…" He stops himself from saying, *your back*.

Something painful balls up in my ribs.

How am I going to leave again? Everyone I truly love is *here*. But no matter how much they love me too—I know they don't want me to stay.

Parry tears away fast. He starts walking back to the curb. I grab onto the suitcase, about to head up the path.

"And Zoey…" Parry turns back.

I rotate to see him.

Overwhelming emotion gathers in Parry's green eyes. "Thank you," he says. "For coming here. For Colt. Maybe you can get further than I could."

I never thought I'd actually Agatha fucking Christie myself. But here I am, in the middle of a mystery.

I need October's help.

This feels impossible without her.

"Don't bet on me yet, Pear." It's the last thing I say before trudging up to the Inn.

No bells on the door announce my arrival. A frail lady with dyed jet-black hair occupies an antique front desk. Wispy strands of hair stick up in a high bun, and she sips casually from a floral teacup.

My footsteps are loud, cumbersome. Her eyes snap up before she even lifts her head. And then slowly—like it's made of molten lava—she sets her teacup on the desk.

"Zoey Durand." My name sounds like arsenic on her lips.

"Mrs. Kelly." I step forward to come face-to-face with Mistpoint's most prominent widow.

George Kelly died from anaphylaxis after unknowingly ingesting peanut oil one night. Police couldn't figure out why Kelly's pot roast had trace amounts of peanut oil, but rumor is that Aimee Kelly laced the meal. And since George was a notorious cheater who'd been caught (one too many times) buying drinks to young tourists at The Drunk Pelican, the sheriff's department didn't poke too hard into the case. The town never shunned Mrs. Kelly.

Good for her, they always said.

He got what was coming to him, the Brambillas echoed.

So I'm very aware that I'm confronting a possible murderer—at least it's more probable she killed her husband than my dad killed his wives.

But out of all the B&Bs in town, the Harbor Inn is my best bet to score a room.

One step closer.

And she holds up a finger. "Stop right there."

As if she put a spell on me, I freeze. *Do what she says. Don't cause waves.* I need her help, not her hatred. "I'm back," I say with a half-hearted smile.

"I have two eyes." She picks up her teacup. "And two ears. I was already informed of your return."

Gossiping gossipers. Don't they have something better to talk about? I clutch the handle to my suitcase. "I need a room."

She doesn't blink. I swear she hasn't blinked this whole fricking time! Okay...maybe she is a witch—a fable that Mistpoint Ghost Tours *love* to tout to tourists.

I'm not an idiot though. Witches and vampires don't exist. The only monsters here are the humans that inhabit the town.

"And why should I give you, a Durand, a room at my Inn?" She surveys me like I'm grocery store produce. Ripe or rotten.

I pull my shoulders back, not cowering to Mrs. Kelly. "Because you out of everyone should know what happens when you have someone with power in your corner."

She sips her teacup languidly, almost in boredom. Then she says, "You don't have any power here, Zoey."

"I'm not the same girl who left six years ago. I'm a writer now. I have a book deal with a big fancy New York City publisher, and you know what my book is about?"

Her face pales, already guessing. "You wouldn't."

"I spent a good part of my life watching from the sidelines. I'm the best person to detail the lovely inner workings of the families, businesses, and people of this town," I say, confidence flowing with each word. "So if you want me to put in a good word or two about you and the Harbor Inn—you should really reconsider letting me rent a room."

She stares me down for a full minute, and my palms sweat. Will she call my bluff? Besides October, no one here knows what I studied in college. No one knows about my job in Chicago. It's the pin keeping this façade together.

She finally blinks and reaches for a skeleton key. "It's four hundred a night."

Okay, that shit is *steep*. And I know for a fact that is *not* the rate of a room here. "Really?"

"This is a very popular Inn. Make sure to note that in your book."

I restrain an eye roll. "Of course." I fish out my debit card from my bag. Luckily, I did have a decent paying job back in Chicago. I'm not broke or strapped for cash—just strapped for connections and...*time*. But I'm not loaded. I won't be able to afford more than a few nights here without seriously dipping into my savings.

I pass over the card, and she swipes it into her reader.

When she passes it back, I opt for politeness. "Thank you, Mrs. Kelly."

"It's just Kelly." She hands me the key. "Remember that for your book too." She arches a brow, as if testing out my resolve. Shit, there's probably a part of her that doesn't believe my story. She could sniff out a fib from a mile away.

All I can do is layer on the confidence. Fabricated or not, I choose to believe my own lie.

"I will," I tell her.

"You're in the Edgar Allen Poe room." She continues to penetrate me with her stone-cold gaze, while my stomach nosedives.

Every room at the Harbor Inn is named after an author of gothic literature. Tourists eat that shit up, and they also talk about renting out the infamous "Poe Room" where George Kelly took his last breath.

I don't believe in ghosts.

Not *completely*.

Sort of.

Okay, werewolves and witches seem ridiculous. But ghosts— ghosts could just be spirits who haven't crossed. They could be real.

And I'm aware she's testing me.

Kelly gives me a smile that looks more acidic than charmed. "I'm sure you'll have lots to write about in that room."

I give her a nod, and I swiftly leave her sight.

It's not until I'm heading up the creaky old staircase that I realize what I've done. I just made a deal with the real murderer of the town.

Maybe Parry is right.

Maybe I do have a death sentence.

CHAPTER 13

OCTOBER BRAMBILLA

ooks hustle in the kitchen. Pots clanking and clam chowder bubbling on the stove. I keep to myself in the corner, beating two eggs into a dough mixture for the fried crullers. My head has been spinning all day. Ever since this morning at the lighthouse, I've been replaying my words over and over.

If we had that kind of power, your father would have been banished after he killed your mother.

The words don't pierce my heart—not as much as the utter horror on Zoey's face. Her hurt. Her anger. I deserved every last ounce of it.

What's worse…

I'd say it all a second time. A third. A fourth…

No hesitation.

I'd cause Zoey Durand visceral pain and hurt again and again to protect her. To push her away. Colt was right. If I care about her—love her—then I need to make certain she leaves this town.

She's only safe if she's gone.

Something stings my eyes. *Emotion that I shouldn't be feeling.* I slop dough out of the bowl. "Fuck," I mutter to myself, cleaning up the mess quickly. Before anyone notices.

"There is a zero to negative chance the FanCon tour stops in Mistpoint Harbor," my cousin Isabella tells her younger sister Angela, both short with wild curls and olive skin. "They're only hitting big cities."

"Maybe one of them will realize how awesome our town is," Angela combats, flipping a *Celebrity Crush* tabloid at the middle prep table. She's deserted shucking clams, and unlike her older sister, she wears big wire-framed glasses. "God, Charlie Cobalt is so *hot*."

Before Zoey Durand returned, I've been going through the motions. Numb. Quiet. Tracking the H.M.C. FanCon tour stops has been the only interesting thing in my life. It keeps me somewhat engaged with my cousins.

The most famous families in the world—the Hales, Meadows, and Cobalts—are currently on a bus going from city to city for meet-and-greets. At least *some* of them are.

We all have our favorites, and thanks to Angela waiting in an online queue for two hours, we all managed to snag tickets for the Cleveland tour stop in December, which was in driving distance. The cities are announced at the last minute. So last minute that we all couldn't get off work and had to sell our coveted tickets.

So Angela has been watching where the bus goes next. Right now, it's nowhere near us.

"Charlie Cobalt isn't that hot, not compared to Maximoff Hale," Isabella declares. He is considered the most eligible bachelor of the bunch.

Benny laughs. "You mean the guy banging his cousin?"

I narrow my eyes on him. "It's a rumor—a lie," I snap in defense. Jane Cobalt, Maximoff's *cousin*, just so happens to be my favorite. Which Benny knows. She's the cat lover. The nurturer. And she's cute in her tulle skirts and mismatched sweaters. Though, yes, she's straight.

I was most upset that I couldn't meet her. Apparently, her autograph and photo lines haven't been very long. She's not the most beloved, but that only makes me want to love her more.

I think of Zoey…

And I stir the dough slower. She doesn't follow celebrity gossip like my family does, but if she had to pick, she's always said she's Team Hale. Purely because that notoriously geeky family loves Star Wars.

"There's no way Maximoff and Jane hooked up," Angela says like it's old news, flipping another page.

"It was all over the internet," Benny proclaims as he sharpens his knives. "He had *teeth marks* on his back. From who? He's not dating anyone. But he carried his cousin when her cats ran out of their house—and he was still in his underwear!"

Angela shoots him a look. "You've carried me before the same way. Are we screwing?"

Isabella cringes. "Gross."

Benny looks sick. "Don't even, *Angela*."

My lips ache to rise, and Angela slips me a smile while tying back her hair for food prep. She's protective of all three famous families and generally knows the most. She's the Encyclopedia of Hales, Meadows, and Cobalt knowledge.

Since childhood, we've all bonded by watching the docuseries *We Are Calloway* together, which documents their lives. We follow them on social media, tune into old reruns of *Princesses of Philly*, and subscribe to the tabloids. Honestly, we turn into teenagers again whenever we're passionately discussing and defending them like they're our friends. But we're all in our twenties now and still obsessed.

I suppose they've always been our way out of Mistpoint Harbor. What life is like beyond our cursed town and fried crullers and sleepy winters.

"It's a good thing we all didn't go to Cleveland," Benny reminds us. "It was a shit show. The power went out before the Q&A portion, and Reddit said the autograph lines were *way* too long."

I tune out as Angela defends the FanCon and Isabella professes her love for Maximoff Hale again. Busying myself with work for ten minutes and thinking of Zoey.

Of the lighthouse.

Of her horror-stricken face.

"OB!" Benny shouts.

I flinch, dropping a spatula. "*Benito*," I growl.

"I've been calling your name five times." He glares. "What's wrong with you?"

Heart rate still accelerating, I grab the spatula off the floor and ignore his question. "What do you want?"

"The *mapeen*." He points at the dishtowel behind me.

I toss it to him.

He eyes me in a long, up and down sweep, then shakes his head.

You're fine, October. Fried crullers. *Fried crullers.* I try to concentrate and make more dough while my cousins discuss Isabella's crush on the sheriff's son Liam Carmichael, who works as a firefighter/EMT. They laugh about how many Italians have married Irish around here.

A lot.

Mistpoint Harbor has been settled mostly by immigrants throughout the years. In the 1800s, Irish and French called Mistpoint home. Later in the early 1900s, Italians and Hungarians were attracted to the coastal place. Railroad industry boomed, and so did our little slice of lakeside paradise.

When railroads shut down, many families with railroad workers—including ours—needed to find a way to survive in a decaying town. Mutterings of "curses" already circulated for decades. Strange deaths. Fatal accidents.

But the town only profited off the misery of others when the museum was built. And legends were eventually made.

"I heard that she was a prostitute in Chicago." Isabella's voice snatches my attention in a quick snap.

My heartbeat hikes up again. *Chicago.* They can't be talking about the famous families anymore. They live in Philadelphia.

Zoey.

Zoey lives in Chicago.

Isabella leans against the freezer door and fixes the sleeves to her black blouse. As the hostess of Fisherman's Wharf, she spends most of her time gossiping in the kitchen. Not helping prep for the lunch or dinner rush.

"Nah," Benny says, descaling a pile of walleye. He's the sous chef. "The prostitution stuff is definitely bullshit that my little brother heard from the high school." My shoulders begin to relax. And then he says, "I think she was a stripper."

I drop my whisk and it clanks against the metal bowl.

They all stare at me. Except Angela, who half-shucks clams, half-reads another tabloid.

Isabella winces. "Oh...sorry, October." She slowly unwraps one of the chocolate mints that servers pass out with checks. "I know you were friends with Zoey."

Benny stares into me. "I don't get why. She's a Durand."

I skip over that comment and tell Isabella, "She's not a prostitute or a stripper, so you can stop spreading that around."

Isabella pops the mint into her mouth. "Yeah, yeah, definitely. Gossip ends here, babe." Her brown eyes sparkle. "*Soooo,* do you happen to know what she was really doing in Chicago?"

Yes.

I do.

With the limitations of our rules, talking about our jobs was one of the very few things not off-limits. However, I'd rather take the knife in Benny's hands and slit my throat before spilling *any* information about Zoey.

Angela peeks up from the tabloid. Interested in my response, too.

"No clue," I say in my usual cold, stilted voice.

Isabella bites into her mint. "Bummer."

Angela returns to the magazine.

Benny places a couple pieces of fresh walleye on parchment lined paper. "She's not going to last another day here, and I put money on it. Three hundred bucks to be exact." He nods to me. "You want in, OB? There's a whole group making bets."

Anger tries to pinch me, but I feel more resigned than anything. Even if I love them, I'm exhausted by the predictability of my family and the people in this town.

"No," I say and try to focus on beating the dough.

Isabella asks Benny, "What makes you think she'll leave tomorrow?"

"She's staying at the Harbor Inn." His words send a burst of panic through me.

"What?" I breathe.

Benny frowns. "You don't know?"

After the lighthouse this morning, I threw myself into prepping dessert for tonight. Zoey has been on my brain, sure, but I made certain that I didn't seek out information about her whereabouts.

I shake my head.

"Kelly gave her the Poe Room," Benny explains with a brittle laugh. "That old witch must be trying to force her out of town herself."

Fuck.

I drop the whisk back into the bowl again and wipe my hands quickly on a *mapeen*. "I have to go."

"Wait, what?" Benny scowls. "Who's going to finish the crullers?"

"Danny can do it." I mention his brother who happens to be a line cook. I don't hear Benny's next words. I'm already ripping off my white chef coat, grabbing a snowy white puffer jacket from the backroom, and booking it into the frigid air.

Why would she go to the Harbor Inn? Out of all places! I hop angrily into my Jeep, heat and fury pumping my cold blood as I haphazardly put the car in reverse.

Crash!

I glance over my shoulder. A metal trashcan is tipped over, garbage littering the cement. Only a few cars are parked here in the back, and clam shells scatter the concrete in front of Benny's Subaru.

I leave the mess behind and peel onto the street.

My pulse thumps in a heavy, frenzied rhythm all the way to the B&B. Head whirling, I park the car and storm into the Harbor Inn. I expect to see Kelly—and I'm ready to claw her tooth and nail for giving Zoey a room here.

But the front desk is empty.

Fury still in check, I storm up the old wooden stairs and pass the stained-glass windows and the eerie artwork on the peeling paisley wallpapered walls. At the end of the hallway, I bang a fist on the door with the raven wood carving.

No one answers.

I bang harder.

"Hold on! Jesus." Zoey's annoyance only fuels my anger, so when the door swings open, I don't give her a chance to explain or say the word *hello*.

I barge in like the bitch I am. "What the fuck is wrong with you?" I breathe sharply and look around the room. Her suitcase is open and neatly folded clothes lie on the bed like she's been unpacking.

"I could ask the same thing about you," Zoey barks back, but she's shutting the door behind her.

"You're not staying here." I point a finger at the ground.

Zoey crosses her arms over her chest, and I lift my chin, breathing uneven, strange breaths. Imagining my lips trailing kisses along her breasts—I pop the fantasy out of my head.

"You know what," she snaps. "I'm tired of people telling me where I can and cannot stay. Fuck th—"

"This is Aimee Kelly's B&B, in case you've fucking forgotten," I interject coldly, stepping towards her. "Don't think for a second Kelly won't kill you herself to attract more customers to the 'haunted' room."

Zoey's nose flares. "Please, you can't honestly think she'd actually kill me…" Her voice drifts, considering.

My eyes heat. "This is Mistpoint Harbor. People get away with unspeakable things by blaming it on legends and curses. You used to know that."

She glares. "I still do."

"Good. Then you're leaving." I reroute to her folded clothes and pick them up.

She catches my wrist. "I'm not." She pulls an old Pat Benatar T-shirt from my grip. Her eyes meet my fury. "I'm not scared, Kenobi."

"You should be." I catch her wrist now, feeling her quickened pulse underneath a beaded bracelet. "You should be terrified." *I'm scared for you. I don't want anything to happen to you. I can't lose you for good.* I swallow the rest.

She shakes her head. "Why do you even care? You're the one who threw me out of the shed."

"So you'd leave!" I scream. "To protect you, you idiot!"

She throws up her hands. "You don't need to protect me!"

"Of course I do." *How can I not?*

"Why?!" she yells back.

"Because you're mine!" Those words just come out from my core, unearthed from somewhere deep.

Zoey's face fractures.

I try to redirect. "You're *my* responsibility," I clarify. "You always have been." Since the day I met Zoey in high school and she bowed at my feet, I took that on myself.

I fell for her headfirst, and I've been falling ever since. Even now, when I've spent months lifeless and cold, I hang onto the rage that grows because it's something. Anything. Other than the numbness and empty hollow I've been suffering inside.

How I can feel anything at all is beyond me—but I'm not surprised Zoey is the one burning that ember in my emptied soul.

Her eyes flit across my features. "I don't need you to protect me anymore. I don't need to be your responsibility. I free you from that, October."

No…please don't.

Tears threaten to rise, and I battle them away. "You're going to leave." I yank her T-shirt back and she fights me for it in a tug of war.

"Or what?" Zoey challenges with a jerk of her shirt.

I tug back. "Or I'll make you."

Her eyes connect with mine in a heady beat. Something deeper swims between us, and in a sexy, low whisper, she breathes, "I dare you to try."

My hand flies to her neck on instinct. I grab her by the throat and push her against the wall. Emotions bubble between us, and my heartbeat drops low, thumping against my heat.

A moan catches against her lips as I squeeze the tender flesh against her neck. Her blond hair is wild around her freckled cheeks. Mine is neat around my face. I'm in control.

I'm in control.

Only like always, like from the history of us, she compels me just as I compel her—and we're in a state of undying longing. An unrest I foolishly want to live inside.

Headiness and arousal start to pass from her to me. We're also in a stalemate in this position. My body flush against hers. Her body pinned to the wall.

"*Leave*," I seethe between clenched teeth.

Zoey's eyes are only on my lips. "Is this supposed to make me want to leave, Kenobi?" she whispers, her wiseass smile melded with burning desire. "Because it's doing the opposite."

Arousal swims low in my belly, descending. *Ugh!* I want to leave her. I want to kiss her. I want to keep her safe. I want to *be* with her.

I have no idea who she's been with—she has no idea about my past. Rule #2: Never talk about relationships. But my brain and body are screaming in so much *want.*

I want her.

She's right though, crossing this line will only fuse us further together. Make her want to stay. Make me want to grip her tight.

Let her go.

My fingers twitch on her neck. I can't loosen my grip around her throat. I can't back away. I haven't felt anger or arousal or *anything* in months, and it's intoxicating to be here right now.

To feel.

I can't force her to leave, but Colt's words have muddled everything. I don't want to give her a reason to stay, but selfishly, I can't retreat.

"So you're staying," I breathe out.

Her lips twitch into another smile. "I'm glad you've caught on."

I tighten my grip on her neck and a soundless moan parts her lips. Her hands fly to the back of my head.

"Don't touch me," I command.

Her fingers thread in my hair defiantly, clutching tighter. Her eyes light up in rebellion that sends warmth to my heat.

"If you're going to be in Mistpoint Harbor and you continue to put your fragile life in danger, then I'm not leaving your side," I tell her sharply as I quickly unbutton her jeans with my free hand. "Someone has to protect you. Which means I'm rejecting your proposition of 'freeing' me from that responsibility."

She curses through a moan. Her soft palms track lovingly down my face, along the nape of my neck—shoving aside my puffer jacket—I shiver as she descends the slope of my shoulder and tries to near my breasts. I catch her hands into mine, my heart racing, and I whisper against her ear, "Listen to me, sweets."

"October," Zoey rasps, wanting me.

I want you but I can't. "Don't touch." I kiss her cheek.

She listens this time.

Our lips ghosting, our eyes melting in heady contact, I draw her zipper down and slip my hand into the front of her jeans. Pressing my fingers between her legs. Feeling the wetness of her panties, I cross the "no going back" territory.

"You're soaked." My heartbeat thrums between my legs.

"Because of you," Zoey mutters, biting her lip. "Thank you very much."

"You can thank me after," I refute and slip my finger past the fabric of her panties and into her warmth. She lets out a shuddered gasp before sinking in me, and I bear more of my body against her, my knee bent between her legs. My movements are slow, languid strokes, running gently over her clit—how I like to be touched.

How I'm certain she likes to be touched, too. What I know feels earth-shatteringly, legs-quakingly good.

Slow and sensual.

Suffering underneath the painstaking, drawn out desire.

Zoey grips my puffer jacket that half hangs off me. Her lips brush against my ear and the corner of my mouth.

Oh my God.

I ache for more, but another side of me says, *no.* I twitch away and slide another finger inside of her.

Her breath hitches.

I inhale, heat boiling. Eyes unblinking as though if I do blink, I'll miss a moment I can't recapture, a feeling I need to consume.

Her.

Zoey.

She tries to kiss me, but I back her head up against the wall. Chin raised, she stares at me in complete defiance while I pump my fingers inside of her.

"Kiss me," she begs.

"No."

A growl rumbles through her throat, and her clutch returns to my hair. I don't protest, not even as her grip tightens. She pulls back the strands, my scalp searing. It feels glorious—this tug-of-war with Zoey.

My eyes burn.

Hers sear deeper into me like she's trying to brand my soul. I don't scare Zoey. I've never scared her the way I can easily scare others.

I circle her swollen clit, and she squirms against me. Breathing shallow. *I still know how to make you feel good, Zoey.* She still knows how to obliterate me. Our foreheads nearly meet, but I resist the urge to kiss her.

"Come for me," I demand, back inside her once more.

"No," she says in a mocking tone.

My lips fight off a smile, and I slide my fingers out again to tease her bundle of nerves. Immediately, she bucks up against me, writhes.

"Nonono," she says, more desperate and wanton than before. Her lips part and can't close.

"Do you really mean that?" I ask. Her *no's* have always meant *yes* when we fooled around, but it's been a while, and I need to make sure it's the same.

"No, I don't. *No.* Keep going, *please.*" Her eyes cinch closed, body shuddering.

My own need crawls under my skin. A high-pitched sound catches in my throat, an aching moan that snaps Zoey's eyes open. She cries against me, "October—"

"Shh," I breathe.

Zoey.

Zoey.

Her eyes close again in pleasure as I rub her in a slow, pressured rhythm. She quakes into another aroused cry, originating from the back of her throat and leaving her lips in an uncontrolled wave. She hangs onto me.

I want to hang onto her for as long as I can.

She shudders.

My body tightens and pulsates. I can feel the wetness between my legs.

"*October*," she moans against her orgasm, and I loosen my grip around her throat.

Slowly, she opens her eyes like waking up from a dream. Her hands fall from my head, untangling from my long brown hair. I pull my hand out of her jeans and politely zip them back up and button her together.

Once finished, she grabs my hips and tries to sink down to her knees. I clutch her by the elbow, stopping her.

"Don't."

Confusion warps her blue eyes. "I want to."

"I don't want you to kiss me. Anywhere, Zoey." I back away, and annoyance pulls her face.

"Why?" She searches me up and down. "Is this about you being a so-called ghost?"

I nod once. It's not just that I haven't *felt* anything these past few months. It's that I don't deserve to. I struggle to tell her this.

She crosses her arms over her chest. "What happened, October?"

My throat dries. "Let's just have an understanding between us. You don't kiss me. You don't try to get me off."

Her nose crinkles. "So you're a masochistic ghost?"

I can't help it, I laugh.

Her face brightens at the noise. "The ghost laughs."

"A true miracle," I say quietly, fixing my puffer jacket back onto my shoulders. The Poe room is dreary. Heavy curtains block what little light seeps through the window. An old oil lamp on a rickety end table, right beside an old smoker's chair, adds a warm, haunting glow.

The four-poster bed lies sunken, lumpy. The mattress old and the burgundy quilt hefty and musty. And though this used to be George's favorite room (God rest his sad soul), his widowed wife put a cracked porcelain doll on the antique dresser.

Better to scare the tourists with.

I can't believe the first time I touched Zoey *in years* was in the fabled, haunted Poe room. Not what I would've planned, but when it comes to me and her—our plans usually go out the fucking window.

I strut into the en-suite bathroom. Zoey watches as I wash my hands. Foamy soap slips over my short, manicured nails. Glancing over my shoulder, I ask her, "Did you enjoy that?"

Her cheeks flush. "You couldn't tell?"

I appraise her from toe to head. Her ratty sneakers, jeans torn at the knees, and cropped top over a black long-sleeve shirt. Bracelets jangling on her wrists. Lips shiny with pink gloss. Messy blonde hair tucked behind each ear.

"I want to hear you say it," I admit.

Zoey half-heartedly rolls her eyes, but she's smiling. "I enjoyed your fingers inside me, Kenobi." She gives me a slow, hot look. "I'd enjoy putting mine in you, too. If you'd let me."

"I won't." I turn off the faucet and wipe my hands on a soft hand towel. When I return to the bedroom, I sink onto the burgundy quilt and untie my boots.

"You're staying?" Surprise coats her words.

"I meant what I said. I'm not leaving your side. Not again."

She smiles fondly. "My protector. Right." She glances back to the door. "I told Kelly that I'm writing the book. It was the only way to get her to let me book a room."

I suck in a sharp breath. "You're digging a grave."

"Luckily, I have someone who's promised to pull me out."

"No, I promised to protect you," I say matter-of-factly. "Which means I very well could end up in that grave too."

"Side-by-side, holding hands as the dirt is shoveled on top of us," Zoey says softly and gives me a silly smile. "Who knew you were so romantic, October?"

Her teasing is making me feel…things.

Things I don't deserve.

I need to change topics so she'll stop flirting. Even though I do like this. Painstakingly, I utter the words, "Did you talk to your brother?"

Zoey's smile disappears, replaced with a seriousness. "Yeah."

"And?" For a second, I think she won't tell me. I've been wishy-washy and cruel. I hardly deserve to be let into her life.

But then she says, "I might really need your help."

How?

Why?

Before I can launch a thousand questions, Zoey is walking over to her suitcase. She unpacks a bottle. "We're going to need some wine and Stevie first."

CHAPTER 14

ZOEY DURAND

We get through an entire bottle of Cab and half the *Rumours* album before I finish my highly *detailed* explanation of what happened with Colt. I don't leave anything out. Shit, I even describe the cigarette butts in his ashtray.

And I try my best to keep on course and make sure my head doesn't fall back into the gutter—reimagining October's fingers inside me. An ache remains where she touched.

Sitting across from me on the lumpy mattress, October is patient through the entire account, and only asks for clarification when she's confused. But most of the time, I respond with a simple, *I don't know*. It's clear I don't have all the details because Colt doesn't have them either. It's like trying to solve a mystery without the right clues.

"So I'm going to help him," I tell her. "Either by finding this missing girl or…the last resort, follow Parry's advice and convince Colt that he didn't see or hear anything that night. But hopefully it doesn't come to that."

Hopefully we can find some sort of proof.

"Which is why you need my help," she realizes.

I nod and wait for her to say more.

October runs a finger over the rim of her wine glass. "Is this what you expected to find when you came here?" Concern for me is her first response.

It's been a while since I've actually felt like someone truly cared about me, and it's an addictive feeling. To be loved. I didn't realize how much I'd been missing that these past six years.

It can't last, Zo, I silently remind myself. Mistpoint Harbor is just a midpoint. Not a destination. I can't let myself believe things here will last beyond just a quick pitstop.

I shake my head. "I came here with zero expectations," I admit. "But running headfirst into a mystery wasn't in my top ten list."

She sets the wine glass on the nightstand. "Maybe it won't be much of a mystery. Missing persons sometimes aren't even missing at all."

Her parents.

I know she's talking about them. The day she found out the truth—that her parents abandoned her and Babette for Canada—she called me to meet her on the fishing pier and she released the truth like someone trying to set a caged animal free. I'd never seen October cry before that day.

"Have you ever spoken to them? Your parents, I mean?" I wonder.

Her eyes soften for a second and then I watch her construct wall after wall. "Rule number one," she reminds me coldly. "No discussion of family."

A frustrated sound leaves my lips. "We're really keeping these rules intact?" I raise my brows. "One. You just *fingered* me, Kenobi."

She smiles like she's pleased with herself.

Fuck it, I love when she smiles, so I don't mind that much.

"Two," I add swiftly. "You're already smack dab in my family drama."

She sinks back into a lumpier pillow, considering for a long second. When I was alone in the Poe room, this dingy, gothic atmosphere creeped me out, but with October here, I could live in this room for eternity.

Like we're two women in a 16th century romance. Lace bodices, unwieldy corsets, fashionable stockings—clothes we'd get tangled in and then slowly slip off each other. Only to kiss.

I bite my lip.

Still wishing to kiss her.

Maybe in another lifetime, we held each other bare. We kissed. We made love and woke to a sliver of sunlight in a musty room. The sweet scent of each other was all we needed. All we wanted.

All we ached for.

I'm good at dreaming about October. So good that if I *could* actually write worth a damn, I might just be able to pen the saddest tale about the girl who calls herself a ghost. The girl I'm not supposed to have.

October sighs in defeat. "I tried calling my parents. A couple years ago. I should've left it alone."

I frown. "Why?"

"I don't want to hear what they have to say. Not really. They're better left a mystery." She sits up more, and I reach for her, splaying my hand an inch or so from her hand on the bed. Our fingers brush.

Her narrowed eyes flit up to me like, *back away.*

I don't.

I can't.

She can't.

And I just ask, "Did they say anything? A *hello* or a *how are you?*"

"No." Her voice is tight. "They didn't answer, so I figured they don't want to talk."

I hate that.

For as much crap as my dad has gotten over the years, he never iced me out. Never totally left. Even though he's on a freighter for eight months out of the year, he still always tries to keep in touch with Brian, Colt, and me. I hate that her parents could so easily leave behind October and Babette like they meant nothing, and I can't begin to imagine the pain the abandonment must have caused her.

I left too.

That annoying thought churns guilt through my stomach.

"They're shit," I tell her. *I'm shit,* I want to say.

"It is what it is," she says. "I'm not crying over it. They already had my tears once. They won't get them again."

Wind whips against the heavy drapes and rattles the windowpane. A burst of cold infiltrates the room. I shiver, and October glares at the window like the wind has accosted me. She rises to her feet. "Kelly purposefully hasn't sealed the window in this room." She stomps towards the Keurig on a little oak desk.

"Maybe she thinks freezing your ass off makes you believe in the supernatural." I grab a knitted quilt at the end of the bed.

"I'm sure it's worked on at least one gullible tourist," October replies. She brews a cup of coffee, and then meanders back to my side. "Here."

I take the steaming mug. "Thanks."

"It's hot. Don't sip it yet."

I blow on it instead, making a show of staring hard into her eyes as I do so.

She drills a pointed look into me. Like I'm both maddening her and mesmerizing her. "Zoey."

I smile. "Isn't this what you asked me to do?"

"I specifically remember asking you *not* to flirt." She returns to the Keurig to brew herself a cup. "That seems to be hard for you."

She technically asked me not to kiss her or touch her today—two things I will respect. Whatever is going on with October is deeper than one conversation and fling can cure. I'd rather be patient and truly understand what happened than push her too hard. Especially since I have zero clue what went down.

My mind has already raced through the worst.

Someone hurt her.

Badly.

Assault. Rape. Those words are like knives in my gut, and I don't want them to be true.

"Not flirting is only hard around you," I say without thinking. I drop my gaze while I blow on the coffee again. Face heating.

Once those words leave my lips, I don't yearn for them back. October doesn't know about my relationships in Chicago, and I basically kicked open a door to a heavier topic. But we agreed to toss the rules away, right?

She purses her lips. "Zoey—"

"Rule number two: don't talk about relationships," I say like this one is wedged between my ribs and my heart.

My insides twist.

I'd love to know more about who she dated in Mistpoint Harbor. I assume she's not with anyone *now*. The whole "I'm a ghost" situation doesn't seem like it'd leave any room for another woman. And October isn't the type to hook up with me *while* she's dating someone else.

Though…I guess she could be different now. Six years is a long time.

Nausea rolls through me at the idea that she's seeing someone.

October grabs her coffee mug. "We're done with the rules," she reminds me.

Relief tries to wash over me, grateful we're at least on the same page on the rules front. She returns to the bed, sitting across from me with her legs stretched out to the side.

I blurt out, "I always envied you when we were growing up. I don't know if I ever told you that."

She tilts her head. "You didn't have to. Your emotions are all over your face. It's been that way since we met."

Awesome. I'm an open book while she's welded closed.

I cup my mug tighter, warmth spreading through my palms. "But I'm talking about *before* we met."

She shifts a little, intrigue passing across her eyes. "Before high school?"

I nod. "I knew who you were. October Brambilla, the girl who saved her sister in the library fire. You were a legend, and everyone started talking about you. Girls loved your bravery. Boys lamented that you were a lesbian." We both catch each other's eye rolls, but I'm the only one who can muster a smile. "I asked how they knew you were gay, and someone told me that you came out to your family when you were *ten*. Ten…" I take a breath. "I envied so much how you knew who you were at such a young age. There I was, struggling to figure it all out. But hearing that was actually what motivated me to tell Parry I was bi."

She frowns. "Why have you never told me all that?"

"I don't think I was ever confident enough to," I say honestly. "And then you helped me gain so much confidence that by the time I had enough to confide in you—"

"You left," she finishes.

"It's funny how that works, huh?" I whisper.

She takes a small breath. "I wonder sometimes what it would have been like, if I didn't help you. Maybe you would've never left."

"Do you wish that?" I wonder. My nerves start sputtering, worried about her answer. Does she really wish me to be the old Zoey? The one that could barely stand up for herself.

She shakes her head. "No." Her eyes flit over me. "Every time you show this…*defiance*, I feel a little bit of pride."

I smile. "Just a little."

She pinches her fingers. "A microscopic bit."

"A prideful ghost," I say.

"*Microscopic*," she reminds me into a sip of her coffee.

I laugh under my breath, but my head swirls around other questions. *Who have you dated? Are you seeing anyone? Do you want to ask me about Chicago?*

A buzzing sound vibrates the end table, and October reaches for her cellphone. Her brows furrow as she answers the call.

"Amelia," she says quietly.

Hearing that name is like a balloon popping in front of my face. I set the coffee aside and lean back against the lumpy pillows. The broken doll is staring at me.

Definitely need to put that thing in a drawer tonight.

I watch October's face close off to all emotion. Bricked-up. She nods tensely. "Of course, I didn't forget. Can you check on Figgy and Rosemary tonight? I'm out…" Her eyes dart to me. "With an old friend…yes, that one…I know…*I know, Amelia.* …thank you. Their pellets and chop are in the same cupboard. Yes…" After another second, she ends the call with, "See you tomorrow."

She hangs up the phone and places her cell on the nightstand. "We should sleep." She stares at her mug. "The coffee might have been a mistake. We're going to have an early start tomorrow."

"We're?" I question.

She tilts her head. "I'm not leaving your side, remember. And if we're going to find answers for Colt, the best place to start will be at the Lock Ceremony tomorrow."

I should be happy that October is going to help me, but I'm tripping over the other part.

"The Lock Ceremony is *tomorrow?*" My stomach overturns.

She nods and takes a couple pillows off the bed, tossing them
to the floor. "You'll have to participate if you want to get in good
graces with the townspeople. Which is paramount. I can only ask
around about Colt's mystery girl so much before they know I'm
asking for *you*," she explains. "Do you need a lock or a ribbon?"

"Yeah, I didn't exactly remember to pack them on my way here."
Shit, how could I have forgotten the date of the Lock Ceremony?
It's something that happens *every* single year.

"We'll stop by my place and pick them up. I have to get my
crown anyway and give Thistle medicine tomorrow morning." She
says it so casually, but if I didn't live here for eighteen years, I would
probably think she's batty as hell.

"Thistle?"

"A duckling. She'll likely be back to full health in a few months."

I smile, just imagining October setting the little duckling into the
lake. Just like she did years ago when we were in high school.

Some things don't change. A warmth of nostalgia cocoons me. Until
she takes an extra quilt from the closet and tosses it on the floor.

"Wait—" I start.

"We're not sharing the same bed, Zoey."

"You don't trust me?" I wonder, hurt starting to blossom in my
chest.

Her eyes lock with mine, and it's hard to pull away. Hard to blink.
"I don't trust myself," she says. "And I don't deserve you." She walks
to a smoker's chair and switches off the oil lamp, bathing us both in
darkness. "Goodnight, Zo."

My heart pounds hard and loud in the quiet. "Night, Kenobi," I
whisper back.

Unsaid things haunt me all night, and the fact that she's close but so far away feels like the antithesis of comfort.

I don't deserve you, she told me.

What exactly does that mean? I thought she was pushing me away for my benefit, but I'm beginning to realize it might just be because she's punishing herself.

CHAPTER 15

ZOEY DURAND

"Mingle. Smile. Try not to act like a social parasite," October tells me when we walk down steep wooden stairs to the pebble-scattered, sandy shoreline of Lake Erie. Home of the Lock Ceremony.

I catch sight of her tight scowl on our descent. "Is that advice for you or for me?"

She zips up her white puffer jacket. "I can't remember, were you always this mouthy?"

"I grew considerably more loose-lipped thanks to a girl who told me to speak my mind, but I might've always had a pinch of verbal diarrhea."

Her lips twitch.

"Is she smiling?" I grin.

She skips over that and says stoically, "I could use the same advice too. *Mingle.* I haven't been very social since…" Her face turns to stone.

I can only guess, *since her curse.*

"Let's go," she mutters even though we're already *going.* She's a half-second from taking my hand—her fingers brush mine, then vanish. She must think against the handhold. I wish she wouldn't.

Respecting her wishes of not touching, I just stuff my hands in my coat pockets. *Her white fur coat.* She insisted I wear it. I like to imagine because she thinks it's pretty on me. But she said, "It's warmer than the one you packed."

October. Always making sure I don't freeze to death.

I smile to myself. Then I smile at her.

If she notices me, she doesn't let on.

Wind whips at us, and I subconsciously run my fingers over the black ribbon around my wrist. *Feels odd.* The glittery blue tiny lock in my jean's pocket weighs heavy with importance.

Importance to this town.

October unhooked the glittery lock off her middle school diary early this morning. On a pitstop at her house. There is no size requirement for locks. Thankfully.

I was always an observer of the Lock Ceremony. I left before I could ever join, and now that I'm visiting, October thinks a good way to ingratiate myself with the locals is to participate in one of Mistpoint's longest standing traditions.

We step off the last stair and onto the muddy-colored sand.

Welcome home, Zoey.

On the packed public beach, locals begin to turn. They look at me. Stare and gawk. I stare right back, trying to wear October's fur coat like a goddess, but I sense the gorgeous coat is wearing me. Heat builds, and October scopes out the scene with razor-sharp eyes.

People aren't building sandcastles, splashing in the lake, or collecting smooth stones. Instead, white tents are set up with pots of mussels and baskets of crostini. And people really are *mingling.*

Locals chat and top the little toasts with the mussel meat, tossing the shells into the lake. No one eats freshwater mussels, so all the saltwater mollusks and shellfish are typically imported from another state.

White wine is served to the adults, and the little kids and teenagers drink non-alcoholic apple cider in plastic flutes. It's all very fancy.

All very intimidating.

Blue and white streamers blow in the wind from the tops of tents. A live band plays melodic music on violins and cellos, adding to the ethereal charm of today.

"Maybe if they were playing rock, I'd feel *somewhat* in my element," I mutter to myself. "Is it hot out here?" I ask October.

"Hmm?" She's busy eyeing the townspeople like she's looking for successful prey.

I am so not made for this hunt.

I shed her coat and drape the thing over my arm.

October registers my growing fear. "They won't bite you."

"No, I'm pretty sure they'll try, and I'm *pretty* sure I might bite them back."

She almost smiles. "I'll bite them first, sweets."

I hope so.

Blushing at her nickname for me, I breathe in the crisp air. Clouds block the sun, and the wind's nipping chill actually feels good against my black sweater. Today is just as I remember from childhood.

Lots of snide eyes on me.

And my total infatuation with October Brambilla.

Except there is one big difference, besides being twenty-four. Besides the ribbon around my wrist and lock in my pocket.

The difference lies with her.

October is carrying a dazzling crown made of beach glass and broken shells. She's ribbon-less.

An easy way to spot "cursed" locals: they wear crowns at the Lock Ceremony. I'd say about 65% of the attendees are adorning handmade crowns. Anna Roberts and her mossy antler crown is seriously freaky.

She wears the imposing thing like she's been dubbed Antler Queen.

Anna is Amelia's uptight mom. She has deep, striking red hair that'd rival the Little Mermaid herself. Amelia only inherited a smidgen of her mom's red hue in her own heap of brown.

I watch October keep her beach glass crown in her hand. Caution and unease somersault my insides. When she picked up the crown this morning, reality struck me like a lightning storm.

October is *officially* cursed.

That means she's in the historical museum. One trip over to the famed Museum of Curses & Curiosities and I'd know exactly what happened to her.

Despite the urge to ditch the ceremony and Road Runner my ass over there, I struggle to go behind October's back. A part of me hesitates to read about her curse in a book. I don't want this town's twisted version of what happened. I want to know from *her.*

But I also have bigger concerns than probing into October's history.

Benito Brambilla, October's twenty-nine-year-old cousin, is currently eyeing me like I'm a spoiled mussel in his pot.

"I'm going to pick Anna Robert's brain," October says, already on the move. "See if she's hiding anything."

"Should I…right," I say to myself, watching my safety net just beeline with zero hesitation to the most *intimidating* woman on the beach. The Antler Queen herself.

That is October. Afraid of no one.

I exhale. "We have to split up, Zoey. They won't tell October shit if I'm hovering. And…I'm talking to myself. Great." I eye Benito again—or rather, *Benny.* I remember his nickname.

Fur coat splayed over my arm, I march my ass towards him with the best "I own this town" Brambilla impression.

He's not impressed. "Zoey Durand."

I hate how he says my name. Like I'm bottom-feeder scum. "Benny." I force a smile.

His well-kept hair and wrinkle-free peacoat over a Polo is the classic upper-crest style in Mistpoint. The most I remember of Benny is that he was in Colt's grade. And Colt complained about him.

All. The. Time.

Benny is an antagonistic asshole.

He's obsessed with me.

Can the guy get a fucking life that's not infatuated with mine?

Now I'm face-to-face with Benny, and if he's still obsessed with Colt, then maybe he knows pertinent information that I might need.

He's standing behind a big pot of bubbling broth. And he scoops mussels into a paper bowl, looking seconds from spitting in the food.

So I'm genuinely surprised when he hands me the mussels without hocking a loogie in the broth.

"Thanks," I say with another tight smile. And I peek over at October. Several feet away, definitely out of earshot, she's talking quietly with Antler Queen Anna. That's her best friend's mom. So clearly, she might have the best *in*.

"Aren't you supposed to have a notepad?" Benny's voice steals my attention.

"Uh…am I?" I make a confused face. What is he talking about?

He narrows his eyes. "Isn't that what authors do? Jot down notes?"

Oh.

Fuck.

The fact that Benny already knows my cover story is a sign that the gossip networks are thriving more than ever.

I tap my temple. "I've got it all up here."

His lip curls in a snide smile. "I guess taking notes doesn't really matter, right? We all know you're going to over-inflate that moldy-ass pub of yours." He swings his head towards a sandy area where outdoor couches and chairs—brought over from everyone's patios—circle a small, rocky lakeside firepit. Town royalty lounges there, mostly Brambillas and Roberts. But I also see Sheriff Carmichael and his wife among the group.

Is he trying to intimidate me with his posse of Very Important People? *It's working.*

No it's not!

I try to arch my shoulders. Try to appear tall. *He's way taller.* "There was a bad storm recently, I heard."

Now he makes a confused face. Like small talk is a weird concept for someone like me. "There's always storms."

"One where a girl might've been caught out on the lake? That doesn't happen very often."

His smile slowly grows. "You've been talking to your brother, haven't you?"

"I don't know what you're—"

"He's been rambling for weeks now. About a mayday call and some imaginary girl." He laughs. "It's actually kind of sad. How far gone he is. I always imagined he'd go down a dark path—booze, maybe drugs—but I never thought he'd lose his *mind.*"

I'm boiling.

Benny tips his wine to his curved lips.

Just as I open my mouth to curse him out, Benny jumps in to say, "About your book."

"Keep my book out of your mouth," I snap, really meaning to say—*keep my brother out of your mouth.* Whatever. I'll take it.

I maintain my fiery stance.

Benny looks surprised. But he doesn't listen. "I thought you'd like to know that Effie already tried to call a couple New York publishers to get your book cancelled."

What?

"She did *what*?" October slips into our conversation. I just now notice that Antler Queen Anna is gone.

Benny tips his head to his cousin. "See, this is why you don't ditch dinner service early. You'd have all the good gossip."

October sucks in a tight breath as he passes her a bowl of mussels. "Thanks for the tip, Benny." Her voice is dry.

I steal a basket of crostini as we begin to leave, and October grabs my hand (fuck yes!)—but Benny also clasps my other wrist (fuck no). With darkened eyes, Benny quickly and quietly whispers to me, "If you want to help your brother, like we all do, then you'll remind him to move past these delusions. No one wants to see him suffer."

"Benny," October says in a scathing, icy tone. "Let her go."

He releases me. "Think about it, Zoey."

I'm thinking about something. Like how can I believe Benny? How can I believe that this town cares about Colt enough to *not* want him to suffer?

They've placed him in the lighthouse to be miserable. Right? That was their goal. So why would they want Colt to be anything other than a madman?

I'm so fucking confused.

I tell this to October while we pull away from the white tents. Loitering between the congested firepits and the food.

"Benny might not know anything more than we do," October says and deserts her mussels on a high-top table.

"So he's actually concerned about Colt's mental wellbeing?" That seems extremely far-fetched.

"I don't know." October looks disturbed.

"What'd Anna say?"

"I asked her about an Augustine Anders, and she said to drop it. That was all."

I tense. "So she knows *something*?"

"I think so, but she's not going to tell me the truth, Zoey. Whatever Anna Roberts is hiding, the entire town council is likely involved."

"Does this mean the girl is real?"

October shakes her head, looking doubtful. Her stomach must be knotting because she leaves her mussels behind as we walk towards blankets spread on the beach.

I study Effie at a firepit, her blue-green beach glass crown similar to October's. She laughs light-heartedly with Milo Brambilla, who I know is Effie's brother. So who am I more afraid of—Effie or Antler Queen Anna?

I want to say Anna, but *Effie* is the one digging into my cover story.

She's her own brand of pretentious and haughty. I'd say the women are like two peas in a pod, but I really don't know them that well. And my dad always mentioned Effie and Colt's mom being best friends. Nothing about Anna.

"Do you think Effie figured out why I'm actually here?" I whisper to October.

"No, she wouldn't be able to keep her mouth shut if she did. It'd be all over town."

True.

But it's a little unnerving that Effie will go to the lengths of calling a fucking New York City publisher to sabotage this book. I'm a little miffed. More for the fact that she's trying to *ruin* my fake career.

Who does she think she is? Seriously. Plus, her nosiness might actually blow my whole cover if I'm not careful.

October suddenly stops. I almost knock into her shoulder, but I halt quickly. Following her gaze, I realize the problem.

Amelia Roberts.

Miss Mistpoint is sitting all alone on a crocheted blanket. Clearly enough room is left for another butt. I can take a single solitary guess who Amelia saved the spot for.

Her eyes already pin to October in impatience. They practically throw out SOS signals saying, *get over here before I look like I have zero point zero friends!*

October rotates to me, and I'm transported back to high school.

Back to those days where she had to choose Amelia and her friends over me. Sometimes there wasn't a choice. Sometimes October took my hand and dragged me with her, but other times, it was clear that no matter how much sway October had, I was *not* invited.

By the epic stink-eye coming from Amelia, I'm pretty positive I have not been offered a silent invitation. More like a stay-away postcard.

"Zoey—" October starts, and I feel like this is the beginning of a pity letdown.

"Don't worry about it, Kenobi," I say quickly, uncomfortable heat baking me. No way can I wear her coat right now. "I'll meet up with you after the ceremony."

Her thick, beautiful brows furrow together. "I told you, you're not leaving my side."

"You already left mine," I mention how we literally just split up. I swear pain cinches her face.

"For recon," I add fast.

She swallows hard. "If it were up to me, I'd just be protecting you here, not trying to play *Clue*. But you love Colt, and I promised I'd help you."

I smile. "I appreciate it, Kenobi. I really do." She could've said *no*, but she knows how much my brother means to me.

"You'll come with me then," October says like an order. A demand. A come-on.

I'll come with you then. "Yeah, yes…" I'm nodding, then I realize, "Wait—we're going to Miss Mistpoint's blanket?"

She nods. "Amelia doesn't bite. She's all bark."

Before I have a chance to reply, October heads towards her best friend. She expects me to follow. And against better judgment, my feet carry me forward.

The closer I come to Amelia, the more her back arches like some territorial cat ready to spring and claw an enemy.

The only thing keeping her talons at bay is my protector—who shields my body before saying, "There's room for Zoey." October doesn't phrase it like a question.

With pursed lips, Amelia makes a show of fixing her shell crown. Red carnations are woven throughout. I've attended enough Lock Ceremonies to know the flowers are a status symbol. One she's unmistakably boasting.

Carnations signify those who've won the title of Miss or Mister Mistpoint in history. Like I give a shit that Amelia is flexing her Nancy Drew status. She even wears a wool trench coat and messenger bag. Packed, I'm sure, with "essentials".

"Amelia," I greet flatly.

She ignores me and looks up at October. "There's really no room for her."

"Then I'll sit on the sand," October says.

Amelia sucks in a breath. "Then I have to sit *beside* her."

October arches her brows. "Your choice."

Blowing out a resigned puff of air, Amelia scoots to the far edge of the blanket to make room for October and me.

Amelia only relaxes when October wedges between us. Blocking Amelia and me from sharing breath.

I balance the paper bowl on my lap and dip my crostini into the broth. "What's your damage, Amelia?" I ask her. "We're all adults now. Can't you get over petty high school drama?"

October steals a couple of my stolen crostini while Amelia leans forward. I can clearly see the contempt on her face.

"Your family leaves bodies in its wake, *Zoey*. This goes beyond high school." She turns to October. "I don't know why you're dragging her around town like one of your lap dogs. She hasn't been cursed yet, which means Zoey could explode and kill us all."

October replies icily, "She's not a bomb, Amelia."

That we know of.

"Metaphorically," Amelia combats. "She is a ticking bomb."

"She won't hurt you."

Is that it? Is Amelia just *afraid* of me? I stare through her, and patchy red marks creep up her neck.

"Of course she won't." Amelia straightens up, dusting imaginary particles off her pants. "I'm already cursed. She can't hurt me." She snaps a warning look to October, who snaps one back—reminding me that I'm very much six years out of the loop and forever out of their friendship circle.

Something eats at me. Not *jealousy* exactly. I don't just want to be October's BFF. Amelia can be that if she has to claim the spot.

I've always wanted more.

What I feel…is *unease*. Like I'm missing pieces of the picture I need to see, and I'm scared I've been gone for so long that I'll never have time to scramble to find them.

I strain my ears to hear their whispered words.

"She could hurt you too, October. She's not the safest person to be around. Not here, not now."

"I'm not deserting her, and I don't want to desert you. But either you're with us or you're against us, Amelia. Again, your choice."

She's not deserting me.

I turn my head. Hiding my giddy smile. One I had every time I uncovered the pastries October left in my high school locker.

Amelia huffs. But her choice surprises me. She doesn't move.

Music suddenly cuts off. Our attention veers to the shoreline where Antler Queen Anna has silenced the band.

Microphone in her clutch, she presides over the beach. "Thank you all for coming to the 124th Annual Lock Ceremony. As the head of the Historical Committee and a member of the town council, it's a pleasure to see your lovely faces on this beautiful afternoon."

I peek over at Amelia. She's more tensed. Maybe because of my close presence. But she's appraising her mom, not me anymore.

October leans a breathless distance from me. Her lips skim my ear, sending a shiver of anticipation down my arms. Whatever she's about to say, she thinks against and listens to Anna continue her speech.

I try to mask the disappointment. My lips dip into a flatline.

What were you expecting, Zoey? She's not going to kiss you out here. We're not dating. We can't be anything.

She touched me. She's helping me. And I want to help her feel something other than terrible, awful numbness.

I look at October the same time she turns to me. A tender but explosive, soundless second pumps my heart with molten affection. Her eyes grip onto mine like she's falling.

We breathe shallowly.

On the blanket, I inch my fingers over to hers.

She inches hers to mine.

That's it, Kenobi.

"In a few minutes, we'll begin," Anna declares, "grab some mussels and take a…" Her voice trails off suddenly. People are muttering around us.

Reluctantly, almost painfully, I detach from October's gaze. She follows suit, and I'm on edge as I look around…oh…

"Shit," I mutter under my breath.

I find the source of everyone's attention.

Brian and Colt. My brothers.

They've arrived.

CHAPTER 16

OCTOBER BRAMBILLA

*E*very town has its outcasts, and if some stranger stumbled onto this beach, they'd be able to pinpoint those unlucky few.

The crowd has grown silent at Brian Durand's arrival. But this year, most of the curiosity is pinned to Colt, who's been cooped up in the lighthouse for weeks. Wild, unkempt hair. Skeletal, gaunt frame. Shadowed eyes.

He's a fucking wreck.

Jittery. Like he hasn't slept.

Worse than yesterday morning, when he called me a heartless cunt. He already texted me a lengthy, rambling apology with typos and more emotion than I expected. I forgot he had my number, but we exchanged them for "emergencies" when I was a teenager.

Emergencies pertaining to Zoey.

Colt knew I was her closest friend in high school.

I knew he was a semi-reliable brother.

If she was in trouble, I promised to call him or Brian or even Parry. "Whoever you can get ahold of," Colt said.

"Sure," I replied. Back then, he didn't hate my friendship with his sister. Which he discovered was actually "more than friends" after he caught us kissing on the fishing pier. Colt just hated my last name, and in order to like me, he thought of me as a Brambilla exception.

One of the good ones.

And time and time again, I proved him wrong. I am a Brambilla. I'm just like the rest of them, and I don't denounce who I am.

Just like he's never denounced who he is. A Durand. Sometimes I think we're more alike than he realizes.

Zoey watches her brothers with knotted brows. "They came?"

"They're here every year."

She's not too shocked. For as awful as most locals are to the Durands, they're still members of this community. They're allowed to take part in traditions.

Anna Roberts regains composure. "Take a seat everyone and we'll begin the ceremony with the newly cursed."

I intake a breath. Glancing briefly to Amelia, then to Zoey. I almost whispered to Zoey the truth about Amelia's relationship with her mother. How nothing is good enough for Anna. Amelia could turn the lake into wine and her mom would balk that it's a merlot and not a cabernet. And then she'd criticize the lack of effort for not reaching Lake Superior.

But I didn't tell Zoey.

Amelia wouldn't want me to, and she's been too good of a friend to betray. Especially at the snap of a finger.

Not far from where we sit, Colt and Brian join Parry on a beach blanket. Parry is one of the few men wearing a crown of red carnations. Most Mister Mistpoints have died. A sinister fact that is often recited on museum tours.

That one, I can't drum up to anything other than coincidence. Zoey, I'm sure, would call it a cursed *fate*.

Colt tugs anxiously at his unruly hair. He barely acknowledges anyone but his best friend.

Brian, on the other hand, is zeroed in on us. Shell crown nestled in his hair, his eyes land directly onto *me*.

It's hard to ignore the seething glare. I remember the day Zoey announced she'd be leaving for Chicago. We were sitting on Brian's boat, eating the grilled walleye he caught that morning. He spit out some bones into the lake and then turned to me. "You want her to go?"

Of course I didn't want Zoey to leave, but I wasn't going to trap her into staying in a town that hated her family. I'd never be able to live with myself.

"I want what Zoey wants," I said diplomatically, "and if that's Chicago, then I'm Team Chicago."

"You're Team Get the Fuck Off My Boat," Brian spat, pointing towards the docks.

"Brian!" Zoey yelled.

I was already standing up. "No, it's okay. I'll let you two talk," I whispered to Zoey. She gave me a look like *don't go*. But I knew she didn't need me to confront her brother. She had a backbone. I saw her grow one over the years.

Before I climbed off the sailboat, I looked at Brian one last time. His glare was as intense as it is today. Accusatory. Like I fucked him over. Like I held power to make Zoey stay and instead I opened the door and kicked her out of the Harbor.

All I know is that Brian Durand used to hate my family more than he hated me. Until that day. After Zoey left, I became the number one Brambilla on his long shit list. And Brian, he's just another cursed Durand in the history books.

BRIAN DURAND

Cursed at Age 30

Sole Survivor of a car crash that killed three other former Mistpoint High football stars

Nine years have passed since the crash, and the town hasn't recovered. Even though one of Sheriff Carmichael's sons was behind the wheel, most of the town still blames Brian for the loss.

Zoey watches her brothers and Parry intently. *I wonder if she'd rather join her family than be here with me and Amelia.*

Without thinking, I splay my fingers over hers.

Her head jerks to me in surprise. Lips caught open.

I open my mouth, heart ascending to my throat. "I'm not forcing you to stay," I whisper tensely. "If you'd rather be with your brothers—"

"No," she cuts me off quickly. "Brian practically gave me a one-way ticket out of town. I'm definitely not welcome over there."

"You're not welcome over here either," Amelia grumbles under her breath.

I shoot her a look, hoping Zoey didn't hear.

Zoey is only focused on me. "And I don't...I don't want to leave you either."

My heart is filling at a heady rate. *She's making me feel.* I don't deserve any love. I swallow an ascending lump, about to shift my hand away, but she clasps ours together. Her eyes ask, *is this okay?*

Yes.

What am I doing?

Zoey thinks I'm so strong, but I don't have the strength to say no. I don't want to say no.

I want her here.

Without thinking, I take her hand in mine. I hold her tighter. Feeling the beat of my heart thump madly, passionately.

Anna Roberts returns to the microphone. The band plays a low melodic tune, and everyone's whispers fade into the wind.

Anna addresses the beach. "For those that have been cursed since the last ceremony, I ask you to stand." With a motion of her hand, certain individuals rise.

LOVE & OTHER CURSED THINGS

My heart freezes over. Quickly, I let go of Zoey. Cold slices through me in painless, numb waves. And I rise to my feet, feeling Zoey's eyes on me. She's the only one looking. Everyone else stares at Colt Durand.

He's standing and staring off at the lake, unaffected by the attention. Almost somewhere else. Haunted. Lost.

I notice a handful of others on their feet. A girl in a Mistpoint High sweatshirt grips tight to her bejeweled crown. Her hair is fixed in two high buns, and a thick bandage hides her entire left cheek.

TINA RICCI

Cursed at Age 18

Scarred from burning her face on a curling iron

On the other side of the beach, an older man is standing, his grayed beard contrasting his dark-brown skin. He owns the local bookstore, selling just as many trinkets as he does novels.

EDGAR JOHNSON

Cursed at Age 71

Developed hay fever and permanently lost his sense of smell

The wind grows louder, and Anna speaks over the howl, "Today, we recognize those that have seen misfortune, and we welcome them to proudly wear their crowns." She waves us on.

Edgar and Tina place their crowns on their heads, no hesitation.

My palms sweat. Colt locks eyes with me, and something passes between us. An understanding. An acceptance.

I'm a Brambilla.

He's a Durand.

Yet, here we are. The same place. The same outcome.

This town curses us all.

And just like that, we rest our heavy crowns on our heads.

My ears ring, barely registering the change in song. The band plays a more uplifting tune, and Anna Roberts tells us to approach the old wire fence that the lake has nearly washed away. The fence sections off the beach from a dangerous rock wall where boulders slid into the lake. Now water crashes against the slick rocks and sprays the air with mist.

A safety hazard, the town decreed decades ago.

Their solution? Install this rinky-dink, cheap fence to stop reckless teenagers and little kids from climbing the rocks and drowning.

Hundreds of locks cling to the wire fence with desperation, like they're trying not to drift away themselves. After the short trek there, I find my lock near the bottom of the fence in seconds. I can't miss the bright pink metal. Black ribbons are still knotted, some frayed. Others are almost unspooled from the soft crashing waves.

Boots ankle-deep in ice-cold lake water, I fit my small key in the lock. And for the first time since I placed it on this fence when I was eighteen, I unlock it.

It's supposed to be a moment of unburdening, but I will *never* unburden myself from what happened.

I will never forget.

Breath is trapped in my constricting lungs. I fist the lock tight in my hand, then I throw it into the lake. It makes a pitiful *plop* before sinking deep.

When I return to the blanket, Amelia gives me a side hug. "Doesn't it feel good to let that lock go?"

I just nod. Not sure what else to say. Amelia never had to throw a lock in the lake. She was cursed the year she would've been required to place hers there.

AMELIA ROBERTS

Cursed at Age 18

Acquired a sudden and severe allergy to latex overnight

For Amelia's eighteenth birthday, her mom threw an indoor tea party, complete with an archway of rose gold balloons. Ten minutes after Amelia's arm brushed the latex balloon, her throat started swelling.

Luckily, another girl at the party carried EpiPens for her peanut allergy. Amelia's dad administered the epinephrine.

"She's been cursed then," Anna Roberts said. "Right at eighteen."

Parents *love* when their children are cursed exactly at eighteen—the age when curses can begin. There are no years of uncertainty. Of worrying. They know what curse has befallen their child, and that's that.

But *knowing* isn't always better. I can see that clearly in my sister.

I'll never forget the panic in Amelia's eyes when her mom announced that she was cursed. She was more frightened of her mother catching her in a lie than of her near-death brush with latex.

Only I knew the truth at that time.

Only I know the truth now.

Anna thought her daughter was a boring, saintly virgin, but Amelia hooked up with Patrick King in the backseat of his car in eleventh grade.

His latex condom gave her such a bad allergic reaction; she had mascara running down her face—crying about how she was going to die from a dick. We used to laugh about the misadventure. Where I had to drive her out of Mistpoint Harbor to a nearby hospital. Just so her parents would never find out.

And then her birthday party happened, and we stopped laughing. Because the latex allergy mushroomed into the biggest lie.

The two of us knew she had the allergy before she turned eighteen. It couldn't be her curse. But we let Anna Roberts write this one in the books. We let her parents and the entire town believe that Amelia is a virginal, do-gooder daughter who'd *never* lie.

And though Amelia is mostly convinced she's outwitted the powers of the town—that misfortune has skipped over her—I know she's a little scared. Or else she wouldn't be casting side-eyes at Zoey like she's an axe-wielding serial killer.

On the beach, the Lock Ceremony continues with those not cursed yet.

Zoey rises from the blanket. With one brief glimpse back at me, she leaves for the fence.

The urge to rush to her side overwhelms my senses. I claw my fingers into the sand beside me. *Let her go.*

From afar, I watch Zoey take out the blue locket from my childhood diary. My heart swells a little, knowing this is the locket she'll have on the fence. The locket that represents her being free of a curse.

For now.

Dread creeps up my spine.

She unties the ribbon from her wrist. Just to retie the ribbon to the lock. Some eighteen-year-old locals click their locks onto the fence like Zoey.

Out of the corner of my eye, I suddenly see Parry DiNapoli approaching our blanket.

Amelia bristles. "This is why we shouldn't be hanging around Zoey. She attracts fleas."

"Go hang out with my sister then."

Babette is lounging with one of the larger groups of twenty-somethings around a firepit. Chatting and drinking wine.

Amelia eyes them before sighing. "I suppose I should make an appearance." She wanders off, and I'm aware that as much of a pain in the ass as she can be, Amelia Roberts is an introvert at heart who really only has one friend.

Me.

And really, she's been my closest friend these past years too.

Parry raises his brows as he watches Amelia make a quick exit. "I'd ask if I smelled but I'm pretty sure Amelia would call me garbage."

"Landfill," I correct.

"Perfect," he says dryly in a wince. The carnation crown pushes back pieces of his blond hair. Babette used to have the *biggest* crush on Parry when she was eleven, for his looks alone. She'd theorize that his hair would be light brown or darker if he weren't always in the sun. She'd ooh and awe whenever she saw him from a distance.

"He is just so beautiful," she'd decree. *"Like a fine wine."* She'd make a chef's kiss gesture with her fingers.

I was thirteen. At her age, she enjoyed slipping into adult conversations, but she was still a child. The only wine she ever had was at mass, and when I mentioned that, she'd often rebut with, *"Maybe he tastes better than the blood of Christ."*

"And you'll never know, Baby. He's gay."

She'd only smile in response. *"Like you. My sister who loves girls and who girls love back."* She was so proud of me.

The moment I had professed to Babette that I'm a lesbian, she had flung her arms around me with tears cresting her eyes. And she had whispered against my ear, *"I'm so glad you told me."*

I might be older, but with only two years separating us, I often confided in Babette as a friend. Not just as a little sister that I needed to take care of and carry out of burning buildings.

I confessed to her, *"Girls don't love me as much as boys drool over Parry. Haven't you noticed?"*

She sighed. *"Girls love you. They're just afraid of you. They don't realize what they're missing."*

Was I jealous of Parry? He was so many grades ahead of me, but he seemed to attract every single soul under the sun. Even the people in *grades* below him.

Who barely knew him!

It was…infuriating. How likable Parry was. How likable he *is*.

I wasn't trying to be *liked*. That word felt weak. Beneath me. I've always wanted to be feared.

And yet, it backfired. Growing up, I agreed with Babette. I felt that if some girls did like me as more than a friend, they were too scared of me to say anything. I intimidated them. I was unapproachable. Demanding.

Self-aggrandizing.

I didn't want to change. And I never had to for Zoey. She saw the pieces of me that were harder to reach. Softer, vulnerable sides that yearned for affection. For cuddling on the fishing pier.

For the late-night heart-to-hearts.

For the soft, stolen kisses when they're least expected.

She reached me once, but I shouldn't let her reach me again. I'm different now…and she's leaving soon…

I tear the thoughts of Zoey out of my head—I try to, at least. And on the beach, I focus back on Parry. He was Mistpoint's resident heartthrob up until the sailing accident and his grisly scar.

Now he's just another grim tale that people tell.

"Has Zoey filled you in?" he asks.

"She told me enough." I feel eyes on us further down the beach. "We're drawing attention." It's extremely rare that Parry and I talk one-on-one—definitely not at town functions—and Anna Roberts is inspecting us skeptically from a tent.

I also just questioned Anna about the missing girl. How can we be drawing suspicion when we've barely even begun the hunt? Ugh!

I'd like to think that I can go toe-to-toe with Anna Roberts and the town council alone. But I've never tried, and I don't want to fail Zoey. She sees me as the ace up her sleeve.

Parry squats down and pretends to tie his boot lace. "Are you going to help us or just protect Zoey?"

He knows I'd prefer to just ditch the Scooby-Doo mission. "I'm doing both," I say with too much bite. *No takebacks.* "A lot better than you are. I already spoke to Anna." I explain the lack of information she offered and her caginess.

"This isn't good, OB."

"I know."

Parry and I have more in common than just wanting to keep the Durands safe. We're both town cynics. We've seen behind the curtains of Oz too many times.

"This whole thing might be one wild goose chase," Parry says in his smoky voice. "What happens if the goose runs off the cliff?"

"You and I—we'll run off the cliff with the Durands." I have nothing to lose, and though Parry has always been willing to give more of himself to Zoey's family—I feel like I can finally do that too.

I want to be here for Zoey more than I was in the past.

Parry studies me. "You're really all-in?"

"Ye—" I cut myself off and say fast, "Yell at me." Anna is moving closer to us.

He's about to look at her.

"*Yell at me,*" I demand through gritted teeth.

Swiftly, Parry stands and towers over me. "You're *unbelievable,* October. Always the same Brambilla. Can't t-t-t-thhhink of anyone but yourself!" He kicks sand at me.

I glare, dusting sand off my lap like he infected me.

That was a little much.

And I'm wholly impressed. I didn't think Parry had that in him. Internally, I almost want to smile and clap, but I spit back, "What did you think? That I'd be your little sidekick?" I don't even stand up. Like his level is beneath me. "There is a line in the literal sand, *Parry.* You're on one side and I will *always* be on the other."

"Go to hell."

"You're blocking my view," I say flatly, unbothered. I wave him away from me.

"Hey, hey!" Zoey is running towards us in alarm.

Oh no.

"*Leave*," I say urgently under my breath to Parry while I rise to my feet.

Zoey is faster. "What's going on?" She's panting from the run and wedges herself between us, arms outstretched. "Were we not all getting along here?"

"We aren't." I shoot Parry a colder glare.

He struggles to keep the façade and simply spins away from me and Zoey.

Good.

"Let's just rewind," Zoey says. "Parry, *Parry*—let's talk it out—"

"No," I cut in.

Zoey scans me up and down like I've been inflicted with a mortal wound since she's been gone. Like there *must* be a perfect explanation for my frosty shift. And I love her for seeing morsels of good in me—even when I think they aren't there.

"I'm fine," I say pointedly.

"You're both—"

"*Not friends.* None of us are." I glare at her—I hate that I'm glaring. Hurt crests her beautiful face and punctures my lungs.

She rocks back. "Kenobi?"

I hate that I'm pushing her so far away.

It's what I deserve.

"We're fine," Parry interjects to Zoey, and his gaze goes gentle on me. Parry! I could shake him. He's undoing *everything* we've done. The charade we've created—what if they question us now? But I could also hug him.

He's not letting me torch the bridge between Zoey and me.

God, Anna is blatantly observing us now. So is Aunt Effie and Uncle Milo. They're all whispering to the other four members of the town council. And I find myself speaking stiltedly to Zoey. "We're whatever you want us to be."

Two town cynics.

Zoey needs to know all of my suspicions, and this goes further back than this year or the last.

"We need to talk," I add quickly.

"...okay?" Confusion furrows her dark-blonde brows.

"Like now." And I catch her hand and then rush towards the stairs. She trails behind my quick, agile pace. When she trips, I hook an arm around her hips—keeping her upright. Keeping her with me.

The town council is watching as I leave the beach just how I arrived.

With Zoey Durand.

CHAPTER 17

ZOEY DURAND

We need to talk. Four words no one wants to hear. But at least I'm not dating October and this isn't some epic breakup. No worries about that.

With my heart somewhat intact, I've left the beach with her. *We need to talk* is also code for *in private*. Heavy conversations surrounded by gossiping townspeople is a recipe for disaster. And I am a certified walking disaster.

I can't believe I ruined Parry and October's fake fight on the beach. She explains all the details on our way to a more private locale.

I'm an utter idiot.

"You're not an idiot," October tells me for the third time.

"I kinda miss when you call me an idiot," I admit with a smile.

She eyes my upturned lips. "You shouldn't like when anyone calls you an idiot."

"Not even you?" I say with a teasing pout.

"Especially me." She rolls her eyes after a beat. "You're driving me mad, Zoey. Stop it."

"Stop what?"

"Flirting, you idiot."

I touch my heart that nearly convulses in love. "I think you struck me with an arrow. Are you sure you aren't cupid?"

"Shut up and open the door." Her lips have risen.

I gasp. "She's smiling! Call the fucking press." I yell outside of The Drunk Pelican—at literally an empty parking lot, "Celebrity Crush! Come here, come here! October Brambilla is smiling! Put that on your front page."

October goes for a playful shove, but the shove is more of a grip on my black sweater, which turns into me clutching her waist. We sway together, and suddenly, her fingertips are skating down my forearms with slow, electric tension.

Hairs stand up on my neck.

"October," I breathe, an ache in my heart.

She instantly retracts.

Shit.

Why does she keep pushing me away?

"We need to talk," October reminds me. "It's serious."

This is serious too, Kenobi. But I'm under her spell and do as I'm told. "Okay," I mutter, and I use my key to unlock the back door to The Drunk Pelican. It fits like butter.

She gives me a pointed look. "Breaking and entering already?"

"Is it *really* breaking and entering if I have a key?" I ask as I push open the door with my shoulder. I whirl the keys around my finger and think aloud, "Jeez, Brian and I really must be related because he's *definitely* an idiot or lazy or both and never managed to change the keys in the last six years I've been gone."

October peers inside, not moving yet. "You think Brian will be pissed?"

"I think he won't find out. Free alcohol and food are on the beach. He won't be back until the party is over, which gives us time."

She nods, convinced enough. We both try to enter the doorway at the same time and our shoulders get jammed, our hips bump.

"Sorry," we say in unison—like we hadn't just touched earlier. Tension mounts between us, and then it happens…again.

My cheeks heat.

She flushes. "I'm going first," she demands.

"Bossy." I end up taking a step back.

She saunters through the open doorway. "It's so you can watch my ass."

I already am. She has a great ass. Only slightly bigger than mine, and I dream of skating my fingertips along her feminine curves like she's done to me. Biting my lip, I mention, "And you told *me* not to flirt." I lock the back door behind me and follow her into the main bar area. Blinds are drawn shut and the "closed" sign is up.

The entire town shuts down for the Lock Ceremony.

She glances over her shoulder. "Is it flirting if it's a fact?"

"Yes," I say. "It's a flirty fact, Kenobi."

Her lips twitch like she wants to smile again. After I place the white fur coat on a stool, I slide behind the bar and grab a couple of seltzers from the cooler. Rounding back to the main floor, I pass her the can.

Our hands brush for a split-second. I zero in on her fingers. *They were inside me last night.*

Heat cascades, and I want a repeat so badly. To give October what she gave me.

She's currently staring at me with full awareness. Like she's already in my head reading all my dirty thoughts.

"What?" I ask.

Play it cool.

I pop the cap and take a small sip from the cherry lime drink.

"You're asking *me* what?" She applies a thin sheen of lip gloss. "You're the one that's seconds away from a moan."

I'm staring at her shiny lips. "Am not." I dribble the seltzer a little on my chin. Quickly wiping it up with the back of my hand. Blushing. "You're the one who fingered *me*. Tell me that's not all you're thinking about."

"I don't deny it," she says like she's giving a testimony.

Okay.

Progress, Zoey.

I lick some of the seltzer off the rim of my can. Keeping my eyes on her. She watches me, her pink lips parting a little. A want gnaws at me. Her full lips. On my lips

My tongue, licking more than just this alcohol up.

I can't have that. She doesn't want me to touch her. Fuuuck.

This whole thing is torture. Shedding all flirtation, I take a normal sip from the can, and October watches more keenly.

Maybe she can tell a switch went off in my head. That I'm trying my best not to flirt or fantasize because it'll only hurt me in the end.

"Let's talk," I tell her, "like you said." And I slide into the nearest booth. The wooden surface is stained and scratched. Crayons mark it up.

Taking off her jacket, she slips into the other side and pops the seltzer can. "Parry might be right."

"About what?" *Maybe we're not on the same page. Maybe she's thinking about something else.*

"About Colt. That missing girl."

Awesome. Same horrible page then.

October stares hard at the table before her eyes flit to me in a way that says *buckle up.* "I agree with Parry. I don't think there's a missing girl."

My mouth dries. "Why didn't you tell me this last night after I explained everything?"

She glances towards the window, but the blinds are shut. Nothing to see outside. "It was just a *feeling* last night, but today at the Lock Ceremony, I realized Parry understands this town a little better than you." *Ouch.*

I shake my head vigorously. "There is no proof that the town is setting up Colt."

October tilts her head, appraising me like I'm a flower wilting in the winter. "Do you remember the first day of high school? How everyone brings umbrellas because of the leaky ceilings."

My grip tightens on my can, not knowing where this is headed. "Yeah, I remember."

"Why do you think the pipes bust every year on the same day?" October asks me.

I don't believe the ghosts of Lenard Doyle and Madeline Mackay roam the halls, but I'm not a complete cynic either. "Because of weird, strange coincidences," I say into a shrug. "This town relies on them. Some things you can't explain, Kenobi."

"I agree. Some things can't be explained," October refutes. "But I can explain that."

I cage breath.

She takes a small, delicate sip from her seltzer before saying, "The pipes are purposefully loosened on that day every year. The city funds the repairs."

It shouldn't be a surprise that something juvenile and harmless was orchestrated all along. But it feels a little like someone revealing the answer to a magic trick, draining the magical aspect from it entirely.

"How do you know that?" I wonder, even though I have a guess.

"Aunt Effie is a part of the town council. I know a lot of things." She narrows her eyes. "Like the fact that tourism in this town accounts for ninety-percent of its business. We'd all be destitute if it weren't for its notoriety."

"I know the 'town playing a prank on Colt' is a viable theory—"

"One you don't want to believe is true."

I can't deny that. "But we're talking about purposefully making my brother go insane. Making him *think* he heard a mayday call. For what? To maintain the fact that this town is cursed? The motives are a little loose, don't you think? They could do that a million other ways without being completely fucking sadistic."

"Your family is what's cursed," she counters. "It's been generations since a family has had as much misfortune in town as yours. The people here aren't going to let Colt have some docile curse like losing his sense of *smell*."

"You think it's all orchestrated then?" I wonder. "Our curses? Even yours?" *What happened to you?*

Her face goes sheet white. "No. It's not all orchestrated, Zoey. But some are."

Jesus. Christ. I knew some things had to be coordinated by the town—I'm not that naïve—but the ugly parts…I wish I could just pin on fate.

October's cellphone rings loudly on the table. I swear she's a second from rejecting the call, but she freezes when she sees the caller ID. Jaw set, she stiffly presses the phone to her ear.

"Uncle Milo," she greets casually.

Her lips flatline as her uncle replies, and our eyes stay locked the entire time.

"Right now?" she asks.

My brows rise. *She has to go?*

"Fine. Yes. Fine." She pauses before saying, "Bye."

My shoulders are already sinking. "Family beckons?" I try not to sound as bummed as I feel.

"Fisherman's Wharf," she corrects, already scooting out of the booth. "I skipped dinner service last night, and my uncle isn't pleased.

I have to go in early now." She fits her arms back through her puffer jacket. "Will you *try* not to get into trouble while I'm gone?"

I give her a wry smile. "What kind of trouble are we talking about, Kenobi?"

She doesn't share my humor. Seriousness etches across her beautiful cheeks. "I'm not joking about this, Zoey. Don't do something stupid."

"Cross my heart." I make an X over my chest.

She stares harder.

"What?"

"That phrase is *cross my heart* and ends with *hope to die*." She doesn't break eye contact. "Don't die on me, sweets."

Sweets.

It feels like she just laced her arms around me in a soft, melting embrace. Gentle affection threatens to unglue me from this spot at the booth, but she's already leaving through the back door.

"I'll try," I whisper to her shadow.

I appreciate October being honest with me about her theories on Colt's curse. But now I'm more curious about *her* curse. Is hers orchestrated by the town too? *Doubtful.* Something bad happened to make her withdraw.

To make her believe she doesn't deserve to be loved.

Why do you keep pushing me away, Kenobi? The question is plaguing the ever-loving fuck out of me.

I blow out a tensed breath and reach for my seltzer. Before my fingers can touch the can, the bells jingle to the front door. *Shitshitshit.* How is Brian back already?

Should I run for the back door?

Hurriedly, with paranoia leeching my back, I slide out of the booth and nearly trip over my feet. And then I catch my balance. Straightening up. *Totally graceful.*

With a big breath, I'm about to confront Brian, and then I freeze at who I see.

Not Brian.

"Zoey?" Parry DiNapoli stops in the middle of the bar. "What the hell are you doing here?" He glances around like the answer will spring up from one of the dusty corners.

"Having a drink." I point at my seltzer. Strangely, I feel sort of letdown. Did I actually *want* to see Brian again?

I must've been hoping.

"How'd you get in?" Parry asks.

"I had a key."

He nods like it makes sense. "Brian didn't change the locks then."

"What are *you* doing here? The Lock Ceremony was boring enough to bail early?"

"More like breathing the same air as both Brian and Colt makes me wish we lived in prehistoric times and a pterodactyl would just swoop down and scoop me up for its next meal."

I raise my brows. "What a visual."

"I've had enough time to think of creative ways to exit." He lets out a tensed breath. "They bicker. A lot."

"Like a crab and a hurricane. I remember."

Parry nods slowly and rubs the back of his neck. "Brian's a bigger dick to me when Colt is also around. He can't seem to understand that I didn't choose the lighthouse for Colt. I didn't choose any of this. I'm just some guy."

I frown. Is that really how he sees himself? "You're not some random guy. You're Colt's best friend. You're one of the few people in town who didn't completely toss aside my family like garbage. That's *something*, Parry."

"Brian doesn't think it is."

"Why do you care what Brian thinks?" And as he stares right at me with raw intensity, I realize…I *am* an idiot. "You really like him, don't you?"

Parry glances back at the door like he's worried my brother might appear. Satisfied that Brian isn't teleporting into the bar, he turns back to me. "Brian's a royal fucking asshole. But he's lost a lot. *I've* lost a lot. Somewhere deep down, I guess I know what it's like to hate the world enough to want a punching bag. So I'm that punching bag for him, and I'm okay with it only because he's my punching bag." He blows out a strained breath. "I guess that makes me care in some sick way."

I nod slowly, trying to understand. "So you two *do* have this mutual love-hate thing going on?"

"Basically." He eyes me up-and-down, then searches the bar. "Where's OB? I thought she glued herself to your hip."

"The Wharf. Hey, is the museum open right now?" My crap memory can't recall their hours.

"Yeah, the Roberts never close it."

"Not even for events?" I'm a little shocked.

"They won't risk losing a customer. They get a couple teenagers to work for the day. I'm sure no one's there."

Perfect. I grab the fur coat, and Parry's frown deepens. "You're going to the museum?"

"I have a mystery to solve," I remind him. Only this one has more to do with October than my brother.

"I'm coming with you then." He touches the top of his crown. "Mister Mistpoint, remember?" He flashes a magnetic smile.

He had to win an intensive scavenger hunt and mystery to secure that title. Right now, I have zero accolades. Not even some silly high school superlative like *Best Dressed* or *Most Likely to Die Young* (yes, our morbid high school has that one). I think that students thought it was a bigger FU to not give me a superlative at all.

Jokes on them because I'd much rather come out with no title than be pegged as the *Most Likely to Die Young*.

Out of the two of us, Parry has more awards. *Mister Mistpoint, Best Smile, High School Sailing Team Champion*. In the years I've been gone, I'm sure he's even acquired more.

Even though Parry probably thinks this museum trip is mostly about my brother, I won't reject his help. I say into a confident nod, "Let's Nancy Drew this shit."

CHAPTER 18

ZOEY DURAND

*P*arry parks his convertible in the empty parking lot. A couple of bikes are chained to the rack, and when we approach the ticket booth, I realize it's empty.

And then I smell the pungent unmistakable odor of *weed*. Parry and I exchange a knowing look. Teens getting lit in the ticket booth is classic.

"Knock knock." Parry taps on the plexiglass.

"Oh *shit*," a boy curses. Scrambling from the floor of the booth, two scraggly-haired teenagers stand up, wearing lilac-collared shirts. The *Museum of Curses & Curiosities* logo is embroidered onto the breast pocket.

The blond blinks a ton, eyes bloodshot. His nametag reads: Matt Beech.

The brown-haired boy tries to straighten out his half-untucked shirt. "Welcome to the Museum of—" He coughs into his fist.

Okay, I laugh. I see his nametag. Lucas Ricci.

"Guys, we're locals." Parry points to the crown on his head. "We're not here to do the whole tourist thing. We're just looking for our names in the books."

"Yeah," I nod. "We just want to do a quick in and out."

"That's what she said," Matt mutters into a *fake* cough under his breath.

I narrow my eyes. "What are you, ten?"

"Fifteen." He barely blinks. "And you're what…*thirty*?"

Ugh. I hate stoned teenage boys. "Thirty isn't even that old," I tell him like he's not making sense.

He makes a face. "Ma'am, it's *ancient*. That's another lifetime for me."

"Did you just call me *ma'am*?"

They're both snickering.

Parry puts a hand on my shoulder and whispers to me, "They're trying to get under your skin, Zo."

Mission accomplished.

"Can you let us in or not?" I ask.

"IDs. We have to confirm you're locals," Lucas states.

Parry pulls out his license, and while I fish for mine in my leather backpack-purse, I realize that I've changed my address. I'm not a resident of Mistpoint Harbor anymore. But maybe they'll recognize my last name…

Lucas appraises Parry's license in a quick second, while Matt glances at the card from behind Lucas' shoulder. "Checks out," Lucas says.

"DiNapoli." Matt squints as he scrutinizes Parry. "Are you the vampire brother or the squirrel?"

Parry rolls his eyes.

"Squirrel?" I question. That term didn't float around when I lived here.

Matt nods. "When's the last time you've seen a squirrel at night?"

I open my mouth to respond, but Lucas cuts me off. "Never," he says *for* me. "Because squirrels sleep at night. Well…usually."

Matt narrows his bloodshot eyes on Parry. "Vampire or squirrel?"

"You're an idiot," Parry says, snagging his ID back.

"Squirrel," Lucas says pointedly and looks to Matt. "It's daytime, dude."

Matt laughs a slow, clearly inebriated laugh. "Riiiight."

I slide my ID over. Lucas takes it first, and he immediately shakes his head. "Nah, you're not from here."

"I'm a Durand."

"Don't care," Lucas says. "It'll be thirty-five bucks."

"What?" I gasp. "Since when? I thought it was twenty."

Parry gives me a consoling look. "There've been some significant curses in the past six years."

"So I take it business is booming," I grumble and fish out some cash from my wallet.

"I can cover it, Zo." Parry reaches for his wallet.

"I got it." I'm already sliding over a couple of twenties, and I wait for Lucas to give me change. I might be spending a shit ton at the Inn, but I can afford a ticket. Plus, I don't need Parry to think I've been struggling in Chicago. My life there is different, but it hasn't been horrible.

Matt stares harder at me. "Are you really a Durand?"

"No, I just forged a whole license," I snap. "Yeah, I'm a Durand."

"So you're like really fucked," Matt says.

I don't know how to respond to that. Luckily, Lucas hands me back a five. Parry's quick to head towards the double doors.

"Don't forget to fill the comment card on your way out!" Lucas yells at us. Their snickering is the last thing I hear as the doors clank shut behind us.

"Horrible," Parry says once we're inside.

"The worst," I agree. "I forgot how much I hated high school until this moment."

His gaze softens on me. "You know Colt and I wish we were in your grade...or at least in school when you went."

"I know," I breathe. "It's okay. I had October."

He considers this for a long moment. "Sometimes I don't understand her. She wants to protect you *fully*, yet she's embedded herself with the people who shit on you."

"They're her family," I say, defending her like it's the natural thing to do.

"Amelia Roberts isn't her family."

I struggle to find a rebuttal. "I'd…I'd never ask October to reject her friends for me, Pear, and I wouldn't want her to make that choice."

Parry mutters something about how I shouldn't have to ask. How I should come first. But I know October did her best when we were in high school. She did *more* for me than anyone else.

And… "Since I've been back, she's repeatedly put me first," I realize out loud. "She snuck me into her shed for a place to sleep. She dropped work to check on me at the Harbor Inn. Plus, she literally just left the Lock Ceremony with *me* and ditched her friends." *And she held my hand. In front of everyone.*

Parry eases. "Yeah, you're right." He stares off in thought, then focuses on me. "Anyway, I think she wants to be all-in."

"Really?" I perk up. "Like all-in with me? Did she tell you something or…?" I'm distracted as we reach the very center of the museum where a massive *sailboat* is on display. Capturing all of my attention. "What. The. Fuck?"

Vini Vidi Vici is painted along the hull.

Parry glances between me and the sailboat. "Shit, I forgot you've been gone this long. You haven't seen the cursed boat?"

"The cursed boat?" I frown and walk closer to the thing. A placard explains the misfortune that occurred on the sailboat, but I don't bother reading the tale. I turn to Parry. "Aren't there like hundreds of those?" Lots of accidents happen on boats in Mistpoint Harbor.

"Yeah, but this happened five years ago. Mr. and Mrs. Varga were taking a sail to Cherry Island. They crashed into the ferry. Injured ten Mistpoint residents. The boat didn't sink, but Mr. and Mrs. Varga died on their way to the hospital."

"Damn," I breathe out.

"Yeah, it's probably one of the worst accidents to date since…" His voice trails off.

"Brian," I realize. "The car crash." I shudder, remembering since the accident happened before I left. I was fifteen at the time, and I remember how pissed Brian was when he learned the town was going to put the singed steering wheel behind a plexiglass display in this museum. It wasn't his car though—so he didn't have much say.

In the end, Sheriff Carmichael agreed to it.

"He still doesn't talk about it," Parry tells me.

"Can you blame him? He crawled out of the broken window seconds before the car caught on fire. If that happened to me… *happens* to me…"

I'm not cursed yet, and if this museum is anything of an indication, I could be really fucked. I could die.

Or I could survive like Brian and just have the weight of others' deaths on me. Brian had been out having beers with his old football teammates. He was thirty. On the ride home, one of the sheriff's three sons had too much to drink.

Emmett Carmichael was behind the wheel.

As Brian told the cops, a deer leaped into the road. Emmett swerved. Slammed directly into a tree. He died on impact along with his brother Josh.

Liam Carmichael, the resident firefighter/EMT, is really the only Carmichael brother left.

I still can't believe my freshman drama teacher had been in the backseat with Brian. Mr. Owens. One year after I had him in class, he was gone.

I've never heard Brian explain what happened, but I read the report on our online newspaper. *Mistpoint Daily Gazette.* Mr. Owens was pinned behind the driver's seat, and Brian couldn't pull him out in time.

He died in the fiery blaze.

Some days, I wonder if Brian wished he'd died that night. His life only got harder after the accident, and the town wasted no opportunity to remind him that he didn't deserve to be the sole survivor. They'd give The Drunk Pelican fake one-star reviews on Yelp. Teenagers vandalized his catamaran. As the hostess of the Pelican, I remember the bar's phone going off and off and off. I'd answer each time only to receive the ass-end of a cruel prank. "*It should have been you,*" a robotic voice would say before the line clicked.

I tried to answer every single one of those calls.

I glued myself to the phone. Just so Brian wouldn't have to hear them. When he finally realized what was happening, he disconnected the phone altogether.

If anyone asks, I'm glad my brother didn't die. He's grouchy and mean, but he's the one who kept a roof over my head when my dad was on the lake for eight months. Brian made me pancakes in the morning, and he'd help me decorate our little apartment above the bar for Christmas.

He's the one who took me to the local clinic when I told him I wanted to go on birth control. He's the one who baked me an awful, inedible birthday cake for my sweet sixteen. He was the one who *begged* me to stay in Mistpoint Harbor.

So for as much as this town hates Brian Durand, I'll never hate him. Not for a second.

We continue down the hallway, and Parry says strongly, like he's convincing himself, "Nothing that bad will happen to you." But his concern pierces through his seafoam green eyes. *It won't be your fault, Parry.*

I can't fret over a future that hasn't come to pass, and the more I worry about my curse, the more grief I'll cause Parry. So I choose to focus on the task at hand. *Find the books.*

"You're probably right," I tell him while we pass a row of artifacts. A bloody Maroon 5 band T-shirt. A baseball bat fractured in three pieces. A sizzled, fried toaster. And yes, Aaron Brambilla, one of October's many cousins, was electrocuted by that toaster. He survived. October said he was a little skittish afterward, but that's to be expected.

We enter the center room where I expect to find the row of leather-bound books. Instead, a projector plays a film on the wall. Empty chairs and couches face the screen.

"Did they move the books?" I wonder.

"They're further back. This way."

I ignore the grainy image of the town, showing the historical parts of Mistpoint Harbor, like the old railroads, and I follow Parry to the last room. *Here we go.*

A dozen thick, leather-bound books lie on ornate podiums like the most prized relics. Gold decorative lights hang from the ceiling and shine on each one.

Years are etched in each leather cover, as well as the words *Historical Records of Mistpoint Harbor Curses.* Each book features a set of decades. I reach the book at the end of the row. It's already flipped open to the last page.

EDGAR JOHNSON

Cursed at Age 71

Developed hay fever and permanently lost his sense of smell

A photo of an older man with a thick mustache and grayed beard stares back at me. A small section underneath the picture details the life of Edgar Johnson, but I know most people skip over that part. They're just here to see the curses.

As am I.

"What are we looking for?" Parry asks, flipping through the book beside me. "Maybe a relative to Augustine Anders? We could track down her mother's maiden name."

That is what a Mister Mistpoint would do.

My stomach knots. "Before all of that...I need to find October's curse."

He pauses, fingers on the worn pages. "What?" Frown deepening, wrinkles form in the space between his brows. "She didn't tell you?"

I shift my weight. "No, and I probably shouldn't be looking it up either. But I just need to make sure it wasn't something horrible." *It has to be horrible.* She wouldn't be going around professing her ghost-status if the curse was benign.

"Curses are always horrible, Zo," Parry says strongly. "It's why they're called curses."

He's not wrong. I avoid making eye-contact with the thick puffy scar on his face, and I scour the pages of the book. One more page-turn, and I freeze.

The photograph of October steals my breath in the worst way. She's staring right at me with a haunted expression. Eyes that appear soulless but weaponized. *Fuck,* this doesn't even look like October.

Not the October I know.

My eyes fall off her photo and pin to the words.

OCTOBER BRAMBILLA

Cursed at Age 25

Died for 10 seconds after nearly drowning in the lake. Resuscitated by her aunt

She is a ghost then.

"She almost drowned?" I whisper in confusion. Why wouldn't she tell me? It's not something that I'd think needed to be secret.

Parry watches me. "The Brambillas kept the whole thing pretty quiet. No one knows what she was even doing on the lake. Brian has a theory that she was trying to...you know."

My brows shoot up, and pain pierces my heart. "You think October was trying to kill herself?" My whole body feels unsteady. Like one finger-push and I'd keel over like a bowling pin. I shake my head vigorously. "No, that doesn't sound like Kenobi. And it's not something to even joke about."

Parry's gaze softens. "I'm not joking, Zo. I actually take this shit seriously." Concern washes over his face when he realizes how much this is tearing me up. He touches my shoulder gently. "Maybe she was just going for a night swim and tired out or something. It's probably explainable."

My throat swells.

Parry squeezes my shoulder, then side-hugs me. "And if OB will explain this to anyone, I'm sure it's you."

"Doubtful," I mutter. "Very fucking doubtful. Weren't you just saying she's so willing to put her friends before me?" I spin on him.

He clutches my shoulders. "And weren't you just reminding me that she has put you first since you've been back? I'm cautious and protective, Zo—but maybe I've been wrong to be cautious of her. She *has* been there for you."

"Then why couldn't she tell me? Does she think I'd react badly?" My brain is in a blender, and I hear my voice rising. "Why would she be okay with the entire town knowing but leaving me in the dark?"

Parry slowly releases his grip on my shoulders. "I don't know."

I'll have to ask her myself.

I try not to be hurt. What happened to October is awful, and I wasn't here. I left. She doesn't owe me an explanation about anything.

I blink hard to wipe October away for a second. "Okay, let's just reroute our focus." I turn to the books. "Time to get down to hunting for more Augustine Anders evidence."

"Otherwise known as a wild goose chase."

"Yeah, and we'll be the best goose hunters in town. Take that, Antler Queen Anna."

Parry laughs hard at the nickname. "Brian would get a kick out of that."

"You mean Colt?"

"No…" His neck reddens. "I-I-I-I meant Brian."

So Parry *really* likes my brother. I shouldn't keep meeting surprise, but it *is* shocking. Six years ago, I would've never predicted the match. It's a little like hearing Han Solo has a thing for Anakin Skywalker.

Brian could so easily crush Parry's heart. Part of me wants to caution Parry, but I can't pretend to understand what I've missed. I haven't been around enough to offer any advice—let alone *good* advice.

We both agree to push aside our romantic troubles and concentrate on the mystery girl.

Hours pass in the museum. Flipping each page and looking for one relative. Just *one*. Even generations ago. My stomach grumbles in hunger by the time I close the next to last book.

"We should break for food," Parry says.

"And have to pay another thirty-five bucks to reenter?" I make a cringy face. "Not a chance. We only have one more book left."

He opens the oldest book. Leather worn and title faded along the cover. *The first known records of the curses.* It's not the original. The town made a replica so tourists wouldn't damage the first edition, and they purposefully distressed the book for that "ancient" appearance.

The replica has the same info as the original, so it'll work. Huddling together, Parry and I turn each page slowly, my stomach sinking with each name.

When we reach the last page, the last second, and the last name, I take a shallow breath. "Well…there's that. I guess we're right where we started. A whole lotta nothing."

"Not really." Parry shuts the book. "We do know something now."

October's curse. My unhelpful thought intrudes.

Parry can't read my mind, but his expression grows more serious. "Let's says she does exist," he grimaces as though it sounds like a fairytale. "If she doesn't have a relative in these books, it means something, Zo."

It hits me.

My mouth falls open. "She's not from Mistpoint Harbor."

CHAPTER 19

OCTOBER BRAMBILLA

Aunt Effie is relentless.

"I'm doing your friend a favor, October." She has pink curlers in her hair and tightens the strap of a purple fuzzy robe. The matching slippers are *so* Aunt Effie, and I'm shocked she's not in bed.

It's midnight.

My muscles ache from my shoulders down to my feet from a grueling shift after our dishwasher didn't show. Since I'm trying my best to reenter Uncle Milo's good graces, I filled in.

I would've gone straight to the Harbor Inn after work, but I received a text from my aunt that propelled me home.

Aunt Effie: I've scheduled a book event for Zoey.

So now I'm here. At a commanding stance in the quaint living room. Surrounded by hundreds of old Harlequin paperbacks of small-town romances that my aunt gobbles up faster than her morning anise toast.

Truly, stacks of books have spilled out of the shelves and found home in various locations.

Three on the coffee table. Two on an end table. One oddly placed on the creaky staircase. Two in the slipper basket at the door. A small white fluffy Pomeranian currently snoozes on a large hardback on the floorboards.

Sometimes I think she'd sell her soul for a good love story.

Aunt Effie even speaks more dreamily about these books than her own romance with the town's lawyer. Bluntly, she's said, "Steve doesn't measure up in the least. There is no comparison because grand, sweeping, eternal *love* is made for novels, October. It's fictional. It doesn't exist in real life."

I want to believe her. Because if soul-deep love that transcends time and place can't truly exist, then maybe it'd be easier to just let Zoey leave for a second time.

But my aunt's romance collection isn't what whirls my mind at ninety miles an hour.

"You called Zoey *my friend*," I say in astonishment. She's never said one kind thing about Zoey Durand.

"Isn't that what she is?" my aunt questions.

"Yes." *She's more than a friend.* Fuck my hesitance. There is a difference between being private and guarded and being *timid*. I refuse to be *shy* towards my aunt—towards anyone. So I add, "But she's more than a friend to me."

"Clearly. I saw you holding hands."

I can't read the emotion in her voice. And she's avoiding my eyes. *Interesting.*

In high school, Aunt Effie heard rumors around town that Zoey and I were together, and she'd caution me, "Pick another girl, October. There are plenty of better fish in the lake. Don't choose the bottom-feeders. You're a *Brambilla*. You're worth more."

"She's not a bottom-feeder," I'd snap back, and I'd strut away like Aunt Effie wasn't worth *my* time.

Sometimes I'd hear her sigh. Sometimes I'd glance back and see her smile. I like to believe she's proud of the girls she's raised. Of the women we are. Opinionated (Babette more so). Confident. Unflinching, even towards her.

"You and Zoey were holding hands?" Babette asks while sitting on the bottom stair and cupping a chamomile tea. She stirs in extra honey. "When? Where?"

"The Lock Ceremony," Aunt Effie answers before I can. "When they so *rudely* sprinted away."

"Please," I say sharply. "No one missed us. Baby didn't even know we left."

Babette mutters into her tea, "I have major regrets. I would've loved to see you two holding hands and sprinting away. I would've *applauded.*"

God, I love my sister. Figgy and Rosemary are perched on her shoulder. Chirping happily. My lovebirds adore her too.

Aunt Effie moans, "Girls."

"Aunt Effie," Babette counters. "You should be proud of October. She's choosing Zoey over this town's dumb obsession with *hating* the Durands—and you should be proud of me for behaving atrociously and calling Isabella a kiss-ass." She bats her lashes.

"She's too far gone," Aunt Effie mutters to herself about Baby, and my sister and I laugh a little. The sound dies in my throat as my aunt turns on me. "Did you not hear the part where I said I'm doing Zoey a *favor?*"

I cross my arms. "You really think this is a favor?"

"It's a *book event*. For exposure. It could help her on release day."

Oh please. I'm not that easily fooled. "Zoey didn't ask for a book event. And seeing as how you *called* a publisher to get her book cancelled—"

"*I* did not do that," she interrupts hotly and takes an angry seat on the floral-patterned couch. The cushion squeaks, and her fluffy dog, Sugar, perks from her sleeping spot on the book. We all watch Sugar bounce onto Aunt Effie's lap before my aunt's eyes snap up to me. "Who told you that?"

"It doesn't matter who. Why'd you call the publisher then?" I'm willing to give her the benefit of the doubt. I understand how gossip can warp the truth.

Sugar licks Aunt Effie's hand before panting happily. At least someone adores my aunt unconditionally. I watch my aunt pat Sugar's head tenderly. "I called to get information. Something Zoey hasn't provided to anyone in the town. And as far as I can tell, her publishing deal doesn't exist."

I roll my eyes. "You're basing that off a few phone calls? You couldn't have gotten a hold of *every* New York City publisher."

She considers this for a moment. "True. So this book event is better timing than ever. Zoey can promote her little creation, and we, the townspeople, can ask the questions we need to ask. This book is about us after all."

I have her actual motive now.

Babette sips her tea. "Technically it's about the history of the town."

"And we *are* the history of this town, Babette," our aunt declares like it's written in stone. "No book on Mistpoint Harbor is complete without mentioning the Brambillas."

I grind my teeth. This isn't going to end well for Zoey. "And if she refuses to attend this book event?" *Complete with a fucking Q&A.*

Aunt Effie stares me down. "She's *your* more-than-friend, October. You'll need to find a way to get her to the event. I'm sure you can find some avenue to convince her."

Babette raises her brows at me. "I'm sensing another batch of nukadells."

Our aunt scoffs at the word, but she doesn't chastise my sister. "Yes, baked goods might be a good way to cozy up to Zoey."

"Oh, I know another way October can cozy up to Zoey," Babette says, and she raises her fingers in a V-formation up to her lips, demonstrating a vulgar gesture that brings a rare smile out of me.

Our aunt turns sharply.

Babette doesn't stop wagging her tongue between her fingers.

"Babette Louise Brambilla!"

My sister is dying in a fit of laughter. "She's twenty-five, Aunt Effie. She doesn't need ear-muffs." To me, she says, "Though, you could also rely on snuggles. I hear those are better than sex at times."

My heart pangs. Babette has told me that she dreams of being romantically touched, but she can't make that end point. Like she's forever charting a course for land that she sees in the horizon. Endlessly sailing, never able to reach shore.

Aunt Effie has recovered from her heart attack. "Some innocent canoodling won't hurt."

Babette laughs at the word *canoodling*.

I'm on guard. On edge.

"But there will be *no* dating," Aunt Effie decrees. "I will bury myself alive before I attend a Brambilla-Durand wedding. That goes for both of you." She points between Babette and me.

I bristle. There is no point in arguing now—not when Zoey and I aren't even dating, not when we likely never will—but my insides curdle at the idea of choosing Aunt Effie and my position in this town over Zoey.

Babette stirs her honey with downturned lips. "No need to fret. I'm not dating anyone, let alone a Durand."

I won't make any promises.

In my heart, I'd love to be Zoey's girlfriend. But that heart is also dead somewhere in the lake, and I know whatever our future holds, my aunt will likely get the outcome she wishes.

Aunt Effie is waiting with pursed lips for my response.

"You don't have anything to worry about," I say with bite.

"Good."

An intensity passes between us, a reminder. As if she's silently telling me, *Remember, child, I know everything.*

I try to stand my ground.

But she knows far too much.

"I have to go," I say, grabbing a coat off the rack. It's not my favorite white fur coat—that one is with Zoey. But this pink plaid full-length peacoat has earned second place in my heart.

"I'll text you the details of the event," my aunt calls out to me. "Invitations go out tomorrow."

"Goodnight, OB." My sister waves from the stairs.

"Night, Baby." My birds squawk at me in loving chirps before I head out the door. On my way to her.

CHAPTER 20

ZOEY DURAND

I didn't break any rules. She never explicitly told me, *"Zoey, don't go to the museum and find my name."* But then why do I feel like utter fucking garbage? Like I just spoiled the ending of Star Wars: The Rise of Skywalker. Not that October has ever cared that much about the Star Wars franchise, and I'm pretty sure I called her and talked her ear off about Kylo Ren and Rey when it did come out.

So yeah...I already spoiled the whole ending to her. And hot take—I actually really loved that movie, even though I know it's not a fan favorite of the films.

What does that say about me? That I like the unpopular things. Maybe I have bad taste. Shit, that's true. I probably have bad taste.

And again, why am I pacing?!

I stop in the middle of the Poe room. Mr. Kelly's ghost could fly into this room right now, and I don't think it could disturb the guilt that's compounded tenfold. What if October thinks this is some sort of betrayal?

Shit.

Sweat builds under my pits. Deep breaths, Zoey.

A knock sounds on the door. "Zoey?"

Her voice freezes me cold, even if it's the sweetest sounding thing I've ever heard.

"Zoey?" she says again. "Are you asleep?"

"No," I call out and reanimate. One foot in front of the other, I reach the door. October stands before me, searching me quickly from head to toe like she's taking an assessment of my well-being since she's been gone.

"All toes and fingers are accounted for," I try to joke, but I fear the humor falls flat.

She frowns. "What's wrong?"

Can she see the panic in my eyes? I step away from the door, wringing my hands together nervously. "We should talk."

She shuts the door behind her. "I have news too. You first."

"No, you should probably go first." *What I have to admit could destroy us.*

She shakes her head, concern building in her eyes. "Mine can wait." She walks towards the bed and pats the mattress. "Sit with me."

"Yeah, good idea. This is definitely a sitting conversation."

Worry builds in her strict posture. "You're scaring me, Zo."

"Can ghosts get scared?" I wonder, more to myself than to her.

She frowns deeply. "Zoey, I'm serious."

I climb onto the mattress beside her. We sit cross-legged. Face-to-face. It feels a little like our first night in this room together. "I'm just confused is all," I admit. "And guilty. I feel really guilty."

She touches my ankle, her fingers brushing over the exposed skin between sock and pantleg. That single touch sends a wave of warmth through me.

"Just tell me what's going on," she says softly but not at all tenderly. Like ice that's trying its hardest to melt but can't. And fuck, does that almost undo me completely.

I suck in a breath, trying to get my bearings in order to explain my betrayal. "I wish I brought my Grogu plushie." I cringe. "That's not what I need to say, but maybe having it would make this easier."

"Grogu?"

"Baby Yoda," I clarify.

Her nose crinkles. "That creepy little guy. You have a doll of him?"

I nudge her knee. "A *plushie*. It's cute and squishy. And *very* comforting I'll fucking add."

Her lips downturn. "I know I'm not warm and fuzzy like your Baby Yoda—"

"You don't have to be those things," I interject. "You're still this comforting presence in my life, Kenobi."

I didn't mean to be this open and vulnerable with her, but emotion is just pooling out. And I'm not in the business of mopping up *feelings* and tossing them aside. I'm not even sure how to rewind and do that!

Stop freaking out, Zoey.

She leans closer to catch my gaze. Hers is intense. Harsh, but not even close to accusatory or angry. October looks prepared to encase me in her arms and shield me from every evil in this town and this fucking world. "Then why are you so nervous around me tonight?"

I try my best not to avoid her eyes. *Don't be a coward.* I unbottle as much bravery as I can muster. "Maybe I don't deserve you either—"

"Please—"

"Maybe you deserve a woman who's *impressive*—"

"You're impressive," she volleys back quickly, glaring like I'm losing sense of our reality, and yeah, we're both cutting each other off. "You're beautiful—"

"Someone who can *rival* you, Kenobi," I interject again. "Not someone who follows you like a lost pupp—"

"You're not lost, and you're far from being my lap do—"

"You deserve more!" I shout. "You deserve a woman who never left. A woman who would've stood by your side."

"*You* deserve more, Zoey," she retorts forcefully. "You deserve someone who would've put you before her standing in the town. You deserve someone who asked you to prom—"

"I didn't want to go!" I almost start crying. Why am I crying? *What the fuck.* I wipe the involuntary tears away—oh my God, October is wiping them for me. She's touching my wet cheeks, and I let her fingers brush over my skin. I let her stay this close while I say, "I didn't care about *prom*. I didn't care that we did everything privately or as privately as we could. I didn't care that we didn't put a label on what we were—none of that mattered to me. I just wanted you."

I still just want you.

Her eyes redden. "Don't."

"October—"

"Don't tell me I deserve more. Not when *you* deserve the entire seven-tiered cake, and I gave you a crumb."

"You gave me pastries every day in high school."

"It's a metaphor, you idiot." Her voice breaks.

I laugh and cry.

"Stop crying, please." Tears are squeezing out of her eyes. "Why are you still crying, sweets?"

I wronged you. "Because you deserve..."

She's shaking her head.

"You deserve a woman who would've never opened the forbidden fucking book!" It explodes out of me.

October has solidified.

My heart is racing out of my chest and into the bathtub to go hide. *Don't cower now.* Staying on the bed with wet lashes, I manage to say more softly, "I went to the museum to look up your curse."

She quickly retracts her hand from my ankle, from my tear-streaked face. Cold bites my flesh. Pain lances me everywhere. *Please don't leave me,* I want to scream.

Instead, I just ramble, "I'm sorry. I broke. I caved. I did all the things I shouldn't have done, but I just needed to know someone didn't hurt you. I was starting to imagine the worst. And I couldn't take it anymore. I just…I fucking *had* to know."

She pinches the bridge of her nose, her eyes snapped closed. "You shouldn't have, Zoey."

"I know."

"No, you don't know," she snaps coldly. "You don't know anything!" She climbs off the bed in anger. Outrage. Hands fly to the top of her head like she's ascending an 8,000 meter peak.

I hop off the bed and hold out a hand like I'm trying to befriend a feral creature. "Can we *please* just talk about it? I just don't understand, okay? The entire town knows your curse, but you couldn't tell me, why?" I stupidly add, "You drowned?"

A growl rips through her throat and she's the one pacing my room now. I want to console her, but I feel out-of-my-element on comforting someone. People can call October an ice queen all they want, but she's in an elite class at comforting the wounded—person and animal. I don't have those skills in my toolbelt, and I worry if every word I say will sound trite.

Try.

I'm going to try. Because I care enough about her to not want to cause her pain or panic like this. She's muttering under her breath. I can't make out the words, but I'm guessing she's cursing me out.

"I don't know what it's like to drown," I whisper. "I can't even begin to imagine—"

She whips around to face me, and the deadly look on her face steals my words. Steals my breath. I stop cold.

"You don't have to imagine it, Zoey," she whispers, her voice full of ice. "Because it didn't happen."

It feels like I've been punched in the throat. "I...I don't... understand," I mutter. "It didn't happen? What does that mean?"

"It means exactly as it sounds," October says, frustration pulsing through each word. Her hands lace at the top of her head, and she glares at the ceiling. "I never drowned."

My throat dries. "So you're not cursed?"

"I didn't say that."

Fuck. I squint as if I can see through the fog that's overtaking this situation. "Then what the hell happened?" I rub at my splotchy cheeks.

She drops her hands to her side, and her reddened gaze falls to me. "I can't tell you." She winces at herself. "I want to...I really do, but I can't. And what does it matter—you won't be here for long. Once you've solved your brother's mystery, you're gone." October stares me down.

I'm not scared, but I'm dying inside. Dying to say *I'm staying*. Dying knowing that the life I've been creating for six years is in *Chicago*.

It's not here.

It's not with her.

"I mean...that's fair." My voice cracks now, and I mutter again to myself, "That's fair." I look up. "But I don't want to go back to our rules. I want to understand what the hell is going on with you, and if you want more from me, then ask. I'll tell you absolutely *anything*."

October seems to ease. Just slightly. "My sister—she's begged me to tell her the whole story about my real curse. I won't. *I can't*." Those last two words come out choked.

"The only person who knows is your aunt?" I guess.

She winces. "Not by choice."

198

Not by choice.

What does that even fucking mean?!

Before I met October, I probably would have been satisfied with the microscopic bits of information she's providing. But she helped me become something more. Something better and stronger, and I'm not letting her suffer alone.

"Look," I whisper. "I'm not asking you to give me a play-by-play. But you're going to have to give me something. I can't go to sleep tonight with you in this room and all I know is that your curse in the museum is a fucking lie."

"Anything I tell you could put you in a lot of danger, Zoey. It's safer if you don't know."

"Stop protecting me."

"I can't!"

"Try!" We're both crying. "Let me join you, *please*." I step closer. "I don't like that you're on an island on your own...with your aunt."

She almost chokes on a laugh. "Zoey." My name sounds loving but pained on her tongue.

I step even closer. "October."

She doesn't break eye contact from me. "I can't tell you my curse. *I can't*. I'm sorry."

I stop cold. It's a swift kick to the gut. Raw from the inside-out, my chest hurts. Pressure and pressure compounding. Before I can say anything, she takes a step forward.

Not one but two.

Then three.

And then she's holding my hands. "It was the worst night of my life." Her voice is shaky, scared. More scared than I've ever heard her.

I lace her fingers in mine. "It's okay."

She takes a steadying breath. "I was on the lake, and I had to call my aunt for help. She came and...she helped. But she...she *insisted*

KRISTA & BECCA RITCHIE

that I keep my real curse a secret. And when my aunt insists on something, there's very little wiggle room. So she came up with this other story."

"About you drowning?"

October nods. "And when we started telling people, no one questioned it. Not when it's coming from Effie Brambilla."

I frown. "Except for Babette." She mentioned that her sister wants the whole story.

Her face shatters a little more. "My sister knows it's deeper than me drowning in a lake. She can tell I'm different." She drops my hands.

I wince.

She stays close.

We stay close.

That's good. We're still close. My throat feels raw and swollen as I ask, "So this whole *I'm a ghost* thing—?"

"Is true, Zoey." October crosses her arms around her body like she's trying to warm herself. "I died that night. Maybe I didn't drown, but I died. I'm not the same person as before."

"And you can't tell me everything that happened." I don't phrase it like a question this time.

"It'd be worse for you, if you knew." She looks pained again. "I told you as much as I can without feeling like I'm putting you in a compromising situation…" She swallows hard, then shakes her head. "I can't hurt you, Zoey. Please don't make me."

I'm so confused.

All I know is that she cares about me. I care about her, and that has to be enough amid the giant question marks popping out of my head.

"Okay," I breathe.

She shrugs off her coat now.

"You're warm?" I say, surprised.

"A little." She hangs the pink peacoat on the coat hook by the door. When she turns back, I realize I need something more. Or else my terrible imagination will haunt me in this haunted room all night long.

"Wait." I bite my lip in thought. "I just have one question and then I think—I think I'll be satisfied." It's not like she's purposefully keeping me and only me in the dark. She won't even tell her sister or Amelia, and in October's head, she's protecting all of us.

It's just who she is.

She looks me over. "What question?"

"So your curse isn't drowning," I say. "But did someone hurt you?" My chest constricts. Worry forming like a little ball under my ribcage.

She shakes her head. "No."

"Promise?"

"Promise." Her eyes flit around me. "Did someone hurt you? In Chicago, I mean. You never told me about your past relationships."

I shake my head. "My past relationship was nothing special. A snooze-fest, honestly. Plain. Dull. Kinda boring. It lasted longer than it probably should have." Three years. But I don't tell her that. I also don't speak his name out loud. *Ashton.* We work together, so the break-up morphed into a co-worker relationship, then an amiable friendship.

His texts about what I'm doing, where I am, have grown increasingly intense over these past days, and it's been distracting enough that I've debated about blocking him.

"Relation*ship*." Her brows rise. "Singular?"

"Just the one." I raise a shoulder. "You've probably been with more people in the past six years than me."

She doesn't deny.

Okay, that didn't feel as good as I thought it would. She was free to be with a million girls. No, a *billion*. She deserved epic love. Not to wither away and pine after me.

I should be tossing confetti knowing someone else out there probably loved October—probably still loves her, someone who's name definitely isn't Zoey Durand (oh God, do I stupidly love her)—but instead, my face is on fire.

Our eyes are still reddened from our tearful outbursts. And my throat is still scratchy as hell. And I end up rambling, "I mean, my story isn't that entertaining. I sort of fell into a comfortable rut. It lasted longer than it should've…so yeah, there's that." I clear my throat. "What about you?"

Her shoulders almost drop like she's…relaxing? Is she happy that I was only with one boring person?

Or maybe she's relieved I didn't kick her out of my hotel room. Maybe she thought that if I learned the truth (or the fact that she won't tell me the whole story), I'd push her away. But pushing October away feels a lot like banishing happiness. Can't do that, even if I tried.

"PJs first." October routes towards her duffel bag. "You're going to want to get comfortable for this."

"Or you're just dying to see me in my Millennium Falcon panties," I tease.

She tilts her head, curious now. "Is that a type of Star Wars bird?"

I burst out laughing.

She rolls her eyes. "I take that as a *no*." She grabs a musty pillow off the lumpy bed and aims for my face.

I duck and it lands on the floor. "I'm sorry." I hold a stitch in my side. "It's just that your bird-loving heart was so excited about this Star Wars bird. I almost feel bad."

"Almost?" She nears me, abandoning her search for pajamas.

"Almost," I breathe out. "But see, I can't feel that badly when October Brambilla, the goddess herself, shows some signs of being a mere mortal."

She stops a foot away. I have to look up since she's a bit taller. I don't mind that one bit. "You think I'm a goddess." Her voice is a whisper.

"I think you're gorgeous." My heart nearly bursts in my chest from this declaration and from our lips that inch nearer. A teasing breath away, and an ache catches in my throat.

She slips a piece of my hair behind my ear. "So are you." October peers into me like I'm made of heavenly, delicate things. And yet, I start shaking my head.

It's silly to think I could be on her level.

She rolls her eyes again. "I wish you could see yourself how I see you."

"Me? The girl with dry, damaged hair." I don't even know why *this* is my thought—maybe because she just touched my hair. Maybe because her glossy perfect locks splay over her shoulders in magnificent glory. To be a girl and love girls is a wondrous, complex thing. Because in one breath, I'm so *envious* of her. And in the other, I adore her. I want to join her fears and worries and happiness and joy. And while she tries to shield me from everyone's judgment, I want to be her companion and protect her from everyone's jealously.

She spools a tendril of my hair around her finger. "Your beautiful blonde hair," she says like she's defending me from…me.

I almost come undone right here.

Instead, I stand my ground. "My pointy chin that makes me look like a wicked witch."

Her palm falls to my chin in a tender caress. "The point is perfect," she tells me. "If someone calls you a witch, they need their eyes permanently fucking checked."

I laugh. "So my eyes need checked?"

"Your eyes," she says, more seriously than me. "You're the most beautiful thing in this ugly room, Zoey. If you can't see it, it's a good thing I'm here to remind you."

And that—that gets me. *It is a good thing you're here, Kenobi.*

My breath shallows, and my eyes fall to her lips. So close…so, so, *so close.* "Can I kiss you?" I ask, wanting that so badly. The intimacy. The love.

Her palm falls off my chin, leaving a biting cold. "I told you—"

"You don't deserve kisses or sex. Yeah, I remember. But the better question isn't whether you think you deserve it. It's whether you *want* it."

"Of course I do," she refutes. Her defenses rise abruptly. "Of course I want to fucking kiss you, Zoey. I've fucking imagined it ten million times since you've been back, but it's not good timing. You're leaving soon, and I promised myself that I wouldn't."

I'm leaving soon.

That reality still haunts me.

"Have you…" I start to ask, wondering if I should let the question die, but I press onward. "Have you kissed anyone in the past six years?"

She backs up a little. "Yes."

Okay. *Don't let that hurt.* Fuck, it hurts. "What about since you've been cursed?"

I expect a *no,* and she says, "Yes."

"What?" I squeak out. "But you won't…with me?" Pain. *Pain* is choking me out, and I inhale without exhaling.

"It meant nothing." Her eyes suddenly well. "They were just flings."

"Anyone…I know?" I hate how choked I sound.

"No." She shakes her head stiffly. "Most were out of towners…I was trying to feel something, and I couldn't." A tear slips out of her eye. She lets it fall. "I couldn't feel anything for the longest time. I was numb, and then here you are."

Here I am.

"And…?"

"And you make me come alive…you make me come alive in ways I do *not* deserve. And you're *leaving*." We're both trying our best to breathe. "I can't lose you again, Zoey."

"It doesn't have to be soon," I mutter, but I remember the museum today. Parry and I are making progress with the search. As soon as I find evidence of Augustine Anders, I should leave.

"It needs to be soon." She nods to herself. "The longer you stay here, the harder it's going to be to keep up your lie. That's what I need to tell you." She intakes a big breath and explains, "My aunt has continued to put her nose where it doesn't belong."

We fall into the distraction from heavier topics, and I hear all about the book event her aunt is throwing. Just to interrogate me.

"Okay…okay, so I don't go." I outstretch my arms. "Easy."

She shakes her head. "No, you have to go."

"Why?"

"Because my aunt wants me to convince you to come. At all costs. She even suggested…*canoodling*."

I snort. "Canoodling?" I laugh harder. "Wait, is she suggesting you fuck me to get me to go?"

"I don't know…maybe." October rubs her temple in distress. "It's not happening."

"You're not going to fuck me and manipulate me into attending a book signing for a fake book that I haven't written a sentence for?" I mockingly gasp. "What kind of evil monster are you? So unwilling to seduce me?"

"Sarcasm noted," she says pointedly. I swear she smiled a little bit.

"I'm glad. Though I am kind of bummed we can't *canoodle* anymore." I tilt my head while she gives me a look to *shut up.* "Is canoodling off the table?"

"The more you say the word *canoodling,* the more I'm ready to walk out the door."

"Wait, no," I call out. "Don't go without a canoodle."

She laughs at that.

"The ghost laughs." I've said those words before, but I love reminding her she's capable of such a thing.

October touches her lips like it's foreign to her. Her smile falters for a second before flatlining completely.

"I wish you could see yourself how I see you," I whisper to her.

Her eyes flit to mine. Tenderness flowing between us for a second.

I say, "Whole. Unbroken."

She blinks repeatedly like she's holding back tears. Then in a quick second, her armor reappears. Her shoulders lock. Her face goes cold. "We should change for bed." She grabs her pajamas and heads for the small bathroom.

My emotions bottle up. I want to help with whatever's going on with her, but I don't know how. We change separately, and when she returns to the bedroom in her cute pink silk pajama set, she beelines straight for her makeshift bed on the floor. My spirits deflate, and all hope for any *canoodling* being more than a joke vanishes completely.

Just as I'm about to shut off the lamplight, October speaks.

"See you in the morning, sweets."

Her voice is as silky as her PJs, and I fight off my ridiculous smile as I pull the cord to the lamp, shutting us into darkness.

CHAPTER 21

ZOEY DURAND

This fake book isn't going to write itself. That's the mantra I've repeated to myself every single day since October told me about the book event.

And every single day—I have written approximately zero words. Mantra sucks. Into the toilet it goes!

I'm not kicking myself too hard, since I did get shit done. Just not book shit. Instead, I spent the past week hunting down Augustine Anders. And isn't that why I'm here in the first place? I need to solve this mystery, not write a fake book that will never be published.

I searched phonebooks from nearby cities and scoured social media for any Augustine Anders. For as unique as her name is, the search results came up empty. I even tried variations of the name *Augustine Anderson, August Anders, Augustine Landers.* So far there's nothing. Yesterday, I begged the ferry attendant to give me ferry records, but she said they couldn't release them. I was pushy enough that she threatened to call Sheriff Carmichael.

Once October stepped in, the college-aged ferry attendant stumbled over her words—and not just because October is supremely hot. (Although, I wouldn't have blamed her.) She recognized October—knew of her family—and she mumbled, "I, uh, I can't…"

"Why not?" October questioned. "You won't get in any trouble. I'll make sure of it."

"I think I will…uh, you should go. Right now." She checked over her shoulder. Like someone was spying on us.

October pressed on, but the ferry attendant literally *ran*. She left her post, and October, with her eagle-eyes and single-minded mission was two-seconds from chasing this girl down—but I grabbed her wrist.

"Let her go. She's scared."

She made a peeved face. "We were practically poking her with a feather. We were *soft*."

"What do you want to do? Tie her up to a chair? Shine a flashlight in her eyes?"

"That's not a terrible idea." She was still searching for the ferry attendant!

"Okay, we're leaving." I adore October and her wolfish instincts, but I'd rather use them against the town council, not some college-aged girl who's just doing her job.

I realize I'm a shit buddy-cop or buddy-villain (I'm questioning what side of the law we're truly on)—but if Sheriff Carmichael showed up, the chances of only *me* being thrown in jail were high.

"Strange," October said to me on our way back to the Jeep.

"You think the ferry attendant is hiding something?"

"I think someone is telling her to be quiet. It's likely the town knows I'm helping you with your book." So people aren't opening up to October like we'd planned.

We weren't exactly discreet at the Lock Ceremony, but I can't wish for a redo. I *love* that October held my hand in front of the town. I *love* that they realize she's on my side and not theirs.

I waited at the Jeep for October to fish out her keys. "Why would the town council warn or threaten the ferry attendant? Why would

208

they think we'd go here if we were just inquiring about the history of Mistpoint?"

Our questions circled around the same theory. The town council is tricking Colt into believing this mystery girl actually exists. Anna Roberts told October to "drop it" and we're clearly not following demands.

So they're one step ahead of us and trying to hide their evil deed.

But we still have no concrete evidence. And in one week, I have zero new leads. Zero new words in the fake book. All dead ends.

Night has fallen. Clouds and fog shroud the stars, and I hoped to see a twinkling sky and constellations while I'm home. But the dark weather has been diabolical, basically warning me to *get the hell out, Zoey.*

If anything wards me away, it won't be a raincloud. That's for fucking sure. "Is it even customary to have a book event for a book that isn't finished yet?" I wonder as October drives me to the center of town tonight.

The event is in approximately thirty minutes. My palms are sweating, and I've had anxiety-inducing flashbacks to all my failed public speaking moments in high school. Even though my people-person skills have *vastly* improved since I was a teenager. And since I graduated college, I've actually been in the business of being personable. Enthusiastic. Flexible. *Adaptable.*

I might lack tact, but people sometimes find *honesty* refreshing. Though, in this situation, I can't be honest.

I need to be a giant liar.

"She's trying to catch you in a lie," October reminds me. "Are you...?" Her eyes flit to me, then the road. "Are you sweating?"

"Maybe just a little bit," I mumble under my breath, then waft the plaid blue blazer away from my perspiring, nervous body. I borrowed October's cute business attire that includes a matching plaid skirt. It reminds me of the movie *Clueless.*

I did not pack to impress her aunt, but I've seen October rock this outfit like she's fit to rule the world. If I can just channel a fraction of that, I'll be fine.

And I remind myself out loud, "I'm not a *horrible* public speaker."

"You aren't," October says adamantly, like there is no other truth.

"I can do this."

"You can."

"I'm actually kind of awesome."

"You are." October is smiling out at the road, and honestly, her smile does more than our pep talk. My lips begin to rise, warm affection melting inside me, and all my troubles are shoved hard to the wayside.

She's smiling because she cares about me. She doesn't want to see me fail. She let me borrow her outfit.

I inhale these comforting, loving sentiments, and I take an even bigger readying breath. "But maybe I shouldn't read any passages... because I have none to read."

"That's smart anyway. Just answer their questions vaguely. If someone asks, *what is your goal in publishing this book?* You'd say...?"

"I want to be a gazillionaire," I joke.

She shoots me a look. "Try to take this seriously."

I sigh. "Okay...I guess I want to publish a book about Mistpoint to highlight our best landmarks and bring in tourism."

"You guess?"

"Be more confident," I nod to myself. "Noted." I gather my hair in a messy bun. Burning up.

"You can do this," October reinforces. "Just remember the more you make fun of Mistpoint Harbor, the more my aunt will be offended. We don't need to cross her tonight."

"It will be hard not to default to that," I admit, "but I promise I am taking this super seriously. I mean, you brought baked goods. It doesn't get any more serious than that." The sweet scent of buttercream, caramel, and honey drizzle has been torturing me since I climbed into the Jeep. I peek at the delicious, mouth-watering cupcakes in the backseat.

Her hands tighten on the steering wheel. "I'm sure I'll be scolded for it."

I frown. "Your aunt didn't ask you to bring them?" I thought October was instructed to make them for the event, so I'm a bit shocked the baked goods are voluntary.

She shakes her head, eyes pinned to the road.

"So you made them for me?"

"For your event," she counters like I'm being silly.

"You made cupcakes for my fake book event," I tell her, unable to hide my growing smile.

"The event is real," she shoots back in a way that also says, *you're being absurd.* "Even if your book is fake."

"So you wanted me to have cupcakes at the *real* event for my *fake* book."

Her cheeks flush. "What are you getting at, Zoey?"

"I just didn't know ghosts could care. But this ghost seems to care a lot about this event of mine," I say into a shrug. "That's all."

October doesn't say anything for a long moment like she's trying to pick her words carefully. Finally, she says, "All events have to have sweets. It's just an understood thing."

My face hurts from smiling.

She glares at me. "You can stop."

"I can't though."

She rolls her eyes and swerves the car into a parking spot. My smile fades fast when I realize we're here.

THE LOCAL BOOKSHOP, OWNED BY EDGAR JOHNSON WHO no longer has a sense of smell, contains long rows and rows of hardbacks new and old. Most of the store dedicates itself to selling trinkets, homemade baubles, and then franchised merchandise. Marvel, DC, Harry Potter, Star Wars, The Fourth Degree, and Halway Comics merch take up a good portion of the store.

A handmade banner hangs ominously over a wooden podium. It reads: **LOCAL AUTHOR ZOEY DURAND BOOK EVENT!**

"What'd I get myself into," I mutter and accidently run right into Edgar's wife. Jasmine Johnson, a petite black woman with gray braids twisted in a cute bun. "Oh hi, Mrs. Johnson."

"You like it?" She must've seen me eyeing the banner. "Edgar made it himself. We didn't know the title of your book, so he had to improvise. He was so excited putting it up this morning."

"Looks great." I force an unsteady smile, feeling the sourness from guilt. "Thank you for all the trouble you've gone through; you didn't have to—"

"We're glad to. Edgar and I—we love hosting local events, you know that." She smiles warmly. "You'd spend hours over there in that chair when you were about eight. You remember that?" I watch her point to the worn leather chair, right near the shelves with Star Wars paperbacks.

Mrs. Johnson remembers me? As more than the daughter of the Mother Murderer?

"Yeah, I remember," I breathe. "I loved coming here early in the morning. When the fog wouldn't clear yet. It'd smell like coffee and morning dew and paper…" I trail off, realizing her husband can no longer *smell*. I add fast, "Not that smelling is that important. I mean, there are so many other things I love about this place…the chair— so comfy." I'm dying.

Where is October? I swing my head to the left. That's right—she left to go talk to her aunt. Which is great. She can't witness my demise.

Mrs. Johnson starts laughing. "Oh Zoey, you can talk about smelling the books. You won't hurt that old man's feelings. He lost his sense of smell, not his sense of humor."

I let out a laugh and end up smiling. "Thanks, Mrs. Johnson."

She wishes me good luck before wandering off to say hello to her friends. I'm suddenly reminded that not all the townspeople feed off the curses and Durand hatred. Some just generally enjoy living here.

At some point in my life, I did too.

I'm early to the event. October is busy placing the cupcakes on a glass cake tier, setting up the sweets table and trying to fend off her cousin Benny from eating everything.

Empty, fold-out chairs face the podium. I greet a few attendees as they enter, then do my best to avoid Effie Brambilla. Every time she locks eyes with me, I duck behind a different merch display. Right now, I'm huddled near a shelf of Gryffindor snow globes.

My strategy has worked thus far, but more people start to fill the bookstore—and I really shouldn't hide from *everyone*.

"Zoey."

I jump at Angela Brambilla's voice and sudden appearance right beside me. Jesus Christ. She finds me pretending to be interested in a superhero-themed cookbook. "There you are...did I scare you?"

"Uh...sort of..." I close the cookbook. "What's up?" *Be casual. Cool.*

She skirts over my awkwardness with a breeze. *Definitely a Brambilla.* "I have a question about your book. Who's the protagonist?"

"Um..." I rest an elbow on the shelf with the snow globe. "You know, that part is still in the brainstorming session."

She squints. "The protagonist?" Before I can get another word in, her face lights up. "That's perfect! Because I was thinking *I* could really be the star of the book—"

"Colt!" I suddenly spot my brother towards the back of the store. He's lingering next to a life-size cut out of the Mandalorian. My first instinct was to send out an audible SOS by yelling his name—great.

The chairs are now half-occupied, and the attendees can see part of my body through the shelves. I know this because I can see them. I'm not that big of an idiot.

And everyone is looking at me.

Ignoring the heat of their gazes, I wave my brother over. *What is Colt doing here?* It's late at night. I'd think he's supposed to be in the lighthouse. Especially since he hasn't left since the Lock Ceremony.

He doesn't move. Not even as I exude total desperation.

"Sorry, Angela." I'm about to excuse myself when she gasps at her cellphone.

"There are photos of her." She swipes through the pics. "Oh my God…"

"Who?" I hold my breath. It can't be Augustine Anders, can it? Angela doesn't even known about our search.

"Who?" Angela lifts her gaze. "Don't you know what's going on today?"

Is this a trick question? I answer with some confidence, "My book event."

"In the *world*, Zoey." She makes a disgruntled face. "Lily Calloway and Loren Hale are having a vow renewal ceremony. *Celebrity Crush* is posting pics of her dress. It's only been trending on Twitter all day."

I don't live under a rock. I did hear that arguably the most famous couple in the world would be renewing their vows, all after the FanCon tour abruptly ended. Their children are closer to our age, but the Hales, Meadows, and Cobalts became famous decades ago after a huge scandal with Lily Calloway. They aren't actors or anything.

Just really rich people.

The kind of wealth that doesn't even exist in Mistpoint Harbor.

"I've been preparing for my event, not scrolling through Twitter," I lie to Angela, but I do love that she's more interested in celebrities than Mistpoint gossip. While she's distracted, I slide past Angela and approach my brother in the stuffy back corner.

More hidden behind the podium and impatient attendees.

Colt is swigging from a flask. His body still gaunt. Hair unkempt. "Congrats, sis. What an accomplishment." With the flask in hand, he points towards the banner, barely visible from here. "I can't believe we're going to have an *author* in the family."

"I sense the sarcasm," I say dryly.

"You think?" He swigs again.

He knows my book is fake.

Parry must've told him, and I open my mouth to respond, only for my phone to buzz. My backpack-purse stands out amongst my plaid skirt and blazer, so I left it in the Jeep.

My phone is in my bra. Buzzing.

Colt sees the blinking light in my blouse, then rolls his eyes. "You answering that?"

"I wasn't going to." But it won't stop buzzing. I curse under my breath and dig into my blouse. Colt is neither amused nor salty. He seems curious at the mystery caller.

I tuck my phone closer to my chest as I peek at the texts.

Georgia: We really need you back this weekend.

Georgia: Spring Break rush is coming, then it'll be wedding season. We're fully booked the next two months.

Georgia: You said you would be gone for a couple days. Where did you even go?

Georgia: Ashton is trying to call you.

He did. Five times.

I switch my phone to mute. Not wanting to deal with Chicago right now. I'll text Georgia later and tell her that it might be another week.

"Angry boyfriend?" Colt guesses.

"No."

"Angry girlfriend?"

"No." I stuff my phone back into my bra. "That was just my coworker."

"Angry coworker," he muses into another hearty swig.

"Why are you even here, Colt?"

"Why else would I be here?" He swishes the flask, then tips his head like he's searching for someone behind me.

I look over my shoulder.

No one is there.

He's not okay.

I catch his gaze as he says, "I'm showing support for my only sister. Can't I do that?"

I nod a few times.

He rubs his exhausted eyes. "The better question is why you're back here talking to me."

"You know..." I motion to him. "Showing support for my favorite brother."

"Sure. Captain Obvious." His hands tremble a little as he grabs a pair of black Wayfarers that are hooked on his collar.

Concern throttles me. "Did you eat anything this morning?"

He ignores me, then looks toward the cupcake table. "I'm gonna have a quick chat with your girlfriend."

"What?" I balk. Then I shake out of that shock and say, "She's not my—"

"Just a quick chat," Colt cuts me off and slips on his sunglasses.

I gawk. "I'm single."

"I get that. But if you two are getting back together, I need to do my brotherly duties and ensure her intentions are pure or whatever."

My cheeks flame, and I lower my voice to a hiss. "We were never together, Colt."

He jerks his head to the side, flinching at no sound. Nothing. He rubs at the back of his neck, then mutters to me, "Yeah, right."

Okay, October and I were never officially girlfriends. We just… hung out. Flirted. Kissed. Hooked up a few times.

"Hey, we should be focusing on *you* here."

"Why? It's *your* book event."

"That's true," I mumble.

He flashes a tight smile. "I'll be on my way then, little Zo." He pats my shoulder like nothing in his life is amiss, and I wonder if I've become a good distraction for Colt. My return is helping him obsess a little less on the missing girl.

It reassures me. But maybe I'm just trying to convince myself that this was a good idea. Coming home.

Possibly staying longer.

And now Colt is headed for October.

"Colt. You are not—" My words are cut off by a screech from a microphone.

Oh God. I weave through a few shelves and roll to a complete stop when I see Effie Brambilla at the podium. And the *packed* audience. Not only is every chair occupied, but people are standing in the back, blocking the door to the store with arms crossed in defiance.

Like this is a town hall and they're prepared to air their grievances.

Colt saunters away to grill October. I can't follow him—as much as I want to.

Instead, Effie's intense brown eyes drill into me. "I'd like to welcome Zoey Durand to the podium."

Fuck my life.

CHAPTER 22

OCTOBER BRAMBILLA

Zoey approaches the podium with about as much enthusiasm as a wounded cat stepping into the rain. My heart nearly beats out of my chest. *You can do this, sweets.*

Babette watches beside me as she slowly unwraps her second honey cupcake. "She doesn't look that frightened."

"She looks terrified." My arms are woven over my chest, and I dig my nails into my palms to stop myself from rushing the podium and sweeping Zoey far away from the impending train wreck.

"She could be worse," Babette whispers optimistically to me. "She could be peeing herself. I'd say she's doing a fantastic job."

"At jumping over your lowest bar."

"The bar has to start somewhere, and I'm sending all my good vibes her way." She wiggles her fingers like she's made of magic.

Sometimes I do believe she is.

"OB."

No.

I tear my gaze from Zoey for a split-second to see her older brother. Colt has approached the cupcake table that Babette and I stand behind.

His tortured gaze is hidden behind dark-shaded sunglasses. "We should talk."

"Not now," I snap. Could he have picked a worse time? I'm trying to watch Zoey.

Babette appraises Colt with an up-down sweep. "What's with the shades?" She stuffs the remaining cupcake in her mouth. "You pretending to be cool or something?"

"I *am* cool, *Baby*," he says her nickname mockingly. "Brambillas just wouldn't know cool if it shoved you in a freezer."

I almost glare at him, but my little sister beats me to the staredown. "You come out of the lighthouse for like five seconds and you're already a dick?"

"I'm always a dick," he combats.

"Shut up," I tell him. "Your sister is about to speak."

Sure enough, Zoey taps the microphone. "Hello?" Her voice quakes.

Oh God. I can barely breathe. *She's going to be fine.* Babette wiggles her fingers and nudges my shoulder, trying to lift my spirits. I have faith in Zoey, but this whole charade has gone too far.

The room bathes in awkward silence, and then Zoey clears her throat and raises a hand. "Hi, um, my name is Zoey Durand. As most of you know, I'm writing a book about Mistpoint Harbor. Which is why you all are here." She claps her hands—a high-pitched static noise screeches through the amps.

I wince with everyone else, but not because my ears hurt.

People are still cringing and muttering as Zoey fumbles with the microphone. "Sorry about that. Technology, right?" She laughs at herself, the sound dying. "Anyway, um, the book—it's still in development, so I can't give too much away. You know…copyright. Publisher rules. All that good stuff."

I steal a quick glance at Aunt Effie. Her lips are pursed, and her whole demeanor reads *do not fuck this up for me.* My aunt doesn't want an event planning failure on her town council resume. Even if she's hoping to just catch Zoey in a lie.

LOVE & OTHER CURSED THINGS

Zoey waves a hand towards my aunt. "First off, I'd like to thank Effie Brambilla for putting this together and inviting me here today."

Aunt Effie produces a warm but manufactured smile. "Welcome, everyone. I'm thrilled you're as intrigued in Zoey's novel as I am."

The audience claps lightly.

Zoey catches my gaze, and I nod to her. *Keep going.* She takes a breath and continues, "Instead of a reading, since the book is currently in draft, I'll be taking questions."

Colt lets out an irritated noise. "Why the hell did she agree to this?" He's asking me quietly while snatching a cupcake.

For me, is the real truth.

To be on my aunt's good side, is the answer I should give him. But I'm not entertaining him right now. I wish he'd shut up and let me be Zoey's cheerleader.

"Any questions?" Zoey asks with some confidence.

She's okay.

She has this.

Benny rises from the audience. "What is your book about? Can you give us a summary?"

Zoey smiles. "Great question, Benny. Unfortunately, that's classified information. The publisher doesn't want me to share any summaries yet."

Decent reply.

Benny is glaring. "Okay, then how do we know you're going to accurately depict Mistpoint Harbor? And shouldn't you have gotten permission from the town?" Grumblings and angry whispers fill the audience.

Aunt Effie steps forward. "One question at a time, please."

I'm sure she wants to give Zoey an opportunity to answer every question. My aunt is gathering information like it's made of gold.

Zoey taps the podium. "You know, I didn't think I'd have to get permission from the town because I'm not using real names. Everyone here will be given an alias."

That causes *way* more whispers.

My gaze is darting to every moving mouth and side-eye. I glower at them, as if I can do *anything* from over here.

"What if I don't want an alias?" Angela whines from her seat.

Aunt Effie tries to hush the audience again, and while the whispers grow, Zoey forces a shaky smile and Colt turns back to me.

"Go away, Colt."

He's still here. "So you and my sister are a thing again?"

"What?" I peel my gaze away from Zoey. "No." *Fuck, that hurts.* I wish it didn't. The truth is, I want to come alive with Zoey. I want to stop punishing myself, and maybe I never will.

Maybe I never can, but I don't want to keep hurting her.

Hurting us.

My ribs constrict around my lungs with each sharp breath, and I remember all week how Zoey has tried to reach me. She'd say things like, *"You can keep pushing me away, or you can realize that we're two undeserving girls who deserve each other."*

Her way of saying, *you deserve me, Kenobi.*

Even if I believe that, it doesn't change the fact that Zoey won't be in Mistpoint Harbor for much longer.

Colt frowns at me. "No?"

"She's leaving town after she solves *your* mystery."

"My mystery?" He lets out a dry sound, then whispers, "I didn't ask her to come here, OB."

"No. Your best friend did that all on his own," I grit out hotly. I'm boiling. Furious that I'm falling for Zoey again, and she's just going to leave. Angry with myself because I don't want this to end now, even knowing this will be short-lived. Even knowing that *pain* lies in the wings. Ready for me once she's gone.

Colt whispers, "But if she stayed—"

"She's not staying," I snap. Even putting that option into the air is cruel. Because it won't happen. It can't. And dreaming about a reality where it does paves an even greater pathway to pain.

At least let me spare my heart a *teaspoon* of agony.

"How long will you be in Mistpoint for research?" I tune into the Q&A as another one of my cousins questions Zoey.

"There is no strict time limit. It could be a few days or a few weeks." *Please be weeks.*

"Don't you have a deadline?"

"Yes…" She draws out the word. "But the publisher is willing to work with me." She sounds cagey but confident. Everyone begins to shout again.

"When's the publishing date?!"

"You really can't tell us anything about the book?!"

"Read the first page!"

"Shh, one at a time! One at a time!" Aunt Effie tries to settle down the crowd.

I focus back on Colt, just as he tosses my perfectly good cupcake into the trash.

How dare he. I'm a heartbeat away from calling him a jackass.

But he's…uneasy, bothered by something—a noise, I think. He touches his ear. Maybe the chaos of muddled voices is disturbing him. And I realize he didn't purposefully chuck the cupcake to piss me off.

Colt notices I'm studying him, and he forces a salty smile. "As her big brother, I need to remind you that if you hurt her, I will come for you."

Babette leans over the table. "As October's sister, I need to remind you that if you come for my sister, you're going to be dealing with *me*."

I interject coldly, "No one is coming for anyone," and I try my best to concentrate on Zoey as she answers a few more easy questions.

My sister's phone pings. "Shit, I forgot to put it on silent." She slips the cell out of her purse and reads a text. "Hank wants to meet up for lunch tomorrow."

"The forty-year-old?" I whisper. *Babette.*

"Fifty."

"Excuse me, what?" Colt hears and makes a face. "You're not dating a fifty-year-old."

Babette glares at him. "Since when do *you* have a say in my love life or what I can and cannot do. And for your information, it's not a date. It's a platonic lunch."

"You two are going alone though," Colt assumes.

"Yeah."

"So it's not platonic."

Babette stares him down. "It's platonic. So platonic that you can come with and see for yourself."

"Fine," Colt says into a swig from his flask. "Text me the details."

"I don't have your number."

Colt grabs a Marvel pen from a bookshelf and then looks to me. "Your arm."

My brows arch. "My arm?"

"Yeah, I'm not touching Baby."

Babette seems a little surprised that he'd either remember her aversion to touch or that he's respecting her wishes. Her lips part, and she's lost for words.

"I have your number, Colt," I remind him. "I can text it to my sister."

"Right." He puts the flask back to his mouth, then side-eyes the bookshelf. He blinks hard too many times. He seems drunk.

"Are you alright?" Babette asks.

"No, I'm not alright. Isn't that what you all want to hear? That I'm losing my fucking mind?" His voice rises, and the chairs creak as the audience shifts and ogles Colt.

"Um." Zoey speaks into the microphone, her concern on her brother. "Any other questions?" She tries to draw attention off him.

Aunt Effie struts over to me while the Q&A continues. She tries to grip my elbow like I'm twelve, but I jerk out of the hold and glare.

She recoils a little but lifts her chin and whispers, "This is a shit show."

"You did put Zoey on the spot." We watch Zoey vaguely respond to a question about the length of the book.

Aunt Effie takes a steadying breath. "Yes, well, maybe so. But it's not my reputation she's ruining. If she wants to dig a bigger grave for the Durands, then so be it." She pauses for a second. "This book...she really has a publishing deal in New York?"

"Of course she does," I say coldly. "She has an English degree from a university in Chicago. It's been her goal to be a writer. She wouldn't make it up." Why am I lying for her? *Because you love her, you idiot.*

"I believe you, October," Aunt Effie says quietly. "It's her I don't trust." And then she slips away and furtively whispers to another relative.

A guest asks, "What points of interest will be included in your book?"

"The most popular spots," Zoey answers with more ease. "The Museum of Curses & Curiosities, Harbor Perk, the Wharf—"

"Your dad's shitty bar," Benny adds into a cough in his fist. When he catches my glare across the bookstore, he shakes his head at me like *I'm* the fool for dipping into the Durand pond.

"That shithole is a Mistpoint staple, so *yes*, Benny, that'll be included," Zoey bites back, and I'd smile for Zoey if her brother wasn't stewing in front of me.

Colt pockets his flask. "What's wrong with the Pelican, Benny?"

"Your sister literally just called it a shithole, man. It is what it is."

"Colt," Zoey warns as her brother detaches himself from the sweets table and approaches the audience.

"Yeah, *Colt*," Benny says, a little on edge. "Go home. Eat a donut. You don't look good."

"What's your problem?"

"What's *my* problem?" Benny scowls. "You're coming at me."

"You're sitting there, coughing into your fist like you're fourteen not twenty-nine. Show my sister some fucking respect. She's writing an American classic—"

"*Colt.*" Zoey is beet-red.

"—but you'd rather poke fun at her like she's a monkey in a cage, and she's not going to do whatever you tell her to!"

"Ah, fuck you, man!" Benny shouts, on his feet now. "I've done nothing wrong! You're losing it! Stop embarrassing your sister— don't you think your dad has already done that enough?"

"Stop talking about my sister," Colt grits out.

"You brought her up!"

"This isn't good," Babette whispers beside me, and then Colt barrels towards Benny.

Guests spring from their seats, avoiding the collision between the two men. Zoey's brother decks my cousin, and they brawl over the fold-out chairs. Crunching them beneath their pushes and shoves and rageful fists.

"COLT!" Zoey yells and bangs the gavel to the podium. "Stop fighting!"

Aunt Effie clutches her chest like she's experiencing a first-class heart attack. No one can split them apart and end the fight, and I can't just stand here and gawk.

With urgency, I go to Zoey.

"October," she says as I stand at her side. She flinches as Colt pounds a fist into Benny's face. He's rolled on top of my cousin.

"Give me." I take the microphone from her hand. "If everyone would calm down, I have a secret to share." My voice booms throughout the bookstore, and the shouting morphs into muffled muttering. Curious glances meet me and Zoey. I repeat the words again, and Colt and Benny stop throwing punches.

Zoey's brother stands off of my cousin, whose mouth is bloodied, and Colt dazedly backs away and spins towards the podium. Confusion in his glazed gaze.

"That's right," I say with little inflection. "I have a secret that none of you know. Wouldn't you *really* like to know why Zoey is here?"

Zoey looks horrified. "*October.*"

CHAPTER 23

ZOEY DURAND

What is she doing? If she thinks exposing our search for the missing girl will help Colt—I don't know how! These people are more secretive than October, and they'll just continue to safeguard *everything*. We need to be covert, not show our asses.

Fuck, fuck, *fuck*.

October isn't relenting. Is she on a power trip? Her threatening eyes are eating the souls of the audience, and I'm wilting beside her like a frightened deer. Mount me on the wall! I'm fucking done for.

"I would like to know why Zoey's here." Antler Queen Anna emerges from behind a bookshelf. Has she been at the book event this whole time?

"It isn't to write a book?" Effie questions, her hand cemented to her heart.

October slips me a single, brief look that says, *trust me*. Of course I trust her—how could I not? And so I don't stop October as she speaks into the microphone. "She is writing a book."

What? I try to mask my confusion, but it's fucking hard.

"But it's not focused on the history of Mistpoint Harbor. It's a memoir about us." Whispers gather. "About our love story."

Our love story. My heart skips a measure, and I rest my eyes against October's sentimental gaze. She blinks away the softness to address the crowd. "We used to be together in high school. I've always had feelings for Zoey, and she's recounting our time here."

Effie is stunned.

I'm stunned. October Brambilla just told the most important people in town that we used to be together. That she's had *feelings* for me.

"Holy shit," her cousin Isabella says with a laugh. "I knew the rumors were true."

Colt—my brother.

He's smiling at me. He nods to me like I chose a good apple. A good person. Like October *loves* me how I deserve to be loved, and without a word or glance, Colt drifts out of the bookstore. No one even notices his departure.

October has everyone entranced. "I asked Zoey not to tell anyone what the book is truly about—and I'm sorry if you found her insincere. She is a horrible liar."

I let out a laugh. Jesus, she is a *great* liar. So good that I even believe we've been in Mistpoint just to write our love story.

"Why didn't you want us to know, OB?" Benny questions, using balled paper napkins to soak up his bloody lip.

I think about the real answer. How October probably *just* thought about this ploy. How I was the one with the fake book. I didn't intend to include her in the lie.

I didn't intend to grow so much closer to her while I've been back.

October lifts the microphone to her mouth. "You're all nosy."

Some people scoff.

Some laugh.

She hardly bats an eye. "And I'd rather you stuck your nose in the history of the town than the history of my love life." She cocks a brow. "But *this* interrogation is too much. So now you have answers, and you can leave Zoey alone." She passes the microphone to me, our hands brushing, and I sense the audience scrutinizing our interactions *way* more than before.

My heart is racing.

"Anything you'd like to say, Zoey?" Anna Roberts, one of the most prominent members of the town council, asks me.

"Um, yeah." *I'm in love with October Brambilla.* The microphone is sweaty in my grip. "All I can say…is that this book about me and October—it'll be a *good* reflection of the town. For how much you all seem to despise my family, I still love Mistpoint Harbor. I had my first kiss here. With October at the fishing pier." More whispers. "I guess you'll read about that at some point."

October is smiling at the floor.

My heart is floating towards her. "I dreamed about this place every day I was gone."

I speak more to October. "And being back isn't nearly as awful as everyone makes returning out to be—"

"What the fuck?!" Angela screeches, springing to her feet. "Oh my God. Check Instagram. Check Instagram!"

As more people whip out their phones, Brambillas begin freaking out like a meteor shower is headed for Earth.

"Uh?" I scrunch my face at October.

She whispers, "I have no idea."

Angela is wafting her face, a second shy from hyperventilating. "I can't believe they're together. They're kissing. Did anyone predict this?"

October turns off the microphone in my hand. "This has to be about the vow renewal." *Hales, Meadows, Cobalts.*

"Right." I can tell October is interested. She discreetly checks Instagram before slipping her phone in her pocket.

I smile at her.

"What?" She acts like the celeb gossip isn't newsworthy, but she seems giddy.

"Okay, tell me," I say as I dig my phone out of my bra.

"Maximoff Hale just posted a selfie. He's kissing his bodyguard."

"He called him his lover!" I hear Angela squeal. "That means they're dating. They're totally together."

"Who's his bodyguard?" I ask October and think back to the FanCon in Chicago, trying to recollect if I caught a glimpse of Maximoff Hale's bodyguard. Was he the super tall bodyguard or the bleach-blond one?

She peeks at her phone. "Someone named Farrow Keene."

"What the hell is Jane Cobalt wearing at the vow renewal?" someone says. "She looks like My Little Pony."

October shoots a glare. She's a diehard Jane Cobalt defender, of course I remember.

Now would be a great time to tell October that I bought tickets to the FanCon—that I attended the meet-and-greet and Q&A.

But as soon as I unmute my phone, about to pop up Instagram—I see a dozen missed texts from Georgia and even more from Ashton.

"Shit," I curse. "I have to…I'll be…" I make no sense while I scroll through the shouty caps texts. "I'll be back." I wander away, hoping the event is now officially over. From my stammering answers, to the brawl, to October's big bold lie (that I secretly love)—it's gone off the rails. As expected.

I meander into the storage room and plop onto a couple big boxes of hardbacks. And glaze over the shouty texts.

Ashton: STOP BEING LIKE THIS. ANSWER ME GODDAMMIT

Why is he being such an ass? I send a quick reply. I'm fine. Stop texting me. I've been talking to Georgia.

I also message Georgia and give her more info and an apology. How I think I'll be another week and she's a lifesaver.

Done. I stuff my phone back into my blouse and find myself slumping forward. Face buried in my hands. My head dipping down.

Chicago is catching up to me. I built a life there...

I hear the door creak.

I lift my head out of my knees. "Kenobi?"

"It's just me." October is carrying a tray of cupcakes and takes a spot on the box of books beside me. She balances the tray on her lap.

They're the most *perfect* cupcakes I could ever conceptualize. Not with plastic, wax-looking frosting, but fluffy cream and expertly drizzled caramel. Something meant to be eaten. Not just stared at, which is why she whispers, "Take one."

I replay the book event. How it didn't go as planned at all, and I don't make a move for the cupcake.

Her face nearly breaks. "Zoey?"

"You had to come to my rescue," I say quietly.

"I'm sorry. I should've let you handle it yourself."

I end up smiling softly. "The funny thing is that I like when you pull me from quicksand, Kenobi. You've always been good at that. My Jedi Master."

She rolls her eyes.

I want to laugh, but I'm sullen.

"Why do you look so down?" October wonders. "The book event wasn't that terrible."

I snort. "My brother beat up your cousin."

"They believe our memoir."

"Our love story," I correct, and I watch her fingers inch towards mine. I splay my fingers over October's knuckles, and our hands curl together. *She's not pulling away from me.* I breathe in. "If I could actually write worth a damn, this is the book I'd want to be written."

Her eyes glass. "Me too." She blinks away some emotion, then picks up a cupcake. "You really don't want this?"

"Me? Only a fool could ever reject your cake and cookie." I wear a smartass smile.

She rolls her eyes at the sexual innuendo, then lightly taps the cupcake to my lips and pulls away. "Taste test."

I laugh and run my tongue over the frosting on my lips. "Buttercream," I say wistfully. "My favorite." *She knows it's my favorite.*

She scoops some frosting on her finger and gives me a stronger, more commanding, more loving look that'd buckle my weak knees if I were standing. A heady breath escapes my opened lips. "Kenobi…"

"Open."

I part my lips even wider, and she slips her finger into my mouth. I close my lips around her, sucking off the sweet cream.

I keep sucking even after the frosting is gone. Our bodies fit closer, magnetized to each other. Knees and limbs tangle up together. I keep a hand on her wrist, and her fingers clasp the back of my head.

Arousal and affection spins around us like a tornado. When she slips her finger from my lips, I hear my shallow breath. I claw towards October.

She seizes my cheeks. Resisting. Desiring. Dreaming of what we could be. "Zoey," she breathes.

I am hers.

She is mine, captivated by the grip I have on her heart—and finally, she kisses me. Her soft lips crash against my lips, and years and bottled love *explode* out of us. I feverishly clutch onto October's slender arms, my lungs flooding with quick, overwhelming emotion.

She tastes sweet like sugar. Her soft hands stay on my cheeks, guiding the kiss into a strand of sensual, aching things.

I've missed this—how she kisses me with drawn-out, hot moments. Like one second should last an absolute eternity. Strung with a delicate kiss onto a sweltering kiss onto a hungered can't-catch-your-breath kiss. Until a bracelet of kisses is beaded and clasped around our frames.

Our tongues tangle, our bodies meld, and our lips ghost each other before we go in again.

And again.

I claw forward, lips stinging.

In the next break, October drinks me in, whispering against my lips, "You're so eager."

"You're everything to me." I'm tortured at the possibility of short-lived moments, and I kiss her with greater desperation. With louder love.

October clutches fiercer, kisses harder, and then she pries her lips off my lips. I can't catch my breath. Her hair looks wild from where I grabbed. She's a soft kisser. Not as aggressive as me.

I blush and say, "I'm needy."

She laughs like I'm the cutest thing ever. "I've loved how you've needed me."

We kissed. She kissed me.

I'm in a post-kiss haze. "You're a great kisser, October…always have been."

"You are too, you know." October stares at my lips, then she begins to smile. Soon, she shakes her head at herself. Her smile fades.

"What?" I frown too.

"Kissing you makes me feel things."

"Good things?"

"Things I'm going to miss," she clarifies. "That's all."

My shoulders droop, and I lick my lips, almost able to feel October on them. Almost able to imagine her hands seizing my face with a type of unabashed love people dream of. "You asked me before why I looked so down." I whisper, "I'm sad because Chicago is breathing down my neck."

"You have to go back," October says, doesn't ask. "Don't think about staying."

It hurts. I thought she'd beg me to stay after we just kissed. I try to breathe easier. "What if I want to stay?" *For you. For all the people I love.*

They're here.

"You'll be cursed." Her voice is pure ice.

"So—"

"So it's safer in Chicago, and what about your job, Zoey?" Her eyes plead with me to choose Chicago.

I want to choose her. "It's just a job."

"That's not what you said on the phone."

I blow out a heavy breath. "What'd I say?"

"You don't remember?" She's disbelieving. "You talked my ear off for *two hours* when they hired you."

"I did do that, didn't I?" I smile a little, only because I liked our phone calls. They weren't frequent. We texted more often.

"I could practically feel you grinning," October says quietly. "Zoey Durand, assistant manager of a five-star luxury hotel in the heart of Chicago. A six-figure salary with—"

"Great benefits," we say together.

I smile weakly. "Yeah, it's a really good job."

"Better than anything you can find in Mistpoint."

Isn't that the sad truth. I left this town for more opportunities. A better life. I scraped up the money for college, and when I landed an academic scholarship in Chicago, my future seemed to fall into place. Why stay in Mistpoint Harbor?

For what?

For who?

Her.

"I should've stayed for you," I say tearfully, my voice cracking. "I should've chosen you, Kenobi."

She stares into me. Always intense, always unafraid, even of the things that scare her the most. "I'm glad you left. You needed to go. You *wanted* to go."

"I wish I hadn't."

"You wouldn't be who you are if you'd stayed. You'd be someone else, and I haven't been falling back in love with Zoey Durand from six years ago. I'm falling in love with the woman you are now. Today."

A tear slips from my eye. "I really love you, October Brambilla. I think I've always loved you. I think I never stopped, not a single day in my life."

She wipes away my tear, and she places the most gentle, tender kiss on my cheek. And as our eyes latch for an intoxicating beat, I whisper, "Would you ever leave Mistpoint Harbor for someone?"

"If I loved them enough, yes."

I light up.

Her face twists, then hardens to stone. "That was *before*. Before my curse. I'm not prepared to leave this town. I'll stay here for the rest of my life, Zoey. Nothing and no one can change that."

I sink into the shattered hope.

If our love story were an actual book, I'm afraid it wouldn't have a happy ending.

CHAPTER 24

ZOEY DURAND

He broke into my apartment. Ashton is claiming I gave him a key, but I moved into a different apartment after we broke-up. With new keys, new locks.

And who takes photos of themselves rifling through their friend's shit while the friend is away? He texted me pictures where he's throwing my stuff onto my bed. Asking if I need anything. If I forgot anything.

I told him to stop contacting me. I'm fine. I have everything I need. Get out of my apartment.

I'm ignoring him. Like if I don't look at my phone, maybe Chicago doesn't even exist at all.

Clouds descend, an angrier storm brewing in the distance. I thought that the hardest thing would be that stupid book event I had to stumble through, but it's been three weeks since that day. And October fortified my cover story with a more believable one, so I'm no longer worried Effie Brambilla will book a flight to New York just to sniff out our lie.

My true concern doesn't even lie with Chicago drama.

It lies with my brother.

Not the one I'm helping, but the older, grouchier one.

Brian busies himself around The Drunk Pelican, mostly by bringing in outdoor furniture. Preparing for the nightmare storm. Skies already resemble nighttime and it's only the early evening. Winds howl and thrash against the windowpanes.

October is helping Fisherman's Wharf lock down for the bad weather, and I'm still not invited into the "enemy" establishment.

With only Parry here, Brian hasn't bunt-kicked me out of the bar. He needs the extra hands, and I've been tasked with window duty. Which quickly turned to "bucket" duty when the light rain started.

I set a second bucket on the bar, a steady drip of water trickling from the ceiling.

Brian kicks the door closed and drops two large patio umbrellas on the ground. "That should be the last of it." His eyes lock on mine. "This would be the best time for you to get out of town, Zoey."

I'm currently standing on the bar, squinting at the hole in the ceiling and wondering if I can fix it. That plan suddenly fizzles in my head.

"I'm not finished yet."

"The bar looks great."

I gape. "Not with the bar—"

"You still haven't been cursed," Brian cuts me off. "You don't want to be here for the storm."

No, *he* doesn't want me here for it.

There's a difference.

He saunters towards the windows to double-check my work. *Great.* He doesn't even trust me to do a decent job.

Pots clank in the kitchen. Parry is storing all the food. The Pelican will be closed for the rest of the night.

"I'm not leaving yet. It might take another week—"

"That's what you said *three* weeks ago," he cuts me off *again* and then adds a glare. "I understand you want to help Colt; I do, but at what cost?"

I can't believe Parry told him why I'm here. But he did after Brian's concern kept growing day after day I stuck around. Parry caved a couple days ago. Then again, I think Parry thought it'd ease Brian's worry. It just doubled his irritation.

"We're getting close," I lie.

It's been almost a month, and the only solid lead we've found is from the first week when Parry and I concluded that Augustine Anders can't be a local. We still think the town council is acting suspicious, but there is still *zero* proof.

Truth be told, I'm shit at this whole Nancy Drew stuff. I don't think I can solve a mystery if the culprit pulled down his pants in front of me. But I'm trying.

I'm trying. I have to.

Brian stares at me like he can see through the lie, but he surprisingly doesn't call me on it. Instead, he says, "Colt will be just as messed up if you do figure this all out *and* get cursed in the process."

I honestly didn't consider that.

"He'll be fine."

Brian huffs, then shakes his head. "That kid loves you."

Kid. As though Colt is so young. He's almost thirty, but I guess to Brian, we're all just *little.* I still can't believe he's almost forty.

Time...

How much more am I going to lose when I leave again?

Forever.

A cold gust of wind knocks open a window. "Fuck," Brian curses. I jump off the bar and help him latch it shut.

"Thanks," he mutters.

I step back from the window, closer to him now. Tension between us isn't the fun kind. It feels awfully strained. Like I screwed up our brother-sister relationship beyond repair just by leaving Mistpoint. Even being here hasn't helped much. I don't like being at odds with Brian.

"I know that I'm testing fate," I admit. "And I…financially can't be here for more than a couple more days, so you can rest easy. Kelly is gouging me at the Harbor Inn." I've stayed *way* longer than I intended at the B&B. My savings have been depleted and without a job here, I'll be meeting some credit card debt when I'm back in Chicago.

Not to mention, my perfect, *amazing* job is dangling on a thin string. I had a lengthy talk with my boss, the general manager and head of the hotel, who said if I'm not back by the end of the week, my position won't be waiting for me. He's already been extremely lenient. Most would've already axed me, but Hank has said he has a soft spot for me.

He's also from a small town. Started with nothing. He wanted me to succeed. Even become the general manager one day.

I can't imagine a better boss. And being fired from one of the best luxury hotels in Chicago will put an ugly stain on my resume. I've already told them there was a death in the family. And yeah, I can't believe I lied about someone dying, but to make myself feel better, I've convinced myself that the dead relative is Ghost October.

She's figuratively dead.

So there.

Brian huffs again. "You know I don't feel good about you rooming there."

"Then why haven't you offered me a job?"

"Because you're *not* staying." He glares back, but it softens suddenly as something clicks in his head. "Unless *you've* changed your mind about that?"

Her face enters my mind for a split-second. *October.* I push that thought aside swiftly.

"No. *No*," I say, trying to stay adamant, but my heart is gripping to Mistpoint Harbor. "I'm still leaving once I make sure Colt is okay."

He grumbles something under his breath and collects the billiard balls and cue sticks from the old shabby pool table. He's been conceptualizing all the ways I can possibly die like we're in the movie Final Destination.

I highly doubt an eight-ball will magically fly at my face and knock me dead.

But I'm done arguing. He's on a mission and secures the sticks and billiard balls behind the bar.

I frown. "Why aren't *you* helping Colt?" Anger suddenly surges. "He's your brother, too."

"There's nothing I can do for Colt," Brian says like he's already made up his mind.

I suck air through my nose. Wind roars louder. The door to the Pelican bangs open, and at first I blame another strong gust, but then I see our brother.

Bedraggled hair. Sleepless, bloodshot eyes. Colt looks worse than the last time I saw him half-drunk in the lighthouse. Muttering "Augustine" to himself and "I'm sorry"—when he burst out crying, I didn't know what to do. I just knelt with him while he wept on the dirty floor.

But now, he's not crying.

He approaches Brian with purpose and fury like he *is* the storm coming to wreak havoc.

My brother, the hurricane.

"Give me the keys to your catamaran," Colt demands, hand outstretched towards Brian.

Brian gawks like Colt has eaten a bag of crayons. "It's about to storm and you want my boat keys?"

"Do I need to repeat myself?" Colt snaps.

"Yeah, because you're not making fucking sense!" Brian yells.

"BOAT! KEYS!"

"Whoa…" I sidestep in between them, worried fists might be thrown. "There might be a reasonable explanation for this." I eye Colt, hoping he can give one.

Brian glares. "No, Zoey. There's no reasoning with him."

Colt grimaces and yanks at his own hair. "Fuck you, man. You hide out in this shithole thinking you're better than me—"

"I don't. I never did! But if you start sailing out into fucking lightning and deathly winds, yeah, I'm gonna start thinking I have a bigger brain than you."

The kitchen door whirls open. "What the fuck is going on?" Parry half-jogs out, seeing Colt and Brian squared off. Me, in the middle.

"I need Brian's catamaran keys," Colt explains like it's a simple request. He snaps his fingers at Brian. "Right now. Give them."

"Fuck off," Brian spits out, pointing at Colt. "Go take a nap in the booth. Drink some water—"

"Screw you—"

"Why?" Parry interjects. He's asking Colt. "Why do you need his boat now?"

"Good question," I say tensely.

Colt throws up his arms. "I'm going to go find her. Okay?"

Her. Augustine Anders.

My eyes grow. "Right now?"

"In the storm?" Parry frowns.

"It's been over four months," Brian snaps. "Give it up."

Colt tries to swing. I'm still in the middle, but much shorter. Brian pushes me aside so that I avoid impact with Colt's knuckles, but I end up slamming into the pool table, the edge catching my hip, and then I trip and fall hard on the uneven floorboards. Knees searing.

Shit.

Colt's fist connects with Brian's cheekbone.

"Hey!" Parry pushes himself in between my brothers. He shoves Colt back up into a booth. "What are you doing, man?"

"What are *you* doing?" Colt questions. "Protecting *Brian*. Like he needs your protection? Like he gives a fuck—"

"Cut it out," Brian sneers, then looks around. My breathing heavies, and when Brian spots me on the floor, he kneels quickly. "Zoey?" Concern and guilt wrap up in his eyes.

"I'm okay."

"You sure?"

I see the red welt on his face. "You're the one who got hit."

"I didn't mean to push you that hard," he explains.

"I'm okay," I say again, and he helps me to my feet.

"I've been trying to protect *you*," Parry emphasizes to Colt. "C-c-ccan't you see that?"

Colt nods repeatedly, eyes welling. "Pear, it feels like the same weather patterns. Maybe if I just sail to the point where I saw her—"

"You'll get yourself fucking killed," Parry snaps. "That's what you'll do."

"I need this!" Colt screams.

"You need t-t-t-t-to get a fucking hold of yourself!" Parry yells back.

I watch my brother break. Unravel. His body concaves, face in his palms. If he was made of thread, he'd be frayed all over, a single string left supporting him.

I breathe deeply. "This isn't going to work, Colt. Wait until the storm is over and then we can go out."

Silence.

Nothing but the thrashing rain against the roof and the clattering shutters against the windows.

Not until Colt says, "No." His bloodshot gaze lifts to no one in particular. "If Brian doesn't give me the keys, I won't be at the lighthouse tonight."

"During the storm?" Parry frowns. "You wouldn't leave your responsibility like that. I know you."

Colt's eyes seem blank. Gone. Lost. "Maybe you don't know me anymore, Pear."

Coldness ekes into the bar. Brian shakes his head. "The catamaran hasn't been out past the breakwall in years. Even if I agreed to your suicide mission, you wouldn't make it far."

Colt goes quiet.

In his silence the front door blows open once more, this time it's the wind. Heavy rain accompanies the howling, and then a girl in a pink raincoat sprints into the bar.

October spins and forces the door closed. Brian is quick to help her latch the lock. When she pulls her hood back, butterflies flap inside my body. *God, she's pretty.* Brown hair a little damp from the storm, October turns around, searching for me.

I catch her gaze. "I thought you had to be at Fisherman's Wharf?"

"I left early." She saunters over to me like she needs to be near. "I had to see you."

I almost ask *why*. But I know the answer.

The hair-raising conditions outside are the worst I've seen since I've been in Mistpoint, and I'm not cursed yet. My brother is just as worried, but October is the one hellbent on protecting me. Her hand slips against my cheek just as a strike of lightning cracks the sky.

Lamps and the old holiday lights flicker but stay lit.

And then I steal a kiss. Brief. Fleeting, but she lets me press my lips to her lips. Since the bookstore, October has kissed me more than once. Each one feels like an epic goodbye kiss. Clingy and desperate.

I think the clingy is me. The desperation is her.

Together, we're just a gooey mess. "Like underbaked sfogliatella," she told me last week. I hate to think we're an inedible pastry because I'd totally still eat October out. I even said those words out loud.

"Not before I do," she replied like there is no humanly way I'd kiss between her legs before she'd kiss me there.

Now, in the bar, I'm clinging to another kiss. She's desperate against my lips. Light flickering again, and then a fist pounds the door.

"Hello?! Is anyone here?!"

We break away.

"Is that Baby?" Colt asks.

October is rushing to the entrance. Brian follows, and in seconds, they've unlatched the door and October's younger sister races into the bar. They slam the door shut again.

"Ah, my gloves are soaked." Babette peels them off with her blue raincoat.

"I'll start a fire," Colt says quietly, gathering wood from a bin. He mans the old wood burning stove in the corner.

Brian is staring at him like he's morphed into a new person. He looks to Parry for answers, who mouths *Baby*.

I can't keep up. October returns to my side with her sister.

"Zoey," Babette greets with an air-hug. She's out of breath.

"Did you run here?" I wonder.

"Two miles. I fell twice." She peels wet hair off her cheek. "I have news. Or rather, news for you." She glances at Colt.

He freezes, halfway putting a log on a tiny ember in the stove. "Me?"

"Augustine Anders—OB asked me to do some digging." She glances between me, Brian, Parry, October, and Colt, and we all seem to collectively imprison our breaths. "So I asked around, and Patrick knows a girl in Ashtabula, who knows another girl from Conneaut, who went to Bowling Green, who has a cousin in Cincinnati that knew a girl from Sandusky. And *this* girl from Sandusky has been mysteriously missing—for get this, more than *four* months."

"No way," I breathe.

October is skeptical. "How do we know it's the same girl?"

"They told me her name."

We all wait.

"Augustine Anders."

Thunder booms, then lightening cracks.

And just like that…the power goes out.

CHAPTER 25

ZOEY DURAND

"Don't touch the fire. Don't light a match. Don't even sniff a fucking candle. You know what—don't do *anything*. Just sit there," Brian decrees to me like I'm a walking fire hazard. The Pelican would be pitch-black if it weren't for the tiny fire that Colt stokes in the wood-burning stove. And the candles that October and Parry light around the bar.

Wax drips off wide cylindrical candles onto a round table where Babette and I sit, and I'm not loving being relegated to a chair. But there's not much else I can do.

"The power has been out for a solid thirty-minutes, and I haven't combusted," I tell my brother.

"Be serious."

"I am! I think I'm fine. What's the worse that could happen?"

Babette glances up from her phone. "Lightning could strike you dead. The ceiling fan could crash down and kill you—"

Brian literally drags my chair (with me in it) three feet away from the ceiling fan and the table. No one else finds his precautions unnecessary. Literally, Parry and Colt come in and lift the table, carrying the thing to where I am. Careful not to tip over any of the lit candles.

Babette places her chair at the table like we didn't just shimmy three feet to the left for absolutely nothing.

They care.

I know they just care about me. But I can't be scared about a looming curse. I can't freak myself out or else I will jump at every boom of thunder and crack of lightning. Which, honestly, is more frequent after the power outage and eerie with the glow of fire.

Brian is hawk-eyeing me.

"I'm not moving," I assure him. "See. I'm sitting. I'm breathing."

He grunts, half-satisfied.

Parry brings more chairs over to the table, and October slips in the one closest to me. Her hand finds my hand, and our fingers thread. *She's not leaving my side.* Like Brian, she fixates on every little creak and rustle in the bar. Her clutch tightens whenever the shutters rattle, and I'm fully aware that October is on edge, seconds from pulling me to safety.

The wind whistles like a ghostly spirit is in the Pelican, singing a haunting tune. *I'm not scared. I'm not scared.* I intake a tensed breath. "Let's just forget about the possibility of me getting cursed tonight."

"How about *no*?" Brian shoots back.

I expect Colt to protest. Figuring he'd be *way* more interested in the news Babette literally just unearthed. But he's not trying to dig into Augustine Anders.

I've been gone for six years, and the five people in this bar care more about my life than the mystery we've all been trying to solve. *They love me.* I recognize, in this moment, how deeply I'm loved, and I think I took this feeling for granted when I was eighteen.

When I left.

I didn't realize being *loved* unconditionally isn't found as easily as a one-way plane ticket. Being loved can't be purchased. Only discovered.

Maybe October is right—I needed to go. I needed to experience new things, a new city.

And I needed to come back. To make sense of what's most important to me.

You can rediscover love in Chicago. I have people who care there, excluding my issues with my ex (obviously), but I can't tell if it's the same or if the love here is just a different, rare breed.

Colt, Parry, and Brian join us at the round table—Brian securing his seat on the other side of me. I'm more conscious of how Brian watches Parry sit next to him. How he tugs Parry's chair closer and whispers something in his ear.

Parry nods. They almost seem…*friendly.*

They did kiss, Zoey.

And they do like each other, but I'm just not used to seeing them evade the jugular. Parry tries to slump back, but he recoils as a gust of wind wooshes through the bar and extinguishes the candles on the table. Darkening our surroundings.

Fuck, it's almost nighttime.

The sun should be setting about *now*, but with the gloomy skies and shuttered windows, time is harder to discern.

With the mystery girl, Chicago problems, and my heart being rebuilt and torn with October, I forgot that Parry is afraid of the dark.

Brian didn't forget. Striking matches against the box, he relights the candles.

"You okay, Pear?" I ask him.

He brushes a hand through his sun-kissed hair. "I'm dealing."

On the other side of Parry, Colt squeezes his friend's shoulder in comfort. Just as Parry jerks from a scraping noise against the siding of the bar. He eyes the locked door. It honestly sounds like nails or a machete raking against the building.

"Whatever's outside will pass," Brian says gruffly, sinking back down and shaking out a match. He extends an arm over the back of Parry's chair. He keeps checking on Parry every minute or so.

"Are you alright?" October whispers to me.

I realize I'm clenching the life out of her hand. I loosen my grip.

"Yeah, yeah. I'm fine." *I'm not scared. I'm not scared.* To everyone, I say, "I just want to focus on the missing girl."

Not the eerie noises.

Not fear.

Not *curses.*

Definitely not the waxy candles on the table that remind me of a séance—and I swear if some ghost of Colt's haunted past flies out, I will scream.

"Yeah, I think we should settle this," Parry says, probably also wanting the distraction. He tears his focus off the latched door and onto us. "Baby's intel is four or five people deep."

Babette clearly blushes at his words or the way he says them, and October whispers to me, "The power of Parry DiNapoli."

"You're more powerful to me," I murmur back, and the ice in October's eyes instantly melts. Her overwhelmed reaction begins to flood my lungs, and the flames casting shadows and warm light against our faces suddenly appear less ominous and more romantic.

Strange how that works.

Perception.

Parry looks at October's blushing sister. "So how well can we trust what you've heard?"

"Well enough," Babette says. "It's not like there are any better leads on the table."

"Augustine Anders *is* real," Colt emphasizes. "I knew she was real."

"Then why is the town council acting so weird?" I wonder. "Don't you think they're hiding something?"

October nods in agreement.

Babette says, "Maybe it has nothing to do with Augustine Anders."

"Maybe they already know the truth," Parry theorizes.

"Wait a sec." Brian raises his hands, then turns to Babette. "You said this girl has been missing from Sandusky. Home to Cedar Point, one of the most popular amusement parks in America. It's not what *I'd* call a small town. So how exactly does a girl go missing without alerting cops or journalists?"

"And why was she in Mistpoint Harbor?" October questions.

Colt rests his elbows on the table, cups his hands to his mouth— barely blinking as he stares straight into Babette. Waiting for the answers.

Shit, he's more intense than October.

Babette seems only slightly unnerved. "According to the friend of her closest friend, Augustine Anders has no family, at least none she speaks to. They're distant and live in Texas, for the most part."

Parry frowns. "What about her closest friend? Why didn't she file a missing person's report?"

"That's where things get a little hairy," Babette winces. "The closest friend knew Augustine had planned to sail across all the Great Lakes, and Augustine told her she'd be gone for a couple months, but obviously, it's been longer. The further removed friend thinks something happened to her."

Now I'm frowning. "Why does she suspect something is wrong, but the closer friend doesn't?"

"She thinks it's strange that Augustine hasn't called her closest friend in over *four* months. Not to say where she is or how she's doing. Instead, she's been sending her postcards from various ports around the Great Lakes."

Colt stares haunted at the table. "Who sends postcards anymore?"

"Exactly." Babette laces her fingers on the table. "It's suspicious."

Colt almost breathes in relief. "You should be a detective."

Babette smiles. "You think so?"

Something *clicks* in my brain, and I suddenly perk up. "Wait—what if someone knows what happened to Augustine and they're sending postcards to pretend she's still alive?"

I realize fast that they were all thinking the same thing. Okay, so I'm not special, but I contributed a shared thought.

"How can we confirm that?" Parry asks.

"Pictures," October tells everyone. "We compare handwriting between Augustine and the postcards."

Colt spins more towards Babette. "Can you get your friend-of-friend to send you photos of one of the postcards and something else Augustine has written?"

"Like a birthday card," October suggests.

"I can do that. It'll be a minute." She slides out from her chair, phone in hand. While Babette leaves, just for the wood-burning stove, the rest of us wait for the news.

"She is real," Colt says again, and this time, no one argues. My brother looks near-tears like he's taking his first breath, and my heart aches for how long he's suffered with the uncertainty of what happened.

"We're about to find real answers, Colt," I say, hopeful.

"The worst thing about all of this," he tells us in a choked voice, "she could be dead, and I couldn't help her. This whole time, we've been searching for a dead girl…" He stands abruptly up from the table, just to go behind the bar. Rummaging through the bottles.

Brian shakes his head, his surly expression not so sympathetic, but I'd like to think he empathizes with Colt. Surviving trauma where nothing you could do would save the other person.

I glance over at October. Her hand has gone slack in mine. She's staring faraway at the wall. "Kenobi?" I whisper.

She wakes up, her hand tightening around mine again. "I just…I had a strange thought."

"About what?"

"It doesn't matter. I'm probably overanalyzing everything…it's likely I'm wrong." She's still tense, but another crack of lightning refocuses her energy on me. Especially as I jump.

"Fuck," I curse, then flinch at the rattling door. It sounds like someone is trying to enter.

Parry is unblinking now. He's white-knuckling the edge of the table. *He's scared of people,* I realize what I never have before. *And what they can do in the dark.*

Murderous, horrific things.

"It's just the wind," October tells me and him.

Brian shifts his arm off Parry's chair and onto his shoulders. And my brother begins to sing over the clanging door. *"Oh the old sailor heaves his grief through the tattered sea."* He pounds his boot on the ground to the beat. *"Let him go and be. Oh the old sailor heaves his grief through the tattered sea. What a sight for me. Winds are strong and the soul grows cold. Let him go and be. Oh I'd never do such a thing, my sailor means too much to me."*

Parry starts to calm, and he listens more to the sea shanty my brother is singing to him. When Colt returns to the table, he thumps the bottom of his rum bottle, adding more percussion to our brother's song.

Brian has always had a great voice, but never did I think he'd serenade anyone. Let alone Parry.

October whispers to me, "Your brother really likes Parry."

"Oh yeah he does," I say with wide eyes. The shock should be worn off completely by now, but this entire time, I've started believing Brian could so easily crush Parry's heart. I never considered that Parry could destroy Brian's—that my brother could be in way deeper than Parry.

He finishes singing the sea shanty, just as Babette plops down in her chair. She waves her phone. "And now we wait for the photos."

"How should we pass the time?" I wonder. "You still have Uno cards behind the bar?" I'm asking Brian.

He scratches at his trimmed beard. "What'd you major in?"

"At college? You want to know?"

Brian nods tensely. "I asked, didn't I?"

Okay, I bypass that surliness, and I've gone this long without sharing my life in Chicago with my brothers or Parry—what's one more day? The mystery is unfolding. I'll probably be gone tomorrow. *Need to book a flight.*

My heart is sinking.

"Parry thinks something with engineering," Brian says with another nod to himself.

Parry gives me a soft smile. "You've always been good at math."

My heart is hurting.

Parry looks to his best friend. "Colt has always thought you majored in business."

"Something to do with people," Colt says quietly.

"Really?" My voice carries a tremor.

"You wanted to be social, but no one ever wanted to be around you here. Except for her." He dips his head to October.

I squeeze her hand beneath the table. She squeezes back.

"I thought maybe you'd find that out there," Colt finishes. "More."

More.

The saddest part…I think *more* is sitting at this fucking table with me. But I did need to go out there to discover what has always been here.

"You were right, Colt," I whisper. "I ended up majoring in hotel management, and I'm an assistant manager at this luxury hotel in Chicago—it's a *great* job." *Don't cry.* "The fucking best."

Brian is nodding a ton.

Like way too much.

"Great," he chokes out. "So go back. Once this all has cleared." He motions to thrashing rain on the roof. "Tomorrow."

I am.

I can't say the words.

"She's buying a plane ticket tonight," October says, her hand squeezing the life out of mine now.

My frown deepens.

She narrows her gaze onto me. "That is the plan?"

"Yeah, yeah…" *That is the plan.*

"October and I can drive you to the airport," Parry offers, looking morose, but I almost smile hearing that he included October. The two of them aren't fighting over protecting me anymore.

"Thanks," I nod.

Colt swigs straight from the bottle of rum.

"Pass here." Babette wiggles her fingers a little.

Colt slides over the rum, and she suddenly tosses the bottle over her shoulder. It shatters on the floorboards.

"What the hell?" Colt shouts, glancing backwards at the pool of alcohol and broken glass.

"It's better on the floor," Babette notes like she did him a favor. I am actually happy that Colt won't be drunk in an hour.

"You do realize I can just go grab another bottle. We're at a *bar.*"

Alright, maybe he still will be.

"You do realize that if I know how to throw one bottle, then I can throw two?"

"No—not at my bar," Brian cuts in. "And you're paying for that, Baby."

"That's fine," Babette says. "The cost of not watching this one drink himself to sleep." She side-eyes Colt. "And anyway, Seagull95 purchased five more windchimes off my Etsy shop last night, so I'm feeling flush."

Colt says nothing. He drops his gaze to the table.

Brian makes a strange face. "Windchimes?"

October explains, "She makes them out of beach glass."

Brian is scrutinizing Colt up-and-down. "Uh-uh. And how many windchimes has Seagull95 bought from you?"

"It'd be close to thirty or forty by now."

Brian shifts a candle closer to Colt, seeing his face. "These wouldn't happen to be the same box of beach glass windchimes you told me to hang up outside the bar? Would they?"

Holy fuck. "Colt..." I feel myself start to smile. "Are you Seagull95?"

Babette is in shock. "No...he can't be?" She eyes him. "...are you?"

October mutters, "Upgrade from the fifty-year-old."

"Hear, hear." I've never seen Colt crush on *anyone*. He had one girlfriend in high school, and she epically broke his heart. She dated him as a literal joke. The soccer team pulled the prank on him just to humiliate Colt. They goaded his so-called girlfriend into doing it. But she'd been dating someone else the entire time.

Colt exhales roughly. "I think they're cool."

"You think they're cool?" Babette repeats with a rising smile.

He shrugs. "They're cool, and I bought some."

"You bought a ton," Brian corrects.

I can't stop grinning.

"I thought they'd make this place look less like a shithole," Colt defends sharply. "And when did it become a crime to buy windchimes off Etsy!"

"It's not one," Babette says with a smile. "But you bought mine and you know me."

"So what?" Colt mutters. "I'm supporting a local artist."

"And I thank you for your contribution."

"*Relentless* contribution," October teases.

He glares. "*Thank you*, OB."

"Oh no, the pleasure is all Babette's."

Colt is blushing, and I'm trying so hard not to laugh. He pins his disgruntled glare onto me. "Zoey."

I hold up my hands. "I think it's cute."

He groans, then slides out his chair. About to leave—probably to grab another bottle of rum—but Babette's phone suddenly lights up in the dark.

Colt freezes.

We all go quiet.

She picks up her cell. "I can air-drop the photos to everyone, but I only have Colt and October's numbers."

I've already started taking out my phone. *Fuck, it's dead.* With the power outage, I can't exactly charge it.

"You can pass the phone around," Parry suggests, but color has started draining from Babette's face.

"What?" Colt asks, shifting his weight impatiently. "Is the handwriting a match?"

She lifts her terrified eyes right to her sister. "October."

We all turn.

October is solid ice. She's unmoving. Stoic. "Let me see."

Babette slides the phone across the table.

And I peer at the photo with October. The front of a colorful postcard reads: GREETINGS FROM MICHIGAN! THE GREAT LAKES STATE!

The back has a short, handwritten note in blue ink.

Weather has been great! Might stay out here for longer. I'm falling in love with Michigan. xoxo, Augustine

Nothing seems strange to me. "I don't understand. Kenobi?" She's barely moving.

I squeeze her lifeless, limp hand. My pulse is racing. "*Kenobi.*"

"This isn't Augustine's handwriting." She speaks flat. No emotion.

"How do you know?" My voice pitches in fear. "We haven't even seen the other photo of her real handwriting. We haven't compared anything yet."

Babette has her hands to her mouth. "I…" She's unable to speak. "October."

"We don't have to match them," October says. "I already know the postcard wasn't written by Augustine." She shoves Babette's phone away. "It's Aunt Effie's handwriting."

Her aunt?

Parry rubs his eyes. He was right to believe the town council could pin this on Colt. October was right too, but I don't think she ever suspected her aunt.

"She covered this up?" Colt croaks, eyes reddening. "To turn me into the madman in the lighthouse?"

Babette's face contorts. "Aunt Effie can be rude, among other things…but I never thought she was capable of that kind of cruelty."

"I realize I never asked you," October says to Colt, "but what was the exact day of the mayday call?"

Did Colt ever tell me? I think he just said "around December"— something vague.

"December 23rd," Colt recalls easily. "The day before Christmas Eve."

October intakes a sharp breath. She looks sick.

"October?" She lets go of my hand like she's arsenic and she'll poison me. I try to recapture her hand, but she's pulling back and standing from the table.

She can't meet my eyes. Rarely has she ever looked away. But she's looking everywhere but at me and at them. "I know everything."

"What?" we all seem to say at different times.

"I know what happened to Augustine Anders."

"How?" I ask the loudest, rising to my feet. For a moment, it feels like it's just me and her in the darkened bar. The two of us in a stand-off. Wanting, aching, *yearning* to be close, but a squall and riptide are drawing us so far apart.

"Because," October breathes, "I was with her."

CHAPTER 26

OCTOBER BRAMBILLA

'm cursed. I've been cursed, and the past is swelling up underneath me, suffocating me all over again, and I default to numbness. To the endless nothingness that crawls over my body and blankets me in cold sheets.

Everyone is on their feet. Candles do little to light the darkened crevices of the bar and the distressed features of the five people around me.

"Have you known the truth this entire time?" Parry questions like I'm the enemy. Like I've purposefully fooled the Durands along with the rest of the town.

"She didn't," Zoey butts in, not for one second doubting me. "She's been trying to help me—*us*."

I feel…

I love…

My eyes sting, and I blink a few times. "I didn't realize she was the same girl until right now. If I'd known…" What would I have done?

I look up at Colt. He's breathing hard.

My curse is twisted around his curse. One of us was always going to go down. Self-preservation has been all I've known. Rise to the top of the food chain.

260

No matter who you hurt.

Stand your ground.

No matter the cost.

Thunder resounds and shakes the floor beneath our feet. The ceiling leaks where I stand and drips onto my pink sweater. I don't move.

"I *didn't* know," I say more forcefully. "She never told me her last name, and when I met her, she said her name was Katie."

"October." Babette looks horror-stricken for me, but she tries to soften her gaze. "Her middle name is *Katherine*."

"We didn't know that," Zoey cuts in, voice rising in alarm. "None of us knew that. You didn't know, Kenobi. It's okay." She reaches for my hand, but I can't—I can't touch her.

I step back and clutch the edge of the pool table behind me.

Pain lances her face.

I'm sorry, Zoey.

"How'd you meet this girl?" Brian wonders.

"I met her the day before the mayday call." I drag my gaze across the floor and walls, seeing the docks where she'd been tying her sailboat. "It was a sunny afternoon. She planned to leave the next day. To cross the rest of Lake Erie. A bucket list trip, she said, and I don't know what she saw in me…" I shake my head. "Envy. Desire. But she said I should come along. It'd be an adventure of a lifetime." A ball rises in my throat.

I swallow hard and inhale, "For the first time in my life, I had an easy out. The *easiest* way to leave this town. It was staring *right* at me. I thought about you." I look up at Zoey and try not to break entirely. "I thought of all the adventures you were taking, of all the people you were meeting and new places you were seeing." My eyes burn. I turn to Babette. "I thought about Mom and Dad. I wondered if they really knew something we didn't. If vanishing from Mistpoint Harbor brought them more happiness than staying here—then why am I staying?"

Tears streak Babette's cheeks. "You didn't think about me?"

A knife plunges through me, but I hold her gaze. "I couldn't," I say painfully. "If I did, I knew I wouldn't leave."

She nods, understanding and wipes fiercely at her tears. "So you left with Augustine?"

"With Katie. The next day—the day before Christmas Eve—I climbed onto her boat, and I almost didn't go." *I wish I hadn't. I wish I turned back around.* "The water was rough." I cringe, remembering the way the boat pitched just at the docks. "Katie reassured me it was fine. She's sailed in worse. I asked her for a lifejacket. I wore one. She didn't."

"Why?" Parry shakes his head repeatedly. "The winds were well over thirty knots that day. If her boat was small, it would've easily capsized."

"She was confident," I say sharply. "She convinced *me* to go out in a storm. I believed her when she said she knew what she was doing. I believed her when she said she didn't need a lifejacket. That we'd be fine. Only when we were so far out and we couldn't see land did I realize her confidence was false—and do you know how many times I've pictured telling her to wait? Convincing her to go another day?" I stare off at the wall again. "I didn't though. I never told her to wait, and there we were, in the middle of hell."

I still hear the hellacious wind.

I still feel the freshwater slap against the boat and the spray against my cheeks. The roar of the thunder—so loud, I couldn't hear Katie yell at me to grab lines.

I helped as much as I could. With all I'd known growing up around sailboats.

In the bar, a sudden strike of lightning lights up the shabby space. I don't flinch at the violent sound. I'm in another storm. The one from months ago.

"I never heard her contact the Coast Guard or the lighthouse." This part plagues me. "I never heard the mayday call, Colt. I never connected the pieces between Katie and Augustine because I didn't think Katie ever reached out for help. I didn't think she would. She wouldn't even wear a fucking lifejacket." I hear my voice crack. "Everything happened so quickly once we were out there." I gesture towards the lake. Eyes raw as I blink, as I fight hot tears and emotion that try to swallow me whole. "The boat capsized. I tried to reach for her, but we were swept away from each other. I floated. And she…" I intake a breath, and suddenly, Zoey's hand is in mine.

Zoey.

I start bawling. I can't stop. *I can't stop.* Her arms are around me, and I struggle to hug back, my arms not working. My head spinning. Breath like a knot in my lungs and swollen throat. She hugs tighter. "I'm here. *I'm here.*"

"I left her to die," I choke out. "I left her to die, Zoey—I didn't go back for her." Everything starts to spill out of me like I'm being ripped open. I wait for Zoey to be disgusted with me, but she never lets me go.

She never stops hugging me. "She was already gone, Kenobi."

I've never deserved absolution, and maybe I always knew Zoey would try to free me. Because she loves me as much as I love her—but guilt is a powerful force. Still trying to wrench me under.

I sink to the floor in Zoey's arms. Crying against her shoulder, partially into my hand, and I want to grip onto the woman I love while she's holding me—but I'm *repulsed* with myself. With the person who abandoned a drowning girl. And I can't ruin something as beautiful as Zoey Durand with my flesh and bone and heart.

"It's okay," Zoey whispers against my ear. "I love you. *I love you. It's okay.*"

"It's not okay," I choke. "She's *dead*, Zoey."

"No one would've survived those conditions," Parry says to me. "Not where you were in the lake. You were too far out."

Colt had our coordinates.

"It's a miracle you even survived," Brian tells me.

"Did Aunt Effie bury her body?" Babette asks in a quiet squeak.

I draw my head away from Zoey's shoulder, my face wet, and I realize I'm gripping one of her hands. I'm unable to let go. She wipes my splotchy mascara with her sleeve. Her eyes say, *you better not let go.*

Under different circumstances, I'd tell her that I prefer making the demands. And then I look to my sister. "No."

"Did you?"

I shake my head. "Her body never surfaced or washed ashore." From too far to reach, I saw Katie sink into the darkness of the water, and I never saw her rise. "The current brought me to shore, and I walked to the nearest building. A Dollar Store. I asked to use the phone, and I called my aunt." I speak more to Zoey. "She met me at the shoreline where I ended up. Barely any beach. No one was there. Pieces of the boat were already washing onto the rocks. I was..." I stare off again. "I was distraught, soaked, and as soon as I told her everything, she said, *I'm going to take care of this, October. Don't say a word to anyone. You tell no one.*"

My nose flares, restraining another onslaught of tears. "And I said, *we should find her, shouldn't we?* And she caught my chin and told me, *do you know what you are to people here? You're the girl who saved history books and your little sister from a burning building. You're a hero. What do you think will happen if you tell everyone you were running away from this town that loves you—and you let a girl drown? I...*" I can barely speak. Can barely move anymore. "I was scared…of the possibility of losing the last thing I had left in this town. Respect." I wince. "But I'd lost everything anyway. I didn't care about anything anymore when I came home and things were supposed to be back to normal. Like nothing happened. Like my aunt didn't cover up the drowning. Like we didn't fake my curse in the books. I didn't want to be here while Katie was dead, knowing I did nothing. I wished it'd been me." I force back a sob, but my voice catches again.

Zoey cups my wet cheek. "Kenobi. *Kenobi*, look at me."

With raw, burning, guilt-ridden eyes, I do. And she says, "I'm glad it wasn't you." She's crying with me. "I needed you here. I want you here, and your aunt sucks—"

I choke on a laugh. How is she making me fucking *laugh?* "Zoey."

"She does. She really fucking sucks, even if she helped you in this sick twisted way. I had no idea she put pressure on you to maintain some hero status, but as someone who loves a good hero, Kenobi, as someone who nicknamed you after one—you should know that the best heroes don't always know exactly what to do. They don't always make the *right* choices in the moment. The best heroes are the most imperfect ones because they remind us of what it's like to be human." She wipes the tears off my cheek, and I wipe hers; my heart is filling up again.

"You shouldn't be making me feel better," I whisper, our hands on each other's faces, foreheads touching.

"I don't care," she whispers against my lips. "I will and I am."

"Zoey," I breathe, an apology already written in my eyes.

"What?" Confusion is in hers.

"I have to make this right, sweets."

For Colt.

For Katie.

For myself.

And I say, "I'm going to go to Sheriff Carmichael and confess what happened. I'm going to turn myself in."

CHAPTER 27

ZOEY DURAND

"You can't," I choke out, broken at the thought of October taking the fall for her aunt's cover-up.

"I have to." October slowly stands, and I follow suit, her fingers still hooked with my fingers. That counts for something. She's not pushing me away. I should be relieved that I finally know October's real curse and the truth about Augustine, but this isn't how this is supposed to end.

"October—"

"The town shouldn't be punishing your brother for something I did."

"You didn't kill her."

October glares like she's trying to bludgeon the words into the world, *I let her die.* She could've gone back for her body, but she couldn't have saved her. The only wrong she made was letting this girl become a missing person…letting her vanish.

And I realize…October wants to fix that wrong.

She has *always* had a big heart, and I understand how something like this could've destroyed her. If this is the final piece to putting October Brambilla back together, then I need to be okay with her decision.

Even if it really fucking hurts.

"Sheriff Carmichael might be in on it," Parry says. "I suspect Effie told the town council and they likely involved him."

Brian frowns. "Why do you think more people are involved?"

"Anna Roberts told October to *drop it* when she mentioned Augustine Anders. The Roberts, Brambillas—they all must've known what this would lead to."

Oh my God. "They were protecting October," I say softly.

Guilt has left her features. Replaced with fortified resolve. "I'm going to make this right. I'll go to the police in Sandusky."

Babette is shaking her head, panicked. "Just let this go, OB. No one will know."

"I will," October says strongly. "I will *always* know."

My heart clenches like a fist is squeezing and rupturing the organ, but I tighten my hold on October's hand. *I'm here. I'm here.* I'm at her side, and I'm not letting her do this alone. I'll be with her.

I'm leaving soon. The thought weighs like ten tons of lead inside me.

Thunder rumbles, and the weather steals our focus. Flames extinguish on a few candles. Smoke billowing into the air. A chill slithers down my spine.

Bang!

"Fuck," Parry curses and jumps.

"Was that thunder?" I ask out loud.

Brian eagle-eyes the door, his hand protective on Parry's shoulder. The banging is louder. More incessant.

Colt shares a cautious glance with Brian, and then Colt picks up a shard of glass from the broken rum bottle. And he says, "Someone is at the door."

Babette takes a few steps towards the stove, and October draws me behind her back. "Stay, Zoey."

"I'm fine—"

"Listen to your girlfriend," Brian growls at me.

I'm not correcting him on the title. That's what I wish we could be. *Girlfriends.* And I'm going to pretend that's what we are. Until I can't pretend anymore.

But I ask them, "What if this is just a tourist caught in the storm?"

"We're about to find out without you—back up," Brian waves me further backwards.

Jesus Christ. I go and stand next to Babette. She's slipping on her gloves and then grabs a fire poker. She tosses the weapon to October.

I didn't realize we're in an episode of *The Walking Dead.* As Brian procures a baseball bat from behind the bar, I half expect to see a hoard of zombies bursting through The Drunk Pelican.

Bang!

I flinch at the pounding.

Parry takes a seat on the barstool, trying to calm himself down with a shot of tequila.

If that is a fist, this person is strong. And persistent.

Brian and Colt go to the door together. "Who are you?!"

"I'm from out of town!" I barely hear.

"Don't let him in," Parry says tightly. "*Brian.*"

Brian slips an affectionate look to Parry—I don't know what else to call that look, but then Brian barks through the door, "We're closed! Try the Wharf!"

"Seriously?" October snaps.

Babette shakes her head with a sigh. "Predictable."

"ZOEY?!" the guy shouts.

My brothers slowly turn their heads to me.

I go cold.

I recognize that voice. A voice from Chicago.

"ZOEY?! ARE YOU IN THERE?! LET ME IN!"

I'm freaked out. No—*freaked out* is an understatement to what I am. His anger feels more visceral out loud than just through text. More cutting. I can't move.

October looks ready to skewer him with the iron poker. And she hasn't even seen his face yet. Or heard that he broke into my apartment.

"Do you know this guy?" Brian asks with scrunched brows.

"Yeah." My pulse speeds. "He's sort of my ex."

CHAPTER 28

ZOEY DURAND

"The dull, boring ex?" October questions like he sounds awful. "This is the same guy?"

"That's the one." *Boring* sounds like a total mischaracterization now, but in hindsight, the worst he ever did was make me fall asleep while he was talking. Not exactly red flags like he's been tossing around lately. "He was never hateful or angry." I jump at the banging on the door that continues.

Everyone is looking at me, and I try to explain my three-year relationship in a matter of minutes. "I met him at college, and we became fast friends. He knew my entire family was miles away, so he kind of became that for me. But then we ended up at the same job, and he just kind of always wanted to care for me. Drive me to work. Pick me up. Go out to eat every night. I'd never had anyone always around like that. I guess the only way to explain it was overwhelming." I avoid looking at my brothers or October, and instead focus on Parry. He gives me this warm consoling nod to keep going.

I take a breath. "We dated and it got worse, but I always talked myself out of it. Like I was the silly one for thinking he was being anything but protective. When I finally ended things, I figured it'd be easier to stay friends since we worked together and hung out with the same people. But that was *two* years ago. He hasn't been a problem since the breakup."

After another vicious lightning crack, I end up telling my brothers, "You should let him in. He has nowhere else to go." Why do I feel badly?

He literally broke into my apartment.

He was just trying to look out for me. Right? He's not some serial killer. He's an ass in the rain, and he should definitely apologize. But not while he's standing out there soaked and wet.

I'm a little less freaked out. Rationalizing is good.

I'm rationalizing this.

Colt glares at me. "You want us to let him in? After what you just told us?"

"It's storming outside," I say, my chest tightening. "He wouldn't hurt anyone. Just...only let him in if it's okay with Kenobi." I turn to October. "Is it?"

Her brows arch. "You're asking me?"

I wouldn't be jumping for joy seeing any of October's exes, even if they're just hookups or flings. "Yeah, I'm asking."

Her lip twitches like she wants to smile. "Yes, it's fine. Let the boring ex in, so he doesn't die."

Brian hesitates.

"It's *thunder storming*," I emphasize. "Have a heart, Brian."

"I don't trust this guy, Zoey," he retorts.

"ZOEY?!" My ex bangs his fist repeatedly.

I picture a drenched, bedraggled twenty-four-year-old. He's a harmless wet noodle whose only flaw is probably caring about me *too* much. Right? *Right.* "I'm vouching for him," I tell Brian. "Can't that be enough?"

Reluctantly, after Parry conveys his readiness, Brian unlatches the door with Colt, and they let my ex-boyfriend inside the bar and slam the door closed behind him.

Boots pad across the floor, leaving muddied prints. Boots I recognize. Skinny legs I remember. Lean muscles hidden behind a faded jean jacket—soaked and suctioned to his tall, lanky frame. White, fair skin. Curly windswept brown hair is tucked underneath a wet beanie.

He doesn't take his hazel eyes off me. "Zoey." He exhales a deep breath like he finally found me.

I guess he did.

Seeing him again, I really want to feel less unsettled, and I shift my weight like I'm trying to balance on a rocking boat.

"Ashton," I reply curtly and come up to October's side. She edges closer to me. *Mark your territory all you want, Kenobi.*

He adjusts his Tumi rucksack backpack that must cost at least five-hundred bucks. He's not loaded, but he likes to blow cash on the finer things. I wouldn't be surprised if he rented a luxury car for his drive here.

Ashton notices the glass shard in Colt's grasp. He lets out a shrill laugh, his lip curling like he's disgusted with…me? "You think I'm here to cause fucking trouble or something?"

"I never said that."

"What's that then?" He motions to the glass, then zeroes in on Brian's baseball bat.

Colt scowls harder. "We didn't know who you were, man."

"We still don't," Brian snaps in threat.

Ashton glowers at me like I put my brothers up to this shit. I didn't do anything. Sharp breath leaving my lungs like knives, I throw up my hands. "What are you even doing here, Ashton?"

"Making sure you're fucking alive," he almost shouts. "You didn't show up to work, and then you didn't answer anyone's calls. Fuck—no one has been able to get ahold of you in days, Zoey. This place was the only one I could think you'd run off to."

Lies. Those are *definite* lies.

Why would he misconstrue the truth like that?

I shake my head dramatically back and forth. "Just because I didn't answer your calls doesn't mean I haven't checked in with other people. I've talked to Georgia and to my boss. And I don't need you checking in on me."

Ashton glares. "Seriously?" He takes a step forward. "Did you miss the part where I flew over three-hundred miles just to make sure you weren't dead?"

Why is he putting that on me? My whole body goes cold. Should I feel guilty for worrying him? *I don't know.*

Brian glowers. "You obviously missed the part where no one here fucking cares."

"I definitely don't," October says coldly. At this, she extends an arm across me and begins pushing me backwards.

Brian sidesteps in front of *October.*

Tension in the bar escalates, and I feel more than unsettled now. A tickle at my brain is trying to tell me to listen to my instincts. Trying to tell me that I might be in danger. But I'm trying to reason with that feeling. Trying to make sense of the person I know from Chicago and the person that's standing here.

Ashton tilts his head to look past Brian's shoulder at her. He sizes October up with a quick up-down with his eyes. Contempt rages for some reason. "No one asked you." He glares harder. "*October.*"

Ashton has never been *this* intense. He's been docile. Chill. He is very far from chill right now.

She peeks over at me. "He knows who I am?"

"Um…" *Yeah.* The word is stuck. I don't need to say *yes* anyway. Her lips part in surprise, already realizing that I didn't lock her existence away from my friends in Chicago. Ashton wouldn't even be here if I never mentioned Mistpoint Harbor.

But I did.

I told him about the family I left behind. And the girl who made my life better. The girl who made me excited to wake up and go to school. The girl who made me stronger.

So strong that I left.

I hate how Ashton said her name. Snidely. Grotesquely. Like she's a bad memory when I never said a *bad* thing about her. So I bite back, "Don't talk to her like that. You don't know her—"

"You're lecturing me?" he cuts me off. "I just flew three-hundred miles for you, Zoey!"

I flinch. I recover. And I bite back. "You already said that!"

"How can you not give a shit?! WHAT'S WRONG WITH YOU?!"

The pressure on my chest has grown more intense. I barely breathe. Who did I bring in here? This doesn't feel like the same person from Chicago. Or is he the same and I'm just now seeing him from the perspective of people I actually care about. The horror in Parry's eyes. The anger in Colt's. The utter concern in October's. It shades Ashton in a new monstrous light.

"HEY!" Brian yells at Ashton, right as the power cuts back on. Multi-colored Christmas lights twinkle above us, and brighter lamps illuminate the rest of the bar. The jukebox screeches to a wonky start and begins playing Frank Sinatra's "That's Life" clearly and loudly.

Brian is on a tear towards the jukebox, but he points his bat at Ashton. "Get out of my fucking bar."

"No, I need to talk—" Ashton flinches as Brian smashes the bat against the jukebox. The song keeps playing.

"Brian." Parry jumps off the stool and sprints to my brother. *"Brian."* He steals the bat, just as a fourth hit to the machine shoots sparks from the speakers.

Frank Sinatra is still going strong, and with more sense, Parry yanks the plug out of the wall. The jukebox sputters to silence.

Ashton is *glaring* at me.

What the fuck is wrong with him?

"Leave," October orders. "Or they'll make you."

"Zoey." Ashton only speaks to me. "I need to talk to you. I flew all this way. That's the LEAST I FUCKING DESERVE!" He's screaming so hard spit spews with his words and his face reddens.

I'm shaking. October is drawing me so far away. Her arms are around me.

"GET OUT OF MY FUCKING BAR!" Brian yells back like he can scream louder. He's charging after Ashton with the bat.

Holy fuck.

Holy fuck.

Ashton races towards the door, slipping on the muddied floor. But he screams back, "SHE'S MY GIRLFRIEND!"

I shake my head in cold shock. "We broke up. Two years ago."

"OH YEAH?!" Brian screams at him, shoving Ashton, then unlatching the door. "WELL SHE'S MY FUCKING DAUGHTER! YOU COME NEAR HER AGAIN AND I'LL KILL YOU!!" He throws Ashton out into the storm. He falls on his ass onto the porch, facing the bar. Still glaring at me, even as Colt slams the door shut and latches the lock.

I'm immobile.

Slack-jawed.

My pulse is skidding away from me. "Did you say…?" No. I didn't hear Brian right. I couldn't have heard him right. I'm in shock from fear. I'm terrified. That's all. I gulp the stale air.

October squeezes my hand.

I can't even squeeze back.

Brian breathes heavily, chest rising and falling. He's still gripping the bat. And slowly, he turns to face me. He points at the door. "And that's the last time you vouch for someone."

I try to shake my head, but the movement hurts. "You can't... you didn't just say...are you my...?" My world is tilting. "...I'm your sister."

Brian Durand. My brother with the same rough, turbulent blue eyes. Fifteen years older. Always there for me. Always taking care of me.

I've never seen Brian cry. His nose flares, his eyes pulsing with the kind of emotion that eats the soul inside out. "No," he breathes. "You aren't my sister."

I start to shake my head, the movement gaining friction and speed.

"You're my daughter." He runs his tongue over his molars, then drops his gaze. He pounds the bat a couple times on the floorboards, peeks back up at me.

"I...I don't understand...how that's possible." I whip my head to Colt.

His face is screwed up in confusion. "I didn't know, Zoey."

I look to Parry.

He's wincing a little. "I just found out. Brian told me a week ago. I'm sorry, Zo." He's sorry because he couldn't share the most important piece of information about my life with me.

But he's not the one who should've shared. Frustration, *anger* begins to boil. "Why wouldn't you tell me, Brian? You didn't think that I'd want to know who my real father is?"

How can this be real?

"I was a wreck." Brian has a hard time meeting my eyes, but he does. "I was fifteen, and I got a woman pregnant who was a lot older than me."

"My mom," I realize. "Is she the same woman…?" He's nodding. "So she's still dead?" He's nodding, and my face falls. We've all known the names of our mothers who are buried and gone.

Brian's mom is Hannah Wren. My dad's high school sweetheart. Colt's mom is Mia Vitale, part of a prominent Italian-American family in Mistpoint.

My mom is Bethany Reed. "Wait—my mom was Colt's nanny." I feel sick, already knowing about her from the bits of information I'd been told. "She was *twenty-three*." I always thought my dad was heartbroken after Mia died and found some comfort in Bethany, even though she'd been much younger than him.

The truth is that she slept with Brian? A fifteen-year-old boy? Through my confusion I feel disgust—knowing my mom was an adult when Brian was just a teenager. How could she do that?

"*Twenty-three*," I murmur again, trying to make it make sense.

"I know," Brian nods a few times. "Dad was never with Bethany. I thought I loved her—turns out, I didn't know what the fuck that really meant. But I didn't want her to get in trouble for sneaking around with me, and Dad and I came up with a solution. He'd pretend to be your father, and I'd be your big brother. Of course she was happy about that."

Brian.

His voice is hoarse as he says, "And then she died. In childbirth—just like my mom and Colt's mom—and nothing made sense. I was scared. She had reassured me that she'd know what to do. She'd take care of everything, and now I was left with a baby. Dad saw me… and he just said, '*Son, it's okay. I'll take her from here.*' And I let him raise you until I felt like I could do more than be a burden." Brian shifts, his gaze boring into me as he croaks, "I know you didn't know it, but I always loved you like a daughter. And I got my shit together by the time you were four. I tried my fucking hardest to be there for you."

"You wanted me to stay in Mistpoint Harbor," I realize, tears touching the creases of my eyes. I'm still in a daze.

He nods slowly again. "I always wanted to tell you the truth, Zoey. There were so many days where I thought, *say it now.* But Dad and I agreed that we wouldn't tell you until you were eighteen."

"I don't understand why."

His chest collapses. "Because it was supposed to be your curse!" He's pained. "Zoey Durand. *Didn't discover her true father until her eighteenth birthday.* And I begged you—I *pleaded* with you to stay in Mistpoint so I could tell you." He can't restrain tears. "And then you left, and I thought, *what's the point anyway?* You're gone for good. I'll never see you again. You cut us out because it was easier, and I get that. At that point, I wanted you gone so I could erase the most *painful* part of my life. The daughter I loved and the daughter I fucking lost."

I pinch my watery eyes. "And then I came back."

"And then you came back," he repeats. "I didn't think you'd be here for a week, let alone a month. So I wasn't going to tell you shit. I wanted you out so I wouldn't have to go through the hell of losing you twice, and then I started thinking today, *maybe she will stay.* For your girlfriend. Maybe you'll stick around. Maybe I'll get to tell you the truth. Maybe you'll have a curse that won't put you in a grave or terrorize you in the night. Maybe, just maybe, this will all work itself out." He nods to himself, face caught between something dismayed and something furious. "But it's too late."

"What do you mean?" My voice sounds unfamiliar. Raspy, panicked and pained. "You just told me the truth."

"You're already cursed, Zoey."

"No, I'm not," I refute.

He points at the door with the baseball bat. "You unknowingly dragged a stalker or rageful ex-boyfriend back to Mistpoint with you—that is your fucking curse."

I open my mouth, but nothing comes out. I look around at Parry, Colt, Babette, *October*—none of them seem ready to debate Brian on the status of my curse. And I guess if I were in their shoes peering in, I'd be quicker to see what's right in front of me.

And Brian is right. If I had stayed in Mistpoint Harbor, I would've never been in Chicago. I would've never met Ashton.

I could've had a different curse. The one Brian wanted for me.

Shit, I could've known he was my dad six years ago.

Brian Durand is my father. Processing this will take some time. A part of me feels duped, but the bigger part understands Brian. Because he always let me know who he is, and he's faced so much tragedy in his life—I just had no idea I was a part of it.

"You might need to file a restraining order," Parry tells me.

"Might?" Colt lets out a dry laugh.

"Yeah, yeah, I will." I want to protect myself any way I can, especially when I return to Chicago.

"The rain is letting up," October whispers, and this time, I tighten my hand around hers.

To Brian—my *dad* (so weird)—I nod to him and go through the motions. Still in a state of disarray. "I'm looking at plane tickets tomorrow."

He simply nods back. But he sniffs hard, wipes his runny nose with his shirt. "Here." He digs in his pocket and hands me what he refused to give Colt.

The catamaran keys.

"Save your money tonight. You and October can stay on my boat. It looks like the storm will pass soon. It shouldn't be that rough at the dock."

I stare at the keys. "Thanks…" Should I call him Brian? Is that strange now?

He walks away, leaves into the kitchen. The back door clatters behind him, and all I know is I want to be alone with October. I want to be out of the Pelican and somewhere quiet. Somewhere safe.

CHAPTER 29

OCTOBER BRAMBILLA

"Right now I don't care about myself—"

"You should," I cut Zoey off while I lock the catamaran from the inside. "There is no one you should protect more or care about more or respect more or love more than yourself."

"Shouldn't you follow your own self-loving logic, Kenobi?" Zoey tosses her backpack-purse onto the galley countertop. "Or do you *really* think you care about your safety more than mine? Because you're giving that aft window a nice threatening glare."

I am glaring out of the aft window. On edge knowing her curse is attached to that angry weasel. If he followed us here to hurt Zoey, he'll have hell to pay—I swear to that. But we need to be prepared. I grab the only chair out from under the chart table and I wedge it underneath the door handle.

He won't get in. Not tonight, at least.

I back up from the door. "I'm not the one with the stalker."

"And I'm over-the-moon happy about that." She slips me a small smile, and my chest swells with bittersweet longing.

This might be our last night together. Whatever happens from here, we can't really foresee. Zoey is leaving for Chicago, and my life is headed where I never expected. But I can't rewrite the past, and I'm done living in a dead purgatory.

Zoey opens a few cupboards. "How sure are we that I'm cursed?"

"Seeing as how I asked Colt to escort us to the docks in case your unhinged ex jumped us from the shadows"—I peer into the mini-fridge—"I'd confidently say one-hundred-and-ten percent."

Seven jars of buffalo dill pickles. Fizz Life soda cans. Leftover fried catfish and hushpuppies.

Interesting.

Brian's 42-foot sailing catamaran might be collecting algae on the outside hulls, but the inside is surprisingly tidy. I don't remember seeing much of the inside from the few times I was invited on his boat as a teenager.

Pots and pans are stored neatly in the galley cupboards. The U-shaped booth's dining table is wiped clean. No dirtied clothes or unorganized clutter. And still, the catamaran appears lived-in. Photos dangle on a wire with clips, and the pantry and fridge are well-stocked. We help ourselves to cheese cubes, grapes, and crackers.

Zoey finds a bottle of white wine. "Over a hundred-percent— that sure, huh?" She pops the cork, and I slide two plastic wine glasses over to her while she asks, "What happens if I lose a finger in two years or get in a car accident?"

She knows the answer.

"Hmm?" She has a fucking wiseass smile.

Zoey shouldn't be this cute. Standing there, gesturing at me with her wine glass with a hearty dose of confidence, her messy blonde hair framing her pretty face.

I ease back against the galley stove. "Your first misfortune is your greatest," I tell her what we're told as young kids. What she already knows. "And so it will be written in history."

"And so it will be written in history," Zoey repeats with a short nod. "My dad always told me that to be double or triple cursed usually means you're dead." She winces. "I guess he's not my dad. He'd be my...?"

"Grandfather." I can imagine she's tumbling through a lot of emotions. I felt a mess of them when I learned my parents weren't missing but just willfully gone. I watch as Zoey skates her fingers along the chart table's maps and navigation tools. "Are you angry at Brian?"

"Strangely, *no.*" She frowns. "I just keep looking at Brian's things and thinking, *you're my dad.* This is my dad's boat. My dad's binoculars." She picks up the binoculars, then plucks a photo from a clip and flashes me the picture of a little Zoey, about six or seven, on Brian's shoulders. "He's told me this is his favorite picture—out of all the fucking pictures." Her eyes well. "I just thought he was a grouchy older brother who liked to do shit with me, who brought me to and from school, who cut the crusts off my PB&Js." She passes me the photo.

She's smiling so wide with strawberry ice cream lining her lips. And Brian is caught mid-laugh. I feel my lips rise. "Where were you?"

"Mistpoint's Birthday Jamboree."

The town throws an annual fair in the summer to celebrate the founding of Mistpoint Harbor. Kids love the Jamboree the most, just for the bouncy castles, face painting, and ice cream.

She skims her fingers over the other dangling photos. "Brian has been more present in my life than my dad—or my *grandpa.* Jesus." She exhales. "I guess there's comfort in the fact that Brian isn't just the brother who raised me more. But he's the dad who raised me."

"I like Brian," I admit.

"Yeah?" She sounds surprised. "Because he calls you my girlfriend?" She bites her lip, cheeks flushing. "Because that *might* be inaccurate, but I think it's...amazing." She winces at herself. "You think it's awesome, too, right? Tell me it's awesome." Zoey is nearly bursting at the seams with anticipation.

I tuck my hair behind my ear, my body heating. *Girlfriend.* We've never used titles, but she deserves one even stronger than that. "It's sweet."

Zoey smiles more, but her lips soon falter. We wish. We want. We can't have. She knows there is little to no paths where I end up her girlfriend and she ends up mine. "What was the real reason," she asks, "why you like Brian?"

"He wanted you to stay. Some days I wish I'd been on his side." I run my manicured nail along the rim of the wine glass. "Other days, I imagine that I would've found you." I hold her eager, wanting, overwhelmed gaze that feeds into me like an electric current. Generating arresting, uncontained light.

"You would've found me?" Zoey breathes.

"In Chicago. I've pictured it so many times." I don't look away from her. "I buy a ticket. I knock on your door. You open it and finally see me, and you're so *happy* that my heart feels like it's yanking out of my chest and into your hands. And then you kiss me."

"I kiss you?" She has tears in her eyes.

"You always kiss me." I hear the tremor in my voice. *What are you doing, October?* "I shouldn't tell you this." God, I'm such a fool.

"No, you *should*. You definitely should. Don't close off now."

"You're leaving," I say icily. "I'm going to who knows where—there is no three days from now. There might not even be tomorrow."

"Exactly. What do we have to fucking lose, October? And this isn't all about me, okay? You went through a life-and-death situation in December—"

"I'm not worried about myself."

"So you're not going to turn yourself in to the Sandusky police?" She's not hopeful. She knows what I need to do. She knows I'm fixed to a strong-willed decision and very little will unroot me. Zoey takes a wounded breath. "What if you go to jail?"

"Then that's where I'm meant to be." I explain, "I can't be frightened of the consequences for what I've done. I deserve what's coming."

"You keep punishing yourself...when are you going to stop?"

I don't know.

Maybe never.

"What more should I say?" I open my arms wide as though to show I'm *open*. I'm bare. "How I thought I was so far out of reach of loving the person I've become. The person who would leave her sister without saying goodbye. The person who would leave a dead girl in the water and hide the fatality. And then you...*you*"—I gesture to her. The twenty-four-year-old blonde smartass with more guts than I even gave her credit for—that Zoey Durand. She's leaning on the booth's dining table, biting her lip constantly, staring at me like I'm *more* than the girl who saved her sister. More than the girl who failed Katie.

More than I even thought I could be. "*You* came home. And you see me—God, you see me—you see the parts of me that I so desperately want to love back. And I don't know what to do with that. What am I supposed to do with that—?"

Zoey bridges the distance, her hands slipping along my cheeks. "This." She tilts her head, and like a sailboat softly gliding to shore, she kisses me. The most beautiful kiss of my tragic existence—her lips like soft pillows, pulling me closer. Pulling me into her arms. And I am open, eviscerated, and spilling—because if not now than never.

And I can't live not giving all that I have and consuming all that she has. Just one more time.

I skim my fingers along her smooth jaw.

Her hands slip slowly down my arms until they reach the hem of my sweater. Our lips nudge in earnestness before she lifts off my top, and our kisses reignite in heady spurts between stripping each other bare.

I easily unclasp her razorback bra, and she smiles against my mouth. "You were always good at that."

My heart swells. I slip the bra off her arms while she quickly snaps off my pink push-up. Our panties fall to the floor.

Lips tingle from the force of our kisses, strengthening with desperation—passion that I can't bottle—I want to draw this out forever. I never want this single moment to end. Light rain pitter-patters on the top of the catamaran.

But I mostly hear her heavy, panting breath. My thumping, racing heart.

We devour with our hands, with our tongues. *Zoey.* Her palm travels along the curve of my hip, as if remembering the slope of my body and the fullness of my breasts.

She cups one and kisses my nipple.

I pulse and throb and ache, and I have a handful of her breast, my thumb teasing her perked nipple. A high-pitched sound escapes her reddened lips, "October."

"Zoey," I whisper, my hand descending between her legs. God, she's already so wet, and I slip a finger between her folds.

She squirms into a soft moan, then whispers, "Not fair, you got to touch me last time. Me first." Her fingers lightly descend my belly and to my hipbone, sending shockwaves through me. I shudder and clench, and my mouth parts as I feel her gentle touch on my pussy.

Oh my God.

Zoey ramps up my need, circling my clit, then slipping a finger inside me. I tremble. *Zoey, Zoey.* "*Me* first," I whisper against her more aggressive, clawing kiss that dizzies me. "You second." I guide her backwards until her back touches the dining table.

"Okay, alright," Zoey pants. "You first." She climbs on the table. We're both completely naked, and I could watch her drink in my body all night long. Because that also means I can drink in hers. The cute little freckles. Her slender legs that I break apart. Her soaked pussy that I lick.

She throws her head back. "Whoa, fuck, Kenobi."

"Lie back completely."

She complies, lying flat on the table, and I eat her out like she's the sweetest dessert I've ever tasted. I reach up and massage her breast, thumbing her nipple, and I open my eyes, watching how Zoey bites her lip, breath catching. She eyes the way my back is curved, ass in the air.

I lick and suck, and she quakes, "Holy..."

"You gorgeous little thing," I whisper against her heat, then press a kiss to her inner-thigh. "Come for me."

She shakes her head. "You come first. I want to wait for you...*oh wow,* shit." Her eyes nearly roll. "Toomuchtoomuch." I devour the way her spine arches off the table. The way she thrusts towards my lips. I flick her clit.

"You want it."

"I don't—I do. Fuck!" She gasps into a high-pitched cry. "Kenobi, waitwaitwaitpleasepleaseplease." Zoey moans so loudly, I almost lose breath watching her, and I listen as she jerks her left leg away from me.

"Okay." I stand up, even though she hasn't reached a full orgasm yet.

She has trouble catching her breath. "You are…supremely good at that."

"It's my favorite thing to do," I remind her, brushing sweaty hair off my shoulder. God, my skin is so warm to the touch. Everything about Zoey is torching my cravings into an inferno. My pussy clenches just watching her *breathe*.

Though, her breasts rise and fall with the movement.

Her heady gaze crashes against mine, and we slide together, hands roaming. Feet moving. Lips kissing. She's guiding me to the starboard stairs. Down into the main cabin. We kiss against a wall. Shoving in impatience.

Fuck the bed.

I'd fuck her right here on the floor. But we somehow bump our way out of the starboard hallway and into the cramped bedroom.

Climbing onto the blue comforter, I straddle Zoey and push her back to the mattress. She's out of breath, but she's gripping a fistful of my long hair and yanking me to her lips. She nips mine, and I moan against her mouth.

Zoey and her eagerness and her clawing aggression is the hottest thing I've ever encountered. I try to draw this slower.

So much slower.

So slow that she's able to roll us on our sides, and my leg hooks over the curve of her hip. Our bodies, coated in a sheen of sweat, meld together like perfect puzzle pieces, and I trace the roundness of her bottom before tucking her closer. My palm to the small of her back.

Zoey skims a finger down my lips. Her blue eyes melt against mine, and the love we share flourishes in our embrace.

Instead of there being a first or second, I whisper, "Let's come together."

Her smile says it all. I edge my lips against hers in another soft kiss—all the while our hands dive between each other's legs.

Heat brews, and I ache for her. So when Zoey fills me with two fingers, a noise I haven't heard in so long catches my throat. A cry of raw, overcome pleasure escapes me. She pumps in me while thumbing my clit.

I slip my fingers inside her. She moans against our kiss while I fuck her with the same scalding, leg-shaking pace. Our hips thrust to the movement of our hands, and we bridge ourselves together like we're trying desperately not to part.

We are both gentle, fragile pieces and unbreakable, ever-eternal things. The things that need to love and to be loved, and I don't want her to go.

I don't want this to come to an end.

"I love you…more than my heart even understands," I whisper as we ascend towards an unbearable limit.

"I've always loved you, Kenobi," she manages to say before her voice breaks into a breathy cry. I tease her clit, and she touches the most sensitive spot inside me. Oh God, my eyes roll, and every nerve-ending along my body is lit.

Black spots dance in my vision. Our hips bow. Our backs arch. Our hands hang on. I shudder against Zoey, and she cries against my shoulder. An orgasm ripples through us, one I wish to meet again.

But anyone who lives here knows not to *wish*.

Not to want.

Not to desire.

The longed-for things become lost things in Mistpoint Harbor. And I know I'm going to lose her again.

WE DON'T GO TO SLEEP RIGHT AWAY. LYING NAKED AND hot and sweaty on top of the covers, I twist a tendril of her blonde hair around my finger. "Why do you want to know this so badly?"

"Because it's your *name*," Zoey says like it's obvious. "And every time I ever asked anyone in school, they all had a different answer. *October is named after her birth month.* False. You were born in July. *October is named after her mom's favorite color. October is named after the fall season. October is named after some ancient goddess of harvest.* So what's the truth? Why do you have such a badass name?"

I roll my eyes. "Only you think it's badass."

"That is so not true. I'm pretty sure almost every girl wanted to be renamed *October* in high school. You made the name cool."

"Because everyone was obsessed with me," I say with bitchy flourish. "Even you."

"I was in love with you." She glances from my lips to my eyes, her fingers running playfully along my bare shoulder.

"Where is the line between love and obsession?"

Zoey thinks for a moment. "Wherever my ex is—he's on the wrong, *wrong* side of the line." I stiffen, and she slaps a hand to her forehead, wincing. "Fuck, sorry—I didn't mean to bring up my ex while we're…" She groans into her hands.

"Zoey," I breathe, prying her hands off her face. I straddle her waist to fully catch her wrists and tear her hands upward. "I don't care that you brought up your ex—it just reminded me about the lock on the door."

She eases.

And I let go of her wrists but still straddle her waist. "I never wanted to tell anyone why my mom named me October."

"Why not?"

"Because I liked the mystery. No one knew this little part of me, and I got to keep it all to myself." I explain how some family knows, but not many. My mom left when I was young, and she didn't tell most people. I think she must've been afraid of being judged.

"You don't have to tell me," Zoey says with so much understanding. But if there is anyone I want to share *all* of myself with— it's been her.

I bend down and kiss her cheek before whispering against her ear. "She named me after a character in an old horror movie."

"You're joking," Zoey gasps.

I shake my head. "The girl died in the movie, but I remember my mom saying she loved the name when she heard it." I nearly laugh at her crinkled nose. "See, it's not as interesting as being a goddess of harvest—"

"No, it's better," she interjects.

I scoff.

"It *is* better," Zoey says seriously. "Because it's the truth."

My heart fills to the brim. "Zoey." I want to kiss her again. Make love to her again. Trace the constellation of freckles on her lower back again. And never wake up from this dream together.

She props up on her elbows. "What if I stay?"

I freeze. "What?"

"What if I stay in Mistpoint Harbor?"

I climb off Zoey.

"Kenobi." She rolls towards me. I don't go far. "I'm already cursed. There's no fear of that anymore. So why am I leaving?"

"Your job is in Chicago. There's not much here for you." My voice sounds cold, but a strange pain is biting my insides.

She sits up more, hurt in her features. "You know that's not true."

I give her a sad look. My heart clenching. "I can't be the biggest reason you stay in Mistpoint Harbor, Zoey."

She's quiet. "I can't help it if you are."

"I won't be here!" I shout, my soul shattering. "I'll be behind *bars.*" I touch my forehead, dizzy. How can this be possible? The moment where she could end up back home for good, I'm the one who will be gone. Before she speaks, I say quickly, fervently, "If you stay, I'm *not* changing my mind—I'm still turning myself in, so don't you dare stay for me. *Don't.*" I drill a glare into her, and Zoey nods slowly.

"Okay, *okay.*" She takes a sharp breath. "I don't know what I'm going to do. Maybe I'll go." She stands off the bed. I watch her walk naked towards the door, and my stomach lurches.

"Where are you going?" My voice spikes into a higher panicked register. *Don't leave now.* We have some hours left. I'm kicking myself for running her out.

"I'll be right back." I hear the smile in her voice while she's out of sight, in the hallway. "I have to get something."

I slip underneath the comforter and sheets. Forcing myself not to smother my face with the pillow in agony. I remember the feeling of coming with Zoey. Being so close to the woman I love—and I try, *I try* to push away the nagging, tortured thought of this being the end.

The end of our love story.

The fake book she's supposed to be writing. I wish I could skip to the last page. I wish I could reread the parts where she says she loves me.

Stop wishing. Ugh. I am about to grab that pillow, and then Zoey returns with her backpack-purse. She slings the thing onto the bed and hops onto the mattress that bounces with her weight. And now she's straddling me. Only the blankets slip to my hips, covering my waist and lower.

"I have something for you." She digs into the backpack-purse.

"You bought me something?"

"Sort of. The tickets cost a decent amount, but I had to wait in the longest queue for them. I thought I'd get booted because my internet sucked ass. Somehow, I was lucky in Chicago. Got the tickets, went to the *thing*, and waited in her line, which was actually pretty short compared to everyone else's line. But I got this." She hands me a photo of Jane fucking Cobalt with her messy *signature* in the corner.

My mouth drops. "You went to the FanCon tour and you're just now telling me?!"

"Are you fangirling? Is this what a Kenobi fangirl moment looks like?" Zoey is grinning.

I would shove her off my lap, but I like her there. And plus, I can't stop gawking at Jane's signature. The picture isn't on photo paper. Zoey must've printed this off the internet. Six cats surround Jane, and she cuddles her oldest black cat Lady Macbeth against the crook of her neck.

It's adorable.

I look up at Zoey, my eyes misting. "Our rules—we were never supposed to meet again—but you went to the FanCon tour. Just to get her signature for me."

"Yeah," Zoey admits softly. "I did do that…I guess a part of me always thought, *maybe we would meet again.* A part me always wanted to, and I thought if we never did, then I could mail it to you. I thought about doing that…you don't like it?" She suddenly frowns, seeing me set aside Jane Cobalt's signature.

"I love it," I say softly. "But there's someone's signature I'd love more."

Zoey realizes what I'm implying, and she groans, "Oh come on, I'm not as awesome as Jane Eleanor Cobalt." I'm surprised she knows her middle name, but then again, I've probably mentioned it a dozen times.

I catch her chin, then splay my fingers against her cheek. "No, you aren't," I agree and her chest rises and falls before I whisper, "You're better."

Zoey starts crying. "Fuck me."

"I already did."

She laughs, wiping her cheeks, and we share kisses and tears. Zoey finds a photo of just her among Brian's collection of family pictures. *Sorry, Brian, this one is mine.* It's a photo from her eighteenth birthday.

Colt shoved vanilla cake in her face, and she's laughing.

She signs it with a Sharpie, her tears dripping on the photo. I rub my splotchy cheeks, my throat swelling closed, and we're hugging when she hands me the gift that feels like a real goodbye.

We don't let go.

Her hands tangle in my hair. Mine are lost in hers. "I'll love you forever," Zoey whispers. "No matter where we are or where we go."

CHAPTER 30

ZOEY DURAND

I wake up and October is gone.

I pat the spot on the bed next to me. *Cold.* Did she make a quick exit? Vanish out of thin air? Sitting up, I hold my legs, trying to fight tears.

Knives stab my lungs with each inhale. Is this how she felt when I left? Like the world is sideways, and intaking oxygen is like swallowing razorblades—I throw a pillow onto the ground. Anger—*anger* is better than sadness, right?

Crawling out of bed, I slip on my clothes from last night, and I gather my things around Brian's boat.

My dad's boat.

The photos.

The longer I'm here alone, the more everything slams against me, and I slide down the galley fridge and cry into my palms. *I don't want to leave.*

I can't leave.

Mistpoint Harbor has the strongest grip on me—not because of these stupid curses or some strange, fate-driven chokehold.

But because my family is *here.* Everyone I love is *here.* Time is precious, and I lost six years with them. I don't want to lose anymore.

That's what's important to me. Not a job. Not money.

Just love.

All kinds, and October said not to stay for her—and while I know she'll always be a part of the reason—she isn't the only reason. So I'll reassure her, and maybe she'll accept that.

Stand up.

Stand up.

I force myself on my feet, and I check my phone. Fuck, it's still dead. Figures. I didn't really want to look for flights, so I wasn't in a hurry to charge the thing.

Ready to go, I unlock Brian's catamaran from the inside, and I stop on the bridgedeck and notice something pink on the cockpit chair.

A muffin from Harbor Perk is wrapped in a folded napkin and sits on top of a note. My heart flutters, and I pick up the pastry and read the note that's typed.

> **I love you more than possible, Zoey.**
> **Meet me at the Edge of the World before you**
> **go. Please. - OB**

Does she want to talk? I reread the note. The typed font seems strange, but October always signed her notes with a dash and then her initials. *And* she included a pastry.

What if she's changed her mind about turning herself in?

What if she wants to run away together?

What if she wants to live with me in Chicago?

Or we could live together in Mistpoint Harbor. All the possibilities of a future with October flood me, and hope surges. I'm about to call her, but I click at a dead screen.

"Fuck it," I say to myself. "I'm going to the Edge of the World."
I don't have a car, but I race back into the catamaran and snatch
Brian's keys out of a drawer.

Hurrying off the dock and into the parking lot, I find a moped
parked in its usual spot. Yeah, I'm stealing my dad's moped. Guess
he'll just have to ground me later.

And I ride off towards the woods.

THE CLIFFSIDE WOODS ARE DENSE. FOG SKATES ALONG
the muddy ground, and light rain mists the air. I have trouble making
sense of where the hell I'm going. "October?!" I call out and glance
at my black-screened phone.

I really regret not charging it last night.

I do *not* regret the sex, though.

That was epic.

Taking a big bite of the muffin, I continue my journey through
the Edge of the World. Is that a campsite? No tents. No people. Just
ashy firepits. Primitive camping.

October's white fur coat warms my arms now, but it isn't sensible
with the light rain. Touching the sleeves, they're too damp.

I'm guessing she'll be in her pink rain jacket. *Pink. Pink. Look out
for pink.* And then I hear the squish of boots in mud.

A shadowy figure emerges through the fog. In seconds, I can see.

My face slowly falls. The muffin slips out of my hand, and I
breathe, "You?"

CHAPTER 31

OCTOBER BRAMBILLA

Colt called me at five a.m.

He said not to wake Zoey. Said to meet him at the lighthouse. He needed to talk alone.

To ask me to slip out on the woman I love—that was a *humongous* request that I can't even believe I fulfilled. What fucking possessed me to do such a heinous thing?

I'm glaring at him while he's shirtless and slouched on his tattered sofa. A bottle of OJ in his hand like he's nursing last night's power outage hangover.

"I thought this was *urgent*," I snap. Honestly, I thought I'd walk in and he'd look more desperate to see me. Like he'd be crawling towards my feet. I feel awful standing here and not back in bed with Zoey.

"It is," he says into a swig of juice.

Ugh! "Whatever you have to say better be worth it—because I just left your sister *alone* after I slept with her."

Colt raises a hand. "Spare me the details."

"I wasn't going to give them to you," I say coldly, a quick second from turning around and driving back to the docks.

"OB." Colt sits forward, cupping the jug of juice. He hesitates a little. "Shit, I'm not any good at this."

"At what?"

"Being honest without…poking the bear?" He shrugs and splays his hands open. "I'm not really someone people come to for heart-to-hearts."

"You asked me here, Colt."

"To tell you not to do it." He intakes a sharper breath. "Don't do it. Don't turn yourself in."

I open my mouth. Too stunned to say anything. I never thought Colt would ask me to stand down. To back away from the missing girl that *he* so desperately wanted to find. Well, he found her, and now he wants to act like nothing happened?

He licks his lips. "I prayed to God you'd love my sister with no reservations, no hesitations, as much as she fucking *adored* the shit out of you. I prayed you'd be good to her—that you'd make her happy. Make her laugh, and she'd have the kind of love that you can *literally* write books about. Not just made-up ones."

"Funny," I say dryly and quietly, imprisoning breath.

"Yeah…funny, 'cause I'm not the kind of guy God answers." I didn't realize he was religious, but I don't know Colt on a deep level.

He meets my defensive glare. I'm waiting for him to tell me to get the hell out of her life. And he says, "I never thought to pray for your happiness. I never thought to pray for Zoey to be good to you—I just figured you're October Brambilla. You're the shit, right? What kind of prayers would you ever fucking need?"

I can't speak. Can't breathe. Waiting for the punchline. Waiting for the knife.

"You're a lot like me. The layers." He pats his bare chest. "And if I've learned anything in my twenty-nine years of life, it's that people like you and me—we bleed internally just as easily. We're just better at hiding the damage." He picks at the label on the OJ bottle. "I guess what I'm trying to tell you is that you need to be happy. Not just for Zoey but for you. Stop bleeding yourself out. You want to make this right for Augustine, but she's *gone*. I can't bring her back any more than you can, and trust me, I would try if I knew how."

I finally take a breath. "If I don't turn myself in, the town will always call you the madman in the lighthouse."

"They can call me the pussy-whipped limp-dick shithead in the lighthouse for all I care. I don't give a shit."

I let out a laugh, a real laugh.

He smiles. "Did I make any sense?"

"Just enough." We talk for a while longer about Augustine Anders, the girl that has connected us, the girl we're both trying to let go. I find myself taking a seat on his uncomfortable chair. I never thought I'd like Colt Durand as much as I do in these minutes. Minutes become hours, and I feel more unburdened—until I check the time.

"*Fuck*," I curse. "How is it already eight a.m.? I have to go—" Just as I stand, just as I grab my keys, my phone rings.

Zoey. I'm so sorry, Zoey. I'm about to apologize when I see the Caller ID. *Amelia Roberts.* Frowning, I tuck the phone to my ear, headed to the door, "Amelia?"

"October," she whispers so quietly but so quickly that I have to strain my ears to hear. "I followed him like you asked. He went to the Edge of the World, and she's here."

I stop dead at the door. "Who's there?"

"Zoey—he's chasing Zoey through the woods. He has a knife."

He can't hurt her. He can't hurt her. He can't kill her. I padlock away panic and the visual of Zoey terrified. My fear won't help her.

"Follow them," I tell Amelia and I watch Colt stand up with furrowed brows and confusion.

"I already am," she replies.

"What's going on, OB?" he asks.

To Amelia, I say, "Drop a pin on your location. I'll be there as soon as I can."

"Got it."

I hang up. "Zoey's ex is chasing her through the woods. We need to go now." Colt is already step-for-step with my hurried pace outside. Rain pelts us on our way to my Jeep.

"How do you know where she is?"

"I asked Amelia to track him last night. I gave her his information."

Colt climbs into the passenger seat, cursing up a storm. It's unhelpful, but I don't have time to mention that. "Open the glove compartment," I instruct while I put the Jeep in drive and peel out.

"For what?" He's dialing a number.

"My pistol," I say. His phone rings. "Who—"

He cuts me off before I can finish my question. "We're not doing this without Brian."

"Or Parry," I tell him.

Colt catches my eyes in a brief second. "Or your sister."

I nod.

We finish this together.

CHAPTER 32

ZOEY DURAND

What the hell. What the hell! *What the hell?!* Shock and adrenaline pump viciously through my veins while I'm running for my *fucking* life through dense, foggy woods. Mud suctions my boots into the earth and slows me down.

Shit! I force my legs upward. I keep moving—I have to keep moving. Breath catches in my throat, and I speed forward into the thick fog. Light rain pelts my cheeks and hair. Too hot from panic, cold barely touches me

"ZOEY!" he yells.

Hairs prick the back of my neck. My toes almost catch a log. "Fuck," I choke out. *Don't trip. Don't fall.*

I hug a tree trunk to catch my balance, and then I keep moving. *Don't stop.*

When Ashton first emerged through the woods, I was whip-lashed.

I never thought the note and pastry could be a set-up because I wanted *so badly* to believe October had a change of heart. I just saw what I desired most. Not thinking about how I'd told Ashton about October's notes from high school. The pastries.

I even showed him a note that I kept.

He would've known how to replicate her messages. He knew exactly how to trap me, and I'm guessing he asked a local about the woods around here. They would've mentioned Edge of the World. Or he could've used Google.

"What's wrong with you, Zoey?" Ashton said like I had some sort of vendetta against him. *"I've been so nice to you, but you can't even try to be kind to me? Not for a second."*

I bit back a retort about how tricking me into meeting him is the very inverse of *nice*. And how I learned to stand up for myself and I'm not going to let *him* walk all over me.

Instead, I thought the smarter thing would be to ignore the backbone I'd grown, and I just tried to apologize. *"I'm really sorry for hurting you, Ashton. I really am."*

He let out a shrill laugh with the shake of his head. *"No, you aren't. If you were, you would've come here for me. I wouldn't have had to pretend to be that bitch."* I must've glared because he added, *"Yeah, that's right. You only love her. You've only ever loved her. How do you feel stringing other people along? Do you get off on it?"*

I shook my head repeatedly.

"How many others have you humiliated? I can't be the first."

I couldn't speak, and I doubt anything I said would've convinced him. He made up his mind.

And then he drew a hunting knife out from behind his back. As a power play? To try and scare and humiliate me? To kill me? I didn't wait to chat and figure out that he hates me enough to hurt me. It's really, *really* clear he does!

I bolted.

I'm still running, and I can't tell how much distance separates us. Not through the fog.

"I wasted years on you! FOR WHAT?!" Ashton screams, his voice an echo through the maze of tree trunks.

304

Branches rake against my cheek, blooming pain in my face, but I don't stop moving. *Where the fuck am I going?* How could I be so stupid? Hot tears scald my eyes, and it hurts to breathe.

I don't even care if love makes me do idiotic things.

I don't even care if I die because I love October more than humanly imaginable.

And I hear her icy voice in my head, *"Don't die for me, Zoey. You better live for me."*

Okay.

Okay. I put myself in this horrible position, but I'm not rolling over. I'm not that person. Survival instincts kick in.

I grit my teeth and force my legs higher out of the mud. Running stronger. My pulse thumps so fast, so hard—*I think he's close.*

Twigs crack behind me, and I hear his heavy, rageful footsteps. Braving a glance over my shoulder, I see nothing but gray fog.

And then I collide into a tree.

"Fuck!" I stumble back and fall ass-first into mud. *Get up, get up, get up, Zoey!* I hear October again. Screaming at me, and I pick myself up, clawing into the wet dirt with my fingertips. Globs of mud cling to the white fur coat that I wear.

Just as I stand, his hand wraps around my ankle—and he wrenches me backwards. Ground slips beneath my feet, and I hit the mud hard, gasping for breath.

"This is what it feels like," Ashton says, his voice distant in my ringing ears. He starts dragging me by the ankle like I'm a dead carcass. My belly skids against the wet earth and soggy brush.

"Stop, stop!" I yell, trying to kick out of his grip. Trying to claw into the mud, but he's sprinting and the earth scrapes against my palms and fingers at a dizzying speed. "HELP!" I scream, eating mouthfuls of dirt. "HELP!"

"No one's coming for you, Zoey." His hateful grip hurts on my ankle. Like an iron vice is clamped against me.

I try to flail.

I try to dig.

His hatred is mightier than my desperation.

My eyes burn and glass with fear. "WHAT'S WRONG WITH YOU?!" I yell at him, lungs burning.

"WHAT'S WRONG WITH YOU?!" he screams back at my face, pausing long enough for me to kick his nose with my freed foot.

"Argh!" He makes a pained noise, but just as I scramble to stand, he captures my ankle again and wrenches me back down. Dragging me harder. More forcefully.

I suddenly see a signpost with a warning symbol. *No.* "The cliffs," I choke out. "There are cliffs up ahead, don't—"

"You don't think I know that?"

Is he going to throw me off the fucking cliff? I scream out as I dig harder, clawing my way back to the signed post.

"Stop! Moving!" Ashton yells, and he slashes his knife at my leg. Pain sears, but I barely see blood seep through my jeans. I'm still clawing.

Still digging.

Get away from me. Get away from me!

I jerk to a motionless state at a sudden, violent *bang.* A gun— someone just shot a gun. Did he...am I...?

Another bang resounds. I flinch as a shotgun shell skids near my cheek.

"ZOEY!" I hear my name in the distance. *October.* October is calling me. My heart tries to flood with more than just fear and adrenaline.

"ZOEY!" Brian yells. I can't see him. I can't see Parry or Colt or Babette, but I hear all of them.

I whip my head back behind me, Ashton's grip still tight on my ankle, but he's stumbling backwards, staring wide-eyed at his shoulder. Blood soaks through his khaki cargo jacket. Right as I scramble to pull away, Ashton trips over loose rock and he begins to fall.

Taking me with him.

I shriek.

"ZOEY!" October screams.

I'm sliding. I'm sliding! *I can't slip over the edge. Don't slip over the edge.* On the other side of the cliff is a drop into endless oak and hickory trees. As Ashton stumbles backward, his weight is yanking me towards the edge, and he clutches me—not like a parachute.

But like he's ready to die with me.

I kick him.

I kick and kick and kick like this is the last breath I might take. I'm so close to the fucking edge when my foot rips out of his grip. I roll quickly onto my ass and scuttle backwards, digging my elbows and heels into the dirt.

Before I can see Ashton fall backward, hands are underneath my armpits. "Don't look!" Brian shouts and pulls me so far away from the edge. We're back in the thick, muddy woods. Away from rock. Fog conceals the cliffside again, and I can only hear the breakage of tree branches and a final *thump*.

I try to catch my breath. I'm in safe hands that try to bring air to my starved lungs.

"I have you. *I have you.*" Brian helps me to my feet, his hands hovering over my trembling body while my chest rises and falls, and I try to make sense of what just happened. He's studying me head to toe. "You're bleeding."

My leg... "It's not that deep." And I lock eyes with Brian—I lock eyes with my dad—and something powerful overwhelms every piece of me. Burns my gaze. Swells my throat.

My dad is here.

And I just feel in my heart of hearts—that everything is going to be okay. And isn't that what dads do? They make things feel okay.

"Don't leave me," I choke out and toss my arms around him. He's so surprised by the hug, it takes him a minute to hug back. But when he does, his arms tighten tenfold around me.

I feel like I'm seven. Knees scraped up from tripping over my feet. Needing my dad, but there comes my big brother instead.

My dad has been here all along.

When we pull back, I start to ask, "Where's...?" I don't need to finish. I see her. October, Parry, Colt, and Babette are barreling through the morning fog, and they stop when they reach us.

"Zoey," October breathes a strangled breath. I must look like utter shit. She's so beautiful, even with fear and determination icing her features into commanding stoicism.

"There you are," I try to joke, but my voice sounds hoarse. "I thought I was meeting you here..." I'm walking to her.

"I'm here now." She's walking towards me. Until we both begin to sprint. We collide like there is nowhere else to go. Nowhere else that makes sense. When we embrace, we're like her lovebirds landing softly together in a nest.

Safe at home.

My fingers curl around her pink peacoat. I bury my nose into the sweet scent of her hair. She holds onto me—holds me up—until my leg hurts enough that I kneel. October kneels with me. She cups my dirtied, scratched cheeks, and we kiss through silent tears.

I'm covered in mud. "Your coat." I try unsuccessfully to pluck a chunk of mud from the fur. Now brown. "I'll get it dry-cleaned."

She glares like I'm the fool she loves. "I don't care about the fucking coat."

"I do…it belongs to you."

October looks overwhelmed. She places a sweet kiss on my forehead. "Forget the coat, sweets."

Brian, Parry, and Colt are around us as light rain continues to drizzle in the cold. They're asking me about Ashton. How I ended up here, but I shake my head, a mess of confusion about other details.

He was shot, and before I ask them, I suddenly see a gun on the ground. Right beside October.

The bottom of my stomach drops. "Kenobi, did you…?" I trail off, remembering the shotgun shell.

The gun next to her is a pistol.

Our eyes meet.

"I didn't," she breathes. "It wasn't me."

"Then who…?"

Who shot Ashton?

"OB!" Babette calls out, and we all rotate to the right. Babette stands near a wooden sign that warns of the cliff ahead.

She's not alone.

Amelia Roberts is here, and Miss Mistpoint herself has a shotgun slung on her back. She clutches her arms like she's cold, but her green puffer rain jacket looks warm. Her glasses mist from the fog, and mud is caked up to her shins.

Before I speak, a deep, older man's voice echoes in the distance. "Amelia, are you out there?!"

"I'm here!" She rotates to the blanket of fog. I've been gone too long, and I can't distinguish the mystery voice.

"You called him?" Parry questions Amelia.

"I just *shot* a guy. I had to."

Colt is pinching his eyes. "We're all fucked—scratch that, those of us named *Durand* are fucked." And then I realize who's approaching moments before the tall, muscular figure slips through the fog.

Sheriff Carmichael is here.

CHAPTER 33

ZOEY DURAND

Once Sheriff Carmichael checks out the cliffside and Anna Roberts arrives with more police, this part of the Edge of the World is taped off as a crime scene. Rain pitter patters against the tree branches, and even though I look like I was literally dragged through the mud—Brian, Parry, Colt, Babette, October, and Amelia are splattered with dirt like they tripped and fell to reach me.

Like they never slowed. Like they gave *everything*.

I'm also not sure if their bedraggled appearance is incriminating. I'm not a fucking lawyer, but Ashton falling over the edge was partly an accident. That should be obvious, but most of us are still tense.

Us, Durands, especially.

We all hang around a primitive campground with a picnic table and ashy firepit until we're told we can leave. Hopefully that'll happen soon.

Parry is doing a good job of forcing Brian and Colt *away* from the cops. My brothers—or rather, my uncle (scratch that—I'm *never* calling Colt that) and my dad (still strange)—are eager to tell their side of the story so the town doesn't skew everything. But they need to wait to give their testimony of the events until they're asked.

"Is she going to lie and say Brian shot him?" I ask October while she picks dirt clumps out of my hair. We're watching Amelia speak to her mom and Sheriff Carmichael. She's detailing the events, and they all keep glancing over at me like I caused an earthquake in Mistpoint Harbor.

"No, she'll tell the truth." October sounds assured.

Amelia Roberts saved my life. I *never* thought that square on my Bingo card would be filled.

I owe her. Or at the very least, I need to thank Amelia. I might be at the bottom of the cliff if she hadn't slowed Ashton down.

I blow out a breath, still a little rattled from being chased and dragged. I try not to think about Ashton's body. His death. October hasn't left my side. I lean into her and rest my cheek on her shoulder.

October shakes dirt off her fingers. Before she tries fixing my hair again, I catch her hand in mine. "You don't have to, Kenobi." I look up at her.

"I want to," she whispers, and my heart swells before she asks, "Have you wondered how we all knew you were here?"

"It hadn't crossed my mind yet," I admit. "But now it definitely has."

She plucks a twig out of my hair. "I asked Amelia to track your ex. She called me and told me what was happening this morning."

Holy shit.

"Okay, I really owe her," I mutter out loud, and I laugh to myself. "Your best friend is kinda awesome." I wince. "Unless she sells us out right now."

October only seems uneasy when Amelia starts arguing with her mom, and my mind is reeling. I pull a little back from October. Just to meet her narrowed, focused gaze.

"Where did you go this morning, if you weren't the one who left me the note to meet you here?" My stomach sinks. *Was she leaving me without saying goodbye?*

Was she turning herself in while I was sleeping—just so I couldn't be there with her?

Her face falls seeing my hurt build. "Zoey—" She cuts herself off as Amelia approaches us.

"Amelia," I start to share my gratitude.

"It was nothing." Amelia shifts her body to block me out and speak solely to October.

But I butt in, "Why did you have a shotgun?"

"I always bring one to the Edge of the World," Amelia says like it's the only rational thing to do. "You never know what animals might be in these woods."

Right.

Amelia continues, "The better question is why *you* came here with nothing. Not a knife, not a gun, not a taser or even a pen."

A pen?

October shoots her best friend a look to stand down. "Zoey has been in Chicago."

"So everyone in Chicago has no common sense?"

"I have common sense," I chime in. "I just thought I was meeting October."

"In the woods?" Amelia says like I'm a total idiot.

She doesn't know what my heart was feeling. She wasn't there last night! "You wouldn't understand!" I shout in frustration and so loudly birds squawk and fly from treetops. Brian, Colt, Parry, and Babette glance over at me. I mutter out, "I'm fine."

Amelia whispers hotly, "I just tracked you two miles through the woods and shot your ex-boyfriend for you, so I understand *something*."

"Alright," October interjects like we're poking beehives. "Enough. You've both been through something traumatic."

"I'm *fine*," Amelia snaps at me.

"I'm fine too," I snap at her.

We're both crossing our arms in a huff, and October is rolling her eyes. Why does Amelia make me turn into a fucking kindergartener? I get my shit together, and I remember how she helped me.

"Thank you," I say suddenly to Amelia.

"For what?" She bristles.

"For saving my life. I'd hug you but—"

"Please don't." She cringes.

Awesome. I mumble to myself, "Love having that effect on people."

October slips an arm around my hips, as though to remind me that I'm not gross. I'm not unwanted. *She wants me.*

If she did, why did she leave this morning?

October has her own questions, but they're not for me. "Why were you arguing with your mother?"

"Oh…" Amelia rolls her eyes, then ices me out further with a back-turn, but she whispers not that quietly to October, "She was questioning my curse. She kept asking if I knew about a latex allergy before my eighteenth birthday."

October stiffens.

"Did you?" I wonder.

Amelia huffs. "This is a *private* conversation, Zoey."

"You should tell Zoey," October says.

"Why? Isn't she leaving soon?"

I can't say a thing before October tells Amelia, "Regardless, I trust and love her, and you can trust her too."

She still loves me. That counts for something. I know it does. A glimmer of hope brightens.

Surprisingly, Amelia shifts and faces me. "This stays between you and October, but I knew before I was eighteen."

About her latex allergy? Which means… "You weren't cursed."

"My mom does *not* know, and she will *never* know." She casts a furtive glance at Anna Roberts who's speaking intensely to Sheriff Carmichael.

I realize Amelia Roberts was cursed *today*. She shot a man before he fell to his death.

My lips part. "Amelia—"

"Don't."

"Don't what?"

"Don't feel sorry for me." She adjusts the shotgun strap on her arm. "I did what I had to do."

I nod slowly. "Thank you," I say more deeply this time.

She nods back curtly, but I swear her eyes soften. October hugs her friend, and a worse thought hits me.

If Amelia is willing to lie about her curse to her mom, would she lie about what happened today? Just as October and Amelia pull apart, Sheriff Carmichael approaches us.

"Well, that just about does it." He rests his hands on his belt. "I think we have everything we need for today."

Brian's eyes flash hot. "You've only questioned Amelia."

"We don't need any other reports—"

"That's bullshit," Colt snaps.

"Hey, watch your tongue," Sheriff Carmichael rebuts with the shake of his head. "Amelia was the one directly involved"—Parry is rolling his eyes around the campground—"and her testimony is all we need today. You're all free to go."

Brian freezes. "We're free to go?"

"That's what I said." He nods. "This is a clear case of self-defense. If we need you for paperwork, we'll give you a call. But yes, you're all free to go."

October whispers to me, "She wouldn't throw you under."

Amelia came through.

Except I'm not sure we are free. I don't even know where we're going from here. All I know is I want to be with October, but is that even possible anymore?

She slips her hand into mine, and I sense the comfort and love in her grip. Something that screams, *I'm never leaving. I love you. Be with me, Zoey.* But how many times am I going to only see what I want to see?

I am a fool because I choose to believe she's not going anywhere.

I choose to believe it's us, together always, at the end of our love story. I might not be a writer, but I wouldn't want it to end any other way.

CHAPTER 34

OCTOBER BRAMBILLA

"We're all going to The Drunk Pelican. Do you want to come along?" I ask Amelia on our trek out of the Edge of the World. Zoey is further up ahead with her family and my sister.

I can't think about how awful she looks. She's nearly unrecognizable. Like a little mud monster. Seeing her scrapes and scratches still twists my stomach.

The worst parts of me wish I'd seen Ashton fall. I wish I could've pushed him over myself.

"I should go home. Talk later?" Amelia says.

We pause near an oak tree to hug, and I thank her again for saving Zoey. I'd like to think that someday Amelia and Zoey can be friends. Or at the very least, *friendly*.

I have enough time to briefly tell her the truth behind my curse. She deserves to know. When I finish, she isn't surprised to hear that Aunt Effie and her mom and likely rest of the town council have been protecting me.

"It's what they do," she says. "It's what we'll do. Sooner than we realized." She protected the Durands.

For me.

They could've easily been blamed for Ashton's death in some twisted scenario. The town would've loved a more entertaining story where the Durands are the villains.

The children of the Mother Murderer killing Zoey's ex-boyfriend—it would've been a great tale.

A great lie.

I frown at Amelia. "Why would your mom go along with the truth? She gains nothing from this, and I have nothing to bargain. She could've said *fuck October* and thrown me in with the Durands." I've been expecting to be lumped in with them.

"You've been my best friend since we were in diapers," Amelia reminds me. "She *adores* you."

It crashes into me. That this all boils down to love.

I can't help but smile. One of the oldest sayings in the museum is *never fall in love in a cursed town*.

And yet, *love* is the most powerful thing here.

$\mathscr{P}$UDDLES DRY UP ON THE WOODEN DECK OF THE DRUNK Pelican that overlooks the harbor. Zoey and I sit on top of the picnic table with my sister, Brian, Colt, and Parry.

Dirtied. Spent.

But still kicking.

Brian brought out a cooler, and we all drink beers and bottles of white wine.

We watch the clouds clear as the rain stops. Bright afternoon sun finally peeks through and glitters the lake where docked boats sway more gently. The historic lift bridge in the distance lets sailboats pass. Through the windows of The Drunk Pelican, we can hear the jukebox playing Frank Sinatra's "That's Life" again.

I peek at Zoey who smiles out at the beautiful weather. She shuts her eyes and basks a little in the sunlight. I have so much I want to tell her.

The anticipation mounts the longer I wait, but I don't want to ruin this peaceful moment. I splay my fingers over hers on the picnic table.

She curls her fingers around mine, and I look out at the shimmering water. All of us have met grief in this town. We've all lost someone. But those of us born in Mistpoint Harbor are crafted from the things stronger than bone. The things that grow out of ash.

The things that endure.

Stories often told here are the miserable, dastardly ones, but there is good to be found. Reasons to stay. Reasons to love Mistpoint.

The beauty of the lake.

The old endearing bar behind us with a broken jukebox and salty catfish.

The late nights at The Wharf where Uncle Milo puts on Lou Monte's "Lazy Mary" and Julius LaRosa's "Eh Cumpari" and everyone dances.

The people who'd create mysteries to protect you.

The people who'd crawl through mud for you.

The people who have profound love for you.

With the song still playing, Brian stands up with the swig of beer. The sole survivor. Quietly, he leaves inside The Drunk Pelican.

One by one, they go as silently as the next.

Colt gazes out at the sun while he slips off the picnic table. Without looking back, he heads towards his home. The madman in the lighthouse.

Babette ties her hair into a high pony with gloved hands. The girl who hates to be touched. After a quiet wave to me and Zoey, she walks in the direction of the Wharf.

And then there were three.

Parry DiNapoli nods to us in a goodbye, trying to smile, but like the rest of us—we don't know when Zoey plans to fly back to Chicago.

He soaks in the sun before slipping away. The boy who's afraid of the dark. He walks inside The Drunk Pelican.

I sip from a wine bottle. "And then there were two," I say out loud, glancing over at Zoey, her cheeks smeared with mud. "The girl who survived her ex."

Zoey takes the bottle. "And the ghost girl who came alive again." She drinks a hearty swig.

We share a small smile, but my lips flatline. The peaceful moment is coming to an end. "How much time do we have left together? Before your flight?"

Zoey is staring at my lips.

"Zoey," I snap. "You can't seriously want to kiss me right now." God, do I love that she does.

"Sorry, Jesus, maybe your lips shouldn't be so pretty." She blushes. "They're otherworldly." She takes a bigger swig.

I give her a pointed look. "Your lips are something to be admired. Something worth kissing."

"And yours aren't?"

"I didn't say that." I eye her lips, craving to kiss her.

"Don't lie, Kenobi—you don't want me to be more obsessed with myself than I'm obsessed with you."

That is true.

I smile.

"Aw and now she's smiling. I made October Brambilla smile. Call the press again!" She's shouting towards the lake. "Celebrity Crush!"

I stroke her muddied hair. "You're insufferable."

"The ghost loves me." She leans into my hip.

"I do." *I really do.* Our eyes meet in a tender second, and reality creeps back towards us. "You asked where I was this morning. Where I went."

"Yeah?" She straightens up, turning more towards me. Our knees knock. She hugs onto the wine bottle.

"I was with Colt."

"My brother?" Her blonde brows shoot up. "Why?"

I explain how he called me. Asked me to meet him at the lighthouse. How we talked for hours about Augustine Anders and my future. How I'm not going to turn myself in.

"You aren't?" Zoey chokes out, uncontrollable tears leaking. "Fuck, I'm sorry—"

"Don't be." I wipe the creases of her eyes and the tear that tracks through her muddied cheek. Zoey watches me brush my thumb softly against her face.

We both breathe in at the same time.

"What does this mean for us, October?"

This is the part that frightens me. The part where I have no control. Just like six years ago, Zoey can leave me. I might be alone and heartbroken all over again, but I wouldn't trade this time I've had with her. Feeling a kind of love that comes once in a blue moon. And I've felt it twice with the same woman.

How lucky I've been.

How cursed I may be.

I hold nothing back. With everything in my heart and soul, I profess, "I want to be with you, Zoey. I want to be your girlfriend for longer than a night and as more than just a dream. Something long-lasting and real—I want *you* and only you." I take a sharp breath. "But—"

"Shit, there's a *but?*"

We're both on a cliff together, but I'm hopeful we can survive this one too. "Don't leave your job and Chicago for me."

"Kenobi—"

"Don't," I force out. "If you want—if you'll let me—I'd like to come with you."

Her eyes well. "To Chicago?"

I nod, tears clouding my eyes too. I once told Zoey that I'd leave Mistpoint Harbor for love, and I did try. This time, I'd like to try again. For her.

It's always only been for her.

I blink but tears fall. "Alright, now you have to stop crying," I say icily. "You're making me cry."

She wipes at my cheeks with a laugh that fades too quickly. "I can't make you leave Mistpoint. Your sister is here."

"You're not making me do anything." I cup her soft cheek. She cups mine. "I want to be where you are." *Please want me there, Zoey.*

She rests her forehead against mine, laughing into a tearful smile. "You'd come to Chicago for me."

"Haven't you realized? I'd do anything for you, you idiot."

She laughs harder. "I'm so in love with you, Kenobi, and wherever we go, it doesn't matter as much as being together. I'll be the happiest just knowing you're there."

I brighten more than the sun that bathes us, and instantly, Zoey and I draw together in a kiss worthy of fireworks and applause and standing ovations. Worthy of our fake book.

And our real love.

She smiles against the kiss, and our happiness lifts my lips higher. We stay on the deck of The Drunk Pelican. Kissing, finishing off the bottle of white wine, and this might be our last chapter in Mistpoint Harbor. The last time I'm tied to the monotonous fried crullers.

Our new home, new start could be in Chicago, but I just dream of opening a door and seeing Zoey on the other side.

No matter where we are, I've always just dreamt of her. The girl who makes me come alive again.

And again.

EPILOGUE

1 MONTH LATER ♡

ZOEY DURAND

A knock sounds at the front door. *She's here.* She's here—and why am I late for our most important date? Oh yeah, because I dumped liquid foundation on my cotton black dress, tried to rub the spot off and created a massive splotch—then I used a broken hair dryer to dry the thing.

I'm a mess.

At least October would say I'm *her* mess. I smile to myself while I quickly check the state of my hair—half-up and clipped with a gold barrette (prettier than usual)—and then I swipe on lip gloss and grab the bundle of peonies, plus a little pouch of bird seed that I tied with ribbon.

Okay, *okay*, I'm all in one piece.

Let's go, Zoey.

I sprint to the door. Just as another knock sounds, I twist the knob and open. "Hey…" Words are stolen, and I bite my lip seeing October Brambilla in her commanding aura of beauty on the other side.

It's springtime.

The cool breeze blows in, but the pleasant weather is no match for October. Her pink floral sundress is so gorgeous, and her iced eyes melt as they sweep me.

I feel just as beautiful under her gaze.

"Zoey," she greets with a rising smile. Her fingers slip against my cheek, and I clutch the curve of her hip. We've gone through mysteries and squalls to reach this point together—and I've never loved where I am more.

Our eyes embrace before our lips, and I steal the first kiss before she steals the second.

My lips tingle, and my heart flutters. When we reluctantly drift apart, I put the back of my hand to my forehead. "I think I've fainted. Catch me, Kenobi." I dramatically disintegrate in the doorway.

Her lip twitches. "How exactly did you fail drama class?"

"I was staring at you the whole time," I say from the ground. "Obviously."

"You realize I managed a *B* while I was staring at you."

She was staring at me. I knew she took interest in me or else she wouldn't have put notes in my locker, but hearing her say the words double backflips my heart.

October joins me on the stoop, legs curved elegantly to her side. While I'm accidentally flashing my Jedi panties to the street. "Are those for me?" She notices the flowers and bird seed.

"Um, yeah." I'm hot all over as I pass October the gifts.

Her smile flushes her cheeks, and I sense October is just as overwhelmed as me. We've been officially together for a month, and even though today is special, we cherish every day like it's the first and last.

"I think Figgy and Rosemary are starting to like me."

She nods. "Bribing them with treats helps." And then October reveals a couple gifts from behind her back. I was so drawn to

October that I didn't realize she was holding anything. "For you, sweets."

Something swells inside me. I take hold of a bouquet of violets, my favorite flower, and... "A Grogu plushie. You remembered?"

"Of your infatuation with the ugly little thing? Yes."

"He's adorable, thank you." I hug the Star Wars merch.

October laughs, then begins to stand. "Ready?" She catches my hand, already helping me to my feet. I'm in an affectionate daze.

A cobblestone pathway curves outside the door and twists towards the places we know and love most in the world.

The Drunk Pelican. Fisherman's Wharf. Lake Erie.

Our families and the water.

I never returned to Chicago. I just wanted to stay here. To be with the people I love. So I sold my things and broke the lease agreement on my apartment. The only thing I've been missing is my Grogu plushie. Which October must've known. Her gift is perfect. My heart is bursting out of my body.

October is in some kind of loving trance with me. Only broken by another voice. "Girls, you better shut that door—you're letting all the warm air out."

"Give me a minute, Kenobi." I take our flowers, bird seed, and the plushie and go inside the musty lobby. "I'm putting these back here." I tuck the gifts behind the front desk. "I'll get them later. And Kelly, we've been over this, you can't suffocate the guests by turning on the heat to seventy-eight. No one wants to be sweating while they're in their rooms."

Kelly huffs from behind the desk. "They're feeling the ghost of Ronald the Fourth."

"Who?"

"You know," Kelly mumbles. "*Ronald.*" She just pulled that out of her ass.

October slips into the small lobby, shutting the door behind her. "Ghosts create cold pockets."

"Demons, then."

Jesus. "You hired me to *make* money, not lose money. Turn off the heat."

"*Fine,*" Kelly relents.

October is grinning at me. *She's proud of me.* Of the woman I am. I smile back at her. When Aimee Kelly heard what happened at Edge of the World with my abusive ex and how I was searching for a job in Mistpoint Harbor, she reached out to me.

Her husband wasn't a kind man. And she's also rumored to have murdered him, so I guess that endeared Kelly to me in this strange, wicked way. She said she's getting older, and she'd rather someone else do the hard work around here.

I'm the sole general manager at the Harbor Inn. With the hopes to one day own the Inn myself, as Kelly has often remarked how she has no children of her own and this place has to be taken over by someone.

She even gave me residence in a room formerly named after Mary Shelley. October spends most nights with me, and if it weren't for Thistle, the duckling that she's still caring for, she'd likely already move in with me.

I don't blame Thistle. Just hotel regulations about animals. That, I can't break. Not even for October. And while Kelly might be a little prickly, she's been kind and lets me make the important decisions at the Inn.

Like who should bake morning chocolate croissants and nightly Italian cookies.

"See you tomorrow, Kelly," October says. "I'll be in the kitchen around six a.m."

"I look forward to seeing what you come up with next, October, honey. Those beignets yesterday were decadent."

"I still dream about them," I chime in.

She rolls her eyes. "You dream about everything I bake."

"I have lots of dreams, Kenobi. I can't help that you and your pastries fill all of them."

She tries to restrain a smile. "You're too much." She catches my hand.

"She means to say that I'm just right," I call back to Kelly as October draws me towards the door. I wave goodbye.

Kelly is smiling before busying herself in a Mistpoint Harbor newspaper.

My first new hire was October Brambilla. Fisherman's Wharf lost the best pastry chef, and I whisked her away to dazzle guests with morning and nightly sweets. To work alongside October at the Harbor Inn has been a dream come true. Guests *rave* about her desserts, and each time, October gets a little emotional.

But no one has been more sentimental over us staying in Mistpoint Harbor than Brian. My dad (getting more used to that) shed more than one tear. "You're lying to me," he said repeatedly until he finally believed the news and gave me the biggest bear hug.

Parry was ecstatic when I said I was sticking around, but I made a joke about how I'm not ready to call him a stepdad.

He groaned, "Stop now, Zo."

Brian was laughing in the background. Partially from seeing Parry in distress. They started bickering after that.

Cutting ties with Brian, Parry, and Colt again would've been devastating. Seeing them all at the Pelican makes me happy. Even Colt leaves the lighthouse more than he used to.

Possibly because Babette hangs around our family bar more often, too.

At the Harbor Inn, I shut the door behind me and October, and I smooth out my black dress that flies up with the wind. "Shit."

October tugs my dress down for me.

I blush. "Thanks."

I fix the strap of her purse that slips off her shoulder.

She tucks a flyaway hair behind my ear. Then I thumb her tiny smudge of red lipstick I caused from kissing her.

When we finish, October smiles, "We're all good to go."

I nod, and hand-in-hand, we steal loving glances and walk towards the Pelican. Towards the lake. Where we'll grab a bottle of wine and sit on a picnic table. Staring out at the sparkling sun over the water. Just like we did one month ago. Just like we promised we'd do every month on the day.

To remember the happiest moment of our lives. Where October and I chose each other. Where we continue to choose each other.

And whatever fate has in store, we write our own legends now.

A NOTE FROM THE AUTHORS

Love & Other Cursed Things spawned from an idea years ago about two girls who fell in love in a cursed town. We adore all things coastal and Nancy Drew, so combining our loves with the epic romance of October and Zoey has been a dream come true.

While the town of Mistpoint Harbor is fictional, we were inspired by the small town on Lake Erie where our mother was raised. Ashtabula, Ohio will always have a warm, cherished place in our hearts. You can even find the real life Harbor Perk along the popular Bridge Street. While there are far less curses and misfortune here, the family bonds, Italian-American roots, and Lake Erie magic are still well and alive today.

ACKNOWLEDGEMENTS

First and foremost, thanks to our magical mom who is always the first to read our stories. Your help in bringing Lake Erie to life was invaluable. This one will always be extra special because of you.

Thank you to our agent, Kimberly, who has found this book a great home in audio.

Thanks to our Aunt Bonnie for all the Harbor Perk knowledge and for shipping us some of that delicious coffee roast, and thanks to the owner of Harbor Perk, Kelly.

Thanks to the Fizzle Force admins—Lanie, Jenn, and Shea—for championing this little novel. We call it "little" because it's outside of the big sphere of the Addicted/Like Us world, and yet, you three still shout from the rooftops like it's something much bigger. We're so grateful for that.

Thanks to the readers who spread the word about this one. From bookstagram to booktok and everything in between, we so appreciate all the love and gorgeous edits and videos. You all continue to astound us with your talent! Big thanks to Haley @ wearecallowaydoc for the gorgeous art leading up to the release of *Love & Other Cursed Things*—you made Zoey and October come to life.

Thanks to our patrons over on our Patreon for your continued support. We're able to keep writing full-time and write more often because of all of you. We feel like broken records saying it, but we truly can't stop…Thank you from the very bottom of our hearts.

And big thanks to you—the reader—for picking up this novel. It's outside of our epically long series, but we love it just the same. And we're so incredibly appreciative that you took a chance on Zoey and October's romance.

All the love in *every* universe,

xoxo Krista & Becca

CPSIA information can be obtained
at www.ICGtesting.com
Printed in the USA
LVHW012356240122
709211LV00004B/74